BLUE JESUS

BLUE JESUS

A NOVEL

TOM EDWARDS

ACADEMY

CHICAGO

Published in 2009 by
Academy Chicago Publishers
363 West Erie Street
Chicago, Illinois 60654

© 2009 Tom Edwards

Printed in the U.S.A.

Library of Congress Cataloging-in-Publication Data
on file with the publisher.

Dedicated to
Wanetta, Wanda, Helen, Ann, Dorrie,
Freida, Shirley, Dawn, Georgann,
and especially my mom,
Evelyn Harrington Edwards.
They are the original Harrington Girls
of Comfort Corners

ACKNOWLEDGEMENTS

In writing Blue Jesus, I am enormously indebted to Ms. Cathy Trost, specifically her article in Science Magazine, November, 1982, "The Blue People of Troublesome Creek: The Story of an Appalachian Malady, an Inquisitive Doctor, and a Paradoxical Cure."

I am also thankful for the insight, wisdom, kindness, and inspiration of Ruth Richards, Brenda Lee, Tony Dow, Ray Walters, Jeannette and Scott Depoy, Stephen King, Dolly Parton, Larry Craig, Libby Whittemore, Bibi Whittemore, Skeeter Davis, Patrick Cuccaro, Scott Benson, Amy Miller, Steven Carr, Liz Brock, Liz Lee, and especially Joe Rawlings, who never lost the faith I had to write a book to find.

FORWARD

This is a true story. You probably read about me in the newspapers: "Blue Jesus Miracle Raises Lazarus Boy." I'm Lazarus Boy. My miracle happened in Comfort Corners, a small town in the North Georgia Mountains. The story began when I was eleven and continues to this day. The memories are forever. It's all true, even the parts I made up. Ask anybody who was there, they'll say it's true.

Life started spinning out of control right after Mama died of cancer. One minute we were in an Atlanta hospital, and the next thing I know we were standing by an open grave way up in the northern notch of Georgia. We buried Mama high on a hill that overlooks the entire valley. She could look down on the town, the Bitterroot River, and even the farm where she was born. She would like it up here. I wasn't so sure about me.

Pa said we were moving up to Grandma's to get a fresh start, but I know it was because our house in Atlanta had too many memories. The night before we moved, I saw Pa sitting on the back porch holding one of Mama's slips in his hands and crying. He sat a long time, and then went to the garage, got a shovel, and buried the slip in the back yard. I waited until everybody was asleep, and then I dug it up. When I'm holding that slip it's like I can hear Mama whispering me to sleep. "Good night, Buddy. Tomorrow's going to be a great day." That was when I felt safe.

Country school in Rabun County is different from my school in Atlanta. Up here the fourth, fifth, and sixth grades share the same room. I even go to school with coloreds. That's how I came to share a desk with a blue boy named Early. His real name is Earl Lee Finch, but everybody calls him Early. He's two years older than me and the first blue person I ever met.

Ever since I can remember, Mama told me stories about the Blue People of Troublesome Creek. The doctors from Atlanta that study the blue people say it's a recessive gene trait, some science thing about their blood that makes them special. Maybe that's true, but the minute I laid eyes on Early, I knew he was different.

My first day of school, I was helping Early work his arithmetic problems. He was having trouble on account of he's sort of slow. He's not retarded like some folks say; he's just a little slow with his book learning. When I leaned over to help him with his "goes-into" figures, he took both my hands in his and held tight for a minute. I felt my palms grow warm, then hot, like I was touching a stovetop.

"Don't be so serious, Buddy. It's going to be all right. You got a new best friend," he said, soft and private.

The words froze the blood in my veins. I jerked my hands out of his, jumped up from my desk, and started to back away. Early was looking right at me, but his eyes didn't focus. He was looking off into the yonder.

"Don't be so serious, Buddy." It was Early talking, but it sounded exactly like my mama. At least that's the way it touched my heart.

"Buddy, have you got something to tell the class?" asked Mrs. Runyon, our teacher.

"No, m'am, it's just something scared me," I muttered. It was my first day of school and already I was sticking out.

"Long division?" All the kids laughed. I hate it when people are sarcastic just to get a laugh, especially when it's aimed at me.

"No m'am," I said, my face stinging.

"Are you still scared?" she asked. Her tone had a cut to it.

"No m'am."

"Well then, I suggest you sit back down and get to work."

I sat down, my face stinging with embarrassment. Early was bent over his figures and was concentrating pretty hard.

"What did you do to me? Why'd you tell me not to be so serious?" I whispered. I had to know what just happened.

"It just come to me," Early said, smiling.

"Why did your hands get so hot?" I asked, looking at the bright red scald marks on my hands where his fingers held so tight.

"They do that sometimes," he said. "Did I hurt you?"

"No," I answered. "What did you do to me?"

"I got a notion about you is all. Sometimes I can see things a'fore they happen."

"Well, quit it," I whispered. "You scared me." After that we were quiet for a time. I couldn't tell him he sounded like my mama. That was my secret. However, there was one thing I had to know.

"Are we going to be best friends?" I wanted him to say yes so bad.

"We already are," he said, his face lighting up.

I was eleven years old when I moved from Atlanta to Comfort Corners. Not only did I step back in time, I found myself in a country of mystery, superstition, and miracles. A thirteen-year-old blue boy named Early became my guide, my best friend, and eventually, my savior. This was the boy they called Blue Jesus.

CHAPTER 1

The day we found the dead baby was like any other hot August day in Georgia. School was out, which meant I spent most of my days alone or with Early. We were all eating breakfast when I looked out our kitchen window and saw him wandering up our road. He waited for me out in our backyard, playing with the laundry Grandma had drying on the line.

When Grandma saw him, she yelled out the screen door, "Early Finch, get away from them sheets, and come in here for a biscuit!"

Early just waved at Grandma and started up the path to the barn. Early never comes in our house when my pa's home. It's not that Pa ever did anything to him, but Early's got instincts about people. He knows Pa doesn't trust anybody, especially anybody blue. Pa says blue people are slick as greasy water and the Lord marked them blue as a warning for us to keep away. I say if the Lord was marking people, He'd start with the criminals and work His way down. I suspect my brother Will would be about number one on His list.

I found Early stacking wood beside the barn. "You okay?" I asked.

"Pa come home drunk. He's getting worser," he said, giving me a half grin, and then we took off down the road. He didn't say anything more. He didn't have to. That's the beauty of the friendship plan.

I wasn't sure what we were going to be doing this morning, but one thing I did know, we wouldn't be seeing anybody else if we could help it. Every time I go to town, I get beat up. There's always some older boy calling me a sissy and smacking me around until I cry. Making me cry is a game all the big boys like. I'm almost as popular as baseball.

In that respect, Comfort Corners is no different from Atlanta. When you're different from everybody else, you get picked on. Sometimes I feel like I'm not really living at all, just occupying as little space as I can so people won't notice me. Early avoids people, too, especially other kids. They call him bait trash because his family owns the bait farm south of town. I feel bad for Early, but I can't stick up for him because then they'd turn on me. I'm not proud of that, but it's the gospel truth, and I'm known for always telling the truth. Ask anybody, they'll say it's so.

This morning we started out for the river. Early likes exploring, especially by the town dump. It's my favorite, too. On a good day you can find all kinds of stuff. One time I found a cracked 78 rpm record of *Sentimental Journey* by Miss Doris Day. It's one of my favorite songs, right up there with Debbie Reynolds' *Tammy*, which is from the movie *Tammy and the Bachelor*. In my opinion this is the best movie ever made.

Early and I crossed the river up by our house and walked along the west bank heading for the town dump. When we passed the cut-off to the cemetery, I waved up the hill to Mama. Further along River Road we were still hidden by the trees when we heard some yelling. Right off I knew it was Butch Calkins, this nasty redneck who is responsible for most of my misery. I don't know what I ever did to Butch, but ever since I moved up here he's been after me. I avoid him every chance I get, but I'd swear Butch spends most of his life thinking up new ways to torture me. Just the sight of me seems to set him off.

If there's a bunch of kids around when Butch has pounded me to the ground, he always lets me go once I start to cry. When we're alone, he won't let me go until I kiss him. He knocks me down, and then throws himself on top of me. I don't think this is right. I'm only eleven. He's at least fourteen and way bigger than me. Grandma says Butch is cussed mean because he's Dutch Christian Reform and his mother's from Wisconsin, which makes him half Yankee. Everybody knows Dutch Christian Reforms don't like anybody but other DCRs.

Early and I squatted down in the woods on the edge of the dump and watched Butch and some other ninth grade boys, one of them was Early's oldest brother, Leon. The boys were shooting their .22s at cans and other junk down by the river, cussing real bad and smoking cigarettes. I was surprised Leon was there because Butch doesn't usually hang around with blue people. We watched the boys for about an hour. By then the mosquitoes were about to chew me up.

All of a sudden the boys high-tailed it for town. I made Early wait and count to one hundred just to be sure they were gone. It takes Early a long time to count to a hundred, and I was ready to go by the time he hit sixty, but, better safe than sorry, so I waited. Even after Early ticked off one hundred, I made him stand in the open for a minute. I'm not proud of this, but I was in no mood to get beat up. When I knew for sure the coast was clear, I came out of the trees and we walked down to the dump to explore.

I could tell right off the dump didn't have anything new. The trash was all smashed down like it'd been there for some time; the magazines were musty, the tin cans rusted and filled with water. Early and I pushed over an old Frigidaire and a bunch of magazines fell out. They were mostly *National Geographics*, a few *Ladies Home Journals*. I hoped there'd be some movie magazines. I was keeping a scrapbook on the Lennon Sisters, who are four famous

Catholic singers on the Lawrence Welk television show. They are my favorite singing sister act, and as good as the McGuire Sisters, who are a whole lot older and much more sophisticated.

Early took off for the river and I lost track of time. I was reading an old *Screen Secrets* story about Ava Gardner, a Southern movie star, who is one of Hollywood's most misunderstood actresses. I was at the point in the story where Ava is talking about what she is looking for in a loving marriage when I heard Early holler.

I looked down by the riverbank and saw Early pointing at something on the ground. It's so weird the way I remember it. Early was standing there pointing, looking back at me. His mouth was open like he was trying to scream, but there wasn't any sound coming out. I got a sick feeling in my stomach, and I knew it was something bad.

I tried to run over to Early, but it was like my legs wouldn't work. I was moving all wobbly, like in slow motion. With every step it seemed like Early got further and further away. I saw him bend over and reach for something, but then he sank to his knees like the wind was knocked out of him. When I got up beside him, I saw it was nothing.

"For crying out loud, Early, you scared me to death. It's just a dumb old milk pail!" I yelled.

Early didn't say anything. He shook his head and rocked back on his heels, clutching his middle like he had a stomachache. When I looked closer, I saw there was something kind of bluish-white in the bucket. Early pulled the pail closer, and that's when I saw the two tiny legs, all drawn up and perfect, like a plastic doll baby.

"Is it a real baby?" I asked.

Early reached out in that timid way he has and pulled the baby out on the ground. I could see it was a little boy. The baby's eyes were closed, and he still had his belly button cord hanging down.

"It's dead," I whispered, then my knees gave way and I hit the ground, biting a chunk out of my tongue when my jaws snapped shut. Early just nodded his head and pulled the baby into his lap.

"Stop touching him. We got to get the sheriff," I whispered, spitting blood out of my mouth.

Early held the baby to his chest and started to moan, rocking back and forth. "Baby's hurt," he kept saying, "baby's hurt."

I was so scared, I took off like a scalded cat. I ran to the top of the hill, screaming for help, aiming for the Watrous place. Miss Pink Watrous came out of her kitchen door with her hair all done up in home permanent rods. I ran right into her and her body stopped me cold.

"What're you yelling about, Buddy?" Miss Pink barked.

I couldn't catch my breath and just kept sucking air. To this day I don't know what possessed her, but Miss Pink hauled off and slapped me across the face. Her hand caught my cheek and made me bite my tongue again. I just stood there looking up at her, stunned.

"Buddy, what's wrong?" Miss Pink yelled.

"Me and Early found a dead baby in the dump," I said.

I must've been convincing because Pink bent over, grabbed my face, and said, "Say it again."

"Me and Early found a dead baby in the dump."

"Holy Jesus," Miss Pink said, and threw me out of her way as she ran to the house. I wanted to follow her to make sure she called the sheriff, but I just stood there shaking, smelling the stink of Pink's home permanent solution in the air. I knew I should go back and stay with Early, but I couldn't move.

"Matt Williams is on his way," Miss Pink yelled, running toward me. "Now Buddy, you take me there."

I don't even know if I heard her. I remember looking at her hair all rolled up tight in blue plastic curlers with bits of paper on them. I couldn't even remember how I got there.

"Buddy, show me!" she screamed, smacking me one more time.

I burst into tears and spit more blood out of my mouth. Miss Pink grabbed me by the arm and dragged me back toward the dump. As we crossed River Road, I pulled away from her and ran as fast as I could back to Early.

"Buddy Dean, you wait for me. You know I got bad feet!" Miss Pink hollered.

When I got to the crest of the hill that overlooks the dump, what I saw made me stop in my tracks. Early was bent over the dead baby, and it looked like he was talking. How could he stand being that close to something dead?

Miss Pink caught up with me, puffing and groaning from her run. I know she was scared, but she must have been mad at me for leaving her behind because she raised her hand to smack me again. I ducked the blow, she swatted air, and the two of us started walking down the hill. As we got closer, we could hear Early.

"Don't you fret little feller, you're going to be fine," Early crooned to the dead baby.

Miss Pink and I took a few steps closer, then we saw Early press the baby against his chest, one hand on the baby's head.

"Jesus, Mary and Joseph," Pink whispered. The next sound we heard was a baby crying.

Early looked up, smiling at me and Miss Pink. He kissed the baby on the forehead, laid it on the ground. He looked up at us and said, "Baby's good now."

The three of us watched that baby come to life, his little chest rising and falling with every breath. With each breath he got pinker and pinker. All of a sudden he opened his eyes and let go with a scream that cut to the quick. Early pulled his hands away from the baby and started shaking them in the wind.

"Hot hands," he said.

The baby sat in Early's lap and quieted down a bit. Miss Pink and I leaned a little closer, looking over Early's shoulder. The baby looked back at us, and I think the sight of two scared white faces and one blue one must've been too much. He opened his mouth and started squalling again.

Early put his little finger in the baby's mouth and it started in trying to nurse. Suddenly we heard a "plink" as one of the permanent rods fell off Miss Pink's head. It landed next to my foot still covered with hair. Miss Pink and I stared at it for a second then looked at each other as if we couldn't believe it. Then another rod hit the top of my bare foot.

"Damn it to hell, I've burned up my hair!" Miss Pink screamed. She tore off for home, dropping permanent rods along the way.

"Well, boys, what we got going on here?"

The sound of Sheriff Williams' voice gave me such a start I yelped and jumped about a foot in the air.

"I asked y'all, what's going on? Where'd that baby come from?" The sheriff reached out and grabbed me by the back of the neck and pulled me to him. "Buddy, what happened here?"

"We were exploring, and then Early found the baby. It was dead when we found it. Early breathed it back to life." I was babbling, but there was no stopping me.

"What are you telling me, Buddy? What'd Early do to that baby?" Sheriff Williams knelt down and we were face-to-face.

"That baby was dead, I know it was," I said. "How could Early make it live again?"

"I suspect it weren't really dead. Earl Lee, where'd you find that baby?"

Early pointed at the milk pail. Matt Williams bent over, picked up the pail, and scratched at some dried blood.

"Was that baby warm or cold when you found it?" he asked Early.

"Cold. It were all blue and not breathing. He looked like me," Early answered, rocking back and forth with the baby in his arms.

"Well, boys, y'all better come along with me. We got to get this baby over to Doc Rodger's. Early, can I trust you not to drop that child?" Early nodded, and we all climbed up the hill and got in the sheriff's patrol car. Early cradled the baby all the way through town.

At Doc's, the grownups took over, and Early and I were told to stay on the porch and keep our mouths shut. We sat in the swing and didn't say a word.

All of a sudden Early started to cry. This was a loud crying, like he was gulping for air. It must've spooked the sheriff, because he

came out on the porch and knelt down by Early, and kind of pet-
ted him on the back. He reached into his back pocket and handed
Early his handkerchief. It didn't look clean to me, but Early took
it anyway.

"Buddy, you got any idea whose baby that is?" The sheriff
asked, coming around to my end of the swing.

"I was just trying to figure it out. He's pinked up so we know it
doesn't belong to anybody blue."

"That's what I was thinking," Sheriff Williams said. "But
who'd leave their baby in a dump? You hear tell of any young girl
in these parts in the family way?"

"Nobody I know. Early, you know a white girl that was pregnant?" I asked, giving him a nudge in the ribs with my elbow.

Early didn't answer, he was still sobbing sort of quiet.

"You boys see anybody suspicious hanging around the dump?"

"Yeah, Butch Calkins was there. He had a rifle and he was
smoking." It was out of my mouth before I could stop myself.

"What was that Calkins kid doing in the dump?" the sheriff
asked.

"Who knows? Butch is real wild. Everybody knows that. If I
were you, I'd find out." Finally Early gave me a jab in the ribs to
shut me up. Well, I was nervous and wasn't thinking right. There
was a lot going on.

"He is a wild one all right," the sheriff answered.

I just looked at my feet, knowing full well if word of this ever
reached Butch, I would be beaten senseless.

"All right, boys, I'm done with y'all," the sheriff said, motioning for us to go on home.

We got up and started down off the porch. Matt Williams
called after us, "Earl Lee, was that baby alive when you found it?"
Early looked back at Sheriff Williams and shook his head. "Then
how do you account for the fact that he's inside with Doc right
now, bawling his head off?" The sheriff eased down off the porch
and walked over to Early. "Mr. Early, what'd you do to that dead
baby?" he whispered.

"I touched him," Early said.

Sheriff Williams studied Early for what seemed like a real long time, then he said, "Well ain't this a crock of you know what? You boys want me to carry you on home? Your folks will want to hear about this."

"Thank you sir, we'll get home just fine," Early said.

"Suit yourself," the sheriff said. I knew he was relieved. It was well-known the sheriff didn't take to blue folks on account of he's Dutch Christian Reform. All the blue people in Georgia are Baptist. I'm Catholic because my Pa's kin come from Louisiana, but we're not real religious, which is lucky since there's no Catholic Church in Comfort Corners. The DCRs don't like us either.

"I'd tell you boys to keep quiet about this, but I can promise y'all Pink Watrous has spread this news all over the county by now." With that he got in his patrol car and drove off.

As I watched the sheriff drive off, I could see the steeple of the Baptist Church against the horizon. "Early, just wait till the Baptists find out about the baby."

It took me a minute to realize Early wasn't behind me. I looked back toward Doc Rodger's house and could see him peeking in the office window.

"Early, come on," I hollered.

"I want to see the baby," he yelled back. Then he knocked on the window. He waited, then knocked again.

Finally Doc opened the window. I couldn't hear what he was saying, but he was smiling. They talked for a couple minutes, and then Early leaned in the window, his butt and legs hanging out. He stayed that way for a bit, then disappeared into Doc's office.

I waited for a time, and then headed for home. I knew the sheriff was right about Miss Pink spreading the word about the baby. I also knew when my pa got wind of this, he wouldn't be happy.

Pa's always saying, "Stay out of trouble, and don't tell people everything you know." I don't know why he says that; I'm only eleven and I don't know that much. Pa won't admit to it, but I know why he wants me to stay low. Fact is, I embarrass my father.

He doesn't want me drawing attention to myself because I'm such a sissy. I think he figures if he ignores me, I'll just disappear, and that way he won't have to explain me to his friends. That's why I try to stay out of Pa's way and not call attention to myself. Finding a dead baby in the dump is big news. Pa's going to be mad.

As I headed toward town, I was thinking about running away from home. I figured the best way for me to get to Hollywood, California, the entertainment capital of the world, would be to hitchhike to Atlanta, and then take a Greyhound Bus. I was just puzzling out how I could save money for the trip when Early ran up behind me and slapped me on the back.

"Baby's good and healthy. I knew he would be," Early said.

"Early, you scared the bejeezus out of me!" I yelled. I had to stop a minute to catch my breath. I bent over to clear my head and could feel my pulse pounding in my temples. It's a good thing I'm young and healthy or what happened today could've given me a heart attack.

"What's bejeezus?" Early asked.

"I don't know. Grandma says it. I think it means you scared the crap out of me," I said, "and you did. What were you and Doc talking about?"

"Nothing." Early and I walked on, both of us lost in thought. Finally I couldn't stand it and I had to know what he did.

"Early, how'd you make that baby breathe again?"

We were right in front of Eat, which was Comfort Corner's only restaurant. It's really just a diner with a neon sign on the roof that says "Eat." I never thought much about it until my cousins came up here from Sandersville. They thought a restaurant named Eat was the funniest thing they ever saw.

"Hey, we're going to Eat to eat!" Then they'd scream and laugh. If that's the funniest thing they ever saw, they need to get out more.

"How did you do it?" I asked, looking Early right in the eye.

"Buddy, I can't talk about this no more." He turned and walked away. I couldn't believe it. I was his best friend, and we'd just been through the biggest thing to ever happen in the whole entire county, and he doesn't want to talk about it.

"Well, I want to talk about it. You owe me an answer," I yelled.

Early just kept walking toward home. I tried to grab his arm to get him to stop, but he jerked away, and started running. I kept up with him as best I could, but his legs are a lot longer than mine. I was running fast, but all of a sudden I got a stitch in my side, and started doing that limp-run catch step that always makes me laugh when it happens to somebody else.

"Early, stop! I got a stitch! Stop a minute, will you?" I gasped, out of breath and bent over in pain.

Early slowed down, turned back to look at me, then walked back to where I was, bent over, red-faced, and out of breath. I sat down in the middle of the road, exhausted. We didn't say anything for a few minutes, but I didn't care. I couldn't breathe and probably couldn't talk either. I got distracted by an ant hill and was watching them scatter every time I dropped a few grains of sand on their castle. They sure are fast.

"Sometimes I know what's going to happen. Things just come into my head. When that happens, I can do things. I can make things happen," Early whispered lowly. "You can't tell nobody, Buddy."

"I won't have to after today. Everybody is town is going to know what you did." We sat in silence for a few more minutes. Those ants were digging away like mad, working to rebuild their hill.

"Early, is it magic; like casting a spell?" I asked.

"More like a burning feeling that tells me what to do. It's sort of like an itch. Usually it's in my head, sometimes my hands, sometimes my eyes. It don't hurt, though. The feeling comes on me, and then I know what I need to do," he said, shyly, looking up at me as if he expected me to laugh at him.

"The way you talk about it makes it sound like you're doing something holy," I said. It did, too. It sounded just like one of those "Lives of the Saints" stories the nuns in Atlanta were always reading to us.

Early took off, and I followed after, walking in silence. When we got to the end of my road, Early turned around and headed back towards town and the bait farm. He'd come way out of his way to walk me home. As I watched him walk away, the sun glinting off his white hair, I knew without a doubt that Early Finch reached out with his blue hands and gave that baby life. The instant that baby cried, I knew my friend Early had been touched by the hand of God.

CHAPTER 2

I began the long walk up our road, dreading each step that brought me closer to one more fight with Pa. Our house is a big old giant that sits back from the road, perched up a small hill, and nestled back into the gentle rise of the mountain. The front yard is dotted with weeping willows, and it's really pretty in the spring and fall.

The homestead has always belonged to my kin on my mother's side, and there's been a Harrington farming this land since long before the Civil War. The house is at one end of a broad valley, and from our front porch you can see the river wind down the valley all the way into town. The barns and chicken coop are behind the house, almost hidden from the road. Grandma has her kitchen garden behind the house and her flowers in the front yard. She said this makes the house look friendly.

The farm used to be much bigger, but through the years a lot of the land has been sold off. Grandma has a colored man named Gizzy Hosler working for her. Gizzy is colored black, not blue. He farms a little more than seventy acres in apples; that's our money crop. Come picking season we get a bunch of Mexicans that come all the way up here from Florida to help. Gizzy has twin daughters, June and July, in my class in school. Next to Early, I like the twins best.

When we moved up to Grandma's, Pa thought he was going to take over managing the farm, but I heard Grandma tell him apples are finicky and Gizzy knows best. Pa told her it's disgraceful that she lets a colored man run her farm, but Grandma said she's not trusting the apples to anybody but Gizzy. I don't think Pa will ever get over that.

Grandma's house is real old; hot in the summer; cold as ice in winter. It's got two stories with a wraparound porch in the front, and another porch out back. I've got my own room and don't have to share with Will. My room is upstairs in the back, and it's got a hidden crawl space that goes the entire width of the house. Will got the best room upstairs. It's in the front of the house and has a balcony that overlooks the front yard. He can see the river and all the way into town from that balcony.

That August morning I dragged my feet all the way up the road. I could see Pa waiting in the kitchen, cradling his yardstick, seven empty beer bottles on the table. I was still shook up about the baby and in no mood for a fight, so I snuck around to the front door and headed upstairs.

"Buddy's home!" Will yelled. I didn't even see him in the front room. "Hey, Pa's been waiting for you. Pa, Buddy's home!"

I sat on the bottom step and waited, knowing what was going to happen. Pa came into the front room from the kitchen, Grandma trailing behind him, holding a dish rag and wiping her hands. Isn't it funny the things that catch your eye? I remember thinking, Grandma's hands are always wet.

"Well, I bet you're proud of yourself," Pa said. "The little sissy boy thinks he's a big hero. What've you got to say?"

What can you say to something like that? I just stared at my feet. It's times like this that I really miss my mother. She wouldn't let Pa do this.

"Buddy, you had dinner?" Grandma asked.

"Buddy Boy don't need no dinner. Buddy Boy won't be eating any supper either. Buddy Boy is going to get a whipping, and then he's going to bed." Pa brought the yardstick from behind his back, and I knew I was in for a beating. But, true to form, Pa had to torment me first. He waved the yardstick in front of my face, smacking it against his palm.

"How many times do I have to tell you to keep out of trouble? You know what your problem is, Buddy? You don't never listen. You're always showing off, prissing around with that retard blue boy. I told you, I don't want you hanging around with him. Ain't you got no pride?"

"Lyle, let the boy alone," Grandma said. She started to say more, but Pa cut his eyes at her.

"I didn't do anything. Early's the one that saved the baby's life." I was still looking at my feet, thinking I'd need new shoes for school, waiting for the yardstick to fall across my back.

"No, you didn't do nothing except run all over town screaming for help, just like a little girl!" Pa kept smacking his hand harder and harder with the yardstick. "Pink Watrous said the way you were screaming, she thought some woman was being skinned alive."

"I was scared," I said. "I never saw a dead baby before."

"Was it a boy baby or a girl?" Will asked.

"Shut up, Will. I'm not done dealing with your little sister here," Pa said. He grabbed my arm and pulled me off the stairs. I stumbled and fell to my knees. Out of the corner of my eye I saw Pa's foot coming toward me. He booted me in the rear and I skidded across the front room.

"Looks like I got to teach you to mind your own business." Pa raised the yardstick, and I could already feel it across my back. This was a feeling I knew too well.

"Don't you dare hit this child for doing the right thing!" Grandma sounded like she had seen enough. When she got that tone in her voice, even Pa wouldn't cross her. I didn't see it, but I bet she was giving Pa her two-finger point.

"Stay out of this, Lena," Pa said, turning back to me, waving the yardstick closer and closer.

"Hey y'all, there's a car coming up the drive!" Will said. "Some woman is driving. I can't make out who she is. Looks like a Buick."

This news took the edge off Pa. He looked down at me, looked at the yardstick, and then said, real quiet, "You make me sick to my stomach. Now get out of my sight."

I scrambled to my feet and ran through the house, out the back door, and up toward the barn. I didn't even look back to see who the company was. I wanted to scream and laugh at the same time. Pa didn't beat me this time, which in my book makes it a good day. Sure he roughed me up a little, but that's what fathers do. Early's daddy does him the same way. Grandma says Pa's mean because he wants to toughen me up. It's not working. I can't help the way I am. If I could, I would.

I planned on hiding out in the barn until it was time for bed. I sure didn't want to give Pa another excuse to whip me, but curiosity got me and I needed to know who came to visit. I went down to the garden so I could see the driveway. Will was right, there was a big green Buick parked in the drive. I was twisting my head, trying to see into the kitchen window, when the back door slammed, and Will came out on the porch.

"Buddy, get in here! Somebody wants to talk to you!" he yelled.

Oh God, I was in trouble. It was probably somebody from the jailhouse come to take me in for questioning about that baby. I hear there's a reform school for bad boys that you get sent to if you break the law. I didn't break any laws, but maybe there's something about finding a body in the dump that's against the law. I'd be dead in a day if I got sent to a school for rowdy boys like Butch Calkins.

When I got up to the back steps, a youngish, curly-headed lady came out on the back porch. She had a white skunk streak in the front of her hair that was very dramatic. It made her look like a movie star.

"Buddy, I'm Carla Watkins from the *Dixie Bugler*. I was wondering if I could talk to you for a couple of minutes." Well, she seemed nice enough, and the closer I got the younger she looked.

"I don't have much to say," I muttered, looking around for Pa. I knew he was waiting for this woman to leave.

"Is there somewhere we can go to talk?" Miss Watkins asked. "The paper would like to do a feature story about you finding the baby."

I led her over to the picnic table we've got set up in the side yard. As we walked I could smell her perfume, which hung around her like a cloud. I didn't really want to talk, but I figured she wouldn't last long once the mosquitoes got a whiff of that perfume.

We got situated at the picnic table and Miss Watkins took out a notebook and pen, then she took a deep breath, looked at me real serious and said, "Tell me about the baby."

I told her what happened, just like I told Matt Williams. She listened all polite and didn't butt in. When I got to the part about Early bringing the baby back to life, she looked at me like I'd lost my mind.

"Well, was the baby dead or not?" she wanted to know. "The baby at Doc Rodger's house right now is the picture of health. Was the baby breathing when y'all found it?"

"No m'am, not until Early touched him and breathed him back to life."

"Mouth-to-mouth resuscitation?"

"I don't know. Maybe. I guess so, but that baby was all cold. I think it'd been dead for a while."

"Until Earl Lee Finch, brought him back to life? Is that what you're saying?" Miss Watkins was writing like mad with one hand and swatting skeeters with the other.

"Yes, M'am. Early breathed on him and he started to cry." That's exactly what happened, and so that's what I said. I wasn't going to lie to the woman. "How'd you get that streak in your hair?" I asked.

"It's a birthmark. Now, Buddy, this is quite a story," she said, playing with that thatch of white hair. "Quite a story."

"It's not a story, it's the truth. I'm known for telling the truth. Ask anybody. They'll tell you I don't lie."

"I'm not calling you a liar, Buddy, it's just that I'd like to talk to the Finch boy and get his side of the story."

"Early won't talk to you," I said, knowing the minute Early got sight of this city woman with skunk-streaked hair, he'd run and hide. "He's blue. They don't talk to nobody unless they have to."

"Well, I'm going to write a story about this whether he talks to me or not. How'd you and Early like to have your picture in the paper? I'd run it right alongside my story. You boys are heroes."

Okay, she got me on that one. I wanted my picture in the paper more than anything in the whole entire world. Usually I try to stay out of sight, but having my picture in the paper was the chance I needed to prove myself. If everybody thought we did something good, maybe Pa'd leave me alone.

"Well, maybe I could convince Early to talk to you, but you'd have to let me go first and bring him to you. There's no way his daddy would let him talk to somebody from the newspaper."

"That'd be fine. I can drive us over right now," Miss Watkins said, swatting at a cloud of mosquitoes swirling around her head. As we walked toward the house, I could see she had two big mosquito bites on the backs of her arms. Will was standing on the back porch pretending like he wasn't interested.

"Will, Miss Watkins's taking me over to Early's. Tell Grandma, okay?"

Will nodded and watched us walk down the drive toward the Buick. I didn't see Pa anywhere around, but I figured he was watching us from an upstairs window. He'd be real mad at first, but once he saw me named a hero in the newspaper he'd be all right.

Miss Carla's Buick is the nicest car I've ever been in. All I've ever ridden in is a Ford pickup that belongs to my pa, an Atlanta city bus, and the Nancy Hanks, a train that Mama and I took to

visit my Aunt Shirley in Sandersville. My Aunt Dawn in Greens-
boro got a brand-new Chevrolet, and I almost got a ride in it once,
but I got so excited, I threw up. Aunt Dawn suggested it would be
best if I didn't ride in her automobile until I was older and had a
bit more control. I've also ridden in a school bus, but I don't really
think of that as modern transportation.

We headed down Highway 28 through town. I sat up real tall,
so anybody looking at the car would be sure to see me. At first we
were really quiet, then curiosity got the best of me.

"Who told you about the dead baby?"

"A woman named Pink Watrous called the paper. She said we
might want to interview her, too, but she said we couldn't take
her picture on account of a bad home permanent. Was she at the
crime scene?"

"Yes m'am. Miss Pink called the sheriff. Did you interview
him?" I was starting to get excited. This was getting to be a pretty
big event. I knew when we found the baby people were going to
get upset. But the way things were taking off, this could be the
biggest story this town had ever seen.

"Sheriff Williams said he didn't have an official position until
the case was solved," Miss Carla said. She sure did talk like a
reporter, but up close I could tell she was young. I figured she was
probably just out of high school and this was her first real job.

It didn't take long to get through town. We passed the colored
cemetery and turned up Bluetown Road, heading up the mountain. When we got to the end of Early's drive, I made Carla (she
asked me call her that. See what I mean about her being young?)
drop me off so Mr. Finch wouldn't see the car. I hiked up to the
house, stood out in the yard and threw stones against the porch,
waiting on somebody to come out. The Finches have two vicious
hound dogs named Duke and Buster tied up under the house.
They'll tear your leg if they get a chance.

The hounds got a whiff of me right off and started up howling.
Early's mama came out on the porch and whacked one of them
with a broom, and they both slunk back under the porch. I was

glad it was her and not Early's daddy. I know she likes me. Miss
Finch is a tall woman, what Grandma calls stringy, with almost
white hair and sky blue skin. Her name is Emma, which I think is
real pretty. Early's daddy is a medium blue, except when he's been
drinking, then he looks like somebody dipped him in ink.

"Early's out in the barn, Buddy, looking after his new calf,"
Miss Finch reported. "What y'all up to on such a hot day?"

"Nothing much," I answered, and took off for the barn, the
less said the better. It was pretty obvious she hadn't heard about
the baby.

"Buddy, now quit that running!" Miss Finch hollered after me.
"You'll catch a heat stroke."

I found Early mucking out the barn. He didn't have his shirt
on, and I was sort of shocked at how skinny he is. Well, he's been
scrawny since I met him, but I think he's lost even more weight.

"Hey," he said. "Are you all right?" What he was asking was
how bad the beating was.

"Not too bad," I answered. "Early, I know you won't like this,
but there's some woman wants to talk to you. She's waiting at the
end of the road. She's from the newspaper."

"Buddy, I ain't talking to no strangers," Early said. He picked
up his T-shirt and slung it over his shoulder.

"I told her that, but she said she was going to try anyway. She
wants to put our pictures in the paper. She called us heroes for
saving that baby. Of course I told her you were the main hero, and
it was because of you the baby is alive." I was laying it on thick.

"I don't want my picture in the paper, and I ain't going to be
telling nobody what happened," Early said. He turned away and
pulled his T-shirt over his head.

"Come on, Early," I pleaded, "I want my picture in the paper.
We're heroes. This is our chance to show the big kids that they
can't push us around anymore. Please."

Early looked at me like I was the most pitiful creature he'd
ever seen. "Buddy, them kids are going to push us around no mat-

ter what. That's the way it is. Finding the baby ain't never going to change that."

"Early, please." I was shameless. I pouted. I kicked at some cow pies. Finally I pulled out the big guns. "I thought we were best friends."

"You ain't going to give up on this, are you?" Early asked, knowing full well I'd pester him until he gave in.

"We're going to be famous!" I screamed. "Follow me."

I led Early back to Miss Carla. Their talk went about as good as could be expected. She was a little put off on account of him being blue, but she handled it pretty good. Early looked scared to death. He never once looked Miss Carla in the eye. When she finally got him to open up, he told her exactly what he did. He lost her when he got to the part about touching the baby back to life.

"You touched him back to life?" she asked. "I don't understand. What exactly does 'touching back to life' mean?"

"I just knew I could help him if I touched him. I put my hands on the back of his head and held him close. Then the baby started crying." That said, Early sort of shrugged. "That's all."

Miss Carla didn't write anything down. She opened her mouth to ask a question, then shut it again. She looked at me, then back to Early, like she was digging for the right words.

"Well, this is just extraordinary," she sputtered. "Extraordinary. You boys should be very proud of yourselves. You're both heroes."

Early didn't say anything more, just stared at the ground, drawing circles in the dirt with his big toe. I knew he regretted talking, and it made me feel bad.

"Now, can you boys come into town tomorrow and have your picture took? My story will run on Thursday, and I want to get the film developed and the photo ready."

I said right off that I could be there any time she wanted.

"No offense, m'am, but my daddy wouldn't want me to have my picture in your paper. I'll have to say no." Early didn't look happy.

"But it will be a very good story," Carla insisted, "very positive. You're the reason that baby is still alive."

"It were the good Lord saved that young'un, not me," Early said, then he turned and walked back home.

Carla and I watched as Early walked away. From the way his shoulders were slumping, I knew he felt bad. When he finally turned the corner and disappeared from view, Miss Carla and I took a deep breath. It was sort of like we were swimming under water when Early was still in sight.

"Buddy, is what he said true?" Carla asked.

"Yes, m'am," I said. "Early's got special powers. He knows things before they happen. It's like magic."

"Magic or a miracle? There's a big difference. I say this is a miracle, and people have got to hear about it," Carla said. She climbed in the Buick and rolled down the window. "You need a ride home?"

"No, m'am, it's not far." I said. I wanted to think of a new strategy for getting in the house without Pa knowing. "I can hike it."

"I'll see you tomorrow at the community hall," Miss Carla said. "We'll get your picture made around one o'clock. Is that all right with you?"

"I'll be there." Carla put the Buick in gear and took off. As her car headed down Bluetown Road, I cut through the woods for home.

It was after eight o'clock when I got home. The lights were on in the kitchen, so I sat outside on the picnic table and waited until I was sure Pa had gone to bed. I snuck in the kitchen door, went around to Grandma's bedroom and knocked on the door.

"I'm home, Grandma."

"I was worried about you, Buddy," she said. "You know, your Pa don't mean what he says. He just gets scared."

"Scared of what?" I whispered. Pa's got good hearing, and I didn't want him sneaking up behind me.

"He's scared about raising you without your mama around. He wants to make sure you grow up right." Grandma smiled and pulled me into a hug. "Now young'un, it's time for bed," she said, kissing the top of my head and pointing me toward my bedroom.

From the stairs I could hear Pa and Will snoring. I don't know how Mama ever slept with Pa, his snoring is loud. Will just sort of whistles through his nose, which usually makes me laugh.

When I finally got between the covers, it hit me how exhausted I was. I wanted to sleep more than anything, but I couldn't turn my head off. I started thinking about what Grandma said. If Pa is scared he wasn't bringing me up proper, I've got a hot piece of news for him. Being hateful and mean is no way to bring me up.

This was making me sad, so I started thinking about getting my picture in the paper. I figured I'd wear my good blue jeans and a clean white T-shirt. I could almost see the picture and imagined everybody's reaction. This would sure teach that white trash Butch Calkins a lesson.

I was excited, but underneath something was tugging at my heart. I tried to tell myself that getting Early to talk about what happened was a good thing. But, I knew I did it for myself. I can be selfish that way, which is a big fault I'm working on. I wanted my Pa to see me as a hero, not just an embarrassment. Truth to tell, I sold out my best friend because I was afraid of my father. This was a decision I would regret the rest of my life.

CHAPTER 3

I woke up early and listened for Pa. I waited until I knew he and Will were gone so I'd have the bathroom to myself. I wanted to make sure I had time to get ready for my picture without somebody banging on the bathroom door. My hair was growing out from the scalping Pa made me get every spring. For the first month of every summer, I go around looking like the county nurse heard I had head lice. When I get old enough to move away from home, I'm going to grow my hair out like either Elvis Presley or Tony Dow on Leave it to Beaver, which is a television show I don't get to watch anymore because nobody up here has a TV. Butch Calkins has long blond hair and looks sort of like James Dean. That's another reason I hate him. It's been my experience you can't trust anybody that good looking.

Thanks to Grandma, my T-shirt was sparkling white, which I thought would look good because I'm sort of tanned from swimming. I started to put on my new jeans, but they were so stiff I decided to go with my cut-off bib-alls. I know they make me look country, but long pants would just make me sweat. I didn't want my picture took with me looking greasy.

"Where's Pa?" I asked Grandma as I flopped down in one of the kitchen chairs. "He and Will go off somewhere?"

"Well, good morning to you, too, Snooty Britches. How come you're all dressed up?" Grandma didn't miss much.

"I'm getting my picture made for the *Bugler*. Miss Carla's doing a story on me and Early. Where's Pa?" If I was going to get a whipping, I wanted to get it over with before I left for town.

"Your Pa said he had business and left about an hour ago," Grandma answered. "He's probably finishing up some work on that cabin at the lake. Will went with him. You know, Buddy, I think your Pa feels bad about what happened yesterday."

I didn't say a word. Grandma put a jar of apple butter and some thick slices of her bread on the table.

"Your Pa is afraid for you is what it is. He's seen what can happen to gentle boys like you. He just don't want nothing bad to happen," Grandma started in, but I cut her off.

"Anything bad that happens to me is because of Pa. He's the only one beating up on me." This wasn't really true, but that's the way I felt. "You know, it's not my fault Mama died."

"Buddy, you don't think your Pa blames you for that, do you?"

I didn't answer. I spread some apple butter on my bread and chewed. I didn't want to talk about Pa. I wanted Grandma to stop pushing, but she will worry a problem to death.

"Buddy, don't jerk away from me," Grandma grabbed my head and forced me to look right at her. "Your pa don't blame you for your mama passing." Grandma has a way of looking in a person's eyes that's like Superman's x-ray vision. I swear she can see what I'm thinking. Mama could do that, too.

"I know," I said. I did, too. Right after Mama died Pa was nice to me. We went out to the cemetery and planted flowers on Mama's grave, and he told me and Will that God took Mama, and it was nobody's fault she was dead but His. That gave me the creeps, and I expected Pa to be struck dead by a bolt of lightning, but nothing happened. Maybe God wasn't listening, or maybe He'd just given up on us Deans. With Pa hating God for killing

Mama, I'd say the best plan is for all of us Deans to stay out of God's way.

"Buddy, look at me. Things ain't going right for your Pa because work is slow and he still misses your mama. That's all it is. Your pa loves you. You know that, don't you?"

I kept quiet. Well, I was quiet on the outside; inside my head, I could hear myself screaming, Pa's supposed to love me. I'm his son. I knew Grandma was waiting on an answer, but I didn't say a thing. I stuffed a big hunk of bread in my mouth and swallowed hard.

"Buddy, I asked you a question," Grandma said, cutting her eyes my way. I resisted looking up and chewed my bread. "Well, you're a stubborn cuss," Grandma finally sputtered, "just like your daddy."

"I ain't nothing like Pa. Nothing!" I yelled, jumping out of the chair. "That's why he hates me. We ain't nothing alike, and we never will be!" I rubbed at my eyes, trying to hide my tears.

"Maybe you ain't alike in all ways, but you both got tender hearts," Grandma said, taking a balled-up Kleenex out of her apron pocket and wiping my eyes. Okay, it's not that I'm all that nervous about germs, but I had pink eye once, and God only knows how long that Kleenex had been in her apron. I twisted out of Grandma's arms, flew out the screen door, and realized I didn't have any place to go. I paced back and forth on the back porch for a spell, and finally sat on the steps.

After awhile Grandma came outside and sat beside me. We looked out over the backyard, the weeping willows, the clothes-line, picnic table, and way out back to the barns, chicken coops, and the mountains beyond. I sure do live in a pretty place.

"You know, Buddy, I sat here once with your daddy when he was courting your mama," Grandma started in. I could tell this was a long-ago story, but since it had Mama in it, I didn't mind. "Your pa had a five-day leave from the Navy. He hitchhiked up here all the way from New Orleans, and he come with a wedding ring in his pocket."

"I know this story Grandma," I interrupted, "Mama said no, and so Pa chased her into town, cornered her in the general store, and said he'd strip naked and run down main street unless she said yes."

"That's the made-up part of the story," Grandma said. "What really happened is your mama had another man courting her, and she told your daddy no. He was heartsick and come out here on this back stoop and cried like a baby. After about an hour of his boo-hooing, your mama took pity on him and said yes."

"Why?" This wasn't the story I'd heard. I found it sort of thrilling that Mama could've married somebody else. "Do you think she really loved him?" I didn't expect Grandma to tell me the truth. She's a grownup, and they always say what they think you're old enough to understand, no matter if it's the truth or not. I can understand a whole lot more than grownups think.

"Maybe not at first, but I think your mama grew to love your pa, and after you boys came along, her love for you flowed over onto him." Grandma stood up and ruffled my hair. "There's a lot about your pa you don't know," she said, moving across the porch to the screen door.

Grandma went inside and I struck out for the barn. I had two calves, Honey and Blossom, I was raising that summer in 4-H. I sort of like 4-H and I'm crazy about my leader. Her name is Dusty Lewis, and she's the local veterinarian. She's got really short hair and smokes a pipe, which I used to think was weird when I first met her, but now I'm used to it. Miss Dusty smokes Cherry Blend tobacco she buys special from Atlanta.

Dusty Lewis lives with Florence Goss, who is a waitress at Eat, and both of them are raising Florence's five kids from her marriage to Ronnie Goss, who is doing time in Memphis for armed robbery and attempted murder. It was in all the papers nationwide. Ronnie was billed as the Hillbilly Kid because he robbed a bank in Gainesville, and got away with eight thousand dollars and the security guard's radio. When the police asked him why he stole the radio, Ronnie said, "It was playing a Hank Williams tune, and I love ol' Hank." If that's not hillbilly, I don't know what is. Ronnie was a local celebrity even before we moved here to Comfort Corners. I bet Early and me finding the baby is going to make folks forget the Hillbilly Kid.

I was in the barn mucking out the stalls, singing "Tammy" to Blossom and Honey, when I heard something strange. I held quiet for a bit, and then heard a low moan coming from the hayloft. I climbed up the ladder that's attached to the silo, stuck my head up into the hayloft, and found Early lying on the hay, holding his stomach and rocking back and forth.

"What in the Sam hill are you doing up here?" I asked, "And why didn't you say nothing when you heard me singing to them cows?" I was embarrassed.

"Buddy, I'm hurt," Early said. He rolled over onto his side and drew his knees up to his chin. I climbed up into the hayloft and knelt beside him.

"Where?" I asked, and Early pointed to his stomach. I reached out and touched his shoulder, and he give out a groan of pain. I lifted his shirt, and what I saw broke my heart. Early's pa beat the living tar out of him. His back, stomach, and shoulders were covered in bruises that were raised up in blue-black welts.

"Why'd he do it?" I asked.

"Somebody told him about us finding the baby, and he got real mad. He was drunk and whupped me pretty good. I runned away from home last night, and this was the only place I could think to come."

"Why didn't you come in the house?" I couldn't believe Early had spent the night in the barn, in pain and all alone.

"Your pa was home, and I know he don't like blues," Early said.

"Well, Pa's gone, so I'm taking you inside to Grandma. Can you walk?"

"I think so. I'm a bit tender is all." Early tried to get up a couple of times, and finally I got under his shoulder and helped him to his feet. He was leaning on me, and with every step a moan would escape. I knew he was bad off, but I still had to get him down the

ladder. I went first and he sort of sat on my shoulders, and I eased
him down. I was hanging on for dear life and almost lost my footing a couple of times. Even though Early's skinny, he's heavy, and
at least a foot taller than me. When we got outside, I started hollering for Grandma. I saw her stick her head out the back door,
and I waved and yelled louder. She must've known something bad
happened by the way I was carrying Early.

Grandma met us halfway, and she helped me lug Early into the
kitchen. She sat him down in a chair and helped him take off his
shirt. When Grandma saw the bruises, she let out a gasp, and I
could see her eyes well up with tears.

"Your pa do this?" she asked. Early nodded, and Grandma
knelt down in front of him and took his hands in hers. "Don't you
worry none, Early. You'll stay here with us for awhile."

Early looked at Grandma, and when he saw she was crying, he
started in to bawling too. Grandma cradled his head against her
chest, and they both cried. Pretty soon I was crying, too. Well, it
was a very touching moment and doesn't have a thing to do with
me being tenderhearted or a sissy. Anybody would've cried. Well,
probably not Butch Calkins.

Grandma got some soap and hot water and cleaned Early's
bruises. She fixed a poultice of mustard greens and Vicks VapoRub,
wrapped him up in a pillowcase, and put him to bed in my room.
When they were walking up the stairs, Early leaned his head
against Grandma's shoulder, and I could tell he was still crying by
the way his shoulders were shaking. Once she got him in bed and
got two aspirin in him, Early looked like he might could relax.

All of a sudden he jerked and tried to sit up in bed. "What
about Mr. Lyle? He won't want me here."

"You let me worry about Mr. Lyle. When I'm done with him,
you'll be welcome here as long as you want to stay," Grandma
said, easing Early back down on the pillow. She reached out and
wiped his brow with a cold washcloth, and picked some hay out
of his hair. "What you need now is sleep. You think you can you
do that for me?"

Early smiled and sunk deep into my pillow. He closed his eyes and give out a deep sigh. I think he was asleep in less than a minute. Grandma and I stayed in the room a bit longer just watching over him. His breathing got deeper and deeper. Every once in awhile his legs would give a jerk and he'd moan, but for the most part he was sleeping hard.

Back in the kitchen, Grandma went right to the phone and called the law. "Matt, this is Lena Harrington. I've got Early Finch out here. His Pa beat the bejeezus out of that poor boy, and I'm calling the law on him." Grandma waited for Matt to finish talking, and then she started in again.

"I think you're dead wrong, Matt. It is my business, and it's the county's business, too, when one of our young'uns gets beat up. And I don't care if that child is blue, red or green. You got to do something. Now I'm making a formal complaint against Finch, and I expect you to act on it."

There was more talking, but I quit listening. I went out on the back porch and sat in Grandma's rocker. This was supposed to be a great day, but all I could feel was this dark sadness creeping in on my heart. I know why my Pa is rough on me, but Early's father had no call beating him. Early was a gentle boy, like me, but he wasn't a sissy. His only fault was a healing gift, a magical gift, his pa didn't understand. If you ask me, Early and I really struck out in the father department.

Grandma came out on the porch and stood beside me for a minute. I rocked away, not saying a word. Finally she gave me a nudge, and I got up so she could sit down. I sat on the floor beside her, and her fingers reached out and played with my hair.

"What's Pa going to say when he finds Early upstairs?" I asked.

"I don't really care," Grandma said. "That boy is going to stay here until he's healthy, even if I have to fight the county to keep him."

"What about his folks? Won't they wonder where he is?"

"I sent Matt Williams out to Early's house. He'll tell Emma where Early is and what needs to be done. If Matt has any sense, he'll take Burrell off to jail and lock him up. Now, don't you have to get into town to have a picture made?"

"Shouldn't I stay here and help you with Early?"

"Early's going to be fine. Right now he needs some sleep, some healthy eating, and time away from that miserable bait farm," Grandma said, standing up, pulling me to my feet. "Now, you head on off to town, and while you're down there pick me up a can of baking power. If I can't put ten pounds on that boy with my biscuits, then I ain't half the cook I think I am." She reached into her apron and gave me a dollar bill. I started to turn away, but Grandma pulled me back in a tight hug, and kissed the top of my head. We stayed that way for a minute; then she turned me around, gave me a swat on the behind, and pushed me toward town.

As I walked down our road, I felt the dread lifting. Grandma was in charge, and there was no way Pa would take a stand against her. Will couldn't do anything. He was scared to death of Grandma, ever since she caught him in the bathroom with one of Pa's girlie magazines and threatened to cut his thing off if he ever looked at smut like that again.

I turned onto the county highway that followed the river into town, picturing reading about myself in the paper and being the center of attention. I was almost happy, lost in my dreams, when I saw Butch Calkins. He was on his bicycle, a cigarette hanging out of his mouth.

"I've been waiting for you, girlie," he yelled. He was smiling in that trashy way he has, flipping his blond hair, eyes squinting against the sun.

I knew I couldn't outrun his bike, so I just stood there looking at him. I wanted to run. In fact, I was desperate to run, but I was so scared, I couldn't make my feet do what my brain was saying.

Butch rode up to where I was standing, and I watched him pull his fist back. I felt the pain like an explosion from my head to my toes. I hit the ground, and when I opened my eyes, I could see fireworks dancing all around my head. Butch was on me right away and busted me a good one in the mouth.

"You ain't nothing but a tattletale bitch, and I'm by God going to teach you a lesson!" Another punch; my right eye and cheek; more fireworks.

"Go on, cry. You know you want to. Come on, girlie boy, let me see them tears." Butch kicked me in the stomach, and the force of the blow rolled me over, off the road, and down into the ditch. He was on me again. "I said cry, girl!"

I couldn't cry. I couldn't do anything but lay there and moan. I reached up and touched my face. My fingers came away sticky with blood.

"Don't kill me, Butch," I said, but the words came out sounding funny, like my head knew what to say, but my lips wouldn't work.

Butch sat on my chest, pinned my arms over my head, and slapped my face time and again. He was quiet for a minute, and I thought he might be done, but then he hawked up a big gob of spit and let it drool down onto my face. I didn't fight back. I took it because I knew I had to. It's the same feeling I get when Pa's whipping me.

After a couple more slaps, Butch got on his bike. "You tell anybody I did this, and I swear to God, I'll kill you." Then he was gone.

I didn't have the energy to get up out of the ditch, let alone walk into town. I laid there for about ten minutes, staring up at the sky, dizzy and hurting. Once up on my feet, I headed down to the river. I could feel my right eye closing up on me, and each step sent slivers of pain right up my spine to my head. I took off my t-shirt, dipped it in the water, and rinsed my face off. By the blood on my shirt, I knew I must look a mess. I cleaned myself up as best I could, and started off for home. I dreaded having to tell Grandma what happened. Pa would tell me I deserved it.

I walked a few yards down the road, but something stopped me. I knew that if I went home and acted like this beating was no big deal, there'd be no way I could look at myself in the mirror ever again. Then it came to me like that thunderbolt in Butch's fist, and I knew what I had to do. I had to go into town and have my picture made looking as bad as I did. I wanted everybody to see what Butch Calkins did to me.

It seems I've spent my entire life trying to stay out of Pa's way, trying to be invisible at school so the bullies would leave me alone. This wasn't working. Being invisible could get me killed. My mama wanted a life for me that was bigger and better; I know that because she told me so. I think I just wanted to matter to somebody, anybody.

I turned and headed back toward town. With each step, I became more determined. At least I hadn't cried in front of Butch, which is a pretty big deal. Once the bigness of what I was doing sunk in, I realized this could turn out to be a great day after all. This was the day I stopped being afraid.

CHAPTER 4

It was slow going, but with my one good eye I made my way into town, limping over North Bridge, heading straight down Highway 28. I was in front of Ed Runyon's gas station when a blue pickup truck pulled up beside me.

"Buddy, are you all right?" It was Dusty Lewis. She had Florence in the truck and all of Florence's kids in the back. It looked like they were on the way to Doc Rodger's because Laurie, Florence's oldest girl, had a rag tied around her hand, and it was soaked with blood.

"I'm fine, now leave me alone," I said and kept right on walking.

Dusty drove beside me real slow and kept yelling out the window for me to stop.

"Buddy, if you don't stop right this minute, I'm going to get out of this pickup and beat the living crap out of you."

"Somebody already done that Dusty," Florence said.

I didn't stop, but I slowed down. Truth is, Miss Dusty sort of scared me. I knew she wanted to help, but I wasn't stopping.

"Go away and leave me alone," I yelled back at the truck. "I'm fine!"

Apparently Dusty didn't believe me. She pulled the truck right across my path and screeched to a stop, knocking all the Goss kids on their butts. In a second she was out her door and by my side.

"Who did this to you?" she demanded.

"It doesn't matter. I'm getting my picture made for the *Bugler* and I can't be late." I tried to limp around Dusty, but by this time Florence had come up on my other side. She pulled her hanky out to wipe my face and was working up a good spit.

"Well they sure ain't going to take no picture with you looking like this," Dusty said, "because Baby Boy, you ain't pretty. My God, Florence, look at that eye of his puffing up. Whoever smacked you had dead on aim."

"Honey, hold still, and let me dab at your lip," Florence fussed, wiping at my split lip and cooing, "Now that ain't so bad is it?"

"Has Aunt Lena seen you?" Dusty asked. I couldn't answer because Florence was still working on my split lip. "I didn't think so. Well, get in the back of my truck and I'll take you to Doc's and let him look at you."

"Forget it. I'm going to the community hall and have my picture took." I pulled away from Florence and started off for town. "Y'all don't understand, I want people to see me like this," I yelled over my shoulder and turned toward town.

I never looked back. Over my shoulder, I heard Laurie Goss whine to her mama, "What about me, I'm the one bleeding to death."

"Oh shut up, Laurie. We'll get you to Doc's in a minute." Dusty turned the engine over and roared back onto the road. "Give 'em hell Buddy!" she yelled out the window.

As I walked past the Dutch Christian Reform Church, I saw a couple of people standing by the parsonage. They looked sort of shocked when they saw me, but they didn't speak. I didn't expect them to since it's known all over town we're Catholic.

Across the street Harold Biehl, the postmaster, was taking letters out of the drop box in front of the post office. When I passed by, he stood up straight, hands on his hips, and let out a low whistle.

"Buddy, are you all right? Should I call your grandma?" he asked.

"I'm fine, so don't go calling nobody," I snapped. I started to brush pass Mr. Biehl and then got to feeling bad. Just because I was hurting was no cause to be spiteful. I liked Mr. Biehl, and he's always been nice to me.

"I'm sorry Mr. Biehl, I didn't mean to get snotty. I've had sort of a rough day."

"I can tell. What can I do to help?"

Those were the words I was dreading. Those were the words that started the tears, and once I started I couldn't stop. I cry when I'm in pain, and I cry when people are nice to me when I don't expect it.

Mr. Biehl put his arm around my shoulders and ushered me toward the post office. At the front door we met Miss Pink on her way out. She had a yellow chiffon scarf tied around her head. She stopped right in front of me, and there was no way I could avoid her.

"I'm not speaking to you Buddy Dean on account of you ruined my hair," she snarled. She bent over to say something really hateful and got the full effect of my puffy eye and split lip. "Lord above, what happened to you?"

When I didn't answer, Miss Pink cut her eyes over to Mr. Biehl. He just shrugged.

"Well, I'm sorry you got yourself beat up, but don't think I'm going to forget about what you done to my hair," Pink said. I thought this was pretty cold. There's nothing like a baldheaded woman to hold a grudge.

Mr. Biehl took Miss Pink by the arm and guided her out to the sidewalk. "Pink, you leave this boy alone. I got to get him over to Doc's."

"Ain't nothing Doc can do but clean him up; maybe take a stitch or two. Damage is done." Miss Pink gave me a hard look, then turned on her heels and headed across the street to Helen's Hairport.

"That's a bitter woman," Mr. Biehl said as he led me inside the post office. "Now Buddy, let's get you over to Doc's. We can go out the back."

"I think I'm going to throw up," I moaned, my stomach roiling. I was all sweaty and hot. It was like I had no balance and was floating in space.

"Right in here," Mr. Biehl said, pushing me into the little bathroom.

I sank to my knees and let it fly, until I had nothing left but the burn of bile. When I looked in the bathroom mirror and saw what Butch had done to my face, the tears started again. I looked pretty bad. No wonder Miss Dusty and Florence were worried. My bottom lip was split wide open and a couple of my teeth were loose. My nose was crusted with blood, and my right eye had all but swollen shut. There was a deep cut on my chin, and I was bleeding from the top of my head where I hit the road.

Mr. Biehl knocked and came in the bathroom. He watched me try to fix myself up for a few minutes and then said in a low voice, "Doc's got to have a look at that lip Buddy. You ready to go?"

"Don't you have to stay in the post office?"

"Nah. The post office runs itself. Ain't nobody likely to come in now that it's noontime."

"Maybe we'd better go then," I told Mr. Biehl. I thought at first I could walk it, but my right eye was getting worse, and I could hardly see.

Mr. Biehl led me out the back door of the post office, which is probably illegal since it is a government building. This is the first time I'd ever been any place so official, and I couldn't see a darn thing because of my eye. We went across the alley to Doc Rodger's, but his wife said Doc was over at Eat to pick up a quick dinner because he'd just stitched up Laurie Goss, who cut herself on a broken milk bottle. Mr. Biehl left me with Mrs. Rodger and said he'd be back in a minute with Doc.

Mrs. Rodger told me to make myself comfortable, so I sat in the swing on Doc's front porch. I knew she wanted to ask me what happened, but she just asked if I'd like a glass of iced tea.

"No m'am, thank you. I guess my mouth's pretty sore right now."

"I didn't even think of that Buddy, I'm sorry," she said. She waited a few minutes because I guess she didn't want to leave me alone. Finally she asked, "How's your grandma doing? She canning this summer?"

"She's just fine m'am. I expect she'll be putting up everything same as last year." All this small talk was killing my mouth, but I didn't want to be rude. "What happened to the baby? Is he all right?"

"That baby is the sweetest child that ever drawed a breath," she said, and her face just glowed up. "We got him in the front room, want to see?"

I nodded and she took me inside to see the baby. She had him propped up with pillows on the sofa. He was drooling like mad. I leaned over him and patted his head.

"Hey there, little baby. Remember me?"

"We call him Andy, after Doc's father. I think the county is going to place him in a foster home, but I'm after Doc to let us keep him. This precious boy has all but stolen my heart."

Doc came in, his napkin tucked under his chin. "My God, Buddy, I've seen road kill that looked better than you," he said, moving my head toward the window so he could take a look. I could see his lips get tight, so I figured I was in for a shot or some stitches.

"So, what do you think of our young cowpoke?" Doc asked, bending over and giving the baby a kiss. Little Andy looked around like he knew we were talking about him. "Ain't he a dickens?" Doc chuckled.

Doc turned his attention back to me. His fingers worked over my head, poking at my swollen eye, moving down to my lip. "It's worse than Harold said," Doc sighed, and then he got down to business. "Mr. Buddy, let's move into the office and see what we can do about this lip of yours."

Doc sat me on his examining table and turned the light full on my face. His fingers traced my busted lip and with his face so close to mine I could smell the fried chicken on his breath. He made me unbutton my bib-alls and felt my ribs and poked at my stomach.

"Well, you're lucky you've got nothing broke, but your mouth is going to be plenty sore for a week at least. I don't want you eating nothing that you got to chew. Let's see if you can keep them front teeth. We may want to get Dr. VanMeeder to take a gander at your mouth."

Doc rummaged around for a minute, then turned back to me and said, "I'm going to numb up your mouth and put a couple stitches in that lower lip to keep it closed. This might hurt a bit."

It hurt more than a bit, even though I was numb. When Doc was done stitching me up, he pulled his chair up beside me and looked me full in the face. "Who did this to you?"

"Butch Calkins," I said. No use lying to Doc. With my swollen lip and being all numbed up, I was lisping more than usual. Doc didn't laugh or anything even though it came out sounding like Buth Calkinth. "He was mad on account of I told Matt Williams that he was in the dump right before we found the baby."

"Well, you didn't lie did you? There was no way you could withhold that information from the sheriff." I liked the way Doc thought. "Buddy, you don't suppose Butch got some girl in trouble do you?

"Butch is always in trouble," I said. "He's wild and runs around. Grandma says that's what comes from living in a house with wheels on it."

"That's not the kind of trouble I meant," Doc smiled. "I mean does Butch have a girlfriend? Did he get a girl pregnant?"

Boy, did I feel stupid. Here Doc was talking to me like I had some sense, and I was acting like a dumb kid. This was something I never thought about. Butch got some girl pregnant, and then tried to get rid of the baby. He's a murderer and he's going to jail. Things were looking up.

"I bet that's what happened!" I eased off the table. "I bet that's exactly where Andy come from." Then I felt sorry for Doc and Mrs. Rodger. "I'm really sorry if Butch turns out to be your Andy's daddy."

"Andy's not ours yet," Doc said, "and there's no proof that Butch had anything to do with this. We'll leave that to Matt Williams." Doc got up and put his needles away. I could tell by the clock on his desk that I had about a half an hour before I was to meet Miss Carla to have my picture took. I sort of wanted to hang around Doc's and play with the baby, but when we walked outside the office, guess who was sitting in the living room with the baby on her lap—Pink Watrous.

"I'm still mad at you Buddy Dean," Miss Pink said.

"Miss Pink, I'm sorry if all your hair fell out, but it's really not my fault," I said. "You got distracted is all from having to save that baby and be a hero."

"Well, I guess," she huffed, "but it's going to be six months at least before I can leave the house without a hat." Then she sliced her eyes at me and I could see she planned on holding a grudge for all six months.

Doc put his arm around my shoulder, and together we walked out onto the front porch. "I'm going back to Eat and try to finish my dinner," Doc said, "What's this day got in store for you, Buddy?"

"I'm getting my picture took for the newspaper," I answered. "They're doing an interview and a story about me and Early finding the baby."

"How's Early doing?" Doc asked, giving me one of those looks that grownups give each other when they want the truth.

"Well, his pa beat him up pretty bad. He spent the night in our barn, but Grandma's got him inside, and she says he's staying with us until he's better."

"Your daddy won't mind?"

"Pa don't know, but Grandma says he'll be okay with it."

"Then I'd trust your grandma," Doc chuckled. He got that grownup look again, leaned over so he could see me eye-to-eye,

and asked, "Buddy, did Early bring that baby back from the dead?"
I knew he wanted me to tell him exactly what I thought in my
heart of hearts.

"I believe he did, sir," I answered.

"That's enough for me," Doc answered. Then he reached out
and shook my hand real formal like and took off across the street
for Eat. I cut across Schoolhouse Road and went in the side door
of the general store. I still had to get Grandma some baking powder and I wanted people to see what Butch Calkins did to me.

Mozelle Landry was working the register. She's a high school
girl and a cheerleader, but I don't think she's very smart. Every
time I run into her I always say, "Good day Madam Mozelle,"
but she never gets it. I guess she doesn't know any French. She's
popular and very stuck up. I don't understand that. However, she
is very pretty and has a big chest that all the boys talk about.

"Buddy, what happened to your face?" I started to tell her, but
Mozelle started talking again. She didn't really care about me. "I
heard all about what you and that retarded blue boy done. Folks
are calling y'all a couple of heroes. I didn't believe it at first, but
the sheriff says it's true."

"Early's not retarded. Mozelle, I need some baking powder."

"Back shelf, next to the flour and corn meal. Why are you talking so funny?"

"Doc numbed up my mouth so he could take some stitches."

"Oh Buddy, we got the new *Screen Secrets* in. I saved one out.
You're the only one up here that reads this stuff."

I got the baking power, and when I got back to the counter
Mozelle had the magazine laying on the counter. Lana Turner was
on the cover. This was not a big selling point with me. According
to Mama, Lana starred in the worst movie Hollywood ever made,
The Rains of Ranchipur, which we saw at the Fox Theatre. It cost fifty
cents because it was a special showing. In that movie Lana wore a
turban, and Mama said she was much too tan for a white woman.

"Now Buddy, tell me about finding the baby," Mozelle said.
"It's all folks been talking about."

"It's just like you heard, I guess. We were in the dump, Early found the baby and brought it back to life," I said, flipping through *Screen Secrets* trying to get in a quick read before Mozelle made me buy it.

"What do you mean, brought it back to life? The baby's okay isn't he? I heard Doc's keeping him."

"The baby's doing fine. They're calling him Andy after Doc's father." I love giving people news they don't expect. I looked around and saw about five people had gathered up front by the register to listen.

"I guess it was a miracle," I said. "That baby was dead, and Early touched it and it started to cry."

"I heard one of y'all performed that mouth rescue thing and breathed him back to life," somebody said. It was Imadeen Landry, Mozelle's homely old-maid sister.

"Was that baby dead or alive when y'all found it?" This come from Janice Lambert, whose son Danny is in my class at school. Danny is a natural at sports, and I like him because he's nice to me even when nobody else is around. "Ain't no raising the dead without some sort of mischief involved."

"We didn't do anything wrong. Early pulled the baby out of an old milk pail, and after he held him awhile, the baby started breathing. Early gets feelings, and his hands get hot, and he makes things happen. He just did a miracle is all. He's got a gift." I was attracting a crowd. There must have been about twelve people gathered by the cash register listening to me. Nobody seemed to care that I was beaten to a pulp and had a face that looked like raw meat, all they wanted to hear about was the baby. I will admit that once I got an audience I might have gotten a little carried away.

"Well now, y'all know Early's blue, and he's got special powers. He can't explain them, he just touches things and makes miracles happen. He gets a feeling deep in his soul, his hands start to tingle and get hot as a stove top, and then he zaps a person just like electricity." I had the crowd in the palm of my hand, and I was just getting warmed up.

"It's the devil's work," is what I heard hissed from the front door. Everybody stopped. It was Bart VanMeeder, the Dutch Christian Reform circuit dentist. He was known in four counties to be ornery and spiteful.

"Devil's work! The dead don't rise lessen the good Lord above does the laying of the hands." Dr. VanMeeder came inside the store, and everybody parted ways to let him pass. "And where was that baby found? In the dump is where. Think about that, will you? Human waste cast off by demons. We need to find where that baby come from."

Dr. VanMeeder was starting to lose the crowd. Nobody wanted a sermon, and nobody liked him anyway. The fact the baby was alive was reason to rejoice, not be suspicious and hateful. A couple of people spoke up against Dr. VanMeeder, and then everybody started talking at once.

I could see things were taking a turn, so I started to inch away. I figured I could get out the back door and over to the community hall and nobody would know I was missing. The last thing I heard was, "That retarded blue boy worked a miracle, and folks have got a right to know." With that I slipped out the back door.

I limped my way across Schoolhouse Road and headed up to the community hall. Miss Carla was sitting on the front steps waiting on me. Sitting next to her was a huge Kodak box camera.

"Buddy, what happened?" she asked, standing up and running toward me. "Look at your face."

"I got beat up, but it's not that bad" I said, trying hard not to lisp.

"By who?" Miss Carla asked, trying to hide a smile.

"I know I'm talking funny. Doc numbed up my mouth. You can laugh if you want to. It was Butch Calkins that done it. He was one of the boys in the dump before me and Early found the baby. I told you about him. You'd better put that in your story too. And tell people that he beat me up, and I got seven stitches in my lip."

Miss Carla took me by the hand and led me to the steps. We both sat down, and she turned to me and looked real serious.

"Buddy, are you sure you want your picture in the paper looking like this?"

"I'm sure. What Early and I did is a good thing, and I want folks to know about it. I want everybody to know about Butch Calkins, too."

"That boy's a minor. I can't put something incriminating in the paper that would name him. That's just not the way things are done in the newspaper business." I started to say something, but she stopped me. "However, I can say that the sheriff's office is investigating some youths who were seen in the area just prior to the discovery of the baby's body."

"You won't name names, huh?"

"I can't. What this boy has done to you is criminal, and I hope Matt Williams calls him out on it, but I can't be putting his name in the paper."

We sat there for a couple of minutes. I was disappointed, but then I realized everybody would know it was Butch that did it. It's common knowledge he's always picking on me. You ask anybody who hates me the most, and they'll name Butch Calkins. News like this gets around.

"So, are we going to take my picture?" I was ready. I wanted the story to run in the paper, and I wanted people to know I was a hero.

"I guess we can," Miss Carla answered, "but don't you want to put on your T-shirt first?"

"It's all bloody," I said, pulling the shirt out of my back pocket and showing her.

"Eeoou, Buddy, don't. That's gross."

"I know. It's ruined. It was my best shirt too. I wanted to look good for my picture, so I sort of dressed up."

"Well, you'll still look good," Miss Carla said, but I could see in her eyes it wasn't true. "Now, where shall we take your portrait? You think it'd look nice in front of the community hall? I know, we could go back to the scene of the crime and shoot it in the dump."

"I don't want to go back there," I said. "Right here is fine." Carla set up the camera, and I practiced a couple of poses. We were just about ready to take the picture when a couple of high school kids went by on their bicycles, whistling and calling me girlie. I pretended not to notice, but Carla turned and watched them ride away. She didn't say anything about it, which I thought was very polite.

"I'm not going to look too country in my bib-alls and no shirt am I? You can tell me true, it won't hurt my feelings."

"Tell you what, I'll get a close-up on your face and we won't see the bib-alls at all. Okay?"

It was perfect. Let them see my split lip, swollen eye, cut chin, and smashed up nose. I wanted them to read my story, and Early's, too. Let them see how heroes get treated.

"Smile," Miss Carla said, and I just stared at the camera. There was no smiling with this lip. "Got it. Now, one more. Good. I think that's going to turn out great."

Now that the picture was took, I got wobbly legs. I don't know what come over me, but it's like all the energy in my body had run out and I sort of fell down. Carla ran over and tried to help me up, but I was so dizzy I couldn't even stand. She eased me back down, and I leaned against the community hall sign and waited for my woozy head to pass.

"Put your head between your legs if you're dizzy. I read somewhere that's supposed to help," Carla said.

I put my head down, but all the blood rushed to my eye and lip and I could feel my pulse pounding in my cuts. I leaned back against the sign. Carla sat down beside me and patted my hand. That didn't help. I closed my one good eye and remembered that this was a good day. This was the day I stopped being afraid.

"Buddy, get in the car. I'm driving you home."

All the way home I kept thinking, I will never be scared again.

CHAPTER 5

"Pink called and told me you got beat up," Grandma yelled from the back door. As I got closer, and she got a good look at my face, I could see her lips tighten into a thin, white line. That was the look she got when she said she was cut-to-the-bone mad. "It was that trashy Calkins boy weren't it? I've had it with that family, and I aim to do something about this right now." Grandma yanked me inside the kitchen and went right to the phone. If she called the sheriff I knew Butch would kill me.

"Grandma, please don't call the sheriff, and don't tell Pa either." I must've sounded pretty desperate because Grandma put the phone back on the hook. She sat in a kitchen chair and pulled me close so she could examine my injuries.

"Where is Pa?" I asked. I knew he wasn't home because I didn't hear him hollering about Early being upstairs.

"Don't know. I haven't seen him since he left the house early this morning. I think he might have a girl somewhere abouts." Grandma examined my injuries, clucking, "I can't believe you, of all people, let somebody take your picture looking this bad."

A girl? Mama's only been dead two years, and it just doesn't seem proper that Pa should have a girlfriend so soon. If he was

51

going to take up with a girl, it'd be nice if he introduced her to me and Will.

"It looks like Doc did all right by you," Grandma said, standing up and kissing the top of my head. I was still stunned with the news about Pa and some woman I didn't know. Grandma took notice and gave out with a big sigh. "Oh don't look so shocked, Buddy. You didn't expect your father to stay single the rest of his life did you? He's still a very young man."

"He's not that young," I said. Pa was thirty-seven, which seemed old to me. "Besides, it's not fitting."

"Of course it is. It's only natural Lyle would want someone to share his life. It's going to happen Buddy, whether we like it or not."

"Don't it bother you, Grandma?" After all, Mama was her daughter. I know sometimes Grandma gets sad when she looks at me and Will. She says I'm more like Mama, but I know Will looks like Mama, too. Will also favors Pa, but I don't look a thing like him.

"It's time marching on, darling, and there ain't nothing we can do about that. Grieving is different for everybody. Right now it's time for your pa to move on. We can't fault him just because we ain't ready."

"Do you still miss Grandpa?"

"Lord, yes. Every now and then I forget he's passed. I catch myself setting an extra place at the table or making something for supper I know he'll like. When I catch myself, I imagine it's Ray talking to me, trying to get my attention." Grandma turned to me and looked serious for a minute. "Do you ever feel your mama, Buddy, like she's right over your shoulder?"

"Not really. I talk to her every night, but I don't know if she hears me."

"Oh, I think she does. I think she'd be real proud of you for helping Early save that baby." Grandma picked up my hand and squeezed it between her palms. "It's your daddy's time to find somebody new. That don't mean he didn't love your mama. Men don't show their feelings like women. That's what makes us different."

Grandma had a point. Boys aren't supposed to cry, but it's okay for girls. The only way Pa could cry was to hide out on the back porch when he thought we were all asleep. I can still see him sitting on our back porch in Atlanta, crying over Mama's slip. Fact is; we all changed after Mama died, but I think Pa changed the most of all. Sometimes he gets so sad he won't get out of bed for days at a time. When he finally comes downstairs, he's mean, won't say a word except to swear at us, and then he disappears, gone drinking. Grandma says that's his way of coping, the same way writing in my diary helps me.

"How's Early doing?" I asked. "Does Will know he's here?"

"Yes, and he's just about driven me crazy with questions. I finally told him this was my house and I could have anybody I wanted for company, and if he didn't like it he could move out." I'm sorry I missed that, but I bet Will went right to Pa and told him Early was upstairs in my bed. "Now go up and see Early while I get supper on the table. See if he's ready to take some nourishment."

I hesitated a second before I went into my bedroom. It was strange to think about somebody else living in my bedroom. I opened the door and saw that Early was propped up in bed looking at one of my Nancy Drew mystery books. I knew he wasn't reading it, on account of Early gets confused by a bunch of words on a page. When I came in, Early's eyes lit up for a second, but when he saw my face he set his jaw and shook his head.

"Butch Calkins?" he asked. I nodded. "You knew it was coming didn't you?" I nodded again. "Did you cry?" I shook my head. Early smiled, "Good for you, Buddy."

"You feeling better?"

"Tolerable," Early said; then he held out the Nancy Drew mystery and shook his head. "What's this?"

"Nancy Drew. It's a mystery story," I said. I love Nancy Drew. She's smart, clever, very popular, and always gets her chums Bess and George out of trouble. If I was in trouble, I'd want Nancy Drew to help me out.

"If you want, I'll read some to you after supper." Early was looking at my favorite Nancy, *The Hidden Staircase*, which was the second book in the series, and the most exciting.

"You can read it if you want to, just promise not to get mad if I don't understand everything," Early said.

I promised, but this was risky. Once I tried to explain television to Early. I told him all about "Leave it to Beaver," and how much I liked Tony Dow who played Beaver's brother Wally. Early didn't get it at all. The whole concept of television was beyond him. He got it in his head there was some family that actually lived in a box. We went over it several times until I started to get tense. Finally I told him Wally and Beaver were my neighbors in Atlanta. He understood that.

I don't know what's going to happen the first time any of these country people see a television. There's a couple of folks up here that have been to Gainesville and seen a movie, and Miss Pink has actually been to New York City and Radio City Music Hall. She said it was the thrill of a lifetime.

"Your brother come in to see me," Early said, "He was looking for you."

"What did he say?" I never could tell about Will. Sometimes he was just like Pa and beat me up, but other times he just left me alone, like I was invisible. He and Pa are so much alike. Grandma says Will's problem is hormones, and what with him being fifteen, he's got too many of them. She says I'll get hormones when I get older. If they make me act like Will, then I don't want them.

"He said your pa is going to have a fit when he sees me here. Then we talked a bit. When Aunt Lena come upstairs and found him in here, she smacked him upside the head and he ran out of the house. I like him, Buddy. I think Will's nice."

"You don't know him. Believe me, he ain't nice." That was the trouble with Early. He liked everybody. He even liked Butch Calkins until he saw me getting punched around once, but even that time he said I had a smart mouth and was asking for it. Early says he can see both sides to any story, but I think a best friend's job is to see my side of the story.

"What'd you and Will talk about?"

"Finding the baby. He wanted to know what happened. I told him what we did. That's all. What does Nancy Drew do?"

"She solves mysteries and helps people like old widows and stuff," I answered. "Will wasn't being mean to you, was he? If he was, all you have to do is tell Grandma."

"We was just talking. I thought maybe he was like your pa and didn't like blues, but he seemed all right to me. Says he wants to be a ball player when he grows up."

"How long were you talking?" I've known Will for almost twelve years and I never knew he wanted to be a ball player. He'd probably be pretty good at it. Of all the sports in the world, I guess I understand baseball the most. Everybody says I throw like a girl, but I hit good. My catching needs work.

"We was talking for a goodly time, and then I fell asleep on him," Early said. "He brought me a glass of water; then Aunt Lena caught up with him. Did you get your picture made?"

"Yeah. Miss Carla says it's going to be right next to the story when the paper comes out on Thursday. I told a few more people all about what you did to save the baby. Everybody in town thinks you're a hero."

"Buddy, I don't want folks knowing what I can do. They won't understand. How many people did you tell?"

"Oh, not that many," I lied. "I was just talking about it in the general store, and maybe one or two people heard me."

"Mozelle?" Early may be slow, but he knows Mozelle will talk.

"I might have mentioned it to her; her sister, too. Really, that's about all." If Early knew how I shot my mouth off all over town, he'd never forgive me. I just figured everybody would talk about it for a day or two, see the story in the paper, call me a hero, and then forget about it. The more I think on it, I reckon that's exactly what's going to happen.

I heard the back screen door slam, and both Early and I were quiet for a minute trying to hear if Pa had come home. When we heard Will ask what was for supper, we both breathed a sigh of relief. I was hoping Pa would come home after Early and I were asleep so Grandma could have it out with him in private. Every time Grandma and Pa fight, it's about something I did. One time I heard Pa tell Grandma that I was the thorn in his side he'd regret until the day he died. Grandma told him if he ever said that again he'd be dead a lot sooner than he thought.

"Buddy, get Early out of bed and get on down here for supper!" Grandma yelled up the stairs.

Early was wearing an old nightshirt of Grandpa Ray's, and it hung on him like a tent. He kept pulling the bottom down so it'd cover his legs, and when he swung his legs off the bed I could see why. From the bruises and busted up skin on the tops of his thighs, I knew Early's pa must've whipped him with a stick of stove wood.

"Buddy, quit looking at me like that and help me stand up." Early got to his feet, but he was still pretty wobbly. We were just starting downstairs when Early whispered, "My pa don't know any better is all."

I knew Burrell Finch wouldn't beat his hunting dogs the way he done Early. I bet if anybody cared enough to ask him, he'd say he done it to learn Early a lesson. I know it's not right, and I swear I'll get back at Mr. Finch if it's the last thing I do. Seeing Early hurt touched my heart even more than when my pa hits me.

"I didn't hear any water running in that bathroom," Grandma said as soon as we hit the kitchen. "Early, you sit right here, and Buddy, go wash your hands. I didn't put plumbing inside for nothing you know."

Early sunk down into one of chairs at the kitchen table. Will was sitting right next to him, looking down at his plate and not saying a thing. When I got back from the bathroom, I took my regular seat, which was across the table from Early. Grandma sat at the head, like always. Pa's chair was empty, but there was a place set for him. Will reached out for the bread, but Grandma stopped him with a look.

"Will, pass the bread to Early. Company first."

Early smiled at Will as he took the bread, then the butter. He put a slice on his plate and with that done, it was every man for himself.

"Aunt Lena, don't y'all give a blessing a'fore you eat?" Early asked. Grandma, Will, and I sat there with our mouths full, looking embarrassed.

"We aren't a churchy family, Early," Grandma explained. "I used to be Baptist, and the boys were brung up Catholic. I guess somewhere along the line we just sort of give up on church."

"No reason not to say thank you," Early said. That just killed me. Nobody ever questions anything Grandma says or does.

"Well, come to think of it, you're right. We got us a lot to be thankful for; this food, and for the fact that both you young'uns are still alive." Grandma shook her head in amazement, "Early, would you favor us with a word of thanks?"

Early bowed his head. We did likewise. I felt sort of silly, and cut my eyes over at Will. He let out with, "Oh, brother," rolled his eyes upward, then bowed his head.

"Dear Lord in heaven who gives us all good things, thank you for this food. Thank you for taking care of Buddy when he was beat up. And thank you for bringing me here where I feel safe. Amen."

We all said a quiet amen. Then the back door slammed.

Pa came through the mud room and into the kitchen. "Smells good in here," he yelled, then he stopped short and stared at the three of us gathered around the table. "What's he doing here?"

"I live here," I said.

"Shut up, Buddy." Pa didn't like smart talk. "Early, I want you to get on home."

"Lyle, Early's going to be living here for a time. Why don't you and me go out in the front room and talk this out?" Grandma said.

"The hell he is, and there ain't no talking to be done. Early, I asked you polite, now I'm telling you to get out of my house." Pa kept smacking his hat against his leg. I knew his palms were itching for the yardstick.

Grandma jumped up from the kitchen table, knocking her chair backwards. When it hit the floor, it sounded like a bullet going off.

"This is my house. My house. Don't you ever forget that." Grandma was around the table and poking Pa in the chest with her finger. He stepped back from her a bit, but they locked eyes and I could tell there was going to be a battle.

"This is your house all right, but who's paying the bills? Who pays the taxes? Tell me that, old lady." Nobody stands up to Grandma when she's mad. I couldn't believe this. Pa and Grandma faced off in the kitchen, and this was exactly what I didn't want to happen.

"Upstairs," Will whispered to me and Early.

"You stay right there," Pa said, looking straight at Grandma, his breathing long and deep. Grandma didn't back down either.

Will got up from the table, and with a jerk of his head he indicated that Early and I should follow him out on the back porch. We both stood up and started to leave.

"I said stay put!" Pa lashed out with his right hand, aiming for anybody. I took it in the small of the back, right where Butch kicked me. The pain knocked the wind out of me.

"This ain't about Buddy, so leave him alone," Will said. "Come on you two, let's go," Will led the way out to the back porch, me and Early trailing behind. Early was limping pretty bad, and I could hardly see because of my swollen eye, but we made it to the porch swing.

Early and I sat and rocked for a time. Will was perched on the porch steps. It was tense. Grandma started in on Pa, and he gave it back as good as he got. Then they must've moved into the front room because we couldn't hear them anymore. It seems like we sat on that porch for a long time, nobody saying a word.

"You don't suppose he killed Grandma, do you?" I was starting to get worried.

"Shut up, Buddy," Will said.

"This ain't good. I got to go home," Early said.

"You can't go home until you get better," Will said. "You go home right now, you'll get another beating. Don't worry, Early, Pa'll come around. He's not as bad as you think." This was the most I'd heard out of Will since Mama died. It was like I didn't even know my brother anymore.

"Will, thanks for sticking up for me," I said. Usually Will and I didn't talk, but since he seemed like a different person, I thought I'd try.

"Bite me," he said. No, he was still my brother. "I just can't stand to see a bully get the best of somebody weaker. So, who did that to your face? Butch Calkins?"

"Yeah."

"What'd you do to him?"

"Nothing."

"Yeah, you did," Early said. "Remember? You told the sheriff Butch was in the dump. That's why he's mad. You put the law on him."

"I figured it was something like that," Will said. "You always got to be shooting your mouth off. I heard you told everybody in town about Early's hot hands, and how he made magic and brought that baby back to life. That's all folks are talking about."

"Oh, Buddy, no," Early moaned.

"Jesus, Buddy, don't you ever think?" Will asked.

"Well, that's exactly what happened. I might have exaggerated a little bit, but it was mostly true. Early, you did bring that baby back from the dead. You're the one that said you can do things like that."

"Folks can't know," Early said. "I told you that Buddy. Why'd you tell everybody?"

"It wasn't everybody. It was just a few people. Don't worry, it'll blow over once the story runs in the paper."

"People talk," Early said, "and then people got to blame somebody."

"There ain't nobody to blame, excepting the fool who left her baby in the dump," Will said. "That's what's criminal. Now you two morons shut up. I'm going to check on Grandma and Pa."

Will got up and circled around the porch to the front of the house. Early and I rocked in silence for a couple minutes.

"You shouldn't a told, Buddy," Early whispered. "There's going to be trouble."

"What kind of trouble? You're a hero. You saved the baby's life."

"I see trouble. I don't know what kind yet, but I can feel it out there waiting on me." Early got up from the swing and limped to the far end of the porch. He looked up at the night sky and took a deep breath. It was like he was casting about for answers in the air. "There ain't no good going to come of this," he said, "it's already in the air."

"What's in the air?" I asked, coming up behind him. I took a deep breath and didn't feel anything strange. It was a typical Georgia summer night, humid, with a soft-feeling breeze and a bit of heat lightning. "Are you sure trouble's coming?"

"I know it. I can always tell. Mama says for me to keep quiet about it, but I know what's out there." Early turned back to me and I could see tears falling down his face.

"Look Early, if this is because I told people what you done, then don't worry. I'll go into town tomorrow and tell everybody I lied. I didn't mean to get you in trouble."

"Buddy, this ain't about you. If you didn't tell, they'd a still found out. This is just me. You know how you got trouble because you're soft acting, like a girl? I got trouble because I got the sight, and I can do things; knowing things, healing things. Folks get scared of what they don't know."

We both stood at the end of the porch and looked up at the sky. There were a million stars overhead, and the silhouette of the pines on the hill cut the horizon like the edges of a saw. I could see the Big and Little Dippers, Orion's Belt, and the North Star. Those are the only stars I know. Early and I stared up into the night sky, peaceful for a minute or two, both of us, it seems, waiting for the trouble he knew would come.

Our quiet was broken by the slamming of the screen door, and Pa come raging out the back. He didn't see us right off, but when he looked over toward the driveway, he saw our shadows on the lawn. We looked tall, strong, and mighty.

"You should be mighty proud of yourself, Early," Pa said, "saving that baby like you done. You got a right to be here, and I'm sorry for what I said. I'll be sleeping in the barn from now on, or until you're better." Pa started off toward the barn, a pillow and blanket under his arm. He stopped, turned back and yelled, "You done good too, Buddy."

That one caught me off guard. This was the first time I could remember my pa telling me I'd done anything worthwhile. Grandma and Will came around the side of the house and up to the back porch. Grandma had her arm around Will's shoulders. Usually Will don't like to be touched, but it seemed like he was leaning into Grandma.

"I told you Pa would come around," Will said. "He's just going to be sleeping out in the barn to give us some more room here in the house." Will slipped out from under Grandma's arm and came up on the porch. He went right up to Early. "He ain't leaving because you're blue."

I thought that was nice of Will. Of course Pa was sleeping in the barn because of Early. I knew as soon as folks got wind of Early staying out here, they'd start talking. Pa had to sleep in the barn for show. He didn't want none of his friends to think he'd gone soft on blues.

"I think it's time you boys headed up to bed," Grandma said. "It's been a long day for everybody. Early, you take an aspirin. Buddy, you make sure he does."

We all turned and started in the house, but Grandma stopped us. "Don't nobody say good night? Don't nobody bother to give an old woman a hug?"

We must've looked mighty guilty because Grandma laughed and waved us up to bed. "Go on with the lot of you. I'll see y'all in the morning."

I turned to go back inside the house, but Grandma called after me, "Did you hear what he said, Buddy? He said you done good."

I nodded, and then I felt the tears start to fall. I waved at Grandma and turned back inside. I've got to quit crying so much. No wonder people make fun of me. Soft-hearted is one thing, but there must be something wrong with me; maybe I've got a tear duct problem. Everything touches my heart. I know boys shouldn't be like that, so I'm going to try to change, but it'll have to be later when all this mess is over.

Early was already in bed by the time I brushed my teeth. When I got in bed I looked at Early's arm lying next to mine, and it reminded me of the globe at school, where the blue Atlantic Ocean meets the pink coast of the United States. My skin looked so pale next to his blue arm with its tiny white hairs.

"Huh?" I asked. Early was mumbling under his breath.

"Praying," he said, and kept on mumbling. When I heard his amen, I knew he was done.

"You pray every night?" I asked.

"Course I do. Don't you?"

"Not since Mama died. Pa's mad at God, so until they patch things up, I figure God won't be listening anyway."

"You got that wrong, Buddy. He sees and hears everything." Early reached over and handed me *The Hidden Staircase*. "Read me to sleep."

I started with Chapter 1, "A Rude Visitor." Early drifted off to sleep right in the middle of Chapter 2, "A Warning of Trouble." When I cut off my lamp, Early was sleeping like he didn't have a care in the world. I was just about asleep myself, then I remembered I had forgotten to tell Early what I found out about myself today.

"Early, wake up. I got something to tell you." I shook his shoulder, and he came awake with a snort. "I got something to tell you."

"I was dreaming."

"I know, but this is important. Early, today is the day I stopped being afraid," I whispered. "Not of Pa, not of Butch Calkins, or anybody else, or anything. This is the day I changed."

"But everybody's afraid, Buddy. Everybody. Why do you think your Pa and Butch act the way they do?" Early let out a tiny wheeze and was fast asleep once more.

Was this true? Was everybody really afraid? Early said trouble was coming because he could feel it. I let my body go limp and tried to feel the trouble so I could put a name to it. Sleep got me first.

CHAPTER 6

"Buddy, you better go over to Early's and get him some clothes. Tell Miss Emma he's going to be staying with us for a spell." Those were the first words out of Grandma's mouth when I came downstairs for breakfast. Then she turned my face toward the window. "Looks like you're going to heal up just fine." Early was sitting at the table eating a bowl of oatmeal with bacon crumbled in.

"Early's pa scares me . . ." Then I stopped. I wasn't going to be afraid of anything. If I was true to my word, this was my first test. "Okay, I'll go."

"Me, too. Maybe it won't be so bad if they see me," Early said.

"You could get the dogs off me," I said. I wasn't going to be afraid any more, but I didn't plan on being stupid. Those hounds were mean.

"Early is staying right here. You'll have to go alone. I thought about it all last night, and it just seems like the right thing to do." Grandma was determined.

"I'll go right after breakfast," I said. "Is Pa in from the barn?"

"Been and gone," Grandma said. "Your brother, too. They went up to check on Gizzy and see how the apples are coming along.

"What am I going to do?" Early asked.

"Rest. You concentrate on sleeping and eating. We got to put some weight on those bones." Grandma put a plate of hot biscuits on the table and buttered one for Early. "You got lots of healing to do, Early. I fixed you a spot on the front porch where you can lay in the sun."

There was a knock on the front door. It took us all a minute to recognize it for what it was. We never get company out here. I jumped up from my chair and ran to answer the door. First I peeked out the window to see who it was. I come face-to-face with a white woman and two kids staring back at me. They had their hands cupped around their eyes for a better view. I squealed. All of us jumped.

"Is this where the blue boy lives that saved a baby's life?" the woman asked the minute I opened the door. No hello. Nothing else.

"Who wants to know?" I had read enough Nancy Drew to know you never answer a question from a stranger straight off.

"I'm Carol Disbrow, and these are my boys, Ozzie and Vic. We're from over Alden way. I want that blue boy to bless my children. Talk in Alden is, he's got a healing touch. My boys are both bleeders." She pulled the kids to her so I could get a good look at them.

The boys did look sickly, but I didn't know if Early could help. Luckily I didn't have to answer because Grandma came to the door.

"There's no blue boy living here," she said. "Who told you such a thing?"

"I heard about him in Alden. When I got in town the cashier at the general store told me a retarded boy performed a miracle," Mrs. Disbrow said.

Mozelle! I told her Early wasn't retarded. She always gets stuff wrong.

"There ain't no retarded blue boy living here. Now I'm sorry you wasted your time, but we've got work to do. Good day to you, and good luck with your children." Grandma shut the door in the woman's face.

Mrs. Disbrow and her boys kept peeking in the windows, but when they didn't see anybody blue, they gave up and drove off.

I started for the kitchen, but Grandma grabbed the collar of my shirt and yanked me back. "Who'd you tell?"

"Nobody." She give me a look. I buckled. "Well, maybe I told a few people; but just Mozelle and a couple others in the general store. Not many." I was lying and she knew it.

"Do you know what you've done to that poor child?" she asked.

"It's going to be in the paper, and the sheriff was asking around about the baby, so folks were going to find out. Besides, Miss Pink told a lot more people than me."

"Pink. I might have known." Grandma held me close for a minute. "This has got me feeling edgy, Buddy. Now you run over to Early's and get his clothes. Ask his mama does he take any medicines I should know about."

I was halfway down the drive when Grandma yelled out the front door, "For God's sakes Buddy, don't tell nobody else!"

I thought that was unnecessary. Grandma knew I felt bad about telling on Early and having Mrs. Disbrow and her two bleeder boys coming to the house.

I started off to the Finch Bait Farm, which was way on the other side of town. I kept thinking about Early and what he could do. When I come up on Runyon's Gas Station, Ed Runyon himself came out to the street to ask me about Early and the dead baby. Mr. Runyon doesn't look so good. He's in bad health and wheeling around a canister of oxygen with tubes and a mask. They say two heart attacks and a stroke will do that to a man. If I was him, I'd stop smoking.

"Buddy, tell me about Early and the baby," he wheezed.

"I can't talk now, Mr. Runyon, I'm choring for Grandma," I said, cutting across the street toward the post office. I got to the middle of Bridge Street, which is the main road through town, when I saw a crowd pointing my way. I ducked around behind the gas station and ran between the Dutch Christian Reform Church and their parsonage, which was just an old Quonset hut they bought at an Army-Navy salvage in Gainesville. I sure wouldn't want to live there.

"Buddy Dean! You get up here! I got something needs asking." It was Helen Adams at the Hairport. She was sitting out back having a cigarette and reading her *Ladies' Home Journal*. She's a real Yvonne DeCarlo type.

"No time, Miss Helen," I yelled, and cut behind Eat. I could hear her yelling at me, but I was running so fast I couldn't make out what she was saying. I ran through the parking lot of the Methodist Church, past the white folk's funeral home, and cut down to the river bank so I wouldn't have to talk to any of the men at Joe's Pole, which is my least favorite place in town. Will says the name of the barber shop is dirty, but I don't get it. He explained it a couple of times, but I think that's just stupid.

I was halfway across the bridge at the south end of town when Matt Williams spotted me from the courthouse. He was out front washing the patrol car.

"Buddy, get your tail over here!" he yelled.

I thought about running, but decided against it. He was the law, and the thought of having to go to reform school with a bunch of rowdy boys made me queasy. I ran toward the courthouse, but got a stitch in my side and had to rest. I bent over to catch my breath, and some sweat ran into my eyes.

"Sweat! I got sweat in my eyes Mr. Matt. It's burning!" I was jumping from foot to foot and had my eyes screwed shut. Mr. Williams threw me a wet rag, and I used it to wipe my face.

"It's just salt water, Buddy. The sting'll go away in a minute," he said. "God Almighty, Buddy, what happened to your face? You get beat up again?" I nodded. "Well, you look plenty bad, but I hear Early's worse. Your grandma told me he was mighty tore up."

"His pa done it. Looks to me like he used a length of stove wood on him. That's not right."

"No, it ain't. I already been out to the bait farm and had a talk with Burrell. Them blues are strange, I got to say. Wife's nice enough, but Finch is peculiar, quiet acting, like he's hiding something." The sheriff took the washrag back from me and began washing down the hood of his car. I picked up the hose and followed after, rinsing away the soap. It didn't hit me until later that I wiped my face with that nasty old washrag. If I get sick, I'll know why.

"I'm heading up to the bait farm to get Early's clothes. Grandma said I was to tell them he was going to be staying with us. Wish I didn't have to go. Mr. Finch makes me nervous."

"You and me both," Matt Williams said. "Buddy, just how many folks did you tell about Early? We got us a television reporter coming all the way up here from Atlanta. They called this morning and said they want to put me on the air. I don't even know what that means."

Television was coming! Oh my God! This could be my big break in show business. I had dreamed of being on television. I even knew what I wanted to do. I'd be on "Leave it to Beaver" and be Tony Dow's new best friend. I'd fit right in with the Cleaver family, and Tony and I would become best friends in real life. I would be invited to stay with Tony and his family, and we would share a room. We'd go swimming in the pool at night after everybody had gone to bed. I dreamed about this so often that I could actually see it happening.

"Did they say anything about wanting to see me or Early?" I asked, praying the answer was yes.

"Nope. They're a might skittish about creating a sensation. I just hope that television thing don't bring a bunch of strangers to town. Now you get along. Mind them hounds." Matt turned back to washing his patrol car. I headed south toward the Finch Bait Farm.

The turn-off to the bait farm is about a quarter mile up Bluetown Road. There's a tacky sign on the main highway that reads *Finch Bait Farm—Worms & Crawlers—This Way*, with an arrow pointing toward Bluetown. The arrow on the sign is painted like a worm with a sharp head that points the way. Mr. Finch hand-lettered the sign and put lots of silver glitter on *worms and crawlers* so it's really shiny, especially in direct sunlight. I think it looks tacky.

I headed up Early's road, going kind of slow and keeping my ears open for Duke and Buster. I know they let the dogs run free a lot of the time, especially when Mrs. Finch is home by herself. I just hoped this wasn't one of them times.

"Hey, girlie boy, what you doing up here?" Leon Finch jumped out from behind a deer blind that was built up the road bank. I automatically flinched, trying to duck a certain hit. When it didn't happen, I turned to face him and slowly backed away.

"Hey, sissy boy, where you going?" he asked.

"Leon, I can't get beat up today. I'm still a mess from what Butch done," I said. "I'm here to talk to your mama. I come after Early's clothes."

"Sheriff said he was going to be living with y'all for a time." Leon said. "That's good. Pa goes too far, especially when he's drunk."

Leon started up the drive toward the house. I followed after him, but I kept my distance. I wasn't taking any chances. It'd be just like Leon to wait until I was relaxed, then sic the dogs on me.

"Is Early bad off?" Leon asked.

"Yeah. Grandma's doctoring him, but he's still plenty sore. Your pa got him bad. Who else is up at the house?" I asked.

"Just the girls," Leon answered. "Pa's off hunting."

Early has two sisters, Louann, who's Will's age, and Pocket, around six, I think. They're all blue, like Early. I can't imagine naming a girl child Pocket. I bet it was Mr. Finch's idea as some sort of joke. What's she going to do with a name like that when she grows up? Pocket's a real pale blue, but Early is expecting she'll darken up like the rest of the family. Grandma says she's six years old, and if she was going to darken she'd have turned. That's the way blue people work.

When I saw Miss Emma outside hanging up wash, I knew I was safe. She likes me. When she saw me coming up the path, she stopped what she was doing and started down toward me and

Leon. Pocket was making mud pies in the front yard. She didn't have a stitch on. That killed me. She wasn't even embarrassed about it and just kept playing in the mud. Boy, if company caught me naked, I'd run and hide.

"How's my young'un doing?" Miss Finch asked.

"Hey, Miss Emma," I said. "Where's them dogs?"

"They've gone off with Burrell, hunting," she answered. "You got no call to be scared, Buddy, though from the looks a you, you already been put through a wringer. Your pa get after you?"

"No m'am," I answered, "just an accident." I didn't feel like telling her about Butch. "Grandma says Early will be okay, but he needs to rest up some. She sent me to get his clothes. I'm supposed to ask if he's taking any medicines she needs to know about."

"No, he don't need no pills or nothing like that," she said, then turned to Leon. "Go inside and pack your brother some clothes. Put in a jar of blackberry preserves for Aunt Lena." Leon went inside, and Miss Emma pulled me a little bit away from the house. "I been so worried about that child, I ain't slept none these last two days."

"He's bruised up pretty bad, a lot of swelling. Grandma says he'll be okay, but it'll take some time. Why'd Mr. Finch beat him like that? He could've killed Early."

"He was crazy with shine and didn't know what he was doing. Somebody come up pretending to want worms, but then they asked for Early. Said they wanted him to lay hands on them for a cure. They told us about y'all finding the baby, and what Early done. Burrell thinks they just come around to stare because we're blue."

"Well, y'all aren't the only blues around. If people come to look, there's plenty in town to stare at," I said. That made me mad. Strangers' curiosity is no excuse for beating your son half to death.

"Did Early bring that baby back from death?" Miss Emma whispered. "I got to know, Buddy. Did he?"

"Yes m'am, I believe he did." I answered.

"Praise Jesus! That child has the gift. I knowed it right off when he was born. My Early's a special boy. You know that, don't you, Buddy? Early's been hand-picked by Jesus."

I heard a door open and Louann, Early's older sister, come out on the front porch. She's a pretty girl, in a blue-trash, tomboy kind of way. I bet with some proper clothes and a visit to the dentist, she'd turn out real good.

"Hey, Buddy, how's my baby brother doin'?" she asked, coming off the porch. "Y'all taking good care of him?" I allowed as how we were, and then she handed me a sack. "Here's Early's clothes. Some of them's dirty, so y'all have to do some wash, but this ought to keep him."

"You know, you can come over and see Early any time you want. I know he'd want to see you. Miss Emma, I know Grandma would like a visit."

Louann and her mother cut their eyes at each other. I knew why. Pa had a reputation with the blues. They knew who they could trust and who didn't like them. Grandma and I have a good reputation with blues, as far as I know. Will's is okay, but I bet once Early starts talking him up it'll get better. Butch Calkins has a bad reputation with everybody.

"You tell Early we miss him," Louann said, "and we want him home as soon as he's better." Louann turned and scooped Pocket out of the mud. "Mama, why do you let Sister run around naked? It ain't proper."

"She's just a baby," Miss Emma said.

Louann took Pocket to one side of the house and the rain barrel. Pocket seemed to know what was coming. She started up squealing and back-peddling as hard as she could. Louann was determined. She held Pocket with one hand and ladled water with the other. Pocket's squeals turned to giggles, and then the girls started splashing each other. Miss Emma watched her girls, and a smile cut across her face. She looked so young when her husband wasn't around.

"Miss Emma, I got to go," I said. "I'll tell Early you said hey."

"Buddy, give him a kiss for me," she said, "but not when he's awake, that'll scare him. Wait until he falls asleep, then kiss his cheek for his mama. That'd make me feel better."

I said I would, but I didn't promise. Early and I are best friends, but that don't include kissing. I've never kissed anybody but Mama and Grandma. There's a picture of me sitting on Pa's lap and he's kissing me, but that must have been a real long time ago.

I headed down the mountain and backtracked my way toward town. I stayed on the east side of the river. I didn't want to go into town. I didn't want to see anybody else and have to explain about Early. I walked along the river and came out on Harrington Road, walked past the south orchard until I got to our drive. I didn't see Pa's truck in the front yard.

Grandma had fixed Early a bed by shoving two of the big porch chairs together and covering them over with quilts. He was fast asleep. I leaned over and kissed his forehead. "That's from your mama," I whispered.

"That's real sweet of you, Buddy," Grandma said, coming around the side of the house.

"Well, I promised his mama I'd give him a kiss from her," I said, embarrassed. "Don't tell Early."

"I won't. How's Emma?"

"Okay. She sent along Early's clothes," I said, indicating the feed sack.

Grandma pulled out Early's clothes: two t-shirts, one pair of bib-alls, some underwear, socks, and a raggedy long-sleeved shirt with a clip-on tie still attached to the collar. That must be what Early wears to church. Grandma shook her head and muttered, "We got some wash to do," and then she pulled out a Holy Bible and a jar of preserves.

"Emma's preserves, best in the county," Grandma said. "Don't know what to make of the Bible. Can Early read good enough to get through this?"

"No m'am. He don't read good at all, but he remembers when stuff is read to him. Maybe she just wants him to have it," I answered. "Grandma, Miss Finch says that Early's been hand-picked by Jesus. She says he's got a healing gift."

"Blues are a strange lot, but you know that. Blue and Baptist is a dangerous combination. There's a lot of superstition around them folks. As for Early having special powers, you'd know that a heap better than me. You were there. Do you think he healed that baby?"

"I thought he did, but now I'm not sure. Maybe it's like the sheriff says, and the baby wasn't dead, just in a coma or something."

"Babies are delicate. I don't know how long one that young could survive outside and still be alive."

"Then maybe Early really is special," I said.

"Of course he is. We just have to wait and see how special. I already know how special you are." Grandma makes me feel good about myself, which I think is her biggest talent. She makes everybody feel good. When I get old like her, I hope I can do that.

"I been sleeping," Early said, yawning and stretching out on his makeshift bed.

"You sure have," Grandma answered, "and now it's time to eat. Y'all ready for supper? We're having pork chops and corn out of the garden. I got to fatten this scrawny blue boy up. Buddy, I've got mashed potatoes for you. Doc said you're not to be chewing until your teeth settle back in your head."

This was weird, it was too early for supper, but maybe Grandma wanted to force as many meals down Early as she could while he was living with us. It was when we were sitting at the kitchen table eating supper, then Pa's truck come up the drive, around the house, and up to the barn. Then I understood. Grandma wanted to feed me and Early and get us out of the way; then she'd take care of Pa and Will. That was fine by me. I have a hard time digesting when there's a lot of tension in the air.

"How's my mama?" Early asked as soon as we were upstairs. "You didn't see Pa, did you?"

"Your Pa was hunting. Your mama's fine. Misses you. Louann and Pocket, too. Your mama says you got the gift to heal. Can you put your hands on my eye and heal me?" Well, it was worth a try.

"It don't work that way, Buddy."

"Why not? You could try. Just put your hands over my eye for a minute and see what happens."

"I can't control it like that. It's like when all of a sudden your eye starts in twitching or you get an itch. When it comes on, I feel like somebody's talking in my head. Then my hands get hot, and all of a sudden I just know what's going to happen, or a voice tells me what to do."

"Have you had any of those feelings since you been here with us? Do you see anything happening to me? Can you read my fortune?"

"I don't want to talk about it any more," Early said. He pulled off his shirt and pulled Grandpa Ray's nightshirt over his head. It looked to me like the bruises on his back and stomach were starting to fade, but he still moved tender.

"It's too early for bed," I said. It was only about six-thirty. I sure didn't want to go to bed before the sun went down. "Are you tired?"

"I don't hurt so much when I lay down," Early said. "Hey Buddy, what happened to Nancy Drew? I was thinking about her all morning."

"I knew you'd like Nancy Drew. I got into Chapter Two, but then you fell asleep. Want me to pick up where we left off?"

"Yeah, but don't get mad if I fall asleep again." Early crawled into bed and settled back against the pillow. I sat at the foot of the bed and picked up *The Hidden Staircase*.

I finished Chapter Two and only had to explain a few things. I continued through the next few chapters, and it was right at the beginning of Chapter Five, "Strange Happenings," that I heard Early's snores. I put Nancy down and got ready for bed.

In the bathroom I tried to brush my teeth, but they were still pretty loose. My eye was starting to open up a bit and the bruises were turning from purple to blue. My nose was puffy-looking and sore, but I didn't think it was broken. In the mirror I saw the face that was going to be in the newspaper. This was the first time I could remember that I didn't hate looking at myself. My bruises made me look like someone else. I looked dangerous. I liked that.

I got into bed and watched Early, wishing all the while I could see inside his head. I never knew anyone who could do healing. Maybe Early had a direct line up to God, and here I was, a Dean, lying right next to him, and on the outs with the church. I got to thinking that if God was out there at all and paying attention, chances are He was watching over Early. I was within striking distance, and odds were pretty good He'd notice me too. Maybe this was a good time to start praying again. Mama used to make us say our prayers, but after she died we just sort of forgot.

"Dear God," I whispered, "please forgive me for not going to church and being mad at You for taking Mama. Please watch after Early and me and Grandma. If You really want to help out, don't let me get beat up anymore, or Early either." After that I felt pretty good. I was going to ask for a trip to Hollywood, but I figured I'd start out small with the stuff that really matters, then work up to the big things later.

I leaned over and kissed Early's forehead for his mama, then rolled over and closed my eyes. "Night Mama," I said, and drifted away, dreaming of hound dogs, worms, Tony Dow, and magical hands.

CHAPTER 7

The next morning Early was on the front porch talking with Will, who was dressed in his baseball uniform. When I saw the sky and the rolling clouds, I knew rain was heading our way.

"You got a game?" I asked. Will didn't answer, he just looked at me like I was the biggest fool on two feet. This talking to my brother is sort of new to me and it's going to take some practice for me to get the hang of it.

"Will's got an away game," Early said, "if it don't get rained out."

"Maybe the storm will pass over," I said. The words weren't an inch past my lips when the sky was split by a bolt of lightning that left the air stinking of electricity. I give out a yelp, and from the backyard I could hear Grandma's squeal. Then came a rumble of thunder that shook every window in the house.

Two more bolts of lightning lit up the sky, and then it was like someone dumped a bucket of water on us. The rain came straight down, making a curtain between us and the road. Grandma came out on the porch and watched with us. We all jumped every time the lightning hit. About ten minutes later Pa's truck pulled alongside the house. He jumped out and ran for cover. By the time he hit the porch, he was soaked through to the skin.

"You ain't going to be playing no ball on a day like this," Pa said.

"Maybe it'll clear," Will said, and another bolt of lightning cracked overhead. The house lights flickered, held for a minute, then cut out.

"Field'll be too wet to play," Pa said and pulled up a chair.

Grandma got everybody some iced tea, and after that we just sat on the porch and watched the storm. The rain cooled things down a might, and the shadows grew long and deep, isolating us on the porch. Fourth of July fireworks are nothing compared with a Georgia lightning storm.

I looked sideways down the porch and saw everybody staring up at the sky like it was some big movie screen. I think this was the first time we all sat together without fighting since Mama died. Of course it helped that nobody was talking, but it was a nice feeling. I knew there'd be plenty of time for fighting once the storm passed.

The heavy rain left us in dark shadows, but I could still see Will, Pa, and Grandma pretty good. Early had all but disappeared into the dark blue of the day. Looking out in the rain, I thought I could see pinpoints of light, but then they disappeared. Another bolt of lightning hit so close to the front yard that we all looked to see if the ground was smoking.

"That's too close for me," Grandma said, "I'm heading inside. Y'all can stay out here and get fried up, but I ain't that foolish." Grandma gathered up our tea glasses and started inside. Another lightning strike, the biggest one yet, cut the sky and lit up the entire front yard.

I was looking down our driveway, squinting trying to see those lights again when I heard Early's voice from the shadows.

"Aunt Lena, something's fixing to happen. Stay with me." His voice had a tone that made everybody turn and look at him. In those blue shadows Early was almost invisible.

"Oh Honey, it's just a storm, that's all. You've seen plenty of these," Grandma said. "Come in the house with me, I'll keep you safe."

"Storm's a going over," Early said, getting to his feet and walking to the edge of the porch.

Sure enough, the rain stopped like somebody turned off a faucet, leaving a thick fog for the sun to burn off. I love Georgia after a hard storm. When the cold rain hits the hot dirt it's like an explosion. The world is covered in a thick fog that makes everything look hazy, just like a dream sequence in a movie. Toward town we could see the tail end of the storm passing over the mountains, the clouds rolling before the rain, like they were being chased.

I thought I heard something in the front yard, so I squinted through the fog, trying to see the end of our road. Then, walking out of the mist, I saw Dr. VanMeeder and two other men, all elders in the Dutch Christian Reform Church, wading through the fog. Pa saw them too.

"Lena, looks like trouble," Pa said, moving to the edge of the porch. "Take Early inside. Will, Buddy, come with me," Pa said, walking down the front steps into the yard. I was so stunned he included me, I didn't turn around to see what happened to Early and Grandma.

"Howdy, Bart. Boys. What y'all doing driving through a mess like that? That's a twister kind of storm." Dr. VanMeeder took off his hat and stepped forward. The others held back a bit.

"We've come to see that blue boy," Dr. VanMeeder said. "We want to do some praying over him and save his wicked soul."

"Bart, there ain't no wicked blue boy here," Pa said. "The only boys I got are white ones."

"Liar!" Dr. VanMeeder screamed. Nobody calls my Pa a liar.

"He is not lying," I yelled. "We sent Early back home. Pa don't like blues. Everybody knows that." I'm a good liar under pressure.

"Shut up, Buddy. I can handle this," Pa said, under his breath.

"Damnation will come to them that harbor the devil and his evil ways," Dr. VanMeeder said, falling to his knees. The other men knelt behind him. "We been to the sinner's house. We know he's lodging here with y'all. Bring him before us, false powers and all."

"Bart, go on home. I bet Lydia and the kids are scared senseless after this storm." Pa turned us back toward the porch.

We only got a couple of steps when Dr. VanMeeder jumped to his feet and ran at Pa, grabbing his shoulders and pulling him to his knees. He pushed his Bible against Pa's chest, yelling, "You will burn in the eternal flames of hell, Lyle Dean, lessen you accept Jesus Christ as your Savior. Turn that blue boy over to us, and let us pray for his salvation!" The other men jumped up too, but they hung back.

Pa pushed Dr. VanMeeder away and got to his feet. I thought for sure he was going to punch him, but he held back. I could tell he was mad because the vein in the middle of his forehead was flicking.

"We're the only chance that blue boy has. Now stand aside and let us save his soul," Dr. VanMeeder hollered, holding his Bible over his head with one hand, thumping his chest with the other.

"If y'all are that young'un's only hope, then the devil might as well claim him now, 'cause boys, there ain't no God. There is no Jesus Christ. If there was, He'd have struck y'all down for the fools you are. Now get off my land!" Pa yelled, grabbing me and Will and hauling us up on the porch.

"Blasphemer!" Dr. VanMeeder moaned, "Oh ye of little faith. Lord Jesus, what nest of evil have I uncovered here?" Dr. Van-Meeder's voice gave out and he was left babbling something about sin and disgust that didn't make any sense. I bet what Pa said scared him. It's one thing to think about there not being a God, it's another thing to say it out loud.

"Lyle Dean, beg the Lord for forgiveness or rot in hell. I say, pray now or face eternal damnation!" Dr. VanMeeder was screaming. Seems he found a second wind.

"Bart, there is no hell. There ain't no heaven. When I die, my body's going to rot and sink right back into this earth. Now y'all get on back to town." Pa pushed me and Will toward the front door, but he stayed behind, turning to face Dr. VanMeeder and the other men. "Y'all leave the Finch family alone. They done nothing to you."

Pa stayed on the porch until Dr. VanMeeder and the others drove away. Then he sat on the front step, watching and waiting. When the car was out of sight, Pa's shoulders collapsed, and he dropped his head in his hands. That fight with Dr. VanMeeder made me see my Pa in a new light.

I heard the front screen door open and saw Early walking toward Pa.

"Mister Lyle, they gone?" Early asked. He walked right up to Pa and put his hands on his shoulder. I couldn't believe it. He wasn't afraid at all. I couldn't remember the last time I'd touched Pa.

"Yeah, Early, you got no reason to fret," Pa said. Early eased himself down so he was sitting beside Pa. I'd bet you money that was the closest Pa's ever been to a blue person. Grandma, Will, and I went out on the porch.

"You done good by me, Mister Lyle," Early said, "but you're wrong about Jesus. He's out there." Then Early reached out and grabbed Pa's hand and held it tight between his palms. Pa started to pull away, then he got a strange look on his face, and it was like all the fight was drained out of him.

"Miss Rebecca says you're not to be grieving no more. You got to get along with your life, the boys too," Early said, speaking low. Then he reached up with one hand and pushed Pa's hair back from his forehead, just like Mama used to do.

"Is she okay? Is Becky all right?" Pa asked, his voice all scratchy.

"She's just fine and saving a place for you in the yonder," Early answered, then he let go of Pa's hand, closed his eyes, and let his head sink down to his knees. Pa looked like he was caught in a dream and couldn't wake up. He looked at each one of us, shook his head like he was trying to knock the visions out, opened his mouth to speak, but nothing came out.

"I got me a headache," Early said, "right between my eyes." When nobody said anything, he looked first to me, and then to Grandma. "What happened? Did those men go home?"

"You had a spell," Grandma said.

"My hands are hot," he said. "What'd I do?" he asked, like he was dreading the answer.

"You didn't do nothing bad, son," Pa answered, "nothing bad at all." He got up, reached over and patted Early on the head, then walked off toward the barn. I figured he had some thinking to do.

"How come you know our mother's name?" Will asked. "Did Buddy tell you about her?"

"She come to me. I seen her," Early answered. "My head hurts. Can I have some water?"

Will went for the water, but just before he went inside, he cut his eyes at Early. I could see he was upset. Early tried to stand, but halfway up he just sort of folded up and collapsed. "My legs won't work," he laughed. Grandma and I helped him up and over to his bed on the porch.

"I don't want you talking for my mama no more," Will said, handing Early a glass. "It ain't right to be talking for the dead."

"I don't mean no harm, Will," Early said, gulping the water.

"It ain't right," Will said, jumping off the porch and heading down the driveway. As he ran off, I noticed he's getting taller and more muscular, looking more and more like Pa every day.

"Did I hurt him?" Early asked.

"He's tender is all. When it comes to Becky, we all are," Grandma said. "She was called to Jesus too soon."

"Did Mama look happy?" I asked.

"It's not like I can really see her," Early said, "it's more like I feel her, and she talks to me. A lot of people talk to me."

"Like who?" I wanted to know.

"That's enough, Buddy, we got to let Early rest," Grandma said. I was surprised she didn't want to hear from Grandpa Ray.

"I need a nap is all," Early said, closed his eyes, and was out like a light. He sure does fall asleep easy.

"What are we going to do about this child?" Grandma asked, aiming the question at nobody in particular.

"Who you talking to, Grandma?"

"Nobody. Everybody. Oh, I don't know," she answered. "Good Lord, was that the strangest thing you ever saw?"

"Not really. Early bringing the baby back from the dead was a lot worse. Well, not worse, better. You know what I mean. How about Pa? At least he didn't haul off and smack Early."

"He was surprised is all. Men can't handle surprises, they like to plan things out. Your grandpa was that way. Women are better at spur-of-the-moment stuff," Grandma said, going over to check Early. She leaned over and felt his forehead with the back of her hand, checking for fever.

"Not a breeze anywhere. Are you hot, Buddy?"

"Well, yeah, it's got to be about three hundred degrees out here," I said. It was, too. That rain didn't cool things down a bit. Once the sun came out and burned off the fog, it made everything feel close and sticky.

"Why don't you take your inner tube and go down to the river? Bet that'd cool you off," Grandma said.

"Okay. You want to come with me?"

"Child…"

"Come on Grandma. You don't have to swim, just go wading. It's pretty down there."

"Just go wading," Grandma snickered. "Buddy, I have so much work to do I don't know which end is up. Now you run along and have fun."

I turned to go inside, but there was something I needed to know.

"Grandma, do you believe in God?"

"Yes, I do," Grandma answered. She didn't hesitate a bit.

"I'm trying to," I said, "but I'm still upset about Mama."

"You'll figure it out," Grandma said, "but not today. Now go swimming. If Early wakes up and feels good enough, I'll send him down to the river. It'd do you boys good to get away from the house."

What she meant was, it'd be a good thing for me and Early to be gone by the time Pa came to his senses and tried to beat some sense into us with the yardstick. I sure didn't want to be around for that, so I gave Grandma a quick hug and took off for the river, the inner tube slung over my shoulder. It wasn't until I was across Highway 28 that I realized I'd forgotten my swimming suit.

Bitterroot River is wide in spots with some white water down by the bridges in town, but slow and lazy up by our house. There are big rocks in the river, so it's not so good for boats and canoes, but it's perfect for tubing. I love floating down the river from our house to North Bridge, walking back up and doing the trip all over again.

I got to our swimming hole, stripped off all my clothes and jumped in. The water was so cold it made my ears ring. My legs were numb for the first ten minutes, but I got used to it and started paddling around. I like to get face down on the tube, grab hold of some weeds that are sprouting around a sandbar toward the middle, and just drift back and forth, studying what's going on under water.

There's all sorts of stuff to see at the river. It's fascinating watching nature going by. I love water bugs. They skip along on top of the water and never sink. They don't pay attention to anything that gets in their way; just skitter over everything. If you hold real still, they'll crawl over your arms like they can't tell the difference between skin and water. If I wasn't going to be a movie star when I grow up, I think I'd like a job with nature.

"That's the pinkest ass I've ever seen!" Danny Lambert yelled from the top of the bank. He caught me naked! I was mortified and slipped off the inner tube and tried to hide. I hoped he'd just make fun of me and go away.

"You ain't peeing in the river are you, Buddy?" Danny started down the riverbank, heading my way. He had a swimming suit and a towel with him, but he threw those on the bank and started to peel off his clothes. "It's so cussed hot, I told my pa I was going for a swim," he yelled, twisting out of his jeans.

I could feel my face getting tight, and my heart was about to hammer a hole through my chest. Nobody has ever seen me naked, except for Early when we go swimming, and even then we never look at each other. Well, sometimes I peek at him. He is blue, after all.

"I ain't afraid of you, Danny! If you plan on beating me up you'd better forget it," I said, trying to sound tough. "Doc Rodger said that after what Butch done to me, one more smack and I might go blind." It was a lie, but it was a good lie and made perfect sense. Danny could tell by looking at my face that I'd taken quite a beating.

"Buddy, have I ever beat you up?" he asked, running full out, his thing flopping from side to side, and jumped in the river. I couldn't believe it. Danny Lambert has hair down there. I don't. Early's got some, but it's white and fluffy looking, and besides that, he's older than me. Maybe there's something wrong with me. I'm tall enough, but pretty skinny. Danny's got muscles and hair on his legs too. I've sure got a lot of catching up to do.

"Damn! It's cold!" Danny yelled, coming up for air. I couldn't look at him, I was so embarrassed. He didn't care. He swam over and grabbed at my inner tube. "Let me get on this thing until I get used to the water," he said, jumping on the tube and splashing me with water. "My God, Buddy, don't this feel good?"

I pulled away, trying to hide my privates. Will calls that area down there "my boys," which I used to think was really funny, until my boys were out in the open for anybody to see. I didn't want Danny to see that I still looked like a little kid.

"Hey, where you going?" Danny asked, "You know I ain't going to beat you up. Get over here and let me look at your face." Danny kicked off and headed my way. I was trapped. I couldn't get out of the water because then he'd see me for sure. I had to tread water and stay low.

"Why are you being so nice to me?" I asked. I hated being suspicious, but given the number of times I'd been beaten up, it was best to ask.

"Because I like you. Man, Calkins beat the snot out of you," he said, looking at my black eye. "I'll pound that punk for this." Danny flopped over on his stomach and rested his chin on the edge of the inner tube.

"Your friends meeting you here?" I asked.

"Nope. Just you and me. Hey, is it true what they're saying about you and Early finding the dead baby?"

"Who told you that?" I knew word would get out, but I wanted everybody to read about it in the newspaper. That'll be the official version.

"Mozelle Landry, but everybody's talking. Folks are saying Early touched the baby back to life. They're calling him a miracle boy. The DCR boys are calling him a devil child, but nobody listens to them."

"What are they saying about me?"

"That you helped. Oh yeah, Miss Pink is going around saying you're the reason she's baldheaded now. Is that true?"

"It's her own dang fault her hair fell out, and I'm sick of hearing about it," I said, forgetting all about being naked for a few minutes. "She gave herself a home permanent and left it on too long."

"Then it is true," Danny said, floating the inner tube closer. "Buddy, did Early work a miracle?" He whispered, like he was afraid to say it.

"Maybe," I answered. Danny didn't say anything and we floated side by side for a time.

"What were you thinking about when I saw you ass end up?" he asked.

"Stuff. The baby. Having my picture in the newspaper."

"I heard you talked to that newspaper lady. You're going to be famous when that story comes out. Funny, ain't it? I'm going to know somebody famous. Two people, counting Early. You ever think about being famous before Buddy?"

"Yeah. Sometimes." Only every day for the last six years of my life, but I sure wasn't going to tell Danny Lambert I planned on going to Hollywood and being a famous movie actor.

"Do you miss Atlanta?" he asked.

"Yeah, I do. A lot. I really miss the television and movies and going to the record stores. There's a whole lot going on I'm missing out on because we moved up here."

"What about your city friends?" Danny asked as he floated closer.

"Oh, well yeah, course I do. You ever been to the city?"

"Nope. Been to the 4-H fair over to Gainesville, but that ain't even a city. I been reading up on going to New York City to play baseball for the Yankees. Your brother and me have been talking about going together." I was learning more about Will every day.

"Man, my balls have shrunk up to nothing," Danny said, jumping off the inner tube. "Come on, I'll race you to the bank."

It was no race. Danny took off and seemed to fly over the water just like the water bugs. I was holding the inner tube in front of me so he wouldn't see me naked. As much as I hate to admit this, I really do run like a girl. I just don't get the hang of where your arms go.

Danny got to the top of the bank and watched me stumble up behind him. "Buddy, I know you're naked," he laughed. "You don't have to hide." I just blushed, kept the inner tube in front of me, and struggled up the bank as best I could. When I reached the top I found Danny, flat on his back, lying in the sun. I peeked again. He also has hair in his armpits.

"Lay down and dry off, Buddy. The sun feels so good," he said, toweling off his face and flopping back on the grass.

I wanted to stay, but the thought of lying out naked next to somebody else made me so nervous, my heart started pounding again.

"I got to get on home and see to Early," I said, pulling on my bib-alls. "His pa whipped him pretty bad and he's been having spells. Grandma's taking care of him."

"So he is staying with y'all. Hey Buddy, is he having miracle type spells or is he just sick?"

I don't know what it was, but suddenly I got a feeling like I was sick to my stomach. Danny Lambert has always been pretty good to me, but today he was being too nice and asking too many questions.

"Why are you asking me all these questions? Why do you want to know about Early?"

"I was just worried about y'all. I heard Butch Calkins whupped your tail, and I wanted to hear about the baby. Buddy, there's a whole lot of people that want to know about Early and the baby."

"Like who? The article ain't even come out in the paper, and that's the official version of what happened."

"Folks are gathering around the court house, and Miss Pink is telling them what she knows. The sheriff says a television reporter is coming up from Atlanta, and another one from Chattanooga, and even some from Nashville. He said they're going to put him on the television news."

"Are people talking about me?" Not only a television camera from Atlanta, but now Chattanooga and Nashville. Matt Williams was the luckiest man in Rabun County, and he wasn't even smart enough to appreciate it.

"Well, yeah, you goof. That's all people are talking about. They say you and Early are best friends. They want to talk to you, too."

"The television people?"

"I don't know. Mostly it's the people that want to find Early. How long is he going to be living with y'all?"

"I don't know yet. Why?"

"A lady from Chattanooga paid me five dollars to find out where Early's been hiding out. She'd already been up to the bait farm and old man Finch set his dogs on her. This is a pretty big deal, Buddy. Five whole dollars!"

"Don't you say a word about this to anybody," I yelled, grabbing my inner tube and taking off for home. I took about ten steps then turned back and yelled, "What do they want with Early?"

"Another miracle," Danny answered. He got up and started putting on his clothes. "Buddy, why are you so mad?"

"You know what Early's like. He can barely talk to people he knows. What's he going to do with strangers after him?" I started running toward the house. I had to warn Early.

"It was five dollars, Buddy," Danny yelled after me.

I kept running. When I got to the gravel road, I realized I'd left my shoes back at the river, but that'd have to wait. I had to get back and warn Grandma and Early before Pa found out. This would make him furious.

As I got closer to the road that leads up to our house, I saw five or six cars parked by our mailbox; people standing around looking up at the house. I didn't recognize any of them, and I know everybody in town, white, colored, and blue. I cut across the field in front of our house.

"There he is!" I heard somebody scream, then all hell broke loose. A man and two women came running across the field toward me, somebody else in a car started honking the horn.

"Buddy, run for it," Pa yelled as I got close to the house. He was standing on the front porch, holding his shotgun. "Throw the inner tube down and run," he yelled. That's exactly what I did. I hit that porch full out, tripped on the front step, and slid all the way to the front door on my belly, picking up about a hundred splinters along the way. Pa grabbed me by the back of my bib-alls and threw me through the front door.

There were about five people in the front yard, all strangers. Pa was walking toward them, cradling his shotgun in his left arm. Grandma and I couldn't hear what they were saying, but nobody looked happy. Two of the men started backing up, holding their hands up just like in a cowboy movie. Another man and two women tried to run past Pa and get up to the porch. That's when Pa fired the first shot.

I peed my pants. (The only reason I'm telling this part is because that's how serious a situation it was, and if this ever goes to court, I want the truth on record.) The strangers took off for the main road, crouching low, running for their lives.

"Get off my land!" Pa yelled, firing off two more shots over their heads.

"Lyle, that's enough. They'll call the law on you," Grandma said, sticking her head out the screen door.

"Can't put a man in jail for protecting his family, and that's exactly what I was doing. Jesus, did you see them run?" Pa laughed. "I doubt they'll be back." He sat down on the front step, resting the shotgun on his knees. "Buddy, you all right in there?"

"I'm fine, Daddy," I yelled. I had run to the bathroom for a towel and was cleaning up the mess I made. "What'd they want?"

"Early," Pa said. Danny was right; they wanted another miracle.

"Where is Early?" I asked Grandma when she came back inside. I was trying to hide the towel behind my back, but she knew what I'd done and held her hand out for it.

"It's okay, Buddy. I was scared, too," she whispered so Pa wouldn't hear. She gave me a kiss on the top of my head and said, "Early's upstairs. Go up and tell him what's going on."

When I got upstairs, I found Early sitting on the floor underneath the window in Will's room. He looked just like he did when I found him in the barn all beat up. I knew right away he'd been watching, and probably listening too, because the window was open.

"Early," I whispered, "are you all right?"

"They gone?" he asked.

"Yeah, Pa run them off."

"They scared me, Buddy."

"Me too." I didn't tell him I peed in the front hall. "Hey, you better not let Will catch you in here," I said. "He's touchy about his room."

"He said I could come in anytime I wanted," Early said.

Okay, I don't even know who my brother is anymore. Will never ever, under any circumstances, lets me in his room.

"Well, okay then," I muttered. "Do you know what was going on out there?"

"Yeah," he said. "They want me to touch them."

"I guess they do," I said. There was no use denying it.

"It don't work that way, Buddy," Early said, getting to his feet, and going out on the balcony off Will's bedroom, searching the front yard for strangers.

"Pa won't let them get you, Early. You saw what he done. Besides, in a day or two things will get back to normal." If I told him that people were gathering in town, and television reporters from Atlanta and Tennessee were coming, Early might've jumped.

"It ain't over, Buddy. Things ain't never going to be the same."

Early left me standing on the balcony and went downstairs. I heard the screen door open and he went out on the front porch. After a minute I heard voices and knew he was talking with Pa. Since I didn't hear Pa yelling, I left them alone and went to my room.

The rest of the day was pretty boring considering the excitement we had earlier. Early and I went up to the barn so I could look after Blossom and Honey.

"Do y'all have any idea what's going on in town?" Will yelled from the barn door. "There's folks from all over the state looking for you two. The sheriff even had to deputize Ellerd Gregory for crowd control."

"Shut up, Will," I hissed, cutting my eyes over at Early, who was staring at my brother like he had three heads.

"Oh, yeah, well, I guess it's not all that many people," Will said. Boy he's a bad liar. If he's ever called to testify in court, they'll be able to tell right off if he's lying.

"I can't talk to strangers, Will. Don't make me," Early said, sinking down, sitting on the feed bin. I thought he was going to cry, but he just folded his arms on his knees and put his head down.

"You don't have to talk to nobody, Early," Will said, coming in the stall and kneeling down.

"I don't feel so good. Buddy, I think I'm going to throw up," Early said, gagging.

"Go on, sick it up, Early. Nobody here cares." Maybe my brother can't lie, but he's pretty good in a crisis. He helped Early stand up and lean over the end of the stall. Early moaned a little bit then let fly with a stream of puke that shot clear across the stall to the wall of the barn.

"Heave it up, Early, this is the perfect place for it," Will said, holding onto Early so he wouldn't fall. Early gave up a bit more, then sort of collapsed. Will helped him back in the stall.

"Can I get you anything, Early? You want some water?" I asked, feeling pretty useless.

"I need to lay down," Early said.

"You want to lay down here or up to the house?" Will asked.

"We better let Grandma look at him," I said, "he might be really sick."

"Nah, he's scared is all," Will said, "Early, you feel good enough to go up to the house?"

Early nodded yes, and Will and I carried him to the back door. When we started up the back steps Early said, "Don't tell Aunt Lena I got sick. I don't want her to worry."

Grandma must've been on the front porch talking with Pa, so that wasn't a problem. We got Early up the stairs and onto my bed, then Will and I got his clothes off and nightshirt on. When Will saw Early's bruises, his eyes got real wide.

Early was asleep before his head hit the pillow. Will and I sat on the bed and watched him sleep for a bit, then Will motioned for me to follow him. We sat at the top of the steps outside my room. Both of us listened for Pa for a minute. When we didn't hear anything, Will started in.

"Buddy, there's all kinds of people in town looking for y'all. They think Early's been sent by God or something. Dr. Van-Meeder and the DCR elders are preaching against y'all on the town square. There's even television people coming up from Atlanta."

"I know. And Chattanooga and Nashville. Danny Lambert told me. There were some folks out here already. Pa fired off a couple shots and run them off. What are we going to do?"

"Nothing you can do, except hide. Maybe the sheriff can kick them out of town or something," Will said. "Pa really shot at somebody?"

"Yeah, three of them. They chased me across the front field and tried to get up on the porch."

"I miss everything," Will said, shaking his head in disgust.

"Y'all come down for supper," Grandma hollered up the stairs.

We started down to the kitchen, but I stopped on the stairs. "Thanks for being nice to Early," I said to Will.

"I'm nice to everybody, Little Brother," he smiled, "you just never took the time to notice."

CHAPTER 8

The Dixie Bugler came out today. Pa brought the paper up to the house, threw it on the kitchen table, cut his eyes at me, and stomped back to the barn.

There I am, right on the front page. The headline reads Miracle Blue Boy Saves Baby in Comfort Corners. My picture is right beside the story, but with all my bruises, it looks like I'm the miracle blue boy. I'm pretty happy with the picture, even if I look like a blue. It's in real sharp focus, and my split lip and black eye look great. Will says I look like an old colored woman with short white hair. I don't think that's funny.

Miss Carla was right when she said she'd write a very positive story. From what I can tell, and I'm not being at all uppity, it seems fair. I give her credit for getting all the facts and names right. The story makes me and Early out to be brave boys who rescued an abandoned baby, which is exactly what I was hoping for. I thought Pa would be real proud of me once he read the story, but I think that's going to take some time.

Miss Carla wrote all the facts, but this is what she said about me. "Assisting with the grisly discovery was Raymond Thomas Dean, a sixth grader at the Comfort Public School, and best friend to Earl Lee Finch. Because of the quick thinking and courageous action of this eleven-year-old, Mrs. Verna (Pink) Watrous was summoned to assist the boys. She promptly did so by calling Sheriff Matt Williams, thereby assuring the rapid rescue of the abandoned boy child."

There was a whole bunch about Early. Miss Carla called him "the gentle blue boy with the mystic healing touch." She named his folks and said where they live, then wrote, "Although Earl Lee was reluctant to take credit for his remarkable feat, acknowledging the Lord above for the baby's recovery, I became certain that without the divine intervention of this gifted and extraordinary blue boy, that newborn child would not be alive."

The story went on to quote a bunch of people guessing who could have done such a heinous thing. I had to look that word up in the dictionary. It means hateful. I was surprised I didn't find a picture of Butch Calkins.

There was a quote from Dr. VanMeeder. He said, "The devil himself has a foothold in Comfort Corners. This is a case of pure evil." Big surprise.

Matt Williams didn't have much to say, only that it was an "ongoing investigation and he couldn't comment." I know for a fact he could comment, because he came out to our house this morning and told Pa he didn't have any leads. Then he said he was leaving Ellerd Gregory in the police car at the end of our road for our protection. Ellerd is the sheriff's brother-in-law and he gets deputized every time something important happens. Ellerd can't read or write. When he gives somebody a ticket, they have to write it up themselves. That's real country if you ask me. Pa feels the same way. He told the sheriff he wasn't having no idiot sitting at the end of our road with a loaded gun, but Mr. Williams wouldn't take no for an answer.

The only other mention I got was right at the end of the story. Miss Carla wrote, "Conflict arose when the witnesses named possible suspects seen in the vicinity of the town dump prior to the discovery of the baby's body. As a result, Raymond Thomas (Buddy)

Dean was severely beaten about the face and body by a local thug. Legal action against this brutal act is pending." I hope that scares Butch Calkins. I really did look pretty bad in the picture.

After the *Bugler* hit the streets, strangers started coming up to the house looking for Early and me. Having Ellerd parked at the end of our road wasn't doing a bit of good. Grandma made us hide inside while she kept guard on the front porch, Pa's squirrel rifle across her lap. There was a scare when two cars made it up the driveway, but Grandma scared them off with a couple of shots.

After this happened a second time, Grandma went to investigate. It seems Ellerd had to take his kids to Vacation Bible School at the Methodist Church and left his post. When he got back he parked across our road and kept everybody away.

Long about dinner time, Will came back from town, out of breath, and full of news. "There's a big television truck from Atlanta in town. I seen the camera and it's huge!" he yelled as he banged through the screen door. "The reporters were talking to the sheriff, and right in the middle of it Dr. VanMeeder and the DCR boys jumped in front of the camera and started shouting about Jesus and sins against nature. It was great!"

"What happened then?" I asked.

"The sheriff pushed Dr. VanMeeder; then all hell broke loose. Everybody was fighting on the town square, even the women, and the television cameras got it all."

"Y'all wash up for dinner, and for once let's have a quiet meal without talking about this mess," Grandma said.

"Early's pa is in town and talking to anybody who'll listen," Will said, washing his hands at the kitchen sink. That got our attention. "He says Early's been kidnapped, but he knows where to find him. I guess that means us. He was making a big fuss, saying that all he wants is his baby boy back. He said Early's been touched by the Lord Jesus Christ Himself and been given special powers. Says he's been this way since he was a baby." Will turned back and saw all of us sitting at the kitchen table staring at him. "What?"

"Is my Pa coming after me?" Early asked. Will realized then he should've kept his mouth shut.

"Nah, I don't think so, Early. He was just blowing off steam. Besides, you know nobody listens to your old man." Will sat next to Early and reached out for his hand. "You're safe here."

"Yes, you are. Ain't nobody going to lay a hand on you as long as I draw a breath," Grandma said, putting dinner on the table. "Now, let's eat and for the love of God, y'all quit talking about what's going on in town."

Since she put it that way, we didn't have nothing to say. The four of us sat at that kitchen table in silence, but I swear we were thinking so hard I could hear our brains working. I was thinking about those TV cameras and the big fight in town.

"What are you boys going to do after dinner?" Grandma asked, trying to start up some kind of conversation. Silence. I guess nobody had any ideas. "Well, somebody answer me," she said.

"I guess Early and me could go up to the barn and look after Blossom and Honey," I said.

"What about you, Will?" Grandma asked.

"I'm going back to town. There's no way I'm missing this. I'm going to see if I can get on the TV."

"Don't tell them you're my brother or they'll chase you clear back to the farm," I said, jealous to the bone.

"I never tell anybody I'm your brother," Will said, snotty to the bone. "Besides, those strangers don't know any locals. I'm just going to hang around to see what happens."

"You ain't going nowhere. You ain't talking to nobody. You're staying put," Pa said, coming in from the barn for dinner. "We're going to wait until this thing Buddy got us into blows over. Understand?"

We nodded. Grandma fixed a plate for Pa, and when she came back to the table she said, "Lyle, people ain't likely to forget what these boys done."

"They'll forget if nobody makes a big fuss about it," Pa said, slanting his eyes my way. "I don't want nobody talking about this.

I don't want no more surprise stories in the paper, and I sure don't want to chase strangers off this farm because of something one of y'all done."

"Mister Lyle, we didn't mean no harm. You got no cause to be shaming Buddy like you do," Early said, aiming it right at Pa.

If it was me that said something like that, Pa would've back-handed me across the kitchen, clean out to the back porch. Early was different. I think Pa was a little scared of him after what he said about Mama.

Pa got up real slow and walked to the back door. All of us watched him, trying to guess what he'd do next, getting ready to duck in case he threw a fit. He stood in the door and waited for a minute. "Early, you're not a member of this family. You're company here, and from now on you're to mind your own business."

"But Buddy's my friend. Mister Lyle, you got no cause to worry. Ain't nobody going to guess how scared you are. These people won't hurt your family." Early stood up and started walking toward Pa. "I can see that real clear in my head."

"I ain't scared of nothing or nobody," Pa said, going out on the back porch and slamming the screen door. He turned back to face Early through the screen. "Don't you ever forget that." Early reached out to touch Pa through the screen. Pa flinched. "I don't believe in you. You hear me? I don't believe what they say about you. I don't!"

"You will," Early answered, reaching out and touching the screen where Pa had rested his hand. Their eyes locked and neither one would look away. The rest of us sat at the kitchen table, expecting the worst, praying one of them would give in.

"No Pa, don't!" Early yelled, breaking the tension. It was then we saw Mr. Finch standing on the back porch, reaching out to grab Pa.

Pa turned just as Mr. Finch was about to grab his neck. Pa's arm went up and blocked the punch, knocking Mr. Finch off balance. He stumbled and fell backwards off the porch.

"You stold Early," Mr. Finch yelled, getting to his feet. "Give him back. Early, get out of there; you're going home."

"Burrell, you blue bastard! Are you drunk?" Pa was fighting mad.

"I ain't a drinking no more," Mr. Finch said, "I want my son back."

"If you ain't drunk then there ain't no excuse for you. Now get the hell out of here," Pa yelled, jumping off the porch, heading his way. Mr. Finch backed away, keeping a safe distance from Pa.

"You got no rights here, Lyle. Give me Early or I'm calling the law." Mr. Finch was straining his neck, trying to catch sight of Early. "Early, you hear me, boy? Get out here!" Mr. Finch took a couple of steps up toward the house. I looked around for Early and saw he'd slipped back into the kitchen, hiding. "Don't make me come after you, boy!"

"One more step and I'm going to hurt you, Burrell," Pa warned. "You know damn well I can do it."

"That there is my family you're holding," Mr. Finch said, puffing out his chest, moving toward Pa.

Grandma came out on the back porch and fired a shot over Mr. Finch's head. He screamed and threw himself down on the ground, crawling for cover. Grandma fired another shot right in front of him. The dirt exploded and Mr. Finch covered his head with his arms. "Jesus, Lena, don't shoot no more. I'm leaving. Just let me up."

"Burrell, you get your worthless, liquored-up ass off our land right now!" Grandma yelled, squeezing off another shot right between Mr. Finch's legs. That did the trick. Mr. Finch scrambled to his feet and ducked behind the willow tree in the back yard, well out of range. I had no idea Grandma was such a good shot.

"You ain't heard the last of me," he yelled. "Early, you come on home. You hear me boy? Sissy Boy Dean," he said, pointing at me, "this ain't over!" Now that probably would've hurt my feelings if I had heard him, but when Grandma fired that last shot at Mr. Finch, the blast pretty much knocked out my hearing for a couple of hours. Everything that happened after that was sort of foggy. I kind of liked the feeling of not being able to hear. It was like living underwater.

Mr. Finch took off running, cutting across the back field, and disappeared up into the woods. Every few steps he'd turn back and give us what Will calls the finger, and I'm not even going to say what it's supposed to mean.

Right after Mr. Finch left, Ellerd come up the drive in the police car, lights flashing. I couldn't hear a thing, but Will told me later that Pa blessed Ellerd out for not protecting us and called him an incompetent hick. Seems Ellerd missed the entire thing because he was talking to a carload of pretty girls from Gainesville who were looking for the miracle blue boy.

With Mr. Finch on the run, we all sort of collapsed on the porch. It was like somebody snapped our backbones and we hit the floor. Gunshots have a way of rubbing on the nerves. I was sitting on the top step, shaking my head, trying to clear my ears. I couldn't hear a thing.

"Grandma, I can't hear," I said. "The gun went off right by my ears!" I must've been pretty loud by the look on Grandma's face, but that was the only way I could hear myself.

Grandma's gaze shifted to the front yard, and I turned and saw Pa coming for me. His face was all red and his forehead vein was throbbing. I knew I was in for it. He grabbed me by the arm, yanked me off the top step, and threw me into the yard. I hit the ground chin first, biting another chunk out of my tongue. It was going to be a long time before I'd be able to chew solid food again.

Pa grabbed me up and held my head between his hands and started screaming at me. "See what you done? Do you see what you done?" I couldn't answer because he was squeezing my head. "Answer me," Pa yelled, and that's when the shaking started. He grabbed my shoulders and gave me a couple of shakes so hard my head was bobbing like a puppet. I could barely hear, but I could read his lips when he yelled, "You ain't no son of mine!" Then I must've passed out.

I woke up on Early's bed on the front porch. Grandma was next to me, holding a cold cloth to my head. When I saw the look of worry on her face I burst into tears.

"Why does he hate me?" I yelled. "What did I do that was so bad?" I really must have been loud because Grandma tried to shush me. I wasn't having any of that, "Don't tell me to be quiet! I don't care if he hears me. I want to know why?" I looked around for Pa and saw Will standing by the front door. He looked pretty upset. "What are you looking at? You want to hit me, too?" I screamed, which really wasn't fair considering how nice he'd been. But that was all the fight I had left in me. I started crying and Grandma pulled me to her. I sobbed on her shoulder until I got the hiccups just like a little kid. Grandma rocked me back and forth, rubbing the back of my head, and I finally quieted down and fell asleep in her arms, hating Pa and missing my mother.

I woke up in bed sometime during the night. Early was laying next to me wide awake like he was waiting on me. I have no idea how I got upstairs, but the good news is my ears cleared up and I could hear as good as always.

"Hey," I said.

"Your Pa runned off. Nobody can find him."

"Good."

"He's scared, Buddy. He didn't mean it."

"He hurt me," I said, then the tears started coming again. Early wiped at my eyes with the pillowcase, petting at my shoulder like he was trying to quiet a dog.

"Your Pa's in trouble," Early said.

"For hitting me? Good."

No. Something else. I can't see it yet." Then he reached over and handed me the Nancy Drew we'd been reading. "Catch me up on Nancy Drew," he said.

I turned to Chapter 11, "A Cry in the Night." I kept going and read all the way through the next two chapters before the book fell on my chest and I fell asleep. When I woke up the next morning I could feel my tongue stinging, and my neck was all twisted up and sore. I tried to stretch the soreness out, but my muscles were all tight. I rolled over and found a note on Early's pillow. It was just one word: Home. Early was gone.

CHAPTER 9

I want my life back the way it was before we found the baby and Early started working miracles. Everything's gone from bad to worse, and I don't know how to fix it. First of all, I'm worried sick about Early. Grandma's as upset as I am. When I reported Early had run off for home, I thought she was going to cry.

My Pa has disappeared. He didn't show up for work yesterday and nobody's seen him around town. The owner of the lake cottage Pa was working on is pretty upset because their addition was supposed to be done two weeks ago. Since nobody's answering the phone at our house, he had to drive out to the farm just to yell at Pa. He was real upset Ellerd wouldn't let him up the drive.

Grandma called the sheriff's office and reported Early had gone home and Pa had come up missing. Matt Williams said he couldn't do a thing about Early, but said they'd keep an eye out for Pa. I think Pa was shamed when Early called him scared. Men like Pa don't like to be told they're afraid. They want the world to think they're brave and can handle anything.

It's not that I miss having Pa around all that much, but he is my father and I'm sort of worried about him. I think my life would be easier with him gone; not necessarily dead, just far away for a really long time. Even thinking that makes me feel guilty. I keep hoping things will change between me and Pa, but I'm almost twelve, and I think if he was going to start liking me, he would have done it already. Grandma says there's always room for hope. I'm not holding my breath.

Will says Pa's shacked up with some girl over Ellsworth way, but he said that just to shock me. Grandma isn't talking, but I reckon she knows who Pa's been running around with. There are three widow women in town, but they're a whole lot older than Pa. There aren't any young girls who'd date him, except for Butch Calkin's oldest sister, Earlene, and she's considered fast and cheap by anybody with taste. That whole Calkins family is common as dirt.

"Buddy, get in here!" Grandma hollered out the front door, knocking me out of my daydreams. I ran into the kitchen, Grandma grabbed me, threw me down in a kitchen chair, and pulled up one for herself. She had her purse on her lap, which means business. "I want you to take this money and go find Early," she said, wadding up five dollars in one of her hankies. "You've got to find out if he's all right and try to get him to come back here."

"Grandma, he won't come back. You know how blues are. His mind was made up last night when he run off."

"Well, he's been home most of the day; maybe he's had a change of heart," she insisted. "Now don't let on you have any money or Burrell or one of them kids will just beat you up for it. When you get Early alone, then give it to him." She put her hanky in the top pocket of my bib-alls. "Now get going and don't come back home until you've seen Early." I started off the chair, but Grandma hauled me back into a hug, practically smothering me against her bosom. "Be careful, Buddy," she whispered, then turned me around and pushed me toward the back door.

Getting from our house to Early's wasn't going to be easy. I couldn't take the main road because Ellerd was guarding our drive, and I sure didn't want any strangers chasing me all the way to the bait farm. That meant I'd have to take the river. I got my inner tube and headed straight for the water. I skirted our meadow and hit the river upstream of the swimming hole. I figured I could float downstream to the North Bridge and nobody would see me. I was counting on the high banks hiding me, and besides, everybody in town takes the river for granted. They don't see it anymore.

I pushed off, and the current took me toward town. I made sure my head was low every time I got close to the road. As I turned the bend before our swimming hole, I heard voices squealing. I slipped off the tube and snuck closer and saw the twins, June and July Hosler, splashing around in the water and making all kinds of racket. I tried to sneak away, but July spied me and commenced to hollering.

"Buddy! Hey Buddy, white folks is looking for you! Buddy, come over here and talk to us!"

"Y'all shut up now!" I yelled, giving up trying to escape. "I'm not supposed to be talking to anybody, so don't be asking me any questions."

"Is Early really the Blue Jesus?" June asked. My jaw must've hit the ground, and I could feel my eyes bugging out. "Oh, yeah. That's what folks is calling him now. Didn't you know? They's named him Blue Jesus on account of he can raise the dead. That's what they say. He brung that baby back from the dead, right?" Apparently June didn't understand me when I said don't ask questions.

"Okay, Twin, who's calling Early the Blue Jesus?" I asked.

"Everybody's naming him Blue Jesus. His daddy be the one that started it. Miss Pink, too." June was full of news.

"Miss Pink's taking people to the dump where the body come back to life," July chimed in. "She makes everybody pay a dime and tells exactly what happened."

"Miss Pink is giving tours of the dump?" Good God. Miss Pink had sunk lower than I thought possible. "Is she nuts?"

"I don't think so, but she bald. She blame you for that," June said. "That's on the tour. She even shows the curler with chunks of her hair on it and points out where it hit the dirt."

"We toured yesterday. I liked it." July was getting excited, and her voice was getting high and squeaky. This usually makes me laugh; today it wasn't so funny. "Miss Pink pointed out the holy milk pail, and even showed everybody where you spit blood on the ground. It looked like purple Kool-Aid to me. She showed how Early laid his hands on your head, and told how he healed the hole in your tongue."

"That's a lie," I said. "How could she do something like that without asking anybody?"

"She ask his daddy, and he say yes," June said. When she saw how shocked I was, she kept right on talking. "Oh yeah, Mr. Finch is in on it. They split up the money. He says Early is Jesus come back to save the world. It's good of Early to do that." The way June said it, so matter of fact, really got me. My head was reeling, and it threw me off balance.

"Just think, Buddy, Blue Jesus is your best friend. You sure are lucky," July said.

I let my head sink to my knees. The blood pounding through my ears made me dizzy and sick to my stomach. This just had to be a joke.

"Don't you worry none, Buddy," June said, coming close and petting the top of my head, "this is good for Early."

"Twin, you don't know what you're talking about," I said, snapping out of my initial shock. The thought of Early having to put up with everybody thinking he was Jesus made me want to cry. Nobody as shy as him could handle something like this.

"Don't you get mad at Sister," July said, punching me on the arm, "She's just telling what is."

"Where's Early now?" June asked, "Everybody says he living with y'all up to the big house."

"He ain't there anymore," I said, "but you can't tell nobody. He's got to hide out."

"Ain't nobody listens to us, Buddy, you know that," July laughed. "Where is Blue Jesus?"

"Stop calling him that!" I said, jumping to my feet and grabbing the inner tube. "He went back to the bait farm last night, and I'm going looking for him."

"Watch out for them dogs," July said.

"You wants that we go with you?" June asked. "We could help you look."

"I got to do this alone," I said, climbing on the inner tube, pushing off for the middle of the river and town.

"Be careful by the dump," July said, "Miss Pink is out there all the time showing folks around."

"Let us come with you, Buddy. We can help," June begged. I shook my head, and she started walking toward me, grabbing for the inner tube. "I want to see Blue Jesus! Please Buddy, let me go!"

"Twins, y'all stay here and watch out for strangers," I said, paddling faster. "If I find Early, I'll be bringing him back this way. You can see him them."

The current grabbed hold of the inner tube and carried me downstream, leaving the twins in the shallow water. They kept watch until I rounded the bend. I turned my attention downstream, floating along with my head down, and my ears open for suspicious noises. Blue Jesus. I was disgusted. This would drive Early back up into the hollows forever.

I came up on the dump faster than I figured, so I paddled ashore and waded through the tall weeds until I could see the dump full on. Since I didn't hear any loud screeching, I guessed Miss Pink must be taking a break from her hectic tour schedule. I could hardly wait to tell Grandma. I knew she'd call Pink and bless her hide.

The coast was clear, no strangers, no Pink. I got back on the tube and drifted on. This was the first time I'd been close to the dump since we found the baby. It was sort of creepy remembering everything that happened. I paddled fast and didn't look back. Seeing the place again made me sad. I sure hope the sheriff finds out who left her baby there to die. I want to know who did it, and I want to know why.

The river gets slower and deep through town, and I was able to drift by holding onto the inner tube, letting it hide my head. I passed under North Bridge right through town and didn't see one person. Every once in a while I could hear somebody yelling or talking, but the town looked boring as always, like nothing had changed.

I paddled to the bank and got out of the river right before I hit South Bridge and colored town. I stashed the inner tube under the bridge, then cut across the field and up through the woods to Early's. The closer I got to the bait farm, the faster my heart started pounding. I heard a car coming up the road, so I ducked back into the woods and let it pass. It slowed down, then the horn honked a couple of times, doors slammed, and there was a lot of you-hooing. It sounded like company was visiting up to the Finches.

When I saw the bait farm sign, I could see Mr. Finch had been busy. Home of Blue Jesus was tacked right on top of worms and crawlers and written in that same tacky glitter. This was making me sicker by the minute. Mr. Finch was backwoods ignorant, but he must've been really, really drunk to do something this stupid. This was about money.

I couldn't go up to the front of the house without being caught, so I crept around behind the barn and come up by the clothesline. Miss Emma had sheets hanging on the line and they blocked my view, but I did manage to catch sight of Early sitting on the front porch under another one of those glitter Blue Jesus signs.

There was a line of about eight people standing in the yard, and beyond them, I could see two more cars coming up the mountain road and parking. Mr. Finch was standing by Early, holding a coffee can. Every once in a while somebody would come up on the porch, put some bills in the can, and then go talk to Early. I couldn't hear what they were saying, so I belly-crawled closer until I got right behind the woodpile.

Old man Finch took a couple of dollars from a young girl and motioned her toward Early. "Kneel before Blue Jesus and all your prayers will come true," he yelled, trying to sound like a preacher.

He'd holler at the folks waiting to see Early and get them all riled up about sin and salvation, and they hollered right back at him. Every so often, he'd turn around and take a long swig off a jug of shine sitting on the porch.

More dollars, more people, and finally somebody I recognized. It was Earlene Calkins, Comfort Corner's bad girl. She knelt in front of Early and started to cry. Early leaned over and whispered in her ear, but that only made her cry more. This was fascinating, but I couldn't hear worth a darn and wanted to get closer. I didn't even realize I'd stood up and started walking toward the house. I was just about in plain sight of the porch when I was tackled from behind and hit the ground with a smack, taking yet one more nip out of my tongue. I may never get to eat again.

"Get down, Buddy!" I looked up and saw Louann Finch's blue face on top of me. "If my daddy catches you up here, he'll skin you alive."

"Get off me," I whispered, rolling over and out from under her. "I got to know what's going on. Is Early okay?"

Louann shushed me and we crawled back behind the woodpile. We sat with our backs propped against the wood and waited, for what I don't know. I opened my mouth to ask about Early, but Louann shut me up with an elbow to the ribs. After a couple of minutes, she peeked over the woodpile, and then took my arm and we crawled across the yard to the clothesline. We lay on our bellies under the lines and let the sheets hide us. That Louann is a quick thinker. What we were doing was exactly like a Nancy Drew mystery book.

"Is Early all right?" I asked.

"Look at him. Does he look all right to you?" Louann snarled. She's bad to get an attitude.

"Why's your pa doing this?"

"Look at that coffee can, stupid. It's full of money. Early's bringing in more cash than the bait farm ever did."

"How'd this get started? He only got home last night, and already your pa's made him a circus freak."

"Somebody in town offered Daddy money if Early'd lay hands on him and his kids. Then some more folks drove up here willing to pay to see Early. That's what give Daddy the idea. He stayed up all night working on the Blue Jesus sign and figuring out what to do."

"What's Miss Emma say? Can't she stop this?"

"She don't want to. She really believes Early is Blue Jesus. She's always believed he was different, sent by God or something. You know, Mama and Daddy aren't real smart." I knew.

"Can't you get Early to run away and come back to our place?"

"Ain't no way Pa'd let Early go. He's got big money plans.

"What's he going to do?" I asked.

"She don't know, do you, Lou?" I jumped about a foot in the air and come down next to Leon Finch. I didn't even hear him crawl up beside us. Sister was on his left, sucking on an orange lollypop and twirling her hair. She was naked again. There's just no keeping clothes on that girl.

"Leon, please help me get Early out of there." I was taking a chance asking Leon for help, but I was desperate.

"Do it yourself," he answered. "Early can run away if he wants. Ain't nobody stopping him. I think he likes the attention."

"Are you nuts?" I hissed, not caring if he smacked me. "Look at him. He's miserable."

"Ask Blue Jesus and all your prayers will come true!" Mr. Finch hollered, stuffing dollar bills in the coffee can with one hand, hefting the jug of shine with the other. "Kneel before him and ask for salvation!"

There were only about six people waiting to see Early when Miss Emma come out on the front porch. She gave Early a glass of tea and wiped his face off with a washcloth. Mr. Finch grabbed that washcloth out of Miss Emma's hands and held it out to the crowd.

"Y'all see this! Sweat wiped from the face of Blue Jesus! Sleep with this under your pillow and cure your pains! Blue Jesus guarantees it! Now what am I bid?" He taunted the crowd with the washcloth. I'll be danged if they didn't all reach in their pockets for more cash. "What will you give me for the holy cloth that wiped the face of Blue Jesus? Do I hear three dollars? Ask yourself sinners, is three dollars too much for eternal salvation?" Some fool bid three. "How about five? Will somebody pay five dollars to sit at the right hand of the Lord above?" He got his five dollars. Early looked sick. Miss Emma watched her husband like she had no idea who he was. I thought I was going to puke.

"Leon, please. We got to do something," I said. Leon was gone, left as silent as he arrived. Those blues sure do move quiet. Sister was still working on the orange lollypop and picking at a scab on her elbow. Louann slid over me and next to Sister, smacking her hand away from the scab.

"Get up to the house and put on some clothes," Louann said. Sister ignored her and picked away. "Buddy, if you want to talk to Early, wait until he goes to the outhouse. That's the only time you can get him alone."

"How long will that take?"

"Depends on what he's had for dinner," Louann answered, which made sense to me. I just hoped he'd eaten a big dinner and drunk lots of tea. "I'm going up to the house and get her dressed," Louann said, motioning to Pocket. "You stay hid. For God's sake, don't let Daddy catch you."

"If you can get to Early, tell him I'm out here," I said, turning to Louann, but the girls had already gone, Sister's bare rump flashing in the sunlight as they went around the side of the house.

I waited under the clothesline until it started to get dark, then I crawled back behind the woodpile. My stomach was starting to growl, but I knew I couldn't go home until I'd given Early the money from Grandma and begged him to come home with me. As it started to get dark, the shadows spread across the yard, finally covering me.

I had just about given up on Early. I kept jumping every time I heard something, and this was making me a nervous wreck. The sand fleas had chewed me up pretty bad, and I was sure Mr. Finch would let them dogs loose any minute. I started to pace between the woodpile and the outhouse, counting my steps, and thinking about Nancy Drew and what she would do. One thing I knew for sure, she wouldn't be scared. Nancy always boldly confronted bullies and brought them to justice. I was spooked, I'll admit that, but true to my word, I wasn't going to be scared ever again.

Finally the screen door of the Finch cabin banged open and Early came out on the porch. Mr. Finch followed him outside. "Where you think you're going?" he asked.

"Toilet," Early answered. I was beginning to think he never peed.

"You run away, I'll set them hounds on you," Mr. Finch warned. "You hear me, boy?" Early kept walking. "You hear me?"

Early didn't answer, just headed for the outhouse. Mr. Finch watched him for a bit then went back inside. I waited until Early was in the outhouse before I got up close. I didn't want to scare him, but I sure did want to hurry this up and get back home. I could hear Early going, and this was pretty embarrassing. I figured I'd better wait until he stopped, then I could grab him and take him home with me.

"What you doing out there, Early? Answer me, boy!" Mr. Finch yelled from the front porch.

"Going!" Early grunted, then went back to doing his business. Suddenly it got quiet. Early wasn't making any noise. I kept quiet too. "Who's out there?" he asked, his voice tiny in the night.

"It's me," I answered. "Hurry up and finish. I got to talk to you."

"Get out of here before Pa sees you," he said.

"It's dark; he can't see me. Now hurry up."

Early came outside buttoning up. I grabbed him and pulled him over behind the woodpile. I reached into the front pocket of my bib-alls and gave him Grandma's hanky. "Grandma sent you this and wants you to come back home with me. Let's go before your Pa gets suspicious."

Early looked down at Grandma's hanky and slowly worked it open. When he saw the five dollar bill his eyes got real wide. "Buddy, I can't. Give it back," he said, and turned toward the house.

"Grandma wants you to have it. I can't go back home without you. Now come on!" I got up and tried to pull Early to his feet.

"Buddy, don't pull at me. I can't have nobody pulling at me right now. I got to stay. They's counting on me."

"Who? Your folks? Well, of course they are; they're making money off you," I said. "Now forget about them and let's go."

"I can't go," he said. "Pa said he'd hurt Mama and the girls if I don't do what he says. He'll do it, too."

"We'll call the sheriff. Mr. Williams won't let nothing happen. Now come on!" I really wanted to get home.

"I can't. Tell Aunt Lena and Will I'm okay. Did your Pa come home?" I shook my head. "He'll come home when it's time. Not before."

"I don't care if he ever comes home."

"You got to forgive, Buddy. You got no choice," Early said, smiling at me, like I was a little kid. I'll be darned, but in that moonlight, he actually did look a bit like Jesus; kind eyes, wise, sweet-looking. All he needed was a beard.

"Boy, them hounds is getting ready to hunt!" Mr. Finch yelled into the night. Early and I jumped apart and peeked over the woodpile. We couldn't see a thing except the sheets floating like ghosts on the breeze.

"Early, we got to go. Now," I hissed. He just kept on smiling in that understanding way and shaking his head. It was like he was in a trance. "Early, you ain't Blue Jesus!" I yelled, grabbing his shoulder and giving him a hard shake. "Let's go!"

"Get out of here, Buddy. Them dogs is mean."

"Early, please!"

"Go home. I'll be fine," he said, getting to his feet and starting toward the house. I reached out and tried to pull him back, stuffing Grandma's hanky in his pocket. He jerked away and kept walking, not looking back.

"Here come them dogs!" Mr. Finch hollered, opening the screen. Duke and Buster barked into the night. "You ready to run, boy?"

"I'm right here, Pa," Early said, climbing the steps to the porch and disappearing into the house. Mr. Finch and the dogs followed him in.

I stood in the darkness, watching the house for another hour, hoping Grandma was right and Early would have a change of heart. One by one the lights went out and everything was quiet. I headed down the road for town and home. I didn't have to worry about people seeing me this late at night. My heart was aching for Early, but as I walked through the night air, I felt free for the first time in a week.

I stared up at the stars, trying to see beyond them to where I heard God lives. If He was up there, this was the perfect night to see Him; lots of stars and a pitch-black sky. I didn't see a thing that looked especially promising. Maybe it was time I tried praying again.

Please God, if You're up there watching this, then You know I tried to help. If Early gets in trouble, please help him out. Mama, if you're up there too, put in a good word for me and Grandma and Will. And God, if You're real, and I don't know if You are, then do what You can to get us out of this mess. If You do, then I can believe in You. If You don't, then Pa is right and I got no choice but to think You don't exist. It's up to You. Amen.

CHAPTER 10

Grandma's answer to the Early problem: "Time will tell." I expected more. I figured the least she'd do was call Matt Williams and get the law up to the bait farm to set Early free. Grandma was disappointed that I came home alone, but she didn't look all that surprised. She just sighed and said, "Things run mighty deep between a father and son. Ain't no upsetting the laws of nature."

Up in my bedroom I turned to *The Hidden Staircase*, but I couldn't concentrate on Nancy because I kept thinking about what Grandma said. There's nothing deep between me and Pa, never has been. Pa and Will are a different story. They speak a different language, and no matter how hard I tried, I could never crack the code. Pa just naturally takes to Will. It's like they have a special club I wasn't asked to join. Pa and Will have got a bond between them.

Pa sure didn't have a bond with me. No father wants a sissy son like me. That's the way it was, and the way it always would be. By being a sissy I was going against nature, but there was no way I could stop. My dreams of running away to Hollywood, being a movie star, and meeting Tony Dow had always been enough to get me through my worst days. But Grandma's words "no escaping the laws of nature" made me realize Hollywood would be no different. There wouldn't be any friendship with Tony Dow. Boys like him didn't have friends like me.

"Open the door, stupid!" Will yelled, jiggling my doorknob.

"Go away!"

"Come on, Buddy, open up." He kept jiggling. "What're you doing?"

"Reading. Now leave me alone!" After what I'd been thinking, I was in no mood to talk to a real boy, even if he was my brother.

"It's about Pa," Will said. "You got to help me find him."

Fat chance. As far as I was concerned Pa broke the law of nature too, but I was the one who was being punished. Having him out of the house was a blessing in my book, and believe me, I'm keeping score.

"Go away!" I yelled.

"Open this door or I'm breaking it down!" Will yelled, pounding until my door shook on the hinges.

"All right. Hold your horses," I yelled. I unlocked my door.

Will pushed his way through, cuffing me up the back of my head the same way Pa does. "Dope!"

"If you're going to hit me, you can get out now," I yelled, reaching out to slap at him. He just knocked my hand away. "And if you want to find Pa, go look for him yourself." I flopped down on my bed, picked up *The Hidden Staircase*, and pretended to read. Will sat on my bed and took the book away from me. I grabbed for it, but he pushed me back on the bed.

"Listen to me, Stupid! Pa's in trouble."

"So?"

"So we got to help him," Will said, cuffing my head again.

"Quit hitting me! Asshole!" I yelled. I twisted away from him, jumping off the bed.

I stood across the room looking at Will, ready to run. Will was bent over, hysterical. "I've never heard you swear before," he laughed. "Did you call me an athhole" he lisped, making fun of me. "Jesus, that's the funniest thing I ever heard."

"My tongue has a hole in it, thanks to Pa," I yelled back. "It's hard for me to talk, and I don't think it's all that funny."

"Come on, say it again," Will pleaded, still laughing. "Pleath."

"Stop it," I muttered.

"Thop it?" he mocked, wiping his eyes on my pillow, spreading his cooties all over it. "Okay, now we've got to get serious. Or should I say therious?" I just turned and walked out of my bedroom and down the stairs. "Buddy, come back. I won't laugh no more. Promith!" Boy, that one really set him off, howls of laughter followed me down the stairs and out to the front porch. Actually, it sort of made me smile. I know I lisp even when I don't have a hole in my tongue.

"Hey, Buddy, you doing all right?" asked Matt Williams. The patrol car was parked in our driveway, and the sheriff was coming up the walk to the front porch. "What's got Will so tickled?"

"He's making fun of the way I talk," I answered. "I got a hole in my tongue and it makes me talk funny." Why was the sheriff here? Will said Pa was in trouble, but I figured he was just passed out drunk somewhere.

"Really? I don't hear it," Mr. Williams said, which was just his way of being nice. Even I could hear it, and I'm used to the way I sound. "Can you get Will down here for me?" I nodded and went inside the house and called up the stairs.

"Will, come on down! The sheriff wants to see you!"

"Really? The theriff?"

"Yeah, the theriff! Get down here!" Mr. Williams yelled from the front door. "Where's Aunt Lena?" he asked me.

"Right behind you Matt," Grandma said, coming around the side of the house with a dishpan full of beans. "I was out in the garden picking some beans when I saw you drive up. Here's a mess for your dinner tonight. Sharon'll have to clean 'em."

"Good looking beans, Lena," he nodded to Grandma. "Will, glad you could join us." He aimed that at the front door where Will stood, looking embarrassed.

"What you doing out this way Matt?" Grandma asked. "Ellerd's doing a good job of keeping strangers out."

"I just wanted to check in on y'all, see how you're getting along." He turned to me, "Buddy, talk in town is Early went back home. Is that true?"

"Yeah," I said.

"What about your dad?" he asked.

"Pa's gone off somewhere," I said, looking toward Will for help. He just cut his eyes.

"He and Early leave together?" Matt asked.

"God, no. You know Pa don't like blues. Early left in the middle of the night. His pa's got plans for him."

"Yeah, I heard. I was hoping it was a lie. What's going on up at the bait farm?" Mr. Williams leaned against the porch, lit a cigarette, and inhaled real deep. He blew two streams of smoke out his nose that seemed to go on forever.

"It's just awful," I blurted out. "Mr. Finch is calling Early, Blue Jesus. He's selling visits with Early, saying he can make prayers come true. Folks are lining up, too. I snuck up there and saw about fifteen people waiting for Early to touch them. Mr. Finch is making lots of money, and I bet Early won't see a dime. He even sold an old washcloth Miss Emma used to wipe Early's face."

"Christ," the sheriff said, breathing out more smoke and shaking his head in disgust.

"Can't you do something about it, Matt? It's got to be against the law, him taking money and all," Grandma said.

"It's really a family matter, and I ain't getting in the middle of them blues," Sheriff Williams said. "I might could threaten Burrell with fraud, but that'd be a waste of time. If folks are stupid enough to pay him money, he'd be a fool not to take it."

"But what about Early?" I asked. "He's a prisoner. Mr. Finch said if Early didn't do what he wanted, then he'd hurt Miss Emma and the girls."

"Did you hear him say that? Now tell me the truth, Buddy. Did you actually hear Burrell Finch threaten the womenfolk?" Mr. Williams was studying my face, looking for lies.

"No," I admitted. "But Early wouldn't lie about something like that."

"I can't do anything without a witness, and God knows them blues is clannish. You can bet Early won't be talking against his daddy anytime soon," Mr. Williams said, getting to his feet, and snubbing his cigarette on the heel of his boots. He looked like he was going to flick the butt into the yard, but Grandma fixed her eyes on him. He put it in his pocket.

"Matt, what's the news on that little baby? You got any idea who he belongs to?" Grandma asked.

"Andy? He's good and healthy, knock wood. Cute little feller, and I tell you, Doc Rodger and his missus sure have taken a shine to him. Mrs. Rodger bought him all kinds of clothes and toys, and they're planning on adopting as soon as the circuit judge gets to town. That'd be the best thing for the boy. Good for Doc, too," Matt said.

"What about the mother?" Will asked, coming down into the yard. "Have any idea who she is?"

"If I did, I wouldn't be out here talking with y'all. But I don't want just the mother; I want the father, too. Bet they was both in on it. Shit fire, we've only got—oh, God, I'm sorry Lena. What I meant was, with only thirty families or so in these here parts, plus some odds and ends scattered way up in the mountains, somebody has to know something. It ain't likely some city gal would come up here and toss her baby in the dump. It's got to be local."

"What you got to do is start at the Hairport and ask around. Women notice things men pass by, but don't go scaring everybody in curlers with legal stuff. They'll just clam up tighter than a tick. Ask a few questions, and keep your ears open. Next thing you do is to visit every church and Sunday School between here and Ellsworth, DCR, too. Pert near everybody's church-going up here. They'll know if somebody's come up missing. That's where you'll find your answer, Matt," Grandma said. "You're just wasting your time on the road."

"I know," the sheriff said, "but I got to do something. Seeing that baby in the dump just about broke my heart. Who would do something like that?"

"Somebody young and scared out of her wits," Grandma answered.

"Maybe you're right," Matt said, "but young and stupid ain't no excuse for what I seen in that dump." He started toward his car. "Well, thanks for your time and the advice." He turned back to my brother. "Will, you got any idea where your pa is?"

"Squirrel hunting, I reckon," Will answered, then looked down at his feet, his face turning bright red.

"That right?" Matt asked Grandma.

"If Will says so," she answered. "Matt, how about them crowds in town? They still looking for a miracle from Early and Buddy?"

"Ah, hell's bells—sorry. I got to watch my mouth. Since the paper come out and them television people got hold of the story, the crowds are bigger than ever. We got cars parked on both sides of Bridge Street and traffic running both ways. Never seen that in my lifetime," Matt answered. "I keep praying it'll die down, but everybody's expecting some magic."

"They come looking for something to believe in. They'll start looking elsewhere when nothing happens," Grandma said, reaching down and picking up her dishpan full of green beans. "Now, take these beans home, and tell Sharon I want my dishpan back. Tell her to come out for a visit. It gets mighty lonesome out here with no visitors."

"I'll send her out tomorrow with a bag of pecans. See y'all later," Matt said. He got in his patrol car and headed off down the road.

The three of us watched him drive off, Grandma waving just before he turned the corner. Will and I started inside, but Grandma stopped us cold. "Where's your pa? Tell me the truth right now."

"Beats me." I shrugged, and she turned to Will for the answer. Will wasn't talking. He just looked down at his feet again, red as a beet.

"Answer me, Will. Is he in trouble?" Grandma asked.

"Yes, m'am."

"Well, where is he?" Grandma was getting impatient, working the hem of her apron between her fingers. She does that when she's worried.

"He's up to the colored fishing shack, passed out drunk," Will muttered, finally looking up and catching Grandma's eye. "Gizzy says he can't wake him up, and the other colored men want him out of there."

"Then you boys got to go get him," Grandma said.

"I ain't going," I said, walking up on the porch. "Let him stay there until he sobers up."

"He can't stay there, stupid. The coloreds don't want him," Will snarled. "Gizzy says if Pa ain't out of there by tonight, the other men will call the law on him."

I could understand that. The coloreds, and by colored I mean Negroes, not blues, don't have all that many places to call their own. When some ornery drunk white man that they don't even like passes out in their territory, they get anxious. Can't say as I blame them.

"Will, think you can drive your Pa's truck without getting caught?" Grandma asked.

"Yes, m'am," Will said, perking up. He's been dying for a chance to take the pickup out on the highway, but Pa would never let him because he doesn't have a license. "What about Ellerd?"

"Wait until dark, then take the back road. Ellerd will never see you," Grandma said. "Buddy, you come in the kitchen with me. I want to talk to you...alone." I was in trouble and I knew why. Grandma was going to make a big deal out of me not wanting to go after Pa, but I don't think I'm all that wrong. If Pa was beating up on her and calling her names, I bet she wouldn't want to bring him back to the house either.

Inside the kitchen, I thought I'd get the ball rolling before Grandma had a chance to light into me. "Pa's mean to me. When he's drunk, he's worse. He's just going to smack me around and call me names, so I don't want to go up there and bring him home. Pa'd be happier if Will went by himself."

Grandma didn't answer, she just sat at the kitchen table, her fingers working the hem of her apron. This is what she calls gathering her thoughts. Grandma's theory is that you've got to gather your thoughts before you talk, because if you don't, you're likely to make a fool out of yourself. I waited, but she didn't say anything. I got to thinking maybe I should have gathered my thoughts.

"Grandma, you all right?" I asked. She looked so sad sitting there, her shoulders hunched forward, brows scrunched up to help her think. With the afternoon sun hitting her full on, I noticed for the first time that Grandma was starting to look real old. "Grandma?"

"I'm fine, Buddy," she answered. "But I am disappointed in you." This was going to be one of those talks. I still didn't think I was wrong.

"What I said is true. Pa's just going to be hateful when we try to carry him back home. You know I'm right."

"I know," Grandma said, opening her arms, motioning me to come to her. When I got close, she pulled me down to her lap. I felt sort of silly because I was too big to sit on Grandma's lap.

"I also know that my daughter didn't raise a son that would turn his back on his daddy." She really got me with that one.

"Please don't make me do this, Grandma," I said, my voice all quivery. "Mama wouldn't make me."

"Of course she wouldn't make you do it; she'd expect you to want to do it," Grandma said, pulling me even tighter. "You do know the difference?"

"Yes m'am," I said, squeezing the words out, fighting back tears.

"Your pa ain't done right by you. Don't you think he knows that? He wants what's best for you, but he don't know what's right anymore. Your mama was his north star. She give him direction and kept him on the right path. Since she's been gone, he don't know which way to turn."

"Just because he don't know where he's going is no reason to take it out on me," I said.

"Remember that night when Early said your pa was scared? He's right about that. Your pa knows you don't like him. Your face is just like a map, showing every bump, every turn, and all them feelings running through your mind. Now I got a question needs an answer. Buddy, have you ever told your Pa you loved him?"

"No m'am," I said, squeezing out the words.

"Why?"

"I'm not sure I do." That did it. Tears.

"Maybe things could be different between you two if you told your Pa you loved him," Grandma said, pulling a hanky out of her apron and holding it up so I could blow my nose. I hate it when she does this, but my nose was running so much I had no choice.

"But what if he don't say it back?" I asked.

"Darlin', there's always a chance he won't say what you need to hear, but that's the way life works. This world can't always be what we want. What I'm asking is, are you brave enough to try? Can you be the bigger man this once? Will you do that for me?"

I took a long time gathering my thoughts. I'm not just saying that, I really did give it some serious thought. Trouble was, I just couldn't picture it in my mind. I couldn't picture me standing in front of Pa, saying I loved him. Even thinking about it made me tense, and I felt my face get tight. Finally I took a deep breath and answered, "No."

"What am I going to do with you, Buddy?" Grandma asked, kissing the back of my head, then pushing me off her lap. "You got a stubborn streak running up your spine, just like your mama."

"Mama said I got it from you," I answered.

"Mayhap you did," she said. "Now go out back and help Will get the truck ready. I want you boys back here with your pa before ten o'clock."

"Grandma, I can't."

"I ain't asking, I'm telling. Now go." That was it. She turned and walked out of the kitchen, leaving me standing there, heart pounding, dreading what I knew was going to be a horrible night.

Will and I started out for the colored fish shack about seven-thirty. We didn't have a lick of trouble getting by Ellerd. He wasn't even at the end of our road. He was down by the river, gigging frogs with his boys. He just waved as we drove by. I can't believe the county pays this man a salary.

The colored fish shack is about a mile up-river of our farm. It's where all the colored men go to drink and get away from their wives. Gizzy calls it the colored social club, because nobody's allowed in except for colored men. It's nothing but an old tarpa-per shack that's built on the edge of the river. They've got a small dock and two canoes, but it's nothing fancy.

When we pulled the truck into the driveway, we could see that they had a campfire burning beside the shack. Our headlights swept a long row of colored men, who shaded their eyes with their hands. Will parked the truck, and we walked toward the campfire. Gizzy got up and started toward us. The other colored men drifted back into the shack, tipping their hats as they passed me and Will.

"God Almighty, boys, I am glad to see y'all," Gizzy yelled. "Mr. Will, Buddy, you boys got to get your daddy out of here."

"Where is he?" Will asked, and Gizzy pointed to this lump lying next to the fire. It was Pa. He was wearing a dirty under-shirt, and that was all. I've never seen my father naked before, and this was really creepy. He looked like some drunken bum you see in the movies. "Where's his pants?"

"He dukied in 'em," Gizzy said. "I cleaned him up best I could Mr. Will, but he started fighting me. He's all yourn now, and good riddance to it."

"Buddy, get that blanket out of the back of the truck," Will said, "and hurry." I went to get the blanket, but I sure didn't want to go back. I wanted to go home and forget what I just saw. When

I got back to the fire, I heard Will say, "Gizzy, Grandma sent you this," and he pulled ten dollars out of his front pocket. "She says thanks for watching out for Pa."

"I ain't taking no money from Aunt Lena," Gizzy said, backing away. "I just want to do right by your family. You tell her that."

"She wants you to have it," Will insisted.

"Take it, Gizzy. You earned it," I said.

"No, sir. I ain't taking nothing. Your daddy done good by me and mine. Now we's even." Gizzy turned and walked toward the fish shack. "You boys, be careful. Still got some fight in him." Gizzy joined the other colored men standing on the fish shack porch. They stood there smoking, watching, and waiting to go back to their fire.

"Well, let's get him home," Will said, taking the blanket and walking toward Pa. I followed, keeping my distance in case Gizzy was right and Pa wanted to fight. We got up close, and Will was bending over to throw the blanket down, when Pa rolled over and let rip with a huge fart. Will and I looked at each other, shocked at first, then we both got the giggles so bad we were bent double laughing. Pa was snoring away by the fire, his bare butt aimed at the sky. Will and I were laughing so hard, I started in to wheezing and had to sit down to catch my breath. Will threw the blanket over Pa, and then came back and sat beside me.

"Now I know why the coloreds don't want him here," Will said. That got us laughing again.

"We got to get him home," Will said, after we quit laughing. I knew he was right. The colored men on the porch kept clearing their throats, letting us know we'd stalled long enough.

"You go first," I said.

Will nudged Pa with his foot. "Pa, wake up. Time to go home." Pa rolled over and snored, sputtering and spitting. Will poked at him again. "Pa, come on. Let's go home."

"Leave me alone," Pa muttered, pulling the blanket tight and turning away. Will kicked at him again, hard this time. Pa's hand came out, lashing for Will's foot. "No!" he yelled.

"Pa, we got to get you home," Will bent over and tried to pull Pa to his feet. Pa wasn't having any of it and twisted away. "Well Jesus, Buddy, give me a hand."

"Come on, Pa," I said, but Will hushed me right up.

"Don't say nothing. That'll just make him madder." I took that to mean the sound of my voice would only set Pa off. I was insulted for a minute, then realized Will was right. I'd best keep my mouth shut and do what I could to load Pa in the bed of the truck and get this night over with.

We finally got Pa on his feet and dragged him over to the pickup. He kept walking on the blanket and pulling it down, which exposed him to me and the colored men. This sure was embarrassing.

"Give me a drink," Pa snarled.

"I'll give you one if you get in the truck," Will said. Pa must've believe him, because he wrapped that blanket around his waist and jumped into the bed of the truck, peaceful as can be.

"Give me a drink," he said.

"I lied," Will answered. "We're going home."

"Don't want to go home. Want a drink," Pa yelled. He started coughing really hard, then vomited all over the blanket. "Oops," he said, then passed out.

"That's pretty," I said.

"Pretty sad," Will said. "Get in the truck."

It took about ten minutes to get home. Will didn't even bother using the back road, he went right down Highway 28 and turned onto our road. Ellerd just waved. Grandma met us in the back yard. She took one look in the bed of the truck and said, "You better get him cleaned up and in bed."

"No m'am, he's staying here. I want him to wake up and see what he's done," Will said. Will sounded so grown up all of a sudden. He looked older, too. I guess seeing your father naked and drunk will do that.

"We can't leave him here," Grandma said.

"Why not? You want him inside, dirtying up your house?" Will asked.

"Well, at least he's safe to home," she said. "Now come in the kitchen. I kept supper warm for you boys."

We ate in silence, and after supper Will went upstairs to his room. I helped Grandma with the dishes, and then we played a couple hands of Uno. Both of us were pretty depressed about Pa. He was out in the truck covered in his own puke, and we knew that come tomorrow, things were only going to get uglier. I finally excused myself and got ready for bed.

There was no way I could fall asleep. I kept thinking about Pa and what a mess he was. I tried praying, but gave up. Praying just makes me feel stupid. Early says faith takes practice. I want proof. Early says that comes in time, but time's running out for me. I'm about to forget the whole God thing unless I get some action.

About daybreak, I came out of a sound sleep and thought I heard something prowling around in the back yard. Then I remembered Pa. I went downstairs and out to the truck. He was flat on his back, snoring up at the sky. I watched him sleep for quite awhile. I tried to see parts of his face that looked like mine. Nothing. His nose is long and sort of dips down. Mine's a little upturned. Will calls it a pig snout. Pa's forehead is huge, broad. Mine's little, and not even the same shape. Our eyes aren't the same. We don't have the same mouth. Pa's hands don't look like mine either.

I reached out and touched Pa's head, smoothing back his hair. This was the first time I can remember touching Pa. He had quit snoring and was sleeping peaceful. I let my fingers move along the scar on his forehead he got putting a new roof on the barn. "I'm trying to love you, Pa," I whispered. He didn't say a word.

CHAPTER 11

Pa was gone come morning. He didn't leave a note, just disappeared. I think if I was him, I'd have to go away. He must've been plenty embarrassed when he woke up covered in puke, thinking about what he'd done. I wish he'd said goodbye to Will. He's taking Pa's disappearance pretty bad. I know he feels guilty for not cleaning Pa up last night, but I think he did the right thing.

Truth is, I'm bored. Everybody's depressed around here on account of Pa. Nobody's calling me a hero. There's nobody fun to talk to, and I'm lonesome now that Early's gone. Grandma's upset with everything and is getting mighty snappish. She calls it cabin fever, but it seems to me that we're all just walking on eggs, tension everywhere. I'm trying to help Grandma as much as I can, but I don't think she appreciates it. I was helping with the laundry, sending the sheets through the wringer, when she really let me have it.

"Buddy, the reason we call it doing the wash is because the sheets are supposed to stay clean. Get them off the floor!" Now I know where I get my sarcasm. "If you can't do something right, then just get out of the house," Grandma snapped again. Okay, so maybe some of the sheets did hit the floor, but for crying out loud, I'm not tall enough to hold them up.

"Fine. Suit yourself," I yelled back, going out on the back porch, making sure I slammed the screen door. That sets Grandma off like nothing else in this world. She says the sound of a slamming door makes her skin crawl. That's what I was hoping for. I sat on the edge of the porch to pout and looked over the back field. This late in the summer, the leaves start getting that reddish-brown tinge at the tips, and there's a smell in the air that lets you know that fall is heading this way.

"I'm sorry," Grandma said, coming out on the porch. I knew that screen door would get her. "I've got a lot on my mind."

"Everybody does," I said, real cold.

"You still willing to help your old grannie?"

"Oh, you don't want me to help. Remember? I can't do nothing right," I said, throwing her sarcasm right back at her. She just burst out laughing.

"Buddy, you are so cute when you're mad. Come here and give this grouchy old lady a hug!" I was sort of put out, but I gave her a hug anyway. "That's better. Now I need somebody to hang out these sheets."

"I'm not tall enough, Grandma, they'll just hit the grass."

"Then we'll just shake the grass off after they're dry. Now here, take these clothespins," she said, tying her clothespin bag around my waist, "and do the best you can to keep them out of the dirt."

I dragged the basket of sheets down to the clothesline and got an old bucket to stand on. It wasn't long before I had the sheets batting in the breeze. Grandma sure does a lot of laundry, and I'm the only one that helps. Pa says I'm the daughter he never had. Real funny, huh?

The sheets were moving on the breeze, and I walked down the aisle they created to knock out some of the kinks. In the middle of the sheets, I suddenly realized that nobody could see me. I was enveloped in a cell of white, away from the outside world, locked in my own private clubhouse. I put the bucket in the middle of the aisle and ran outside to check from all angles. Nope, nobody could spy on me.

I took a pillowcase off the line and plunked it on my head. I wore it like a bride's veil and walked down an imaginary church aisle, the adoring eyes of my best friend in the whole entire world, Tony Dow, pulling me onward. We wouldn't get married, of course, because men don't do that, but we'd say vows that announced to the world that we were best friends, and we would do everything together for the rest of our lives. It was like being blood brothers, but with a veil.

So there I was, prissing between the sheets, pretending to be a bride, when I looked up and saw Pa watching me from the hill. I hit the ground flat. I crawled to the edge of the sheets and looked again. Pa looked at me long and hard. I stared back, frozen. Then he shook his head in disgust, hawked up a gob of spit, let it fly, and disappeared into the woods.

I stayed on the ground, staring at the very spot where he had been. I knew I should be embarrassed, but I wasn't. What Pa thought about me just didn't matter anymore. Since Butch Calkins whupped the tar out of me that last time, stuff that would've sent me screaming now just made me defiant. I don't know what I would've done if Pa had come down to the clothes-line and beat me, but I know I wouldn't have been afraid. As a matter of fact, I sort of wished he had. I'd like the chance to tell him that a man caught naked and covered in puke ought not be throwing stones.

"I just saw Pa," I told Grandma when I went in the kitchen.

"Where? Is he all right?"

"He was standing at the edge of the woods. He just watched me for a bit and then went back up the hollow."

Will must've heard me because he came thundering down the stairs. "Where'd you see Pa? Show me," he said.

"He's gone," I said.

"What'd you do?" he asked.

"Nothing you'd understand," I said with a sassy tone that earned me a knuckle-punch between the shoulder blades. "Quit hitting me!"

"Grandma, I'm taking the truck and looking for him," Will said. "I'll stay off the main road and keep close to the woods."

"Go on and go," Grandma said, "but, honey, I don't think your Pa wants to be found."

"I got to try," Will said, grabbing the keys off the hook and running for the truck. He tore out of the driveway and up to the back field.

"How'd your Pa look?" Grandma asked.

"Mad. But he always looks mad to me. He's probably embarrassed we saw him naked," I answered. "Grandma, where do you reckon Pa's been?"

"God only knows," Grandma said. "Maybe he's got a woman. Maybe he's just been off by himself. Don't worry, he'll come home soon."

"That's what I'm afraid of."

"Buddy, things are going to be all right. Don't be so serious all the time. Now what're you going to do with the rest of your day?"

"Thought I'd sneak up to the bait farm and try to see Early. I want to see what Mr. Finch has got him doing today," I answered.

"I think you'd better let Early alone for a time. This mess is for him and his family to figure out." Just then we heard the sound of a car horn, and both Grandma and I went through the house to the front porch. It was Sharon Williams, the sheriff's wife, coming up the drive.

"It's Sharon with my dishpan," Grandma said, waving at Mrs. Williams. "Sweet girl. Oh Lord, she's got the kids with her. Buddy, I'm warning you, if you don't want to talk about Early and that baby, you'd better get going. Why don't you go swimming? Won't nobody be down at the river this early."

I didn't hesitate. I ran out the back door, jumped off the porch, and headed for the river. I had no intention of swimming. I was going to the bait farm to see Early. What Grandma didn't know couldn't hurt her. I went across the meadow and hit the main road, turned left, and headed straight toward town. Ellerd was at his post, keeping watch. I didn't even try to hide, I just walked up to his car and caught him all crunched up on the front seat, napping. His body was all twisted to fit the seat, and he was snoring, dead to the world. I gave the hood of the car a pretty hard slap and must've scared him pretty bad.

"Dang it, Buddy! You scared me to death!" he yelled, jumping out of the car, lurching on unsteady legs. I could tell his body had fallen asleep because he kept stumbling, like he had rubber legs. "I had me a good nap going, Buddy. Why'd you scare me like that?" he asked, stamping his feet, trying to get the blood moving again. Then he looked at me like he just realized I was there. "Hey, you're not supposed to be down here."

"I'm going into town, and you can't stop me," I said, waiting to hear about a hundred reasons why I couldn't go.

"Well, go on then," Ellerd said. This from the man the county was paying to protect me.

"You think it's all right then?"

"Beats me. If I see you running back home with a bunch of holy-rollers on your tail, we'll know you should've stayed put."

"Well, I'm going," I said.

"Good luck. Hey, get me a R.C. Cola from the gas station on your way home, will you?" Ellerd gave me a dime, and I started for town. I was a few feet down the road when he called after me, "Your Pa come home?"

"Yeah," I yelled back, "but he's gone again."

"He sure don't stick to home. What's wrong with him?"

"Wish I knew," I yelled back, then turned toward town.

This was sort of exciting. I was looking forward to having everybody make a fuss over me, but I planned on keeping my eye out for Butch Calkins. It'd be just like him to hide and then jump me when I wasn't paying attention. I wasn't afraid, but I'm no fool either. I was going to play this like Nancy Drew, courageous and true, with a steadfast heart.

The dump was right across the river from where I was walking, and I could see somebody that looked like Miss Pink in a huge straw hat leading a group of strangers down to the river. I guess this was the dead baby tour. I could see two black dots that looked like June and July sitting behind a card table up by the road. They must be working for Pink, taking tickets or collecting money. When I saw Miss Pink pick up the milk pail, show it to the crowd, then drag a plastic doll baby out by its feet, I got a little queasy. Grandma always said Miss Pink was common. Common or not, she drew a pretty good crowd.

Dusty Lewis was at the gas station helping Mr. Runyon change a tire on her pickup. He was lying on the ground studying the tire, his canister of oxygen pumping beside him. Miss Dusty was wearing her veterinarian outfit; white blouse, string tie, men's pants, suspenders, baseball cap; and she had her pipe going full steam. She wasn't happy.

"Ed, you ain't got the sense God give a goose. You stripped the damn lug nuts!" Miss Dusty give the pickup a kick with her boot, then walked over and sat on the bench outside the gas station. She looked up, saw me, and hollered, "Buddy Dean, you get over here!" She knocked the ashes out of her pipe, and when I got close, she pulled me down on the bench. "Let me look at you," she said, breathing tobacco stink at me. "My God, you're a mess," she said, examining my face. "Them stitches are ready to come out so stop and see Doc while you're in town. Where you been?"

"Sheriff had me staying to home," I answered.

"You ain't missed a thing except a bunch of city folks looking for miracles and a Blue Jesus. Well, take a look," she said, pointing down Bridge Street toward town. "The place is crawling with the fools."

"They've been coming out to our place looking for me and Early. Even two bleeder boys from Alden come to get healed. When the DCR men showed up, Pa had to fire some shots over their heads."

"So that's why Ellerd's been parked at the end of your road. If the Lord created a stupider man, I've yet to meet him. Hey, you still planning on showing them heifers? 4-H fair's in two weeks," she said, getting up and going back over to her pickup.

"I don't know. I've been pretty busy with Early and everything," I said, noticing her hair for the first time. "You get your hair cut?"

"Hell, yes. I told Helen to clip me bald. I didn't want nothing to fuss with—shower, and out the door. Florence hates it. Of course, Pink Watrous thinks I'm making fun of her."

"It looks good. Easy. Hey, you take Pink's tour?"

"What do you think?" she said, rolling her eyes. "Florence has been begging to go, but I said I'd leave her if she did. That Pink's got a tacky streak; always did have."

"Grandma says she's common."

"If your grandma heard you tell me that, why she'd tan your behind," Miss Dusty laughed. "Ed, what are your plans for this ol' truck of mine?"

Mr. Runyon rolled his oxygen back to the bench, wheezing every step of the way. He was dragging his feet more than usual, so I guessed it was bad news for Miss Dusty.

"See y'all later," I said, giving them a wave.

I didn't want to walk past the DCR church and risk being called a sinner in broad daylight, so I crossed the street to see Mr. Biehl at the post office. I always like to check out the wanted posters, hoping I'll see Butch Calkins's face plastered up there offering a huge reward, dead or alive. It'll happen too, sooner the better.

"Hey Buddy, where you been?" Mr. Biehl asked.

"Home. Sheriff says there's folks in town looking for a miracle."

"I expect you'd be safe enough. People's looking for Early, not you. You stopping by Doc's to check up on that miracle baby?"

"I guess. Miss Dusty said it's time my stitches came out," I said. "Any more television cameras been in town?"

"Nary a one. They got their story and left a couple of days ago. You missed the whole thing. They interviewed the sheriff and Miss Pink. They tried to get Doc to show them the baby, but he wouldn't even answer his door. Mighty rude, them city folks."

"Anybody ask about me?"

"Not that I recollect. Since Burrell Finch put up the posters, all they's talking about is Early and the revival."

"What revival?

"Turn around and look at the door. Finch has gone too far if you ask me."

On the back of the post office door was a poster all done up in that bait farm glitter. Meet Blue Jesus—Miracle Revival & Hymn Sing—August 30th—8:00—Community Hall. There was a drawing of somebody hung on a cross wearing a crown of thorns, and Early's school picture was tacked on the face. Under the picture it said, "Blue Jesus the Miracle Maker. Prayers answered. Diseases Cured. Receive his healing touch. $3.00."

"This is awful!" I whispered to myself. It was like somebody socked me in the gut. "What does he think he's doing?"

"Making money off his son. Charging three dollars a head, little children, too. That's just not right," Mr. Biehl said, "Ought not to charge for a miracle."

"Early won't do it," I said. "He's too shy. There's no way he can talk in front of strangers."

"He'll do it," Mr. Biehl said. "Blues is a different sort. Early'll do what his father wants."

"I got to get up the bait farm," I said, opening the door. "See you later, Mr. Biehl."

I tore out of the post office and smacked right into Doc Rodger, who was coming in. "Whoa there, Buddy. Where you going in such a hurry?" I couldn't even talk I was so upset. I just pointed at the poster, and Doc nodded like he understood. "I know. Pitiful. Now let me look at that lip of yours." Doc Rodger led me back inside the post office and made me sit at Mr. Biehl's desk. He swung the lamp around close and I flinched from the heat. "Got to admit it, I do good work. Buddy Boy, them stitches need to come out. Harold, hand me your shears."

"Is it going to hurt?" I asked, starting to pull away.

"It'll pull a might," Doc said, pushing me back on the chair, keeping one hand on my shoulder. He took the scissors from Mr. Biehl, tipped my head back, and I heard a bunch of little snips. "Now, this part might tug a bit," Doc said, as he pulled the first of the stitches out of my lip.

"A lot! Hurts a lot," I moaned, my lips stinging.

"No, it didn't," Doc said, like I was too stupid to know when I was in pain. "Ready to go again?" Before I could answer Doc had snagged the last of my stitches and was wiping blood off my lip with his handkerchief. I know I've said this before, and I really don't have a germ phobia, but I hate it when people wipe my face with their hankies. Grandma's bad to do that. I just prayed Doc's handkerchief was clean. He's a doctor and knows about germs, but I'm not so sure. He didn't know he would be performing surgery in the post office, so it's not like he came prepared. I'm going to have to watch my lips to see if they swell up on me.

"There you go Buddy, good as new; handsome as ever," Doc said, turning off the lamp and giving me a pat on the head.

"Yeah, well, it hurt, though," I muttered. "How's the baby doing?"

"Beautiful child," Doc crowed. "Come by for a visit any time."

"Maybe later, right now I got to check on Early. I can't believe what his pa's doing."

"It's that blue taint," Doc said, as if that explained everything. "You better let it go, Buddy. Just chalk it up to the fact that they're different. We'll never understand their ways."

"No, we won't," Mr. Biehl added.

"Well, they're not all that different. They're just people. Mr. Finch never done right by Early," I said, kind of mad. I was disappointed in Doc. I thought he'd want to help. And I don't buy the story about how mysterious the blues are. Doc has lived around blue people all his life. I think this is just small-town thinking, and I expected better from Doc.

"I got to run. Thanks, Doc," I said, closing the door on my way out.

"Watch out for them dogs," Doc and Mr. Biehl yelled after me.

Once I hit the sidewalk, all I could think about was that revival. I knew I had to find Early and get him to move back in with us. Grandma wouldn't care I'd disobeyed her and went to the bait farm. She'd take care of Early forever. Pa wouldn't like it, but he wasn't around. I didn't figure there was any way in this world

Early knew what his pa had planned for him. I was his best friend; I had to warn him.

As I ran through town, I didn't recognize half the people I passed; city folks come to see Blue Jesus, I guess. There was a crowd of strangers in front of the drug store, so I cut across the street and ended up in front of Joe's Pole. Mr. Newsom was sitting out front with Hank Adams. Mr. Adams was a WWII vet with only one leg. He'll show you the stump if you ask him. Mr. Newsom and Mr. Adams both had a chaw of tobacco going. Since I was barefoot, I watched my footing.

"Buddy, your pa stopped in to see me this morning," Mr. Newsom yelled as I was maneuvering tobacco cuds on the sidewalk. "Well, hold up a minute, can't you?" he asked, grabbing my arm and pulling me up short. "Your pa don't look so good."

"Been sick," I said. "I got to run." I saw another poster announcing the Blue Jesus Revival tacked up on the barber shop door. Mr. Finch must've had help because all the words were spelled right.

Traffic on Bluetown Road was pretty thick, and I kept having to walk in the ditch to avoid getting hit. The cars kicked up a lot of dust off that dirt road, so I finally gave up and cut across the woods, through the orchard and up behind the Finch's house. I kept my eyes peeled for the hounds, but they must be keeping them in the house, or there's no way there'd be a long line of people waiting to see Early. I crept right up to the clothesline and stayed hid. The same sheets were hanging on the line.

Early was sitting under the Blue Jesus sign; his daddy was taking money at the other end of the porch. This time it seemed different. Early didn't look so sad, and it seemed to me he didn't mind being the center of attention. He was wearing a white shirt under his bib-alls and looked sort of dressed up. His blue skin was glowing bright blue, and I knew Miss Emma must've scrubbed him down with lye soap.

Every time Mr. Finch would receive money from somebody, he'd yell out their name to Early. Early would walk across the porch, take the person by the hand, and walk them back to the stool. He'd make them sit and then kneel in front of them, taking their hands in his, listening to the secrets they whispered. Every once in awhile Early would reach up and brush away tears, but mostly he listened. After a bit Mr. Finch would holler that time was up, then Early'd walk the person down the front steps. He always stayed one step up, put his hands on their head, and kissed their forehead. They went away looking happy. Early went back to the stool, and it started all over again. It gave me the creeps.

"Hey Buddy! What're you doing here?" Pocket asked, sneaking up on me and laying down. Buck naked again.

"Shh! Get away from me, you're naked," I hissed, trying to stay hid.

"Don't like clothes," she giggled. "Watch what I learned, Buddy." She got up on her knees and started doing somersaults, giggling like mad.

"Quit it," I whispered. "I ain't watching till you put some clothes on." What was wrong with them Finches that they let their youngest run around with no clothes?

I was concentrating pretty hard on Early. The line to see him kept growing. Close to the front of the line was that woman from Alden and her two bleeder boys. She sure is determined. The next sinner to come up on the porch was Nettie Ruth Johnson, the colored dishwasher at Eat. Early spent a long time talking to her.

"Lord, God, but he do know my pain," Nettie bawled, throwing up her hands to heaven. "He see everything. Thank you, Blue Jesus! Thank you!"

Early pushed her back down on the stool and kept whispering in her ear. Nettie was flat out crying, gut wrenching sobs, giving all her sorrow over to Early. Mr. Finch yelled out that Nettie Ruth's time was up, but Early ignored him.

All of a sudden Early stood up and pulled Nettie Ruth's head close to his chest. His head bent back and his mouth opened in that same silent scream I'd witnessed at the dump. Then his left hand went straight up in the air, held for a second, then boom, smacked down on Nettie Ruth's head. Early exhaled a loud gush of air, Nettie Ruth's legs kicked her backwards, and she fell flat on her back.

Nettie's sister started to run up on the porch, but Early held out his hand and stopped her. He helped Nettie Ruth to her feet, and they whispered some more, their foreheads touching. Mr. Finch hollered that time was up, but Early kept right on talking. Nettie started to cry and bobbed her head up and down like she was agreeing with everything Early was saying. Early walked her down the steps, kissed her forehead, and Nettie burst out in giggles. She pulled Early close in a hug and covered his face with kisses. I've never seen a young colored person hug or kiss some- body white or blue. It's just not done. Early didn't seem to care. He laughed as Nettie skipped away, yelling after her to come back any time. Boy, did I have a lot to tell Grandma.

I heard the spank, and then the sobbing started. Leon was hold- ing Pocket with one arm and paddling her behind with the other. "Get up to the house!" he yelled, giving her one last smack to get her going. She took off for the porch, wailing for her mama every step of the way. Leon came over to the clothesline and looked down at me. "You getting an eyeful?"

"Well, yeah," I said. No use lying. "You aren't going to sic them dogs on me, are you?"

"Shut up," he said. He jerked his head toward the porch, "Well, what do you think of this mess we got going on?" he asked, hun- kering down beside me. I'd never really studied Leon up this close before. He's a shade or two darker blue than Early, except for some light blue splotches on his neck and arms. I think he got burned pretty bad once. "Well?" he asked, waiting for my answer.

"I don't know. Early doesn't seem to mind doing it today."

"He's scared of Pa is all. You know how quiet Early is. This ain't right," Leon said. "Can y'all take him in up to your house?"

"That's why I'm here. I want him to come home with me. Does he know about that revival your pa's got planned?"

"What do you think? Pa said not to tell him, he'd just get fear- ful and run away. Buddy, get him out of here before it's too late."

"How? If your pa sees me up here, he'll know right off I'm trying to make Early run away."

"Early's fixing to take a break. I'll make sure it happens soon.
I'll send him out back. You meet him around the other side of the
house. Mama won't say nothing. This whole thing is starting to
scare her, and she wants Early to get away."

"What if your pa catches us?"

"Ain't no way he'll leave that porch if people are lining up to
give him money. Just stay out of sight. I'm going up now. When
Early comes out the back door, grab him and run for your life."

"Okay," I whispered, "but don't let your pa kill me." This
sneaking around was making me tense. "What if Early doesn't
want to go?"

"You got to make him. He'll listen to you. Now I'm going up
to the porch. You wait until I get Pa talking, then you head out."
Leon reached out to ruffle my hair, and I instinctively flinched. I
wasn't used to big boys being nice to me. He just laughed.

"Carol Disbrow! Vince and Ozzie!" Mr. Finch bellowed from
the porch. I saw Early stand up, look straight at Mrs. Disbrow.
He stared at her for a bit, and then shook his head no. He looked
terrified and backed up a few steps. "Carol Disbrow," Mr. Finch
yelled again. Early shook his head again and turned his back on
the crowd.

Leon jumped on the porch then and grabbed Mr. Finch's arm.
He pointed at Early, and then they started arguing. Mrs. Disbrow
got into the fight. She tried to push her kids past Mr. Finch and
kept throwing dollar bills at him. Mr. Finch was busy picking up
the money, pushing the kids toward Early. Early was backing up,
heading for the door.

Leon took his pa by the arm and pulled him off the porch. I
was studying them pretty hard, and when I looked back for Early,
he had disappeared. This was my cue. I ran behind the woodpile
and cut around to the back door. Early was standing on the back
porch, drinking a RC Cola and eating a Baby Ruth. The Finches
were eating store-bought now there was money coming in.

"Early," I hissed, touching his foot through the porch rail. He jumped straight up in the air.

"You scared me, Buddy," he whispered. "What are you doing here?"

"I'm taking you home. Come on, we got to hurry."

"I can't. Pa's waiting on me."

"It's all right. Leon told me to take you home. He'll tell your pa."

"Pa won't understand. Leon don't put things right."

"He will this time. Early, we got to hurry. Come on!" I tugged at his arm. He looked back once, then followed after me. We went up the hollow behind the house and cut across the mountain on the west side of town. This was taking the long way, but I didn't want to risk running into Mr. Finch. I figured Leon could stall him for about fifteen minutes, but when he discovered Early was missing, I knew he'd take the main road and cut right through town for our place. Since it'd take us about an hour to get home, Early wouldn't be there. Grandma wouldn't know a thing, so she wouldn't have to lie. As far as I could see this was a perfect plan.

We set quite a pace at first, climbing straight up the mountain. Maneuvering the mountain path was rough going. Early's got long legs and didn't have any trouble jumping ravines, crawling over and under branches, and seemed to recognize the easiest way to go. I'm sort of clumsy in the woods and made so much noise, I knew Mr. Finch had to be taking the main road. If he was tracking us through the woods, he'd be on us in a second just following my panting, grunting, and yelps every time I tripped and fell.

I made Early stop so I could rest, and we sat high above town, looking down on the river and all the buildings laid out like a jigsaw picture puzzle. We were high up in the mountains behind the school, watching people and cars moving through town like miniature figures on a game board. Everybody down there had normal lives, or so it seemed to me. Early and I were caught up in something otherworldly and bizarre. From a distance our far-away town looked nice, peaceful-like, but I knew the closer we got to town our troubles would just get bigger, like the people and the buildings.

"Are you okay?" I asked Early.

"I think so," he said. "You?"

"Sort of. Pa's run off."

"Do you want me to find him?" Early asked.

"No. I like it when he's gone. Will misses him, though," I said. We sat quiet for a bit, then what Early said sank in. "Can you really find him?"

"I'm Blue Jesus. I can do anything," he answered, smiling in his shy way. I looked at him like he was crazy, and he let one side of his mouth turn up, sly like. He held out his hands like as if he was going to lay them on my head for a healing. I ducked and started to crawl away. I looked back toward Early and he said, "Boo!" That did it. We both started to laugh until we were howling. After what I'd seen on the Finch porch, this made me feel better.

"Should we head down?" Early asked.

"Later," I said.

"Pa'll be looking for me."

"I know, but we got time. It's not so bad up here."

Early and I sat in silence for quite some time, just watching the town. Every once in awhile I'd sneak a look at Early and study his face. He looked normal, like my best friend. He didn't look like the mystical blue boy that brought the baby back to life. He didn't look like the Early that was whispering sacred secrets on the Finch porch.

"Can you really make miracles?" I asked.

"Sometimes," he said, "but Buddy, the miracles are already there. I just help people see them."

CHAPTER 12

It's only been three days, but it seems like forever since I got
Early away from the bait farm. When we got back to our house
Grandma had all the lights on and the house looked like a ball of
fire against the mountain. As we came across the meadow I could
see her pacing on the front porch and I knew she was looking for
me. She was walking mad, digging from one end of the porch to
the other, her fingers working the hem of her apron, gathering
thoughts. I knew I was in trouble.

I snuck Early up to the barn and tried to get him settled. He
wouldn't stay in the tack room where Pa's been sleeping, so I
hauled an old mattress up to the hayloft and made him a place
up there. His hiding place is behind some hay bales, and unless
you know he's up there you'd miss him. I got him a flashlight and
some old Screen Secrets I keep hid in the barn. I know them by
heart and don't care if they get wrecked. There's a water pump
next to the stalls and if he has to go the bathroom there's an old
outhouse behind the barn, or he can just squirt out the door
like Will. I planned on sneaking food out of the kitchen when
Grandma wasn't looking. Near as I could tell, Early's biggest
problem was going to be boredom.

Boy, I can read Mr. Finch like a book. He made a beeline for our house the minute he discovered Early was missing. Will told me he and Grandma had a knock-down, drag-out fight on our front porch. Mr. Finch called Grandma a lying thief, and she called him an ignorant, drunken hillbilly. I always miss the good stuff.

Mr. Finch went into town and came back with Sheriff Williams. Will said the sheriff looked sorry to be confronting Grandma, but said it was his duty and Early belonged at home. Mr. Finch said he wanted to search the house, but Grandma said if he did it'd be over her dead body. She gave the sheriff her word that Early wasn't in the house and promised to call when she found out what happened to him. I came in about three hours later.

My grandma's got an icy stare. I read about somebody with an icy stare in a Nancy Drew. I can't remember the book, but Nancy was confronted with an unkempt stranger with long, greasy hair, a sardonic sneer, and a chilling, icy stare. Tonight that was my grandma. She blessed my hide up one side and down the other. She called me irresponsible, reckless, foolish, and a bitter disappointment to her in her old age. That just wrecked me.

I told Grandma I had no idea where Early was, but I thought she'd be happy he was away from the bait farm. That did it. She grabbed me by the back of my neck and flung me down on the sofa in the front room. She started screeching about how Miss Emma was probably worried sick, that Early didn't have no sense and was probably out wandering the mountains, hungry and scared out of his wits. She lost me on that one. We both knew Early could cut cartwheels over these mountains with his eyes closed.

Then Grandma grabbed my chin, forcing me to look her in the face. "Buddy, I'm only going to ask you this once; where is Early?"

"I don't know."

"You do too, now tell me the truth." I knew she would ask again.

"I don't know," I said.

Grandma came pretty close to smacking me. She was all red-faced and flustered, her lips drawn together in a tight, white line.

I thought she was about to crack, but then she stood up straight, smoothed her apron, and said she was going in the kitchen to compose herself before she did something she would regret for the rest of her life. While she was gone she suggested I take a few minutes and try to remember where I'd put Early.

Grandma went into the kitchen and then the screen door slammed and she was out on the back porch. She must have had a lot of composing to do because I waited almost half an hour. Grandma came in the front door and stood there looking at me. She opened her mouth to say something, then closed it tight. She tried again, and nothing. Finally she came into the front room and held out her arms. I jumped off the sofa and ran into her hug, relieved that she wasn't angry anymore. She held me tight and we stayed that way for quite awhile.

"Buddy, I want what's best for Early. I want him away from that mess at the bait farm, but his kin have a right to know where he is. Now I'm asking for one last time; do you know where Early is?"

"No m'am," I answered.

"Fine," she said, pushing me away.

For the next three days Grandma frosted me out. I could've been invisible the way she ignored me, refusing to meet my eye, avoiding me every chance she got. She was all chatty with Will, which drove me nuts. They don't have a thing in common and I knew she was doing it just to bug me. All I got was the icy stare.

When the sheriff came out to the house the next morning to see if Early had turned up, Grandma didn't call me downstairs, she sent him straight up to my room. She knew that'd drive me crazy. I hate having strangers in my room. Will says I have a sick obsession with privacy, but I don't think it's all that weird. Will also says I'm obsessed with germs, but that's not true either. I just like my things neat and clean, and besides, I think Will's very reckless with his health.

When Sheriff Williams came in my room, he didn't look all that comfortable. I was lying on my bed pretending to read my Nancy Drew. I know he doesn't really like me because I'm a sissy.

Grown-up men and me don't mix well. Sometimes I've seen Pa and the other men in town looking at me like they caught me doing something dirty. The sheriff wasn't doing that today. He was just bobbing from one foot to the other, looking at the pictures of movie stars I've got on the walls, and trying to make small talk by asking who everybody is. I can't believe somebody in this day and age doesn't recognize Arlene Dahl. She's only been billed as the most beautiful woman in the world.

When the sheriff finally got around to asking about Early, I kept my mouth shut. I shrugged like mad to avoid talking. It was kind of fun watching how nervous I made the sheriff. He couldn't stand still, and I knew he was anxious to get out of my room. He asked me a bunch of sheriff-type questions, like where was I the day Early disappeared, what was I doing, who was I with? I just told him he'd have to check with my social secretary. Blank stare. Nothing. Nobody up here gets sarcasm. Finally I told him I didn't remember. That's when he hit me with the fact that if I knew anything at all about Early, then I was guilty of aiding and abetting a runaway minor, which was breaking the law. When I didn't confess, he practically ran out of my room. I'll tell you one thing, if I end up in that reform school for delinquent boys I'm never going to forgive Early.

After that I couldn't do anything right. Grandma wasn't talking to me. Will was never home, either playing ball or fooling around in town. I had Early stashed in the barn, and on top of it all, Pa was still missing. I was a nervous wreck day and night, but from the looks of it, Early was having the time of his life. He didn't have to answer to anybody. All he did was look at pictures in the movie magazines, play with Blossom and Honey, go for long walks in the mountains, and lay around eating the food I snitched out of our kitchen. I was suffering horrible guilt, couldn't sleep, and nobody would talk to me. By the middle of the third day I was ready to snap.

Tonight Will, me and Grandma ate supper together and nobody said a word. I hated it. We're not noisy eaters by custom;

by that I mean we don't talk all that much at the table. Tonight, nothing.

Finally Will pushed his plate back and got up from the table in disgust. "Y'all better settle this thing because I've had stomach cramps for three days!" He went out the back door and after a minute I could hear the pickup take off down the road. Will went off every night, looking for Pa. He drove up and down Highway 28, and even went looking in the colored quarters south of town. The look on his face when he comes in the door all alone just about kills me. Will misses Pa as much as I like having him gone. No matter how this turns out somebody's going to get hurt.

After dinner I couldn't take the tension or guilt a minute longer. "Grandma, Early's in the barn," I said, aiming it at her back as she was doing dishes. She didn't say a word, but I could see her neck stiffen up, and I knew she heard me. She kept right on washing. "Early's been in the barn all along." I tried talking above the water but got no response. I went up to the sink, lay my head against Grandma's back, put my arms around her, and whispered, "I'm sorry." That was what she was waiting for. She turned around and pulled me close.

"I knew all along," she said, kissing the top of my head.

"How? For how long? Why didn't you say something?" I don't get grownups at all. If I knew somebody was lying, I'd call them out on it. I got three days of the icy stare for nothing.

"Wasn't my place," she sniffed. "You and Early are friends. I didn't know what you'd promised him."

"You lied to the sheriff," I said, stunned.

"Not really. I suspected, but I wasn't sure." Grandma took off her apron, grabbed the flashlight off the window sill, "Now let's get Early inside and get some food in him before I call the law."

It was already dark when Grandma led the way to the barn. She went straight for the tack room, but I pointed up to the hayloft and watched her shudder, thinking of the climb. Grandma's afraid of heights and won't even stand on a chair to decorate the Christmas tree.

Grandma took her sweet time getting up in the hayloft. She took the silo ladder one rung at a time, convinced with every step she was going to crash to the floor. She kept calling out Early's name, but we didn't hear a thing. When Grandma finally got on what she considered safe footing, she swept the flashlight across the barn, but there was no sign of Early.

"Maybe he went home," Grandma said. I pointed over to the far corner and Grandma aimed her flashlight at the bales of hay that made up the walls of Early's hideaway. "Earl Lee Finch, you come on out here!" she yelled. We didn't hear a thing, just a little bit of scratching that could've been one of the barn cats.

"Early, it's okay," I said. "You're not in trouble so come on out."

More scratching, then something that sounded like a heavy sigh.

"I ain't here," Early said.

I got tickled at this, but Grandma shook her head.

"You can come out now Early. Nobody's going to hurt you," she said.

"Come on Early," I said, "It's okay. Grandma knows everything."

First we saw a wisp of blond hair in the flashlight beam, and then Early's sky blue face came into view. He squinted into the bright light for a minute, then a smile cut across his face. Grandma and I both laughed.

"Hey Aunt Lena," Early said, grinning in the light. "Buddy said not to tell nobody where I was, and I didn't neither."

"Well it's time you came up to the house and had a bath. You hungry?" Grandma asked, walking toward Early and cutting off the flashlight. "Your mama'd never forgive me if I didn't feed you."

"I could eat. Has Mama been looking for me? She worries about me all the time. Did Pa hurt her?" Early asked.

"Your mama's fine," Grandma said, pulling Early close.

"I been thinking on this and I got to go home." Early started to pull away from Grandma, but she held back, sitting herself on a bale of hay, pulling Early down beside her. "I miss my mama," Early said, and I could hear the tears in his voice.

"Buddy, go on down and look after Blossom and Honey. Me and Early got some talking to do."

"That's okay, they're fine."

"No, they ain't," Grandma said with a little more force. I knew to make myself scarce.

I hate being left out of things. I was the one that rescued Early. I figured that whatever went on between him and Grandma, I had a right to know. He was my responsibility. That's why I only went halfway down the ladder. I figured I earned the right to hear what they said.

"Early, you tell me right off and you tell me true, do you want to go home, or do you want to live with us? You can do either one and ain't nobody going to get mad about it," Grandma said.

I could hear Early blow his nose, so I knew Grandma pulled her hanky out from her apron and was wiping his nose. It had to be the same hanky she used all day long and I knew it wasn't clean. If Early gets the pink eye, we'll know why.

"You know, Buddy and I would like you here with us," Grandma said.

"If I stay with y'all, could I still see my mama?" Early asked.

"Of course you can," Grandma said.

"But what about my pa" Early whispered.

"What's going on out to your place?" Grandma asked. "Buddy told me about it some, but I want to hear it from you."

"Pa makes me talk to strangers, hold their hands, say where they hurt. Sometimes I help. Most times all they want to do is talk."

"Is that why you run away?" Grandma asked.

"Kind of," Early said, so low I could hardly hear. I went up another rung. "Pa calls me Blue Jesus and promises I can heal. Says when I do the laying of the hands they'll be happy. He gets money for it, too. We been eating store-bought. It ain't right getting money for what I do."

"Early, can you fix folks? Can you heal?" Grandma asked.

"Sometimes," Early whispered.

"How?"

"I touch them, and I can see inside. I see the dark places. I take the dark away." Early was whispering, so I risked another rung on the ladder.

Grandma took a deep breath, and I could hear her shifting her weight. Suddenly the flashlight beam hit the ladder. "Buddy, I know you're hanging on that ladder! Now get down and give us some privacy!"

Dang it. I got the feeling Grandma was just getting Early warmed up for what she called a soul-searching chat, and I was going to miss the best part. My grandma has a way of talking you around to something that's for the best, and you don't even know you've been persuaded until it's too late. I didn't know how she was going to talk Early out of going home, but if there was any chance at all, Grandma could do it.

I hung around the barn, mucking out Blossom's stall and giving her a good brushing down, waiting for the big talk to finish up. Every so often I could hear them talking kind of loud, so I'd sneak around to the ladder. Once I thought I heard Early crying, but by the time I got close they were whispering again. Finally I gave up and went outside for some fresh air.

Seems to me fall comes earlier in the mountains than the flatlands. Tonight the air seemed lighter. The weight of the southern summer drawing one final gasp, giving way to a brisk-flowing air that doesn't linger on the body, but sweeps right on past, like it's got better things to do. There's a smell on the breeze; over-ripe apples, pine, hay, all mixed in the night air that rolls down the mountain, past our farm, along Bitterroot River, and I imagined off to the ocean. You start to recognize the signs of fall by smell and touch even before you see the leaves changing colors.

Autumn meant another school year was about to begin; another year of torture at the hands of Butch Calkins. It also meant that I was about to turn twelve. Maybe things would be different for me this year. Maybe this summer the other boys would have grown up enough to know it wasn't sporting to fight someone who won't fight back. Maybe I'll get those hormones that Grandma warned me about. Maybe I'd learn to fight. This year would be different in one way; I wouldn't be afraid.

Our barn sits back from the house, up a small rise right before the tree line. I climbed up on our tractor so I could see all the way into town, checking lights to see who was up, and counting cars that crossed North Bridge heading south into town. When the neon light at Eat went out, I knew it was nine o'clock and things would be shutting down.

That's when I got the idea for a country song. I'd call it "Midnight Girl in a Nine O'clock Town" and send it to Loretta Lynn. It'd be perfect for Loretta because she's got a real common touch. She knows all about cheating women and living on the wrong side of the tracks. Mama said Loretta Lynn is the Joan Crawford of country music.

I was climbing off the tractor, fixing to go inside and start writing my song, when the flashlight beam cut through the dark. I could hear Grandma and Early whispering. Then Grandma bent over, laughing so hard the flashlight beam was jumping all over the place. They were right beside me and didn't even know I was there.

"Took you long enough," I said. They both jumped.

"Buddy, you scared me! Child, you didn't have to wait on us," Grandma said, wiping her eyes with that same nasty hanky.

"What ya'll talk about for so long? What's going on? Is Early going home?" I know I sounded mad, and I really wasn't, but I couldn't get that tone out of my voice. It was a left-out tone. Grandma knew it by heart.

"Buddy, we ain't got no secrets, I promise. Now let's head down to the house. Early's got to take a bath, and then I'm going to feed him."

"Aunt Lena's going to make me noodles called spaghetti," Early said. "Chef Boyardee."

"Do you like spaghetti?" I asked. I wasn't sure Early had ever tasted foreign food.

"Maybe," he laughed.

As we walked toward the house we could see the pickup lights coming up the driveway. When just one door slammed, we knew Will came home alone. Early saw Will walking toward the back door and yelled, "Will, I was hiding in the barn!" He ran toward my brother, threw his arms around Will, and hugged him solid. Will looked stunned.

"Hey, Early! Everybody's been missing you!" he said.

"I'm back," Early said. "I'm going to have spaghetti."

"But first you're going to have a bath. Now get in that house and don't come downstairs until you're clean. Understand?" Grandma said. Early just grinned, turned tail and ran in the house. Grandma walked over and hooked her arm through Will's. "No luck?"

"I don't know where he is," Will said. "I asked everybody. I think somebody's hiding him."

"Who?" I wanted to know.

"What do you care? You're glad he's gone," Will snapped. Well, he had me on that one. "What are you going to do with Early?" Will asked.

"I got to call Matt Williams first thing," she said, "and then I'm putting him to bed. This will all get sorted out in the morning."

"Does he know anything about the revival?" Will asked.

"I told him. Says he wants to do it," Grandma sighed, easing herself down on the back porch steps. "Says he's been called to help people."

"Well, he can't!" I yelled. I couldn't believe what I was hearing. "Early gets scared in front of strangers. He'll start crying, and everybody'll laugh. Grandma, we can't let him do it! You got to stop it!" I could feel tears starting. It wasn't just Early that brought on the tears, it was everything else; the guilt of lying and Pa being gone.

"Jesus, she's going to cry!" Will laughed. "Girl."

"Shut up!" I was crying, and there was no use trying to hide it. "Grandma, please! Everybody's going to make fun of him. We can't let him do it!" It felt like my stomach was folding in on itself.

"Buddy, hush. Everything will be all right." Grandma pulled her hanky out and started toward me. I backed right up. "Besides, if Early wants to do it, we can't stop him. This ain't up to us."

"It's got to be against the law! Make the sheriff stop it!" I yelled, pulling up my T-shirt to wipe my tears. "It ain't right, and you know it!" I must have been getting pretty loud, because Will came over and raised his hand to smack me. I flinched out of the way.

"Don't yell at Grandma. She didn't do nothing." Will started to walk away, then whirled around and knuckle-punched me on the arm. I didn't even see it coming.

"That hurt! If it leaves a mark, I'll get you!" I yelled.

"Ooh, I'm scared. You'll get me? What'll you do then, bore me to death talking about your best friend Tony Dow?"

"How do you know about that? Have you been reading my journal?" That had to be it. How else could he know about me and Tony Dow? I felt like I was going to throw up.

Will just laughed and minced away, lisping, "Tony Dow is my besth friend. I'm going thwimming in histh pool."

"Stop it," Grandma warned.

"I'll kill you," I screamed, running at Will, arms flailing. I hit him right below the waist, and didn't even knock him off balance. Boy, is he muscular. He just laughed at me, like trying to hit him was the funniest thing he'd ever seen. That did it. I pulled back and hit him in the balls with my fist. That got his attention.

"Sissy, girl!" he yelled, twisting my arm behind my back, and then throwing me down in the dirt. "No wonder you don't have any friends!"

"Stop it! Now! Will, get inside!" Grandma yelled. When Will didn't move fast enough, she gave him her two-finger point and jerked her head toward the house. "Now!" Will took the porch steps two at a time and disappeared, giving me one last drop-dead look.

"Buddy . . ." Grandma said.

"He's been reading my journal. Mama gave it to me before she died. He's got no right." I was sobbing at this point.

"I'll talk to Will," Grandma said. "When your pa gets home, he'll deal with Will."

"Oh, Grandma," I said, "Pa won't do anything. Whatever Will does is perfect. I'm the one that can't do anything right. I'm the one he hates."

"Buddy, don't talk like that," Grandma whispered. "Come here," she said, patting the place next to her on the step. I eased toward the porch and she pulled me close. "I'll take care of Will. I promise."

"What about Early?" I asked. "We can't let Mr. Finch put him on stage. Everybody'll make fun of him, like he's a big joke. They'll laugh and he won't even understand why," I sobbed.

"But that's Early's choice, not ours," Grandma said.

"No, it's not. It's his pa making him." I tried to twist away from Grandma, but she held tight.

"No, it isn't. I'm a little surprised you don't realize just how strong Early is. Buddy, this is something he feels he has to do, and it's got nothing to do with his pa. He says he was called to help people."

"But they'll laugh," I said, quiet, sniffing against Grandma's shoulder.

"Maybe," Grandma whispered. I could feel her reaching for that hanky again, so I put a little distance between us.

"I better go to bed," I said, "but promise you'll talk to the sheriff. Tell him it's okay if Early lives here."

"I promise," Grandma smiled. "You go on. I'll send Early up after I fill him full of spaghetti." I started up the steps, my feet heavy, my arm throbbing from Will's hit. "Young man, don't even think about leaving here without giving me a kiss," Grandma said over her shoulder, getting up with a grunt, and brushing off the back of her dress.

I leaned over and kissed her cheek. "I'm sorry I lied," I whispered.

"I'm sorry I sent the sheriff up to your room," she said.

"He doesn't even know who Arlene Dahl is," I said as I headed inside, dead tired and feeling like I could sleep for a year. I could hear Grandma laughing as I went up the stairs.

Early was in the shower singing This Little Light of Mine just enough off key to irritate me. I had to pee like mad, so I sat at the top of the stairs and waited for him to get out of the bathroom. Will kept opening his bedroom door and checking, so I guess he had to pee too. Downstairs I could hear Grandma on the kitchen phone talking to the sheriff.

"Matt, Lena Harrington. Early's staying here at the farm with us. Uh-huh. He was camping out in our barn and didn't nobody know." There was a long pause and then Grandma got a tone. "Oh, for God's sakes Matt, use the sense the Good Lord give you. We can't send him back to the bait farm." Another pause. I could see Grandma's shadow on the dining room floor, and I knew she was pacing. I bet anything her free hand was working the hem of her apron. "He's scared of his pa, that's why. You give that boy back to Burrell Finch and I'll press criminal charges against you. Now, good night."

I was clutching so bad, I couldn't hold it anymore. I banged on the bathroom door, "Early, come on, I got to pee!"

Early opened the bathroom door and stood there, bright blue, one towel wrapped around his waist and another around his head like a turban. "Well," he grinned, "I'm clean. Smell me."

"I believe you. Hurry up, I got to pee. You better get downstairs and eat." I tried to get by, but Early wouldn't move.

"Did you know I'm going to be in a revival? I'm going to help people."

"I know all about it. Are you sure you want to?"

"Got to. It's what I'm supposed to do," Early said. "I got a gift."

"Out of my way, girls," Will said, pushing us away from the bathroom door and locking himself inside. I knew he'd be in there for hours.

"Hey, I was waiting!" I yelled, banging on the door.

"Tough tittie," Will yelled through the door.

"Buddy, if I can help Pa make some money and help people too, then it's all right. This is important."

"Yeah, it's important to your pa. How do you know he just won't drink up the money? He's done it before," I said, jigging from one foot to the other, close to bursting. "We can talk about this later. You go down and eat."

Early went downstairs wrapped up in his towels. He looked like a blue Roman from olden times when they wore togas. It's sure a good thing Pa wasn't home. If he came in the kitchen and saw a half-naked blue boy eating spaghetti at our table, he'd go nuts.

I banged on the bathroom door pretty hard, but Will didn't answer. I knew he was camped out to stay. I didn't even want to know what he was doing in there. I had to move fast, so I went in Will's bedroom and peed in one of his baseball trophies. That'd teach him for reading my journal.

I crawled into bed, and when I stretched my legs out, I could feel just how tired I was. I tried to read, but couldn't keep my eyes open. I didn't even have the energy to turn my light off; I just drifted off to sleep, thinking of ways to get even with my brother. I woke up sometime later in the night and could see Early sitting in my window seat, looking out at the night. He looked like a ghost, a pale blue shape in the dark shadows, his hair and his underpants glowing white in the moonlight.

"Hey, how was the spaghetti?"

"I liked it. Noodles and tomatoes."

"What are you doing up?" I asked.

"Praying," Early whispered. "You still pray, Buddy?"

"I give it up. I never got an answer. I don't think God was listening to me," I said, leaning over to turn on my lamp.

"Don't. Keep it dark. I like the moon. Buddy, I got to ask you something."

"What?"

"What happens if I do this revival and I can't help nobody? What if I don't get the feeling? What'll people do if I don't make a miracle?"

"I don't know."

"Pa's promised everybody I can cure them."

"I don't think people really believe that. I think folks are coming to see you because of the baby. You're like a movie star up here."

"I can't help everybody."

"I know. Just help who you can."

"I can't help them bleeder boys," Early said. In the moonlight I could see tears streaking his face. "I can't fix them."

"Nobody can. It's something they were born with. Now come to bed. We'll talk about this in the morning."

"What happened to Nancy Drew?" Early asked as he crawled over me and got under the covers.

"She solved the mystery. Now go to sleep." I rolled over and shut my eyes. Every so often a little spaghetti burp would hit the air, but by this time Early was fast asleep. I followed soon after.

Somebody was pounding on our front door, hard. The screen door was whapping against the house, and the walls were shaking. My first thought was, Pa had come home drunk and ready to beat me for taking in Early.

"It's my pa," Early said, sitting bolt upright. "He's come for me."

"Shh," I whispered. "It might be my Pa. Come on." Early and I got out of bed and started down the stairs.

"Lena! I got the law with me this time! Lena, open this door! I got something to ask you!" It was Mr. Finch.

"Burrell, shut up!" Grandma yelled right back at him. "Good morning Matt."

"Aunt Lena," the sheriff said, "sorry to get y'all up so early, but Burrell's been pestering me since dawn." Early and I crept down the stairs and peeked around the corner. We could see Grandma and Will standing inside the front door. Mr. Finch and the sheriff were on the front porch. "Burrell here has something to ask you."

"That's what I hear," said Grandma, sarcastic. "Well?"

"Y'all done stold my son," Mr. Finch yelled.

"That's not a question," Grandma said, real dry. Man, when she wants, Grandma's got a tone that can cut timber. "And stop yelling at me. Early run away because he was scared."

"That ain't true," Mr. Finch yelled.

"Burrell, get to the point. I got to go to work," the sheriff pushed.

"What do you want, Burrell?" Grandma asked.

"I want y'all to keep Early for a time. Then I want him back."

"What if we don't want to give him back?" Grandma asked. Early and I went into the front room to see what Mr. Finch would say.

"He belongs to me and his mama," Mr. Finch bawled. "I just want y'all to keep him until after the revival."

"Why?"

"This healing thing is upsetting his mama. Folks are coming to the house night and day, and Emma don't take to strangers."

"There's been a line of traffic going up Bluetown Road to the bait farm, and over a hundred people waiting in line to see Early," the sheriff told Grandma. "Emma don't think it's good for the boy to be talking to strangers all the day and night."

"Well, what's she think about that revival freak show Burrell's got planned? That ain't good for the boy either," Grandma said.

"Blue Jesus is going to help people, make them well. He's special, that one. He can do it, too," Mr. Finch hollered. "It ain't no freak show."

"Shut up, Burrell," the sheriff said. "Now let's get this settled. Lena, are you willing to take Early in?"

"We'd love to have Early," Grandma said.

"Good. Now let's everybody go about their business, and let me get to work. Burrell, does this sit right with you?"

"Iffen she makes sure he's at the revival, and don't try to run off with him," Mr. Finch said.

"Lena?" Matt Williams looked to Grandma for an answer.

"If he wants to do it, he's free to go," Grandma said.

"Early, boy, I see you in there!" Mr. Finch yelled. "Come out here."

"Hey, Pa," Early said, walking out on the front porch.

"They treating you all right?" Mr. Finch asked. Early nodded. "If they don't, you just come on home. Your ma will be down to see you later today. We ain't telling nobody where you is at. Y'all don't say nothing either, unless you want a bunch of strangers on your land. Early, you stay hid until this revival thing is over and done."

"Okay," Early said. "Mama's coming today?"

"Right after dinner."

"Burrell, you about ready?" the sheriff asked.

"I love you, Early," Mr. Finch yelled as he started down the front path to the patrol car.

Will and I went out on the porch and joined Early and Grandma. We all watched the patrol car pull down the road and head off toward town. My head was racing a mile a minute after hearing Mr. Finch telling Early he loved him. I never heard that from my pa. I don't think I ever will.

"Pa's up to something," Early said. He had a troubled look on his face, like he was scared of what was out there waiting for him.

"Who cares? You get to stay with us," I said.

"Your Pa just wants to make sure you're safe," Grandma said.

"That ain't the reason," Early said. "Pa's going to do something."

"What?" Will asked.

"Don't know yet, but it'll come clear soon enough. You can't trust my pa. He's not a good man," Early said.

Burrell Finch wasn't a good man. Everybody in North Georgia knew that. The fact he wasn't to be trusted became evident as soon as we got our copy of *The Dixie Bugler* later that day. One thing's for sure, the next ten days are going to be mighty interesting.

CHAPTER 13

"Look what Finch is up to now," Will yelled, slapping *The Dixie Bugler* down on the kitchen table.

"Blue Jesus Disappears!" The headline of *The Dixie Bugler* trumpeted. Under that, in smaller type, "Vanished Without a Trace! Will Blue Jesus Make the Revival?" There was a picture of Mr. Finch standing on the back porch at the bait farm, pointing toward the woods. The caption read, "Burrell Finch reports Blue Jesus' journey of peace started that way."

"Let me read it," I said, grabbing the paper.

Early sat beside me and kept staring at the picture of his father. "Look, Buddy, Pa looks like a colored man," he said, his fingers tracing his father's face on the page.

"He is colored, you goof. He's blue," Will said. Mr. Finch did look pretty dark in newsprint. "Buddy, read it out loud."

I groaned. I hate reading out loud. From the first sentence it was clear Miss Carla was in rare form.

"Four days ago true believers in the power of Comfort Corner's own Blue Jesus met with bitter disappointment. Standing in line for hours, waiting for magical miracles to descend in the healing words of Earl Lee Finch, known locally as Blue Jesus, their dreams were crushed when Burrell Finch, Blue Jesus' father, had to turn them away."

"Who wrote that?" Grandma asked. "Was it that skinny gal with the skunk streak in her hair?"

"Uh-huh. I get to call her Carla. She told me she believes in the power of the human interest story to bring about social change."

"Oh, brother," Grandma snorted.

"Keep reading," Early said, "but not so fast."

"Among those waiting for an audience with Blue Jesus were Carol Disbrow and her children, Ozzie and Vic. Mrs. Disbrow's children are afflicted with hemophilia, a rare blood disorder that causes excessive bleeding."

"I can't help them," Early said, breaking in. "Them boys are going to die. I seen it, and there ain't nothing I can do."

Grandma turned and stared at Early. I could see Will rolling his eyes as he let out a low whistle. I got the creeps so bad I shuddered.

"Go on, Buddy, read," Early said.

"Faithful readers of *The Dixie Bugler* know this paper was the first to break the story of the mysterious baby that was found in the town dump, and the child's miraculous rebirth at the hands of Earl Lee Finch. It was the power of that miracle that earned him the name Blue Jesus, and stories of his gifts for healing and prophecy have been spreading nationwide.

'Early is a spiritual young man,' his father reports. 'His mother and I realized he had the healing gift when he cured her asthma. That was a true miracle of faith.'

"Pa don't talk like that," Early said. "Besides, it's a lie. Mama don't have what it says there."

"Keep reading," Will said, reaching across the table and knuckling my arm. I didn't say a thing, just stared at him. Finally he broke. "Okay, I'm sorry. Will you finish the story? Please." It was a sarcastic "please" but I turned back to the story and continued reading, thinking about that trophy full of pee waiting in his room.

"That's enough," Grandma said, pulling the paper out of my hands. "I want to get dinner on. Will, you got to carry me up to Gizzy's sometime today. I want to check on the apples and make sure he's got enough Mexicans to pick."

"We can go after dinner," Will said, then he picked up *The Dixie Bugler* and threw it across the table to me.

"Read," Early and Will said together. They looked at each other and both grinned. I still don't understand why they're friends.

I looked at Grandma. She shook her head and said, "Well, go on. We won't have no peace in this kitchen until you finish the story."

"As concerned citizens wait for the return of Blue Jesus, the question is, will he make an appearance at the Labor Day Revival planned at the Comfort Corners Community Hall on September 6th?

"Tickets for the revival have been selling briskly. Mrs. Verna 'Pink' Watrous has been called in to direct the revival, select the music, and oversee the proceedings. Mrs. Watrous has an extensive theatrical background, having traveled to New York City and seen the Easter Show at Radio City Music Hall. She reports that she is planning a spectacular event that will make true believers out of dedicated doubters. 'Miracles will happen. Prayers will be answered,' Mrs. Watrous promised. 'Blue Jesus will appear and believers will be born.'

"'We knew Early was a miracle baby,' Mr. Finch said, as he remembered the fateful day his son came into this world. 'He was born on Christmas Day during a blizzard. Early was born in our barn under a full moon and a wondrous sky full of stars. His birth was a miracle, just like the real Jesus.'

"My birthday's in June," Early said.

"That man has no shame," Grandma said, pulling the newspaper out of my hands and putting dinner on the table.

"We didn't even build the barn until after Pocket was born," Early said.

"So what? I think it's neat," Will said. "Your old man's telling everybody you're the next Jesus. The money's going to be roll-ing in."

"I ain't no Jesus, and it's a sin to say I am. I told y'all he was up to something. What do you think, Buddy?" Early asked.

"I think I'm hungry. Let's eat," I answered. I couldn't trust myself to talk because it all come clear to me. The only reason Mr. Finch wanted us to keep Early was so he could get public-ity for the revival. Once everybody read Miss Carla's story in the paper the revival will be standing room only, everybody showing up to see the Blue Jesus freak. It was a brilliant publicity stunt.

As for Miss Pink being in cahoots with Mr. Finch, that didn't surprise me. Anybody that would give dead baby tours of the dump would be up for something underhanded like the revival. The only thing I can't figure out is if the sheriff is in on it. The paper didn't come out until this morning, so there's always a chance he didn't know the story Mr. Finch was telling. But if he is going along with Mr. Finch, I knew it had to be about money.

"I'm going into town and I'm telling everybody where Early is," I said, getting up from the table.

"No, you ain't. You're going to sit there and finish your dinner. We ain't saying a word about this to nobody," Grandma said.

"But Grandma," I started. She stopped me cold.

"Early, do you want to go along with all this? Do you want to go to that revival?" Grandma leaned across the table and studied Early's face.

"Yeah. I mean, yes m'am," Early said.

"No, you don't," I snapped, but Grandma cut her eyes at me, and Will knuckled my arm. I shut up.

"Are you sure? You don't have to do nothing you don't want to. You can stay here with us no matter what," Grandma said.

"I got to do it now. I can't let everybody think I'm Jesus," Early said. "I got to tell the truth."

"All right then, here's what we're going to do; Early's going to stay up here at the farm, and nobody's going to say a word about it. Understood . . . Buddy?" Grandma stared right at me. I nodded my head, but it just about killed me. I wanted to ruin Mr. Finch's plans more than anything. "What about you, Will? Can you keep your mouth shut?"

"Yes, m'am," Will said.

"Good. Pull the truck around and we'll go up to Gizzy's in a minute." Will cleared his plate and ran out the back door. "Mr. Early, think you can wash them dishes up for me?"

"Yes m'am," Early said.

"Your mama did a good job raising you," Grandma said, giving Early a squeeze as she went into the pantry. She came out with her purse open and counting her money. "Buddy, come here."

"For crying out loud Grandma, you don't have to pay me. I'll keep my mouth shut," I said.

"Lord, child, I know that. I want you to take this money and buy a strongbox at the general store. Get one with a real sturdy lock, one that Will can't pick. Reading your diary was wrong. A boy that's almost twelve has to have a place to lock his secrets away." Grandma handed me a twenty dollar bill. I couldn't believe my eyes. It seemed like play money.

"Twenty dollars! Grandma."

"I'm not saying you got to spend it all, but if it takes twenty, that's what you spend. This is important."

"Thanks," I mumbled. I could feel my eyes filling up with water. It's that unexpected kindness thing.

"If you start crying, I'm taking that money back," Grandma said, pulling me into a hug. "Early, I'm off to Gizzy's. If your mama comes while we're gone, ask her to wait. I want to talk to her."

"Yes m'am," Early answered. "What do I do if Mr. Lyle comes home?"

"Run for your life," I said under my breath.

I know Grandma heard me because she hesitated a bit, trying not to smile. "Tell him to get up to Gizzy's. We've got apples to harvest."

Grandma went out the back door, Early turned to the sink full of dishes, and I headed toward town, the twenty dollar bill burning a hole in the pocket of my bib-alls. I'd never been trusted with this much money before. I was determined to get the best box for the least amount of money. I knew Grandma didn't have a lot of extra money, especially for stuff like this, and I wanted to give her as much back as possible. My birthday was in a couple of days, so I'd tell her she could count the strongbox as my present. The idea of a secret box to keep my papers in was sort of exciting, and a whole lot better than hiding my journal under my mattress.

I was at the end of our road and turning right onto Highway 28 when the sheriff's car came barreling down the road and squealed to a stop a few feet behind me. Matt Williams stuck his head out the window and yelled for me to stop. When I turned around I made sure I looked disgusted.

"Buddy, I swear to God, I didn't know what Finch had planned. When I got the paper this morning, I got so damn mad I almost drove out to the bait farm and beat him senseless. Is Aunt Lena mad?"

Okay, he was innocent. I'm a pretty good judge of character, and I could tell by the look on his face he didn't have any idea that Mr. Finch was going to turn Early running away into a huge event.

"She ain't all that happy," I said.

"She up to the house?"

"No, Will drove her up to Gizzy's to check on the apples. If you hurry you can probably catch them. You know Will's driving without a license."

"That's okay. Will's responsible," Mr. Williams said. "I'm heading back to town, but tell Aunt Lena I stopped in, and for God's sake make sure you tell her I'm sorry."

"Mr. Williams, ain't there nothing you can do to stop this revival? Early's just going to look like a fool."

"Holding a revival ain't against the law, Buddy. Besides, how do you know Early's going to look like a fool?"

"His pa's promising a miracle. What happens when Early gets on that stage and nothing happens?"

"Maybe he can make a miracle. You never know," Sheriff Williams said, gunning the gas, anxious to get back to town. "Don't forget to tell Aunt Lena I stopped by." He tipped his hat to me, caught himself doing it, and hit the gas. I knew he was embarrassed. Tipping your hat is what southern men do to show respect to ladies. The hat tipping sort of gave me the creeps, but even creepier was the sheriff saying maybe Early could make a miracle. If you ask me, that's the power of the press.

I stood on the bank overlooking the dump, trying to see if Miss Pink was conducting a tour. When I didn't see her, I decided to check it out. I hadn't been there since we found the baby and I was curious. I couldn't see a whole lot for Miss Pink to show off. It didn't even look the same, but dumps change a lot. The milk pail was there, and I saw where Miss Pink had put a black ribbon on the handle. I was looking for the red paint on the ground that was supposed to be my blood, but it must've washed away in the rain.

I was kicking over piles of trash, looking for old movie magazines or record albums, when I heard somebody heading downhill on a run.

"Got you alone at last, you lying little girl!" Butch Calkins! I was trapped. I felt my knees give out, and I almost fell over a pile of National Geographics. "You stinking little sissy. Proud of yourself?"

"Leave me alone, Butch," I said, backing up a couple of steps. "You can't hit me in the eye or I'll go blind. Doc said so."

"That's too bad, you piece of shit. Maybe you should've thought of that before you put the law on me. I'm on a year's probation because of your big mouth." I was working my way down to the river. I figured if Butch came at me, I could at least make a swim for it. I'm pretty fast in the water. "Hey girlie, where do you think you're going?"

"Get away from me, Butch," I said. "I ain't scared of you."

"Yes, you are," he said, coming right up to me, knocking me backwards over the dead baby pail.

"Not anymore," I said, looking him right in the eye. And it was true, I wasn't afraid. "I'm not running from you any more. You can't scare me."

"Ooh, I can't believe it, the little girl's not afraid. Looks like I'll have to give you something to be scared of," Butch said, running at me. He tackled me around the waist. We both hit the ground, rolling down the hill until we bumped up against a stack of old tires. Butch got on top of me and pinned my arms down. "Scared now?"

"Get off me," I said. I really wasn't afraid. I was looking up at his face and noticed that he had green eyes and the start of whiskers. I'd never really looked at him this close before.

"You know what you got to do," he said, bringing his face toward mine.

"I ain't kissing you, Butch, so get off me!" I tried to twist away, but with all his weight holding me down, it was hard to move. His lips were right above mine when I bucked my head up. We smacked foreheads with a force that made me see stars. It hurt, but it beat having him press his cigarette mouth against me.

"Jesus, bitch!" Butch yelled, letting go of my arms, grabbing his head.

With my arms free, I was able to sit halfway up, get a little leverage, and push him off my lap. I got up and started to run up the hill. Butch lurched for me, grabbed my feet, and I hit the dirt again. He pulled me down the hill toward him, grinning. He looked crazy, like Pa when he's bad drunk. I know this look. I kicked back and tried to get away, but Butch kept a tight hold on my feet, jerking my body down the hill.

"I like a frisky girl with some fight in her," he said, slapping my face. I didn't say anything, just stared at him. He slapped me again. And again. I felt tears stinging my eyes, but still I didn't cry. "Oh, baby girl's going to cry," Butch said, slapping me again. "Poor baby."

"Butch, you've had your fun. Get off and let me go," I said.

"Say please," he said, still grinning that crazy smile. I knew he wasn't even close to being done with me.

"Stop it," I said, trying to squirm out from under him.

"You like it," he said, bringing his face close to mine, trying to kiss my mouth. I turned my head away, but he grabbed my face and held it still. I squeezed my eyes closed and felt his lips on mine. "See, you like it," he said.

"Let me go," I said.

"Not yet," he said, and I felt his hands on the front of my bib-alls. He started to feel me down there, on my privates. Now I was scared. I tried to twist away, but Butch is real strong. "Just what I figured, a little girl," he laughed. "You ain't got nothing down there."

"Stop it!" I yelled. I could feel his hands undoing the buttons of my pants, and then he was pulling them off. "I'm going to tell everybody!" I yelled, kicking and twisting my body to make it that much harder.

"Well, look what I found," Butch crowed, pulling the twenty dollar bill out of my pocket. "Looks like I got a reward for beating up a sissy!"

"Give that back. It's Grandma's!"

"Not any more," he said, giving one last tug on my bib-alls. They came off, the straps smacking me in the face. "Just to make sure you don't go running into town, I'm taking these too." Butch took the twenty, my bib-alls, and for good measure he pulled my t-shirt off. He left me lying on the ground in my underpants. Halfway up the hill he turned back; "Tell anybody about this and I'll kill you. Understand?" Then he was gone.

I lay there in the dump looking up at the sky, wishing I was anywhere else in the world, wishing I was normal. If I was a normal boy this wouldn't have happened.

"Now's a good time to prove You're up there, God," I yelled. "Kill Butch Calkins!" I waited, but nothing happened. "Let me know You saw this. Please!" Nothing, not even a bolt of lightning. "Okay, then I can't believe in You. Thanks for letting me know I'm on my own."

I was in the dump wearing nothing but my underpants and the beaded moccasins my Aunt Dawn bought me in Cherokee, North

Carolina. I couldn't go back home by the main road because people would see. I couldn't climb the hill of the dump because that would bring me out right by Miss Pink's house, and there was no way I was going to let her see me in my underpants. I had no choice but to turn north and walk the river home. When I got to our swimming hole, I swam across, climbed the bank, and waited in the weeds to make sure there weren't any cars coming. I ran through the meadow, and up to our house. I could see the truck in the driveway, so I knew Will and Grandma were back from Gizzy's.

I waited until I saw Grandma heading toward the chicken coop. After a minute I saw Early running after her. He runs funny, more jumping up and down than going forward. Miss Emma and Louann came following after. I was glad Early's mama had come to visit. I knew it'd make him happy. When they were out of sight, I went up the front steps and into the house. Just as I got to the foot of the stairs Will came into the front room from the kitchen. He took one look at me in my underpants, closed his eyes, and shook his head.

"Calkins, right?" he asked, opening his eyes. It was the look of pity on his face that set me off. I felt the first tear roll down my cheek, and that opened the flood. I didn't sob or cry out, I just let the tears fall down my face. "Did he hurt you?" Will asked. I shook my head. It must've been going up and down and left to right because Will had to ask again. "Buddy, did he hurt you?"

"He touched me. Down there." I couldn't look at Will so I stared at the floor. I was so nervous saying it that my knees gave out and I started to fall. Will reached out and grabbed me.

"Down where? Your dick?" he asked. I nodded. "That son of a bitch!"

"And he took the twenty dollars Grandma give me. What am I going to do? I can't tell Grandma."

"I'll take care of this," Will said, putting his arm around my waist and helping me up the stairs.

"He's crazy. I saw his eyes. He's like Pa. He hates me." My teeth were clicking together, and I couldn't stop shivering. "Why? What did I do that was so bad?"

"Shut up. Pa doesn't hate you," Will said.

"Butch said he'd kill me if I told."

"Don't worry about Calkins," Will said, opening my bedroom door and putting me on the bed. "Now get dressed so Grandma won't suspect anything. She can't know what happened."

"Why are you being so nice to me?" I really wanted to know.

"Shut up and get dressed," he said, leaving me alone.

When I was getting dressed, I heard voices in the back yard. From my bedroom window I could see Will taking to Grandma in the backyard. After a minute they both looked up at my window. I ducked out of sight, but I'm pretty sure they saw me. It wasn't long before I heard the kitchen screen slam. I looked out my window just in time to see the pickup heading toward town. I had to trust Will to take care of things. I didn't have anybody else.

I was right in the middle of a nap when I remembered the pee in Will's baseball trophy. I went into his room, emptied the trophy, and washed it out. Don't get me wrong, I still think Will was wrong for reading my journal, but after what happened at the dump, it just doesn't seem that important. Will's my brother. He can read anything of mine he wants.

Grandma fixed us an early supper, and the dishes were done by six o'clock. There was no talk about the strongbox, change from the twenty, or why Will missed supper. Early and I were in bed by nine o'clock. I tried to get him interested in Nancy Drew, but he knew something was up and kept asking me what was wrong.

"If you want to know what happens to Nancy Drew shut up and listen," I snapped.

"You ain't right. Something happened in town, didn't it?" Early is like a bloodhound sniffing out a clue. "What?"

"Nothing, now let me read," I said, avoiding his eyes.

"Why ain't you looking at me?" Early grabbed the book out of my hands. "Tell me what happened that made you so quiet."

"All right, but you can't tell Grandma," I gave in. I knew there'd be no sleeping until I told. "I got in a fight with Butch Calkins. He took the money Grandma give me."

"That ain't all," Early said, looking me full in the face. I closed my eyes to keep him out, but I could feel his thoughts prying into my head, searching out a secret. There was no stopping Early, so I opened my eyes and let him look. "He hurt you," Early said, his eyes watering, his mouth quivering like he was fixing to cry. "Bad. He's bad."

"It's okay, Early. I'm okay." I whispered.

"Buddy, Butch ain't like most folks. He's bad."

"Believe me, I know," I said, smiling a little in spite of myself.

"Now you got to ask God for forgiveness," Early said, pulling my hands, sitting me up.

"Forgiveness for what?" I asked, pulling my hands away. I didn't want to risk those hot palms and Early reading my future.

"Saying you don't believe. He heard you."

"How do you know that? And where was God when I needed Him? He didn't help me. He didn't do nothing!"

"It's not time yet. God wants you to do the small stuff. He takes care of the big things. You got to know the difference before you ask Him for help."

"Well, Early, when I'm getting the crap beat out of me, it feels like big stuff. If God can't help me then, why should I trust Him to help me later?"

"It's about faith, Buddy. You've got to believe before it happens."

"That's not good enough. I want proof. Until I get it, I don't believe God even exists. The only thing I learned today is that I'm on my own." I flopped back down on the pillow, turned off the lamp, and shut my eyes. I heard Early sigh, like he was going to say something else.

"I ain't talking about this no more," I said. "Now go to sleep." I heard Early mumbling, and I knew he was saying his prayers.

When I woke up my bib-alls were lying across my dresser, and the twenty dollar bill was sticking out of the pocket. My big brother was right, he took care of it. Was this the sign I'd asked God for?

CHAPTER 14

I'm twelve years old today. It's not much so far. Maybe going from eleven to twelve isn't the big deal I thought it was going to be. I'm still the short, skinny, blond-headed boy I was yesterday. I don't think I'm ever going to grow up. If those hormones Grandma told me about are going to hit, they'd better kick in soon. I read up on hormones, and when they hit you're supposed to experience all kinds of changes. I think I'm ready.

I wasn't officially twelve until one thirty this afternoon, but Grandma said we were going to celebrate all day. She fixed French toast. Mama used to sprinkle her French toast with powdered sugar that she called snow icing. Grandma just puts regular sugar on top, but it's still pretty good. Will gobbled his breakfast up and took off before I got a chance to ask him about the twenty dollars and Butch Calkins.

Pa's chair is still empty. As much as I like not having him here, I think it's weird nobody's talking about it. He's been gone over a week, and Grandma hasn't mentioned his name but for a couple of times. I don't want him back, but I know it'd be good for Will. Boys like him need a father.

"Grandma, when's Pa coming home?" I snuck the question out of the side of my mouth just as she took a drink of coffee.

"When he wants to," Grandma said, swallowing hard.

"So, where is he?" I really wanted the answer to that one. If Pa had a woman, I figured I had a right to know.

"Don't rightly know," Grandma answered. "Early, you want more French toast?"

"Yes, please," Early said. "Buddy, I heard some blue folks what are kin to Mama saying Mr. Lyle's got a woman over to Alden."

"That's just great. What kind of woman is she? If Pa plans on making this woman my mama, I think I ought to meet her first, don't you?" Nothing. I hate it when I'm ignored. "Grandma, don't you want to meet her?"

"What Early heard is gossip and nothing more. Now I think we'd be better off not talking about your pa and concentrating on eating. When you're done, you got some presents from your aunts wanting to be opened." I knew Grandma wanted to know about Pa's woman as much as me.

Early eats slow. This drives me crazy. It's not that I'm a fast eater, I just like to get the job done, and then get onto other stuff. Early takes one bite, chews it about a million times, then swallows. This drives me nuts. It was really working my nerves today because I was itching to open my birthday gifts, and then get into town and buy my strongbox. I had that twenty dollars tucked away and it was begging to be spent.

"Well, I'm done," Early said, pushing his plate away. He had a few bites left, but I think with Grandma and me both watching him eat, he got nervous and his stomach knotted up on him.

"I give Buddy my gift yesterday, but I expect he hasn't found the right box yet," Grandma said. "Early, what about you?"

"My present's on the back porch," Early said, and led us out the back door. I didn't see anything at first, then I heard giggling. I walked to the edge of the porch, and two black faces jumped up.

"Surprise!" June and July squealed from where they were hiding. "Happy Birthday, Buddy!" They ran up on the porch and gave me hugs. Colored girls aren't supposed to hug white boys, but I didn't remember that until later. I was real happy to see them, but if this was Early's idea of a birthday present, then it was time I had a talk with him.

"Well, y'all better give Buddy his birthday present," Early said. July handed me a piece of paper.

"It's a birthday card me and Twin made," June said. "Go on Buddy, read it out loud."

On the front of the card the twins had drawn flowers, birds, butterflies, and a huge sun over two black faces and one white face with big smiles. It read, "Burfday Frends." This card really touched my heart, but it also made me wonder about the quality of education those girls were getting at public school.

"Well, read it out loud, Buddy," Grandma said.

"Happy Birthday. We promise to give Buddy Dean singing lessons for one entire year, love June and July." I don't know what it was, but that really got to me. Unexpected kindness again.

"Buddy, you ain't supposed to cry," June said, rubbing my arm and giving it a squeeze. "It's your birthday. Jesus is smiling on you."

"Buddy, you is blessed," July said. "Look at all of us'uns here that love you."

"What you say to that, Buddy?" Grandma asked.

"Thank you, Twins." I had to turn away.

"What else you got to say, Twins?" Early asked.

June and July took me by the hands and twirled me around, while they sang Happy Birthday in two-part harmony. It was gorgeous. When they were done they gave me another hug, and each of them kissed my cheek.

"Buddy, you got some presents in the front room. Girls, Early, come on inside, and when Buddy's done opening his gifts, we'll have some birthday cake." Grandma, Early, and I went into the kitchen.

June and July waited on the porch, afraid to come inside. White folks don't have colored in their homes as company or to socialize. I didn't even think about that until I realized they weren't behind me.

"Twins, come on inside. It's okay," I said.

"My ma'd wear me out iffen she knew we went inside," June said.

"I think your mama would understand," Grandma said. "It's Buddy's birthday. We want you here."

"No m'am. It ain't fitting. Daddy works for y'all. He wouldn't like it." June took July by the hand, and they started down the back steps.

"Stay there, Twins. We'll have the cake outside. Is that okay, Grandma? Can I open my presents outside?" I asked.

"It's your birthday. You can do anything you want," Grandma said.

Early and I hauled all the packages out to the back porch. I sat on the top step and started ripping through the wrapping paper. I could tell right off most of them were books. My aunts know what I like. The first one I opened was from Aunt Dawn. Her card said, "If you tell your father I sent you this, I'll never forgive you. Have a happy birthday." It was a Lennon Sisters book, *The Secret of Holiday Island*. I had no idea the Lennon Sisters had even written a book.

Aunt Shirley sent me *Janet Lennon: Adventures at Two Rivers*. My aunts kill me. They must've gotten together and decided what to get me. I'm so excited. It looks like the Lennon Sisters have written an entire series of books. Aunt Shirley's card said, "Don't tell your father this come from me. If it's got stains on the pages it's because I let Peaches read it first. She says you're going to love it."

I got *Janet Lennon at Camp Calamity* from Aunt Wanda. Her card just said, "Know you'll love this." Aunt Dorrie sent me *Janet Lennon and the Angels*. Her card said, "Love Aunt Doris. P.S. Don't tell your pa this come from me. He won't like it."

There was a long package from Aunt Ann, and when I got it opened, I squealed. It was a real majorette baton. It was balanced, like the type the professional twirlers use, and not the cheap kind you find at the dime store. Aunt Ann's card said, "Twirl away and make me proud. Love, Aunt Ann." She could be my favorite aunt.

She didn't say a thing about keeping the baton a secret. She's not afraid of Pa.

Aunt Helen and Aunt Georgann went in together and sent me two long playing record albums. The first one is by Brenda Lee, who's billed as "Little Miss Dynamite, the little girl with the great big voice." It's called "Emotions." The second record is from Doris Day, and it's called "Cuttin' Capers." I can't wait to hear what Doris Day has been up to. Brenda Lee is from Atlanta, and she was just starting to be a big star when Mama got sick.

"Who wants cake?" Grandma asked.

"I do," Early said. "How about you, Twin?" he asked July. She didn't say anything, and they both hung back sort of shy.

"Everybody's getting cake," I said. "Grandma, can we mix up some Kool-Aid?"

"Course you can. What color?"

"What color you want, Twins?" I asked. "We got orange, green, and purple."

"Purple," July whispered. "I like purple."

"Me too. Grandma, mix up the grape," I yelled into the kitchen.

I was giving the baton some trial twirls, and the twins were looking at the covers of the Lennon Sisters books. Early was studying Doris Day's picture. I think it was probably the first time he'd ever seen a woman wearing Capri pants.

"Close your eyes, Buddy, here comes the cake," Grandma whispered from the screen door.

I screwed my eyes shut. I could hear the screen door swoosh shut and knew Grandma caught it with her foot just before it slammed. I was waiting to be surprised when I heard a familiar voice.

"Y'all having a party back here?" Pink Watrous asked. I saw her coming around the side of the house from the front yard. "I been knocking for the last five minutes. I thought maybe y'all were up to the barn."

With that Pink stopped dead in her tracks. She caught sight of me, the birthday cake, the presents, and the twins, and I think it was sort of a shock. She didn't look all that surprised to see Early.

"Why, Aunt Lena, you're having a regular colored festival back here."

"What do you want, Pink?" Grandma asked, putting the cake down and walking over to the end of the porch.

"I just came up to talk to Early. We got us some things to discuss about the revival is all. Somebody having a birthday?" This was a pretty stupid question, since I had all the ribbons hung around my neck.

"It's my birthday, Miss Pink," I said. "I'm twelve years old today. How's your hair?"

"Fried to a crisp, as you well know, but Happy Birthday anyway," she sniffed. "What are you girls doing down here so far from home?" she asked June and July.

Miss Pink might just as well have slapped the twins. They buried their faces in their arms and wouldn't look up.

"June and July were invited to my birthday party," I said, real cold. I was trying to give Pink that icy stare that Grandma could do. "They're staying for cake and Kool Aid, and they ain't going until they get it."

"Pink, looks like everybody was invited here but you. Now supposing you say what's on your mind, and then you get back to giving tours of the dump," Grandma said.

That stung Miss Pink pretty hard. I could see her face heat up, and she started tearing at the cuticle of her right thumb.

"Early and I have got lots to talk about. I been planning the revival, and his daddy said for me to come out here and talk things over with him. I'm here to tell him what he's expected to do, and when to come into town for the rehearsal," Pink said, starting to stammer at the end, like she was losing steam. "I meant no harm."

"Early, you want to talk to Miss Pink?" Grandma asked.

"Not alone," he said. "Buddy, you come too."

"That all right with you, Pink?" Grandma asked.

"I guess it'll have to be," she said, getting some of her old attitude back. I knew she didn't want me there, but if that was the only way she could get to Early, she was stuck.

"You want some cake, Miss Pink," I asked.

"No, thank you, Buddy," she said, patting her scarf tight by her ears. "I'll just wait out front until the party's over, and you boys can talk. Is that all right, Aunt Lena?"

"Suit yourself," Grandma said. As Miss Pink started around the side of the house, Grandma followed after her. "Pink, I don't want to hear any talk in town about how I'm taking in coloreds and treating them special. You scared these little girls enough, and I won't have you causing them any trouble. You understand that?" Miss Pink nodded and disappeared.

"We gots to go," July whispered.

"No, you don't. Stay and eat some cake," I said. "I want you and June to be here. Don't worry about Miss Pink. She's crazy."

"She don't have no hair," June said. "I seen her working in her garden when me and July was playing at the dump. "She bald like an egg."

"She look like a bald baby," July giggled. "Buddy, we gots to go. We got chores waiting."

"Take some cake with you," I said, cutting two huge hunks. Grandma makes me cakes and pies all the time. I knew this would be a treat for the twins. "I'll pick up the plates when I come up for my first singing lesson."

"We'll learn you good, Buddy," July said.

"Happy Birthday, Buddy," June giggled, taking the plates of cake. The girls skipped up the path to the barn, heading off for home. I could hear them singing all the way, "Peace in the Valley" in two-part harmony.

"Boys, Miss Pink's waiting on y'all," Grandma said from the kitchen door. "You know, y'all don't have to talk to her."

"Pa wants me to," Early said. "Buddy, you come too."

I didn't need urging. To tell the truth, I was looking forward to it. Ever since I'd heard Miss Pink was planning the revival, I'd imagined all sorts of carrying on, with bands, church choirs, fancy preaching, and colored lights.

Miss Pink was sitting at the picnic table in the side yard, smoking a Pall Mall and swatting at the mosquitoes. When she saw us coming, she stubbed out her cigarette and stood up. "These skeeters are fixing to drain every ounce of blood I got. Is there some place more pleasant we can go?"

"Front porch gets a good breeze. Bugs won't get us there," I said.

"Perfect," Pink said, heading up to the porch. "Oh, Buddy, did your little colored girlfriends leave?"

"Yeah, you scared them off," I said.

"Oh, I doubt that," Miss Pink said. "I've had them working for me down at the dump, but I guess you've heard all about that. Seems some people just don't understand the historical significance of what happened down there." It was obvious Miss Pink was a little touchy about the dead baby tour. I bet some of the Methodist ladies in town had blessed her hide.

"Now, this is much better," Pink said, sitting in one of the porch rockers. Early and I sat in the swing.

"Miss Pink, what's Pa want me to do?" Early asked.

"Well, Earl Lee, he just wants you to do what you do naturally. He wants you to listen to people, and help them if you can, of course," she said.

"Then why's he have to do it down to the community hall?" I asked.

"I'm not here to discuss this with you, Buddy. I'm here talking to Earl Lee." Miss Pink was out of Grandma's range, and I guess she felt she could be as snotty as she wanted.

"Oh really? Well, Early wants me here. I'm looking out for him. So, how much money are you making off this revival?" I give her a real icy stare with that one. She shot one right back. I tell you, Miss Pink is no slouch in the stare department.

"Buddy Dean, you have caused me no end of heartache and pain, and I'll not discuss my business with the likes of you," Pink said, with a look that told me I'd better shut up because she was running out of patience. "I will probably be bald for the rest of my life. If any hair does grow back, it'll be all wispy-like. This is your fault, Buddy, and I will never forgive you."

"Miss Pink, you done that to your hair, not Buddy. Let me fix it," Early said, getting up from the swing. He walked over to Pink, snatched that scarf off her head, and slapped his hands on her skull. She really was bald as an egg. As he pulled her head close to his chest, I could hear Early whispering and Pink whimpering. Early said, "You will have beautiful hair." He released Miss Pink's head and her scalp was a bright red, like a sunburn. I knew Early's hands were scalding hot.

"What did you do to me?" Miss Pink whispered, staring at Early, and patting at her scalp. "What happened?"

"I fixed your hair so you can't blame Buddy no more. Don't worry, your head's all right. You'll have hair." Early sat back down in the swing.

"Can you do that?" Miss Pink asked. "Just like that? You can fix me just by touching my head?"

"He fixed your hair, that's all. The rest of what's wrong is up to you," I said. I was running low on patience, too. "Now what's Early supposed to do at this revival?"

"I can't believe what just happened," Miss Pink whispered.

"Believe it. Your hair's going to grow. It's going to grow so fast, you'll probably blame me for that, too. Now, what about the revival?" I really had to know what she had planned so I could stop it. There was no way I'd let her make a fool of my best friend.

"I've got everything written down, and I think it's going to be very nice. I wanted to create something very religious, spiritual-like, something that will stick with these people and have them believe they witnessed a miracle," Miss Pink said, still feeling her scalp.

"You might want to put your scarf back on, Miss Pink. It's going to take a few days for that hair to grow," I said. As much as I enjoyed seeing her sitting on our front porch looking like a melon, I knew she'd be embarrassed. Embarrassed people cause trouble.

"Oh, Lord, yes. Thank you, Buddy," Miss Pink said, putting her scarf on, tugging it down over her ears. "I'm really going to have

hair again?" she asked. Early nodded. Then Miss Pink give out
with the sweetest smile I've ever seen. I never would've expected
it. It was a smile without a catch in it, genuine, appreciative,
and kind. I wished I had a mirror so she could see herself. If she
smiled like that more often, she'd have lots of friends and people
wouldn't make fun of her. It was like I saw the real Miss Pink for
a minute, and I liked her.

It didn't take but a split second, and the other Miss Pink was
back and acting all uppity. She dug around in her purse and
brought out a Bible. "Now Earl Lee, I've marked some passages
I want you to memorize. It's the usual miracle stuff, you know,
Jesus raising Lazarus, that sort of thing. I've also included the part
where you, uh, I mean Jesus, wandered in the desert searching for
the meaning of life. Your pa and I figured that'd tie in nicely with
you disappearing."

"I didn't disappear," Early said. "I'm right here."

"But people in town *think* you disappeared. It's good for business. Everybody loves a mystery. Nobody knows if you're going
to show up at the revival or not. People can't wait to find out."
Miss Pink started digging in her purse again.

"Miss Pink, Early can't read," I said.

"I can, too. I can read lots of words. Too many words get me
confused is all," Early said. He took the Bible from Miss Pink and
flipped through the passages she'd marked. "Oh-oh. Too many
words. I can't do this."

"But your father said you could read," Miss Pink stammered.

"I can read better than Pa, but he can't read at all," Early said.
"Buddy does my reading for me."

"But I've got this entire revival planned around you quoting
scripture. Early, can you memorize? Can you remember things if
they've been read to you enough times?"

"I'm not so good at that either. Buddy remembers things for
me," Early said, smiling at Miss Pink.

Miss Pink was wrecked. She looked from Early to me, to the
Bible, and back to Early. She threw her hands in the air, "I'm ruined."

"But you're going to have hair," Early said.

"Miracles! Sweet Jesus, we still have the miracles. Anybody can read scripture, but only you can perform the miracles. You can help folks, can't you, Early? If they come to you up on the stage, you can lay your hands on them and fix them. Right?" It was like I could see Miss Pink's thoughts rattling around in her bald head, scrambling to rearrange themselves.

"Not everybody," Early answered.

"But most people," Miss Pink said.

"No. Just some," Early said.

"Do you know who?" Miss Pink asked. "The ones you can fix."

"Not right off. Sometimes I get a feeling. Most times it don't work. I knew I could fix your head. I got a special feeling. I felt it in my hands. You got a beautiful smile, you know that, Miss Pink?" Early said.

Miss Pink was speechless for a minute. "Well, thank you. But Early, your father told me..." she sputtered, reaching for more words, then giving out. Finally she turned to me. "Buddy, can you help me?"

"Make a fool out of my best friend? I don't think so," I said.

"I'm not a fool, Buddy. I want to do this," Early said. He grabbed my hands, and I could feel his palms getting hot. "I got a calling to help, and you need to help me." I tried to pull away, but Early held fast. Then it came to me like a dream, and I knew I'd help. I saw it all. Early was on the stage. I saw the colored lights. I heard the music. I had to help.

"What have you got planned?" I asked. I had a nagging suspicion that I'd regret those words. Miss Pink started in outlining her plans, and I was right all along. She never did get over her brush with show business and her trip to Radio City Music Hall.

"I've got the Methodist Choir lined up to sing "Amazing Grace" right at the opening. That gets the ball rolling. Then I figured we'd have one of the choirs sing "Precious Lord, Take My Hand" while Early makes his entrance. I figured he'd enter wearing a white robe. I bet we can get that from Bart VanMeeder and the

DCR choir. If Bart doesn't have a choir robe, I bet he'd give us one of his dentist smocks."

"Are you sure the DCRs will want anything to do with this? They've been preaching against Early since we found the baby," I said.

"That's all changed. They had a bunch of conversions at the church, people accepting Christ into their hearts, and now they want to make sure everyone knows they believe in Early. I really think it's best if all the churches in town participate, don't you?" Miss Pink asked.

"What about the colored Baptists and the Bluetown Baptists? Are they going to be there? Early's blue. His church has to do something."

"Buddy, you know as well as me we can't have whites and coloreds going to the same program. It's just not right. Don't you go cutting your eyes at me, young man. I don't agree with it either, but I'm sorry, that's the way it is. But you give me a good idea. Once we do a revival for the white people, we could do one for the coloreds, and then one up in Bluetown. My God, think of the money that'd bring in!"

"No," Early said. "Blue and colored got to come to the community hall or I ain't doing it. Everybody's got to be together."

"But Early, it doesn't work that way," Miss Pink said.

"Then I ain't doing it," Early said. "White and colored and blue. Together. Tell Pa."

"Early, it's impossible," Miss Pink said.

"His mind's made up. You'd better do what he says, or there won't be a revival," I said. "What you should do is get June and July to sing at the revival. That'd take the edge off it. Everybody in town likes them. They're just little girls. No harm in that."

"I'll have to run this by the sheriff, but it might work. Of course, the DCRs will have a fit."

"So what? They're always mad about something. If they want to be a part of this thing, that's the way it's got to be; white and colored and blue all together." I was starting to like the way this was turning out.

"Well, I'll ask." Miss Pink buried her head in her purse and came up with a notebook. She flipped through the pages. "And Buddy, I've got the boys from the 4-H making me a wooden cross. I figured it'd be real dramatic right at the end, after all the miracles and healing, if Early was strapped to the cross and ascended into heaven while the combined choirs are singing 'Christ the Lord is Risen Today.'"

"That's an Easter song. Even I know that, and I don't go to church. The Baptists will go nuts."

"It'll be real dramatic. Once the cross ascends to the ceiling, I'm going to have a burlap bag full of Joe Newsom's pigeons released just like doves. It'll be like Radio City, only smaller."

"What do I have to do?" Early asked.

"You just have to work some miracles is all," Miss Pink said. "Buddy, is there any way you could teach Early some scripture? I just think it'd be a nice touch and add so much for the true believers in the audience."

"I can't read nothing. I get scared in front of people," Early said.

"I'll teach you something to say. You won't have to read," I said. "Early, is this getting to be too much? Do you really want to stand up there in front of people and try to make miracles?"

"Of course he does. He already said so. He's got a gift. He's got to share it with the world, and don't you try to talk him out of it either," Miss Pink snapped. "Oh, I almost forgot, I asked Doc Rodger to bring 'Miracle Baby Andy', that's what we're calling him, to the revival so everybody can see how beautiful he is. I just know people will want to touch him."

"What'd Doc say?" I asked.

"He said he'd get back to me," Miss Pink sniffed.

"That means no, Miss Pink." Boy, I wish I could've seen Doc's face when Miss Pink asked him. "It ain't right dragging that baby into all this."

"Well, I had to try. It was Burrell's idea, and it would be a nice touch," Miss Pink said with a sigh. She knew it was wrong. "Oh Early, it's going to be fun. I promise. We're going to have a dress rehearsal next week, and I want you full of energy and ready to make a miracle. Oh, honey, don't look so scared. Your daddy and I wouldn't let anything bad happen to you."

The blast of gun fire hit the house right above Miss Pink's head. All three of us hit the porch, Miss Pink screaming that she'd been shot. I pushed Early through the front door, and scrambled behind the rocking chair. I looked between the slats and could see Pa in the front meadow, aiming his rifle right at me. He took a long pull off a whiskey bottle, took aim, and fired off another round.

Grandma came running around the side of the house, pulled Miss Pink off the porch, and they scrambled away, scuttling across the yard to the back of the house. Miss Pink bellowing she'd been shot, and Grandma was yelling for Pink to shut up.

"Pa, put the gun down," I yelled. He pulled off another round, hitting the side of the house and busting out a window box of geraniums. Grandma was going to be mad. "You got to quit shooting, or Grandma's going to call the law!" I yelled.

I wasn't worried that Pa was trying to kill us. My Pa is a champion shot. Even dead drunk and half blind, he never misses.

"Buddy, are you all right?" Early whispered from the front door.

"I'm fine. Stay inside," I said. "Pa, put the gun down, and come up to the house and talk," I yelled, walking to the edge of the porch.

"I want to see Will," Pa yelled back, taking another long drink.

"Will's not home, now put the gun down!"

"I want to talk to Will. Where's Will?" My God, he was drunker than I can ever remember.

"He ain't home. Now put the gun down before somebody gets hurt!"

"Shut your mouth, sissy boy," Pa yelled. "I want Will. He's the only son Becky give me. My only boy." He was mourning Mama again. "You killed her, Buddy! You and God. She died of shame because of you!"

"Cancer killed Mama, not me, and you know it. Now come in the house before you shoot yourself," I yelled back at him. I knew he wouldn't kill me. He was just blowing off steam.

"Buddy, I called Matt Williams. He's coming right away," Grandma whispered from the front door.

"Everything's okay, Grandma," I said.

"Where's Will? I want to talk to Will!" Pa yelled. He put the gun down long enough to take another slug of whiskey. "Will!"

"Will misses you too," I yelled.

"Tell him to come outside," Pa yelled back.

"Early, stand up in the front door so Pa can see you," I hissed.

I could hear scrambling behind me and then he said, "I'm here."

"Pa, Will's right here. Look!" I stepped aside so Pa could see Early's silhouette in the front door. "He wants to talk. Come closer."

Pa leaned over, squinting toward the house. He hung his rifle over his shoulder and starting walking toward me. "Will. How you been keeping? Will? Come on out here, boy!"

Matt Williams' car pulled up our road and stopped halfway up to the house. The sheriff got out of the car and started running toward the house, coming up behind Pa.

"Buddy, get Will out here so I can see him," Pa yelled, slurring his words, stumbling over the flagstones leading up to the front porch. "Will! I missed you, son! Come out here and see your pa!"

I watched the sheriff sneak up behind Pa. I tried to think of something to talk about so Pa wouldn't hear him. "Hey, Pa, today's my birthday. I'm twelve years old today."

"What makes you think I care?" Pa snarled. "You ain't my son. I don't want nothing to do with you. There ain't none of me in you. Your ma told me so the night you were born. You make me sick."

Matt Williams came up behind Pa and got him in a chokehold, grabbing the rifle off his shoulder and flinging it across the yard. He threw Pa down on his stomach and got his handcuffs on him. Pa didn't fight him at all. He just looked surprised.

"Hey, Matt. What are you doing out here?" he asked

"Come for you, Lyle," Mr. Williams said. "You're making a fuss and it's getting dangerous."

"I wouldn't hurt nobody. You know that," Pa said. "I love everybody."

"Jesus, Lyle, look what you done to your family," Mr. Williams said. "I heard what you said to Buddy. What kind of man are you?"

"He ain't my son," Pa whined.

"If I was him, I'd be mighty proud of that right now," Mr. Williams said, turning Pa around and pushing him toward the patrol car. "Buddy, your Pa's going to be cooling off down to the jail. Tell Aunt Lena."

Grandma, Early, and Miss Pink come out on the porch, and we watched as the sheriff put Pa in the car and start for town. The patrol car met Will coming up the drive. Will just turned the truck around and followed behind. That was good. I'd hate for Pa to be alone.

Nobody said anything for the longest time. Even Miss Pink was quiet. Finally Grandma broke the ice. "What he said ain't true, Buddy. You know that, don't you?"

"It doesn't matter," I answered. "I know Mama loved me."

CHAPTER 15

Will reported Pa would be in jail until the circuit judge come to town next week. He was charged with public drunkenness, public endangerment, and reckless and woeful mishandling of a firearm. I didn't care. That's the truth, too, and this was a big step for me. Usually after a scene like what happened, I'd worry about what I had done and how I could fix things. Now I realized there was no way I could fix Pa. He had to fix himself. If and when he did sort himself out, then I'd decide if I wanted him back in my life. Right now, I wasn't especially optimistic.

Poor Miss Pink was a mess after being shot at. She told Doc Rodger's wife she had to have a gin and tonic to calm her nerves. I knew everyone in town must have found out what happened. I just hoped Pink wouldn't gossip about what Pa said to me. I didn't want people thinking Mama got pregnant with somebody other than Pa. Secretly I hoped it was true, but I know I'm Pa's son. That's a sad fact we both have to live with.

I've been working with Early on the scriptures he's supposed to be memorizing. What Miss Pink is calling the dress rehearsal is in two days, and then it's only two more days until the revival. We spent our first day going over and over the Bible passages, and

I came to the realization there is no way Early's going to be able to learn actual scripture. He just can't wrap his mouth around the words and that old-time way of talking. This is really important, because people want scripture quoted exactly as written. If you make a mistake quoting Bible verse, you're just asking for trouble.

Miss Pink had marked John, Chapter 11, Verse 1: "Now a man named Lazarus was sick. He was from Bethany, the village of Mary and her sister Martha." We worked on learning that one phrase all day, but Early couldn't get it. He got frustrated, and then I got all tense and nervous. Finally I gave up and told him we'd have to do something else if we still wanted to be friends when this thing was over.

That night I started reading *Janet Lennon at Camp Calamity*. I was about three chapters into it when the idea come to me that Early could recite the Ten Commandments. I figured that'd be dramatic enough for Miss Pink and also give the DCRs and Baptists something to think about in their own lives. The next morning we started rehearsing right after breakfast. I was working from some old catechism workbooks. We started out at the top, *Thou shalt have no other gods before me.*

Right away there was a problem. Early couldn't say *shalt*. It kept coming out *shout*, which I kind of liked, but it meant trouble because coming up was *Thou shalt not kill, Thou shalt not steal*, and *Thou shalt not commit adultery*. With Early reciting it'd sound like he was commanding the audience to kill, steal, and commit adultery. I kind of liked that, too.

From both a Biblical and theatrical sense, I thought it was important that the Ten Commandments go in order. I've seen enough movies that I know it's important for dramatic effect that you build to a climax. Besides, when you read the Commandments through, you can sort of see where God was going with the whole idea.

Grandma finally put a stop to our rehearsing. She said she'd heard enough Bible to last her a lifetime. Nick of time, too. I was so frustrated, I was ready to scream. Early wasn't any happier. When we sat down for lunch, neither of us was speaking. Grandma made Chef Boyardee and cherry Kool-Aid, Early's favorites. It didn't work. He sat there scowling at me and kicking the leg of the kitchen table.

"Early, child, you know I love you, but if you kick the leg of this table one more time, I'm going to smack you into the middle of next week." Grandma had put up with enough.

"Buddy thinks I'm stupid," Early muttered.

"I never said that. I just said this was going to be a challenge," I snapped back. Well, it was. If he wanted to do the revival so bad, then he'd better start learning.

"You always said people was wrong when they said I was slow, but now you think I am," he said. Well, he had me there. "I'm stupid," he said, his voiced choked up. He put his head down on his arms and started to cry.

"You're not stupid. You're smart. Just not book smart."

"See," Early bawled, "Buddy thinks I'm stupid!" Early jumped out of his seat and flung his arms around Grandma.

"Well, I've heard enough," Grandma said, pulling Early down to her lap. "The Bible's supposed to bring folks together. This ain't right. Now Buddy, think of something."

"Why me? I don't even want him to do the dang revival," I said. "Miss Pink planned the whole thing, so why do I have to fix it?"

"I would think this is answer enough," Grandma said, jerking her head toward Early. "Either you come up with something Early can do, or I'm calling this whole thing off."

"Can you fix it, Buddy?" Early asked.

"Do you still want to do this?" I asked. "There's going to be lots and lots of people watching you." I wanted to give him every chance to back out.

"I got to. They's counting on me," he said. "Fix it."

Miss Pink was going to have a fit. My only chance of escaping Pink's wrath would be if her hair started to grow.

"I'll try, but we don't have much time," I said.

"You can do it. You're smart," Early grinned.

"Fix it, Buddy, but not today. I need a rest, and so does Early. Tell you what, why don't you go into town and look for that strongbox? I'm going to put Early to work in my garden. Early, think you can dig some potatoes?"

"I'm a good digger. Mama says I'm the best," Early crowed. Grandma tickled him, and he started to giggle.

His troubles were over. Mine were just beginning. A trip to town might give me some time to think. I really did want to get a box for my journal and personal stuff, and I'd been hankering to stop in at Doc Rodger's and see Baby Andy.

"Okay y'all, I'm going to town. You need anything, Grandma?"

"Not that I recollect, but Buddy, remember, you can't tell nobody Early is out here. We made a deal with Burrell and Matt Williams. If anybody asks, just say you ain't seen him," Grandma said. "Lord, this just don't sit right with me. All these lies leading up to a revival. It ain't fitting."

Early and Grandma took off for the garden, and I headed into town. I was halfway down our road when Early come running after me, screeching for me to stop.

"Aunt Lena says maybe you'd better stop in to the jail and see after your pa," he huffed, out of breath.

"Gee, what a swell idea," I said, sarcasm dripping off every word.

"Really? I didn't think you'd want to," Early said, mystified. See what I'm dealing with?

"Early, I was kidding. There's no way I'm going to see Pa. Don't you think we've got enough trouble already?"

"Oh," he answered. "Should I tell Aunt Lena?"

"She'll figure it out." I headed for town.

I was just about over North Bridge when Will pulled the pickup up even with me. "Get in," he said.

"Where you been?" I asked.

"Helping Gizzy. He needed somebody to talk to the Mexicans."

"You don't talk Mexican," I said.

"Neither does Gizzy. He said it'd be best if they got orders from a white man."

A white man? Will? Well, I guess as long as Pa was in jail, he was the man in our family. "Where you going?" I asked. He didn't answer. I knew he was going to the jail.

"Where do you want me to drop you?" he asked.

"Doc's. I want to see Baby Andy," I said. We rode into town, and Will pulled over in between the post office and Doc's office. As I was getting out of the truck I said, "Thanks for taking care of Butch Calkins."

"It was easy. Just don't get in his way after this."

Speak of the devil, and there he is. I walked into Doc's waiting room and slunk in the corner was Butch Calkins. Both his eyes were blacked, he had a nasty looking split lip and a sling for his right arm. This was one of the happiest moments in my whole entire life.

Doc come out of his office right then and gave us both a look. "I don't want any trouble," he said. Butch didn't say a word, just got up, brushed past me, and left the waiting room. "Butch get back in here and let me look at those stitches," Doc called after him. Butch was gone. "That boy is nothing but trouble," Doc said, shaking his head.

"Hey Doc. Can I see Baby Andy?" I asked.

"Not today, Buddy. Katherine's got him over to her sister's. They'll be back before supper. Want to stop back?"

"Maybe. I got stuff to do in town," I said. "How's Butch?"

"Ornery cuss like that can take more than what your brother give him." Doc took a good look at my face. "You're healing up right fine," he said. "That Calkins kid just got what was coming to him, if you ask me."

"He's not a nice boy."

"No, he's not," Doc said. "Not his fault though. That boy was raised rough. Trash begets trash. And don't you go telling anybody I said that."

"Miss Pink said you might take Baby Andy to the revival so's people could look at him," I said.

"Oh, she did," Doc said. "That woman is demented. And Buddy, you can tell anybody you want I said that."

"She's a mess all right," I agreed.

"You got any idea where Early got off to?"

"Nope. I ain't seen him," I answered. Doc give me a hard look at that one, and I had to look down at the floor.

"Your grandma tell you to say that?" he asked.

"Yep," I answered before I even thought about it. That's something Nancy Drew never would've done.

"I thought so," Doc laughed. "You better run along. I got things to do. Stop back in if you've a mind to. Andy takes to company."

I went out Doc's back door, cut across Schoolhouse Road and into the general store. Mozelle was working the register. When I came in the side door she screamed, "Buddy, where's Early? You got him out to the farm?" She was hungry for gossip, a regular Miss Pink, Junior.

"I haven't seen him, Mozelle. I just came in to get a strongbox."

"Hardware section. We got two kinds. Bottom row," she panted. She practically ran around the end of the counter and come up on me, grabbing my arm. "I'm so excited about this revival, I'm beside myself. Do you think Early's going to show up?"

"You'll just have to wait and see," I said, bending low so I could get a good look at the boxes. One was red tin and looked like a toolbox. I don't think it even had a lock on it. The other was a cash box sort of thing and pretty flimsy. I wanted something more official looking than that. What I wanted looked like a safe with a lock that'd scare Will.

"I can't wait. Me and my whole family's coming. We already got tickets. Pa had to pay eighteen dollars, but Mama says it's religious so we got to do it. Everybody in town's going."

"I know. Hey Mozelle, are these the only strongboxes you got? I was sort of looking for a safe?"

"You got a bunch of money we don't know about, Buddy?" she giggled. I give her a dry look until her giggles died out. "Well, we got some fireproof ones. They's going to run you about twelve dollars, Buddy."

"I'll take one," I said, pulling out the twenty dollar bill.

"Well, you are rich," she said. "We got one in the storeroom. I'll get it."

Mozelle went in the back and I went up front to the magazine rack. I was looking for a new *Screen Greats* or *Screen Secrets*. They were both there. Lana Turner was on *Screen Secrets* again. I don't get it. She's on practically every month. I don't think anybody has that many secrets, even if you are a big Hollywood movie star.

"I know, Lana Turner, again. That's why I didn't save you one," Mozelle said, putting exactly what I wanted on the counter. The packing box said fireproof, steel-encased, guaranteed safe, and burglar proof. The minute I saw it, I knew there was no way Will could break the lock.

"Twelve dollars?" I asked.

"Uh-huh," Mozelle grunted, wrestling with the packing box. "Buddy, you need this wrapping box?"

"Yeah, I think I do," I said. I really didn't, but I thought if I left it around the house, then Will would know he couldn't crack the safe. But then again, maybe Will would take that as a challenge. "Uh, Mozelle, on second thought, forget about the packing box."

"Well, I already got it in," she said. "You want to get the *Screen Greats*? Debbie Reynolds."

"I think I spent enough money," I said. "Hey Mozelle, how many tickets has Mr. Finch sold for the revival?"

"It's sold out, Buddy. Where you been? It's been sold out since yesterday. Mr. Finch has been telling folks they can stand on the lawn, and he'll open the windows so they can hear. He's charging a dollar for that."

"That's crazy," I said.

"I know. My Aunt Louise is carrying my grandma all the way here from Ellsworth, and they can only get tickets for the lawn. She's looking for somebody to trade for inside sitting. If you know anybody, let me know."

"This is way out of control."

"It's a big deal, Buddy. Everybody's going. If you don't have tickets, you're out of luck."

"Oh, I'll see it," I said. "Miss Pink promised me front row seating."

"I thought she was mad at you," Mozelle said.

"She was until her hair started growing back," I said. "Now all she thinks about is the revival. She's running the whole show."

"Well, of course she is, silly. She's seen the Rockettes. Who else could do it?" Mozelle stared at me like I was a fool for not recognizing that fact. I've just got to get out of this small town before I go crazy.

"Nobody I know," I said. "Thanks Mozelle. The box is perfect."

"See you at the revival," she yelled after me. "Front row seats! You lucky dog!"

I went out the back door of the general store and cut up Schoolhouse Road so I could take a look at the community hall. I stood across the road, directly in front of the Baptist parsonage, and watched as Miss Pink and Mr. Finch moved folding chairs into the hall. There was a huge sign out front (bait farm glitter) that said *Blue Jesus Revival—Labor Day—7:00*. There was a smaller sign that said *Sold Out—Lawn Sitting Only—$1.00*.

Miss Pink saw me standing across the road and motioned me over. "How's it going with the rehearsal?"

"Just fine. Early's going to be real good. How's it going here?" I'm getting to be a champion liar.

"We got no tickets left except for the poor souls that want to stand on the grass. We're leaving the windows open for them. We're completely sold out. Buddy, I'm getting so excited, I don't know if I can wait. Maybe I'll finally get enough money ahead to get back to Radio City. Oh Buddy, it's going to be wonderful!"

"I bet. So how much money is Early getting?" I asked. I'll admit I did have a snotty tone, but she deserved it.

"Well, that's between Early and his daddy, and none of our business, isn't it?" Miss Pink snapped. Her cheeks were flushing up red, and I knew she felt guilty. That's exactly what I was going for.

"Early gets nothing, and you and Mr. Finch are splitting everything."

"Don't you go getting all high and mighty with me, Mr. Buddy Dean. You just make sure Early's here tomorrow night and knows those Bible verses by heart." Push come to shove, Miss Pink can get mighty cold.

"Early will be here, but he sent me to town to find out one thing. Is colored, blue, and white going to be sitting together?"

"We sold tickets to anybody that could afford them. Of course, we been sold out quite awhile. They can always stand in the grass." Miss Pink dug for a Pall Mall. This was making her real nervous.

"Early had better see some colored folks in the audience, or there won't be any miracles. You can't make him do a miracle just because y'all sold tickets. He's got to want to."

"I know," Miss Pink whispered. "What are we going to do?"

"For starters I'd ask June and July to sing. Early likes them, and it'd make him feel real comfortable if they were on the stage with him. They do a real good job on "Sweet Little Jesus Boy." Any blues coming?"

"Early's whole family will be sitting in the front row," she said.

"Who else? Family don't count in something like this. You better have some people from the Blue Baptist Church, or Early's going to be mad." I could see Miss Pink was perched on the edge of a hissy fit.

"I can't do everything, Buddy. I can only suggest it to Burrell, but it's up to him. Now tell me the truth, is Early going to be ready?"

"Early will be ready if y'all are," I answered. "If he doesn't see white, colored, and blue in the audience, there won't be any miracles. What'll people do if no magic happens, Miss Pink?"

"I'll work on it, Buddy, I promise," Miss Pink moaned. "Just make sure Early knows those scriptures. The rest is up to God."

"No, the rest is up to Early," I said.

I left Miss Pink puffing like mad on that Pall Mall. I knew she was miserable, but she could stew in that juice all night for all I cared.

It'd be best if she was scared of what Early was going to do. That way she couldn't push too hard when she realized he didn't know any of the Bible verses and couldn't recite the Ten Commandments.

Early was counting on me to fix things, and I didn't have a clue. The music would cover a lot of time and then, of course, the miracles. All Early had to do was reach one person, smack them on the forehead, and scream "Heal!" and that'd be all anybody would remember. Nobody would care that he couldn't recite John 11 by heart. But, if people were paying three dollars, he had to do something.

I hauled that strongbox all the way through town, and had to stop to rest at North Bridge. It's heavy. I was sitting there thinking about the revival when Dusty Lewis and Florence Goss come by in their pickup.

"Hey Buddy," Florence yelled from the window of the Ford, while Dusty pulled over to the side of the road.

"Where you been at, Buddy?" yelled Dusty.

"Hey Miss Florence, Miss Dusty," I said. "I been around."

"Bull!" Dusty bellowed. "If you'd been around, we'd have seen you!" She sure was loud. "Florence has been down to see Doc Rodger. She's got some aches." I walked over to Dusty's side of the pickup, and when I saw the beer bottle between her legs, I knew why she was screaming. "Buddy Boy, what you think about this revival?"

"It's a mess," I said.

"It's a mess!" Dusty screamed, spitting beer through her nose. That must've stung because her eyes teared up.

"You going to the revival, Buddy?" Miss Florence asked.

"I'll be there," I said. "You?"

"Hell no, she ain't going. None of us is going!" Dusty yelled. "It's a crying shame what they're putting that boy through. Burrell and Pink ought to be horsewhipped."

"Early wants to do it," I said.

"Then you do know where he is," Miss Florence said. "I was so worried when I heard he disappeared. Is he okay?"

"I don't know, Miss Florence, I ain't seen him," I answered. I had to look at the ground so she wouldn't see my eyes.

"That's okay, Buddy. I won't tell," she said. "You need a ride home?"

"Hell yes, he needs a ride home," Dusty yelled. "Buddy, get in the back of the pickup and we'll carry you out to the farm."

I got in the back of the pickup, and Dusty peeled out, coating North Bridge with gravel and a cloud of dust. When we got to the end of our road, she pulled over and I hopped out. I was walking around to her window to thank them for the ride when she peeled out again, pelting me with gravel.

I turned up our road and was almost home when Early jumped up from the ditch. "Boo!" he yelled. "I been waiting for you. Did I scare you?"

"Yeah, you did," I said. Then I looked at Early standing there in the late afternoon sun, and I got so sad. He had no idea what was about to happen. It wasn't right, but I didn't know how to stop it.

"I dug two bushels of taters, and Aunt Lena and me made us an apple pie. We're having meatloaf for dinner. You hungry?" He was jumping all around, excited about me being home. "I cut up the apples, but Aunt Lena made the crust. She said cutting the apples is the hardest part."

"It is," I said. "Crust is nothing to cutting up apples. You slice them thin or thick?"

"I don't know. I just cut them up. Aunt Lena said I done good."

Early looked at me and grinned. In that instant, with the sun shining on his white hair, he had my heart. I had to think of something so he wouldn't be hurt. If people laughed at him, I wouldn't be able to stand it. I can bear almost anything that happens to me. If Early gets hurt, it'll kill me. He's more precious to me than I am.

Right after supper I went to my room to put all my private stuff in my strongbox. I had that Brenda Lee record I got for my birthday playing as I sorted through things. She's real good and loud. On the album cover it says that she was only nine years old when she started performing and supporting her family. I wish I could sing and make money. Will said it's a well-known fact Brenda Lee is a thirty-two-year-old midget, but I know he's lying. I've seen midgets at the county fair, and she doesn't look like none of them. I played the song "Emotions" over and over, until Will banged on my bedroom door and threatened to beat me senseless.

Of course the first thing I put in the strongbox was my journal. Next I put in the letter Mama wrote me before she died. This is the letter where she tells me not to be so serious. I read it a couple more times before I tucked it away. Then I arranged all the pictures I've got of Mama in an envelope and put those in. I folded Mama's slip and put that in the box, too.

Then I found my souvenir booklet from *King of Kings*. Mama and I went to a special matinee screening of *King of Kings* at the Fox Theatre. She let me buy the deluxe souvenir booklet even though it cost one dollar and fifty cents. She made me promise not to tell Pa, and I never did.

Mama and I loved *King of Kings*. After the movie Mama said, "Nobody turns water into wine better than Jeffrey Hunter." That was a good day for us. Her cancer wasn't so bad then.

King of Kings! This was my answer. Early could do something from *King of Kings*. Miss Pink would love that. I had the entire book, and all I had to do was study up on something Early could handle. Of course if I could get Early to turn water into wine, he wouldn't have to say a thing, but that was a long shot. No way around it, Early was going to have to talk to the crowd. I had all night to read my booklet and decide what he'd say.

Once the box was packed, I put it under my bed, but that's just too obvious, and it'd be the first place Will looks. Then it came to me. There's a trap door behind my bed leading to a crawl space. I bet Will has forgotten it's even there. It's a perfect hiding place. At last my journal had a home.

When I got into bed, Early was already asleep. I couldn't concentrate on *King of Kings*, so I picked up Janet Lennon and tried to get interested. I tell you, that Janet Lennon is no Nancy Drew. I love the Lennon Sisters, but I bet they didn't have a thing to do with writing these books.

I cut off my light and tried to sleep, but I had so many thoughts bouncing around in my head, I couldn't sleep. I'd start to drift off, and then an idea would come up on me, and I'd be off and thinking a mile a minute. This much I knew for sure, I needed help if I was going to save Early. I felt sort of stupid asking, but I had to try.

"Dear God. If you're up there and listening, please don't let Early make a fool of himself. Help me to help him. Amen.

"Okay, God. I'm not done yet. I'm begging. Just get us through the next three days, and I'll believe in You. I promise this time. Even though I've been telling a lot of lies lately, I'm usually pretty truthful. You can ask anybody. Really."

CHAPTER 16

The official time of the dress rehearsal was six o'clock. Everybody was late. If Miss Pink had asked me first and done this thing right, she'd have sponsored a covered-dish social with the rehearsal immediately after, and everybody would've been on time. As it was, the Methodist Choir was the first to arrive. The white Baptists were an hour late, and the DCRs straggled in all night long. Miss Pink was a mess.

Getting Early into town without being seen was no trouble. I dressed him up in Will's clothes and put a baseball cap on his head. We walked along the river bank until we got to North Bridge, and then we climbed the hill up to River Road, which put us out by the dump. It was the first time Early had been back.

"Look where we are," he said.

"Yeah. Don't look like there's anything new today."

"I don't like it here," Early whispered. "There's ghosts down there."

"Then let's go," I said, pulling him away. "It gives me the creeps, too."

Early pulled back and stood there staring at the dump for a long minute. "Early, we got to get along. If we stand out here in the open, folks will see you."

"I can't help everybody. You know that don't you, Buddy?" he asked. "Some folks need to be sick. That's the way it works."

"Let's go," I said, avoiding the issue. "We can cut up behind Pink's."

The parking lot of the community hall was half full when we got there. There were a bunch of Methodist men standing by the back door, hiding from their wives and sneaking cigarettes. We stayed low so they wouldn't see us, and circled around so we could see the front of the hall. There had to be at least twenty people just standing on the sidewalk.

Miss Pink stuck her head out the window and yelled, "People, I need you inside!" She was tense. "Right now, people!"

Some people turned to go inside, but most of them just looked her way and kept right on talking. She should've had food.

"When I say now, I mean now!" Miss Pink barked, smacking her hands together. She had moved out to the sidewalk and was pushing people toward the front door. "We've got a lot to do and not much time. I mean it this time, y'all!"

"I don't see no colored people," Early said.

"Blues neither," I added.

"Miss Pink promised me," Early said.

"I bet they'll be there tomorrow night," I said, lying through my teeth. I'd bet anything Miss Pink would go back on her word.

"There's Dr. VanMeeder. He don't look happy," Early said, scrunching down in the grass, folding in on himself.

"Does he ever?" I asked. "Hey, Early, it's June and July! Oh my God, they look so cute."

June and July Hosler were walking up the sidewalk to the hall, and I could tell right away they were scared out of their wits. Their mama must've scrubbed them with lye soap because their skin was glowing. They had about fifteen braids apiece, and their dresses were starched stiff and standing out at 90-degree angles.

"Maybe Miss Pink wasn't lying," I said.

"Girls, get on in here, we're fixing to start," Miss Pink bawled from the front door. The twins joined hands, and ran through the door.

Miss Pink finally got everybody in the hall, and we could hear her bellowing all the way out to the back field. Early and I moved closer, and just as we got to the back door the Methodist Choir started in to singing "Amazing Grace." They sounded real good, but I could tell Imadene Landry was playing the piano. Everything she plays sounds the same.

Early and I snuck down to the basement of the hall while the Methodists were singing. We had to hurry, because once they were done, Miss Pink told them they had to leave. She should know better than that. Nobody tells a Methodist it's time to go home. Even I knew that, and I'm Catholic. Methodists are bad to get their feelings hurt, and besides, they pride themselves on acting proper. Miss Pink was way out of line.

As the Methodist Choir was filing out, we heard a commotion coming from the front door. From the basement it sounded like a stampede. Then everything got so quiet I could hear Early chewing on his thumb nail. I hate it when he does that.

"What's going on?" he asked.

"Beats me, but I'm going to find out," I said.

"Miss Pink will be mad," Early whispered.

I didn't even answer. I ran up the back stairs, cut through the auditorium, and headed for the front door. I had to force my way through the Methodists so I could get a good look. From what I could see, it looked like the Bluetown Baptist Choir collided with a delegation from the Dutch Christian Reform church. That meant the Methodists, blues, and DCRs were all clumped together. That meant blues and whites together under the same roof.

Nobody was saying a word, just looking out the front door. When I saw why I felt my stomach clutch. Coming up the front walk was Ernest Nichols, the pastor of the Negro Baptist church, with about ten of his choir members. Pastor Nichols marched through the door, raised up his Bible and shouted, "Praise Jesus! We have come to witness a miracle!"

If I thought it was quiet before, this was deadly. I swear I could hear Early chewing on his thumb nail way down in the basement.

Methodists and DCRs aren't a shouting type of religion. The Bluetown Baptists looked a little shocked, like they got caught in the crossfire, and didn't know where to turn. In the middle of all this come Miss Pink.

"You Methodists can go on home and thank you. "Amazing Grace" will be beautiful." Nobody moved. Not a word was said. "People, either come in the auditorium or go home. We got a lot of work to get done here!" Miss Pink didn't seem to be afraid of anything. She didn't make a big deal about colored and whites being together either. I bet she was praying nobody would notice.

Pastor Nichols walked over to Dr. VanMeeder and held out his hand. VanMeeder hesitated a bit, but he shook his hand. Betty Crutchfield, the Methodist Choir Director, walked over and extended her hand to Mr. Nichols. I thought that was nice, but that's just like Miss Betty. She's originally from Mississippi, and they are known for their good manners. Then Earl Benson, the pastor of Bluetown Baptist, come forward and stood directly in front of Mr. Nichols. They looked at each other for a minute, then both started laughing. They ended up hugging each other, wiping away tears, and then it was like everything was all right.

"As I said, the Methodists can go home. I need the, uh, well..." Miss Pink floundered. She didn't want to say blue Baptists, and I knew she'd bite off her tongue before she said Negro Baptists. People were waiting for instructions and finally she blurted out, "Y'all come in the auditorium and we'll sort this out."

As she walked past me, Miss Pink give me a look. "Get downstairs. Now!" she hissed, pinching the fat on the underside of my arm and giving it a vicious twist. She's strong for a skinny woman, and I know it's going to leave a mark.

Back in the basement, I could hear the colored Baptists running through "Precious Lord, Take My Hand." After that I heard Mr. Finch start talking about how he would be calling people to come forward to take the hand of Blue Jesus, and that's when the miracles would happen.

"What's Pa saying?" Early asked.

"You can hear him as good as me. Just listen," I said.

"I hear him, but he's not making sense."

"He's saying that when the Negroes sing, the people are going to go up on the stage and see you. That's all. Now shut up and listen."

"I don't want to," Early said, and curled up on the floor. Within minutes, he was asleep.

The twins started in to singing, and I kicked Early to wake him up so he could hear, but he just rolled over. They were doing a fine job on "Sweet Little Jesus Boy." I closed my eyes and leaned back against the wall to listen.

"Buddy, get up!" Miss Pink yelled, jabbing at me with a yard-stick.

Given my history with yardsticks, when I come out of a deep sleep and seen one coming my way, I was scared. I yelled (and I think I screamed "No Pa!" but I'm not sure) and scrambled away. I rolled over Early and smacked my head against one of the concrete support beams in the middle of the room. My head hit so hard, it was like explosions going off behind my eyes.

"Buddy, it's me," Miss Pink said, crouching down beside me. "Rub your head. That'll take out the hurt," she said, grabbing my head and giving it a good rubdown. It did help a bit.

"You okay, Buddy?" Early asked.

"Of course he's okay. Now boys, we got lots to get done. It's almost eleven o'clock. If I don't get to bed soon, y'all'll have to roll me down the hill."

The auditorium stage was all decorated for the revival. I thought it might be tacky, but even I wasn't prepared for this. Miss Pink had gotten the plastic manger statues from the Methodist and Baptist churches and had all the figures standing around a huge manger on one side of the stage. It was sort of weird seeing two sets of Marys, Josephs, wise men, and shepherds. It made for a mighty crowded stable. There was a giant cross hanging from the ceiling directly in the middle. On the other side of the stage, there looked to be some sort of throne. I think it was left over from the high school homecoming dance.

"Now, this is what I've got planned. Early will make his entrance from the manger," Miss Pink started in. "It's got a fake bottom, and he can just climb up and appear before the people. It'll be very dramatic."

"I don't want to do that," Early said. "Why can't I just walk in?"

"Trust me on this," Miss Pink said, a might snappish. I think the rehearsal had sapped every ounce of tact the woman had left. "I know what works. Besides, it'll make people remember you were born in a manger, just like, well, uh, well, you know."

"I wasn't born in a manger. I was born at home. I come early," Early said. "Hey, that's my name. Early!" he laughed.

"But your father told everybody you were born in a barn," Miss Pink said. She looked upset.

"You know he lies," I said. "He'd say anything to make a buck. What's Early supposed to wear? You still putting him in a robe?"

"I've got it right here," Miss Pink said, pulling yards and yards of white fabric out of a box she had stashed behind the stage curtain. "I made this myself out of some old curtains Helen gave me from when she redid the Hairport."

Early took one look at the robe and started shaking his head. "I ain't wearing that," he said.

"And why not? I spent six hours stitching this thing together," Miss Pink said. "Just try it on, Early. Please. It's clean."

"I don't care, I ain't going to do it. I'm wearing my cut-offs." Early's mind was made up.

"We will not have Jesus up on this stage in cut-off shorts," Miss Pink snapped. "Every ignorant hillbilly in this county has shorts. Now I made you a gorgeous robe of pure white, and by God, that's what I want you to wear. That's what Jesus wore at Radio City, and that's what Blue Jesus will wear tomorrow night!"

"I ain't Jesus, and I ain't wearing no robe. I'm wearing my shorts," Early said, slow and deliberate. He wasn't backing down.

Miss Pink and Early stared at each other, testing their resolve. I knew neither one would give. I was getting tired, and all the manger figures were making me nervous.

"Miss Pink, if Early wore his shorts, they might look like swaddling clothes. Or, they might even look like he'd been wandering around for forty days and forty nights. I think that might work just as well as the robe. Besides, it'd make Early more comfortable on stage."

"Swaddling clothes, huh?" She was intrigued. "That might work."

"You could give the robe to Mr. Finch. He's going to be doing the talking isn't he?"

"He'll be doing the introductions," Miss Pink said. I knew she was irked about the robe, but at least her efforts wouldn't go to waste. "All right then. This is the plan. Early will make his entrance from the manger, in shorts, which means you have to get him here early tomorrow so we can hide him. Early, after the Methodists sing 'Amazing Grace,' the spotlight will hit the manger. I've got Joe Newsom all set to recite 'and lo, an angel of the Lord appeared before them and said, 'a child is born to you this day in the city of David.' Or is it Bethlehem? I can never get that straight. Early, that's when you make your entrance. I want you to pop out of the manger, then walk to the center of the stage and start reciting them Bible verses."

"About that," I said.

"What now?" Miss Pink was tired, and her nerves were rubbed raw. She could feel her authority slipping right through her fingers.

"Early won't be doing any talking."

"What do you mean, he won't be doing any talking? He's *got* to talk. Oh, Christ on the Cross! People are paying three dollars. He's got to say something. He's just got to." Pink was sputtering.

"I can't," Early said. "I get scared."

"I been thinking of a way around this," I said. "Now, you've got lots of music to take up time. What if I was to stand behind Early and talk for him? If you keep the lights down low enough, nobody would know it wasn't him."

"Did you even try to teach him the Bible verses?" Miss Pink asked. She was talking quiet now. I knew her feelings were hurt.

"No," I said. She whimpered. "I got something even better. How about if Early does the Sermon on the Mount?" That perked her up. "If he's standing in front of the cross, I'll hide behind it. If I yell, it'll be just like him talking."

"You know the Sermon on the Mount?" Miss Pink asked.

"I learned it for you," I said. It wasn't true, but I knew it'd make her feel better. "It'll be best if I do this for Early. He can talk to the people when they come up on stage, but that's all."

"What about when he ascends on the cross?" she asked.

"When I what?" Early asked.

"The cross is rigged to ascend to heaven. Well, the rafters. We got to set the weights later. Once you ascend to heaven, we'll release the doves."

"What doves?" Early asked.

"Mr. Newsom's pigeons," I said.

"After the pigeons are let go, the Bluetown Baptists will sing 'Christ the Lord is Risen Today.' I promise you, people will weep."

"What if he says that thing about forgive them Father for they know not what they do?"

"Oh, my God, Buddy, I love it!" Miss Pink said. She was starting to get some energy back. "That will have everybody boo-hooing like mad. Now, let's set the weights."

The cross the 4-H boys made was huge. There was a little platform for Early to stand on, and there were ropes to connect his arms. Wires connected the cross to the ceiling beam. Counterweights had been rigged so that with the release of a rope, the cross gradually floated up to the rafters. Miss Pink demonstrated, and I have to admit it was pretty effective.

Early stood on the platform, and Miss Pink and I added more weights on the rigging until Early floated upward. He started to scream at lift-off, and didn't stop until we pulled the cross back down to stage level.

"I don't like that," he said, collapsing in my arms when he hit the stage. "That scared me."

"But, Early, honey, it looks so good," Miss Pink said. "Please try. We'll practice a couple more times."

"Do I have to?" Early asked me.

"No," I said, flinching as Miss Pink reached out for another pinch. "You don't have to do a thing. We can go home right now and forget about this whole thing. It's up to you."

Early gave this some thought, and I could see him struggling. I knew it was important for him to do the revival, but ascending to heaven in nothing but his shorts was more than he bargained for.

"I'll do it," he announced, "but only once. I'll do it tomorrow. You make sure they tie me down good so I don't fall."

"I promise," Miss Pink said. "Buddy, can you yell that forgive them Father line so everybody can hear?"

"I guess so. Just remember to keep the lights down low so nobody sees me. If you put the spotlight on Early as he goes up into the rafters, nobody will even know it's me."

"How do I get down?" Early asked.

"Just like tonight. Once everybody leaves the auditorium, we'll pull you down with the rope that's on the back of the cross. It's simple." Miss Pink fished a Pall Mall out of her purse and struck a match. "Buddy, you want to practice that Sermon on the Mount?" She lit her cigarette and blew thick columns of smoke out her nose.

"No. I'll practice it some at home, but I know it by heart," I lied. "Is there anything else you need to tell us before tomorrow?"

"Nothing right off. It'd be best if y'all got here around five in the afternoon. Just come like you did tonight and stay hid. That worked out perfect. Burrell will be doing the announcing, and I'll be here to direct things. Buddy, with you doing the talking, I'm not so nervous. Early, all we got to get out of you is at least one miracle. Think you can do that?"

"It depends on who wants to see me," he said.

"Buddy, Grandma wants y'all to come home." Will was standing in the middle of the auditorium. I didn't even hear him come in. "Y'all got no business being out so late and making her worried."

"She knows where we are," I said.

"Shut up and get in the truck," Will said, "I'm leaving in two minutes, with or without you." Early ran after Will, and didn't even say goodbye to Miss Pink.

"Looks like we got to go," I said, turning to leave. "See you tomorrow."

"Buddy, thanks for your help," Miss Pink said. She reached out and took one of my hands in hers. She hesitated a minute, and I thought she was going to cry. "Buddy, does your daddy hurt you? Does he hit you?"

"No! Why would you think that?" Of course I knew why. It was that thing with the yardstick. Why did I have to fall asleep?

"I just wondered is all. See you tomorrow." Miss Pink gave my hand a squeeze before she let go. This was the Miss Pink with the beautiful smile.

The ride home was quiet. Early fell asleep with his head resting on Will's shoulder. When we got to the house, Will and I had to practically drag him upstairs. Grandma was already in bed. I knocked on her door to let her know we were home safe.

"How did it go?" she asked.

"Okay," I said. "You going to come?"

"I don't think so. This whole thing has got a carnival taint to it I don't appreciate," she said. "Is Early all right?"

"He still wants to do it," I answered. "I told him he didn't have to."

"You're a good friend to him, Buddy," Grandma said. "Watch after him tomorrow."

"I will. Goodnight, Grandma."

I got into bed and tried to read *The Lennon Sisters on Holiday Island*. Nancy Drew must've spoiled me, and I've gotten used to good literature. These Lennon Sisters books just aren't all that good a read. I still say the Lennon Sisters didn't have a thing to do with writing them.

I practiced the Sermon on the Mount as I drifted off to sleep. I fell asleep thinking about the Beatitudes. That Jesus was onto something.

CHAPTER 17

Neither Early or I slept good. My bed looked like we had been fighting all night long; the covers knotted up and half on the floor. Early had both pillows over his head, and I could still hear him snoring. When he sleeps, he sleeps hard.

As I was getting dressed, Early woke up yelling something. I couldn't tell what, but he jumped out of bed like his drawers were on fire.

"Early, wake up. You're all right," I said, trying to calm him down.

"There's blood. I seen lots of blood," he whispered, shaking all over.

"You had a dream is all," I said. I reached out to touch him, but he jumped away and huddled by the door.

"It was real. I seen blood, and there was a gun. It was real bad, Buddy," he said.

"It was a dream."

"Yeah, a bad one," he said. He tried to smile, but his lips just pulled tight. He sank back on the bed, exhausted.

"You want to talk about it?"

Early opened his mouth to say something, and right away his jaw snapped shut. He shook his head, and his eyes got that unfocused look he got when he was thinking hard. "I can't remember it no more. There was blood is all. I saw a lot of blood," he shuddered. "Why can't I remember?"

"Dreams are like that, especially bad ones. Grandma says nightmares keep us from going crazy."

"How?" he asked, his brow all knotted up. I could tell he was concentrating real hard, trying to bring his dream back.

"I don't know. I guess we dream about being nuts, so when we wake up all the craziness is out of our system."

"Then there ain't no blood?" Early asked.

"Do you see any blood? It was a stupid nightmare. You're just nervous about tonight."

"But I ain't nervous, Buddy," Early said. "I'm supposed to be at the revival. The voices told me that. My dream didn't happen tonight. It happened later. I remember a gun and blood."

"Who gets hurt?" I wanted to know. If Early dreamed it, then I'm taking this as gospel. If there was going to be a gun and blood, I thought we'd better call the law.

"I don't know. It's gone," Early answered. "I'm hungry. Let's eat." He threw on some clothes, ran down the stairs. I stayed behind, thinking about the gun and the blood. It came to me that some religious nut might try to kill Early at the revival. But he said it didn't happen tonight. Still, I suspected somebody was going to get hurt.

"Buddy, come down and eat. We got pancakes!" Early yelled.

I don't get how somebody can switch gears so fast. Early was scared out of his wits two minutes ago, but then it was gone out of his head in a heartbeat. I think about stuff so much that it wears me out. Right now I'm thinking about the revival and what I've got to do. When that's over, then I'll start in to thinking on Early's dream of the blood and the gun.

"Buddy, you ain't swallowed a bite, just pushed that food around your plate. I don't cook for my health, you know," Grandma said.

"I'm not hungry," I said. "Give it to Will."

"Will's ate and gone. He's up at the orchard with Gizzy and them Mexicans. That boy has taken on a lot since your pa's been, uh, well, since Lyle's been gone." Grandma couldn't bring herself to say Pa was in jail. "Will's got a lot on his mind."

"Don't we all?" I said.

"What time is the revival?" Grandma knew what was on my mind.

"Early. We got to get there early, just like my name," Early said, grinning wide.

"What you going to do until then?" Grandma asked.

"I don't know. We got to stay out of sight so nobody sees Early. I guess we'll just stay here until it's time to go. What you got needs done?"

"Plenty, but I don't want y'all underfoot. I know how you get when you're nervous, Buddy. You'll just pick at everybody. Why don't y'all go swimming? It'll be one of the last times you can. School starts in a few days," Grandma said, clearing the table.

"Can we?" Early asked. "I love swimming. Can we, Buddy?"

"Sure," I said, but swimming was the last thing on my mind. School! That meant Butch Calkins, more teasing, more fights, and more trouble.

"I can't swim. Remember, Buddy? You got to watch me good."

"You can have the inner tube," I said. He loves to float face down in the water and watch the rocks. I think he got that from me.

"Early, you wear a shirt. I ain't sending you home all burned up," Grandma said. "And Buddy, just stay around the swimming hole." We started out the back door, and Grandma called us back. "I don't want y'all swimming naked, you hear? Go on upstairs and get some shorts."

It was a perfect day for swimming. The sun was hot, but there was a good breeze coming off the mountains that moved the air around and kept the mosquitoes off. The water wasn't so cold that it made your teeth ache; it was just cool enough to feel good.

When we got to the swimming hole, Early threw off his clothes, put on Will's swimming suit, and climbed on the inner tube. I just sat on the riverbank watching him. He drifted out to the sandbar, just like I knew he would, flopped over on his belly and commenced to picking out stones. I knew his routine, so I moved a few feet back up the bank.

"Here's a pretty one," Early yelled, pitching a stone up on the bank. He buried his face in the water, looking for more. "This one's got diamonds in it!" he screamed, throwing another rock to the bank.

I moved out of Early's range and thought about school. Seventh grade meant I'd be in another classroom. Now that I was twelve, maybe things would be different. I hoped so. Maybe Early and me being heroes would make the other kids be nice. Truth is, I don't think I'd last one more year with Butch Calkins beating me up.

"This is the most beautiful rock I ever saw," Early screamed, throwing another treasure to the bank. "Buddy, help me find more rocks."

I watched Early rooting around for rocks a few more minutes, then put my trunks on and waded out to the sandbar. Grandma was right about this swimming thing. Early was happy and not even thinking about the revival. I wished I could forget, but it was rolling around in my head, along with school, blood, and the gun.

"You got enough rocks," I said, "let's float." I grabbed hold of the inner tube and pulled Early out into the river. The water was shallow enough so our feet touched the bottom. We floated downstream a bit, then put our feet down and worked our way back up to the sandbar. For the longest time we didn't say a thing, just floated. I climbed up on the inner tube and let Early push, maneuvering us over the rocks and back upstream.

"You ready for tonight?" I asked.

"Uh-huh," he said, "but Buddy, there's something you got to know."

"What?" I asked. He didn't answer, just stared off over the river. "You aren't getting scared are you? It'll be just like on your front porch, but with more people. I'll be there, and Will, too. He says he's not going, but I know he won't miss something this big."

"I ain't scared," Early said. "Really." He studied my face for a long time, not saying a word, just looking. I could tell he was starting to get a feeling about something. Then he reached out and touched my cheek. His hand was hot against my face. "Buddy, no matter what happens tonight, you're my best friend. I love you."

"I know. You're my best friend, too. But what's going to happen?" I asked. He kept his hand on my cheek and stared right through me. "What do you see, Early?" I whispered.

"It ain't so clear, but I'll help you, Buddy. I'll do whatever I can."

"I know you will, but you're spooking me right now. What's going to happen tonight?" I flopped out of the inner tube and swam away from him a bit. "Does this have anything to do with your dream? Because if there's going to be a gun and blood, then I'm going to tell Grandma. She won't let either of us go."

"No gun tonight," Early said. "And don't you worry, I'll be there, Buddy. You'll be fine."

"I ain't so worried about me, I'm thinking about you," I said.

Early let go of the inner tube and walked to the sandbar. He sat down and buried his head in his arms.

"You all right?" I asked, sitting beside him. My arm brushed across his back, and he was burning hot.

"My head hurts," he whispered, "just like in my dream. It's so close, but I can't see it."

"See what?"

"I don't know," he said. "There's something out there. I'm supposed to help, but I can't see what it is." He rubbed his eyes with his fists and rocked back and forth. I pulled his hands away from his eyes, and his palms were red hot. All of a sudden Early's hands flipped over, and he grabbed hold of my wrists. He held tight for a second, and then pulled my hands to his face. "After tonight I have to go away," he said, talking into my eyes, "but I'll be watching you. I'll always watch over you, Buddy," he whispered. His eyes rolled back in his head, his body jerked violently, and he fell backwards. His head bounced off the inner tube once, then hit the ground. He was out cold.

"Early!" I yelled, jumping up. I knew this was another spell, but maybe this one made his brain explode, or he had a stroke. "Early, wake up! Please!" I splashed water on his face. "Come on, wake up. Early!"

I didn't see him breathing, so I leaned over and put my hand on his heart. I put my head down and could hear Early's heart pounding steady.

"Hey Buddy, why you listening to my heart?" Early whispered, eyes wide open. He smiled up at me, reached out and touched my face.

"You fainted," I said, "I thought you were dead."

"Still here. Headache's gone," Early said, sitting up. "I feel good."

"You said you were going away," I said.

"Did I?" he asked. "I ain't going nowhere."

"But you had a spell, and you said you were going away," I insisted. "What did you see?"

"I can't know it right now. It'll come later," he said. "Let's go swimming." Early grabbed the inner tube and headed for the middle of the river. It was like nothing had happened.

"Buddy! Are y'all naked? If you are, I'm not coming down there!" Miss Pink was screeching from the riverbank. She was upstream from the sandbar and couldn't see us. "I need y'all to come up to the house! And hurry!" We didn't say anything. "Buddy? Where are you boys?"

"We're naked!" I yelled back. I was in no mood to deal with Pink.

"Get up to the house as soon as you can! I'll be waiting on y'all!" Miss Pink was practically in hysterics. "Buddy, can you hear me?"

"We'll be right there!" I yelled back.

"Stay off the road!" she yelled, "Don't let anybody see you."

What now? Early and I took our sweet time drying off and getting dressed. He collected all his rocks, and added some to the collection. I didn't care how long he took, I was in no hurry to hear Miss Pink's problems. If you ask me, Miss Pink needed a man in her life, or maybe a dog, anything to keep her mind on something besides herself.

There were a lot of cars on the road, so we waited in the ditch until the coast was clear, then scooted across the road, across the front meadow and headed up toward the house. Pink was standing on the front porch waiting on us. When she saw us coming across the meadow, she started screeching again. I couldn't hear a darn thing she was saying, but I saw her waving her arms, motioning us to go to the back of the house. That's when I saw the cars parked at the end of our road and along Highway 28.

I made Early duck out of sight, and we cut up the far side of the meadow, up to the barn and came down the path to the backdoor. Miss Pink was waiting on us, puffing like mad on her cigarette. Grandma was sitting on the back steps, mending my bib-alls. She looked put out.

"What are all the cars doing out there?" I asked.

"They come looking for you and Early," Pink screamed. "We got to get y'all out of here!" I was right. She was hysterical. She took off her straw hat and mopped her head with a hanky. No hair yet.

"Just tell them to go away, or get the law on them," I said.

"I tried that! They won't go!" Miss Pink screeched. "They want Early!"

"You don't have to yell at us, Miss Pink. We didn't do nothing wrong," Early said. He was pretty calm considering he had a hysterical bald woman screaming at him.

"Oh God, I'm sorry. I know. It's just that town is full of people. They're already lined up and the revival doesn't start for seven more hours," she moaned. "I got to get you boys into town before it's too late."

"Too late for what?" Grandma asked.

"For the surprise, of course!" screamed Miss Pink. Grandma cut her eyes at that one, and Pink slowed down. "We got to keep Early hid, Lena, you know that. If somebody sees him, then the whole revival is ruined. Boys, get in my car, I'm taking y'all to the community hall right now."

"They ain't going nowhere until they have lunch. Pink, looks to me like you could use something to eat too," Grandma said, putting down her mending.

"There's no time!" Pink screamed.

"Listen to me!" Grandma snapped, leveling Miss Pink with her two-finger point. "Pink! Y'all are going to come in this kitchen and eat some dinner. While you're eating, I'm going to have Matt Williams chase them cars off. Then you can head into town. Is this clear?"

"Yes, m'am," Miss Pink said. She stubbed out her Pall Mall and took a deep breath. She started to take off her straw hat, but thought better of it and just dabbed at her brow with her hanky.

That two-finger point of Grandma's is like a slap across the face. It was just what Miss Pink needed to knock some sense into her. We all followed Grandma into the kitchen. She started some pole beans to cooking, and put Miss Pink in charge of iced tea. Early's job was to set the table. I sliced tomatoes. Grandma dialed the phone.

"Will, there's cars at the end of my road again," Grandma said. "I want them cleared out right now. Ain't nothing to see out here." Grandma listened for a minute then answered, "No, I ain't going. Like I told Buddy, this whole thing's like a tacky carnival. I don't go to them neither." Miss Pink pretended she didn't hear, but I could see her face flushing up. "Send Ellerd if you have to. We ain't had a minute's peace since this whole mess got started." Grandma hung up. "You boys hungry?"

Lunch was quiet. Miss Pink ate, and then excused herself and went outside for a smoke. She sure does love Pall Malls. Early and I did the dishes, and then went upstairs to change for the revival.

I didn't know what to wear. Early had it easy. He was going to make his entrance in his cut-off shorts. I decided on short pants and a dark t-shirt. I figured that'd be best, since I'm not supposed to be seen.

"I think the coast is clear," Miss Pink called in the kitchen door. "I saw Ellerd running the cars off about twenty minutes ago."

"Then I guess it's time y'all left," Grandma said. She followed us out to the back steps. "Early, are you sure?" she asked. Early nodded, smiling. Grandma pulled him in for a hug. "No matter what happens, you got a home here," she whispered. She pulled me close and gave me a kiss. "I'm sending Will to watch out for you," she said, then whispered in my ear, "Don't let nothing bad happen to Early."

Miss Pink had it all figured out. She put us in the back seat of her car and made us lay on the floorboards. She covered us over with an old quilt and pointed the car for town and the community hall. We couldn't breathe, so we pulled the quilt off and opened the window. Nobody could see us lying on the floor anyway. When I heard the tires rumble, I knew we crossed over North Bridge. I could hear Miss Pink muttering to herself about traffic. It did sound like a lot of cars.

"Jesus!" she screamed, slamming on the brakes, throwing me and Early up against the seats, knocking our heads together. "What in the Sam Hill are we going to do?"

"What's going on?" I asked. I tried to get up, but Miss Pink pushed my head down.

"Stay down! There's at least five hundred people out here! Oh my God, how am I going to get you in the hall without people seeing? There's folks crawling all over the front lawn, and a line from the front door all the way past the Methodist Church." Miss Pink cursed under her breath as she worked her way through the cars on the street.

"Miss Pink, pull up to the back of the community hall and park real close," Early said, "We'll get out and go in one of the basement windows. Ain't nobody going to see nothing."

"Early, there's people all over, even in the back. My God, they've got picnic lunches going in the parking lot. Good Lord!" Miss Pink hissed, "Burrell's selling hot dogs. That snake!"

"Miss Pink, do what I say. Drive slow and park close. It'll be fine," Early said. He sure was calm.

"Just don't hit anybody," I added. Miss Pink cut loose with another string of curse words. For a Christian, she's got a very dirty mouth.

"You're doing good, Miss Pink." Early took control just like that. "Park by the kitchen windows. We can stand on the counters when we go in."

Early coached Pink through the maneuvers. She slid the car up next to the building, but on her first try she got too close, and we couldn't get the car door open. She backed up and tried it again. Perfect. Early opened the back door of the car, took my hand, pulled me out of the car. We slipped through the window and into the community hall basement.

This was just the beginning. We had five more hours until the main event. I checked the community hall to make sure there wasn't anybody around. When I was sure the coast was clear, I got Early and we went up to the stage. I wanted to check out the trap door in the manger, and Early wanted to see the cross again.

Everything was just the way we left it last night. All the manger figures were still there, and the cross was sitting on the stage, waiting to ascend to the rafters. Early checked the cross, went to the side of the stage and looked over the counterweights, then went back to the cross. He stood on the cross' platform and held his arms out, like he was crucified.

"Buddy, tell me again. Once I'm up in the ceiling, how do I get down?"

"There's a rope on the back of the cross. When everybody leaves, we'll just pull you down. It'll be like last night, except you may have to stay up there a little while until everybody leaves. Do you want to try it again?"

"No! I don't like it up high. Just tonight," he said.

"Hey Early, come here and look at the manger. There's a place for you to lay down, and when it's time to show yourself, all you have to do is push this straw aside and stand up."

Early came over to examine the manger. The 4-H boys had done a pretty good job. It looked exactly like a Christmas nativity manger, except it was so big that Mary, Joseph and Early could all fit inside.

"Early, get in there and practice making your entrance. Just lay down and when I say ready, you stand up. I'm going out into the audience to see how it looks." I went out to the middle of the folding chairs and yelled back, "Okay, Early, let's go!" Nothing. "Early, come forth!" I snickered. He didn't stand up. "Early, come on. I want to see how it looks!"

When Early still didn't appear, I went up on the stage and peeked in the manger. I pulled back the straw and found him sound asleep, curled up on the stage floor. Best to let him alone. He had a big night ahead.

CHAPTER 18

"Buddy, I can't find Early," Miss Pink hissed in my ear.

I must've fallen asleep, because I was all balled up and lying on the stage between two Mary's and one of the Wise Men. When I looked to see who was talking, I got confused and thought it was the Blessed Virgin asking me about Early.

"Buddy, where's Early?" Miss Pink shook me full awake.

"Hey, Miss Pink. You look good," I said. She had on a sky blue dress, silver heels, and a dark red hat that looked like a big bunch of roses.

"I thought you were going to watch Early," she said.

"He fell asleep in the manger. How much longer?"

"We're getting close. The front lawn's full, and so's the back parking lot. Folks are getting pushy. Joe Newsom already put the bag of pigeons in the rafters. Leon and Louann are at the front door to take tickets. If Early's ready, then we're going to get Imadene to start playing, and let the folks in."

"You'd better check," I said. I had no idea how long I'd been asleep. For all I knew Early woke up and wandered away. Truth to tell, I was still a little spooked thinking the Virgin Mary had talked to me.

"Early!" Miss Pink whispered, inching toward the manger. "Early, are you in there?" She moved closer. "Early! Get up!" she hissed.

At that moment the straw parted and Early stood up. It was like he appeared out of nowhere

"Jesus Christ!" Miss Pink gasped.

"No, just me," Early said, giving us a smile. The effect was spectacular, and I couldn't wait to see it with lights.

"Early, you gave me a fright, but it looks wonderful. It really does. Now we're fixing to let folks in. Do you need to go to the bathroom? Do you want water? What can I do for you?" Miss Pink was babbling. I think seeing Early in the manger gave her a glimpse of how tonight would go.

"I'm all right, Miss Pink. What does Pa say when it's time for me to stand up? You'd better tell it to me again."

"He's going to say, 'Blue Jesus come forth and shine your heavenly light on this world.' Can you remember that? 'Blue Jesus come forth.' That's when you stand up." Miss Pink walked around the manger, looking Early over like she was planning on taking this show on the road.

"Good Lord, I hope this works," Miss Pink whispered. "Now Buddy, where are you going to be?"

"I thought I'd just stand behind the cross," I said.

"That's good. Well, then, it looks like we're ready," Miss Pink said, taking off her flower hat and mopping her bald head with her hanky. "Burrell, we're ready!" she yelled toward the front door.

Mr. Finch came in the auditorium. He had on the white robe Miss Pink made, but he still looked like a bait farmer on a bender. If I knew I was going to be on stage, I'd at least shave and wash my hair. His hands were trembling, and I knew he'd sell his soul for a jelly jar of shine.

"Everything okay?" he croaked. He didn't look too good to me, all sweaty and sticky looking.

"Open the doors. We're ready," Miss Pink said, smiling real big. Mr. Finch went out to the entryway to open the doors. "Please,

Lord, don't let that blue drunk mess this up," Miss Pink said under her breath. Then she turned to me, "You stay out of sight. I don't care what happens."

The first person through the door was Imadene Landry. The piano was sitting on the stage in front of the curtain, and she went right over and started in playing "A Mighty Fortress is Our God." Of course, being Imadene, this sounded exactly like her rendition of "You Are My Sunshine." She's just not a musical girl.

Mr. Newsom was next. He came right up on the stage to check on his pigeons. "Well, Buddy, is Early going to show?"

"We'll have to wait and see," I said.

"Won't be a show without him," he said, staring up at the rafters. "Well, everything looks good here. I'm stepping out back for a smoke." He wasn't gone but a second when I heard him yell, "Y'all can't come in here. You got to go in the front door! Buddy! Help!"

I ran down the stairs and saw Mr. Newsom leaning against the door, trying to keep people out. He was having a tough time.

"When I get this shut, lock it up," he panted, giving one mighty shove and slamming the door. I snapped the lock. "Can you believe that?"

"They want to see a miracle," I said.

"Don't we all?" he said. "Guess I better head out the front door."

I wandered around in the basement for a time, and then drifted back upstairs behind the stage curtain. I was bored and wanted to see what was going on out front. I peeked through the curtain and saw Early's mama and baby sister sitting in the front row. I think this is the first time I've seen Pocket in clothes. Mozelle Landry and her family were sitting in the middle of the auditorium eating hot dogs out of a paper bag. I bet they bought them from Mr. Finch. Helen Adams from the Hairport and the Runyons were sitting together. Mr. Runyon had his oxygen canister sitting in the aisle. Mrs. Runyon must've dyed her hair to get ready for the school year because it was pumpkin orange.

I went out front, steering clear of Miss Pink, and was standing just inside the main auditorium doors when here come Miss Carla. She had a camera with her and was all dressed up.

"Hey, Miss Carla. You look nice," I said.

"Buddy! Is Early here? Is he going to appear?"

"Don't know. I haven't seen him since he went away," I said. "If he comes back it'll be a true miracle, and only because he wants to help." I'm pretty shameless around the press. I wanted to say something that would sound good if Miss Carla quoted me for the paper.

"I can't wait. What'll they do if he doesn't appear?" Miss Carla asked.

"Beats me, but there's going to be four preachers here. There's no way the Baptists and DCRs will waste an audience."

"Colored and white together, blue, too. This is historical, Buddy, do you know that?" Miss Carla took out her notebook. I wracked my brain trying to think of something smart to say in case she was quoting me.

"It's historical because of Early," I said. "Early told me that miracles come to every color; white, black, and blue. Early said God is colorblind."

"That's beautiful, Buddy," Miss Carla said, scribbling in her book. "What else did Early say?"

"Early said everybody needs to get along and not fight each other." Like I said, I'm shameless with the press.

"I am fixing to bust I'm so nervous," Miss Carla squealed. "My God, Buddy, look. This place is near full, and we've got an hour to go."

The auditorium was packed, with more people streaming through the door every minute. The entire main floor was filled, and there were even people up in the balcony. It was so strange to look up at the balcony and see white and colored sitting side by side. I wandered out to the entrance hall and saw Leon and Louann taking tickets, collecting money, and pushing people through the door. There was a line of people snaking out the front door, onto the lawn, and winding behind the building to the parking lot. Matt Williams had the patrol car parked on the road, and he was directing traffic. There was no way everybody would fit in here.

"Buddy, can you get me in?" It was Florence Goss. She was standing in front of Leon holding out a five-dollar bill, but he was shaking his head.

"I told you Miss Florence, we ain't got no more room; just standing room on the lawn. I'm sorry." Leon looked worn out.

"Come on, Leon," I said, "she won't take up much room."

"If you ain't got a ticket, you ain't getting in. Pa and Miss Pink sold too many as it is," he barked.

"Please. I got money. I need to see Early," Miss Florence said. She looked ready to cry. "Buddy, you won't tell Dusty I'm here will you? She said I couldn't come, but I decided I'm a grown woman, and I'll go anywhere I please. But don't tell, okay?"

"Leon, come on," I whispered, "It's Miss Florence."

"Okay, Miss Florence, but promise me you won't sit down. People paid money for them folding chairs." Leon turned away, and I pulled Miss Florence toward the door. She turned back to give Leon her five dollars, but I yanked her into the auditorium.

"They don't need your money Miss Florence," I said. "Give it to Early if he does a miracle for you."

"Thank you, Buddy," Miss Florence said. "This is our secret. Okay?" She started to say something else, but a big wave of people came through the door and she got swept up in the traffic.

I had seen enough. The auditorium and the balcony were full, and I didn't see how Leon could cram another person in. I headed backstage.

"How's it look out there, Buddy?" Mr. Finch asked. He looked better than before, and when I saw the jug of shine behind his back I knew why.

"Crowded," I said.

"Is Early ready?" he asked.

"I guess. What about you?"

"Just got me a good dose of confidence," he said, showing me the jug. "We're making some good money tonight."

"Is Early going to get any?" I asked.

"He's my son. What's mine is his," Mr. Finch said, slurring his words.

I was all set to say something snotty, but the Methodist Choir came up on the stage, and Mr. Finch got busy. Miss Pink flew by, stopped to say something to me, forgot what it was, and then went after Mr. Finch. I watched her snatch that jug of shine out of his hands, and decided I'd be better off hiding behind the cross. I snuck behind the curtain and walked over to the manger.

"Early, you all right in there?" I whispered. I heard him rustling under the straw.

"Is it time?" he asked, pushing the straw aside.

"Fixing to be," I said. I was right. I'll say this for Miss Pink, she kept the Radio City tradition alive by starting on time.

CHAPTER 19

"Blackout!" Miss Pink yelled, and all the lights in the auditorium went out. I heard a whoosh when the audience gasped, and then there was total silence. Miss Pink waved her arms at Joe Newsom, and he pulled the curtains open. The spotlight hit Imadene Landry, and she pounded out the opening lines to "Amazing Grace." The Methodist Choir, all dressed up in their navy blue robes, marched on stage, and formed a semi-circle around the manger. As they marched in, the stage lights got brighter and brighter.

I stayed hid, but I had a great view of the choir and the audience. Most everybody was singing. If there's one thing country folk know, it's "Amazing Grace." When the stage lights hit all the plastic manger figurines, it was creepy. They all looked like they were about to say something important, and were waiting for a break in the music to spread the news.

The Methodists were winding things up, and you could tell it was the final chorus because Betty Crutchfield, the choir director, walked over and put her hand on Imadene's shoulder, real firm. Everybody really sang out on the last "was blind, but now I see." They held the last note a long time, and then there was another blackout. Pink had Danny Lambert running lights, and he must've hit the wrong breaker box, because even the emergency lights went out. It was pitch black.

The spotlight hit the stage, and there stood Mr. Finch, weaving side to side in that long white robe. He looked eerie standing there, sort of mystical, his blue face glowing in that bright light.

"I was blind, but now I see," Mr. Finch bawled. "I have seen the evil ways of mankind, and I know there is a better path. Some will be called to testify. Others to witness. We are here for a miracle . . . the boy called Blue Jesus."

He wasn't bad. Miss Pink must've practiced him hard. He took a deep breath, and then a blank stare come over his face. From the terrified look on his face, I knew he was lost.

Miss Pink came to his rescue, and hissed from the side of the stage, "He was adrift in the desert!" Mr. Finch missed it. He turned to face Miss Pink and she screeched at him again, "He was adrift in the desert!"

"Oh yeah, that's right . . ." Mr. Finch was back on track. "He was adrift in the desert, forty days and forty nights . . . uh . . ."

"Seeking wisdom and guidance from his father above . . ." Miss Pink yelled. She gave up whispering.

"Say what?" Mr. Finch was drunker than I thought.

"Seeking wisdom . . ." Miss Pink yelled. Mr. Finch was drawing a total blank, rolling his eyes upward, searching for his next line.

"Oh, hell," Miss Pink muttered, and walked on stage, joining Mr. Finch next to the manger. Imadene started playing what sounded like "Angels We Have Heard on High," which everybody knows is a Christmas song.

"Blue Jesus wandered in the desert forty days and forty nights, seeking wisdom and guidance from his father above," Miss Pink said. She was nervous. You could tell because all the rose petals on her hat were quaking. She turned to Mr. Finch, waiting on him to deliver the next line. Nothing. So, Miss Pink faced front, and spoke again. "But are we sinners worthy to receive him? Will Blue Jesus appear here tonight?"

Imadene was banging the bejeezus out of the piano. I think she was playing a hymn, but I couldn't be sure. Miss Pink waited for Mr. Finch to pick up his cue, but he was drawing a blank. Miss Pink rallied again.

"All of us sinners gathered here today; white, blue, and colored, are the children of the Lord." And here it got real dramatic. The stage lights got real dim, and the spotlight got small, so it was just shining on Miss Pink's face. She walked to the edge of the stage and said, "And the Lord Jesus said, 'Suffer the little children to come onto me.'" Miss Pink looked over at Imadene and whispered, "That's your cue. 'Holy, Holy, Holy.'" Imadene struck up the hymn. Miss Pink hissed, "Just two verses."

From the back of the auditorium the DCR choir, with Lydia VanMeeder leading the pack, filed in. They were wearing bright purple robes with white collars and carrying hymnals. I thought that was sort of dumb. It looked like they couldn't remember the words to "Holy, Holy, Holy." Even I know two verses of that. As the choir marched in, the entire audience sang along. Mountain people love hymns.

"Dear Lord, tell us, are we worthy to receive Blue Jesus!" Miss Pink yelled above the music. "Are y'all in a state of grace? For only then will Blue Jesus appear." Now it could have been that spotlight, or the choir, but I swear, standing there in that sky blue dress and rose petal hat, Miss Pink made you believe.

Mr. Finch must've thought so too, because he started in boohooing like a baby. "I want Early! Early, talk to me! Early, come see your pa! Early!" He tried to get at the manger, but Miss Pink held him back. I peeked around the cross in time to see her reach under the sleeve of his robe, and I knew she was giving his underarm fat a mighty pinch.

As "Holy, Holy, Holy" went into the last chorus, the DCR choir formed a line in front of the Methodists. I could see that irked Miss Crutchfield, because she pushed her way into the front line. After awhile all the Methodists were elbowing their way to the front, until both choirs formed a long line from one side of the stage to the other. I couldn't wait to see what would happen when the colored Baptist choir came up on stage.

"Holy, Holy, Holy" ended after two verses and three choruses. The only light in the auditorium was a soft glow from the stage. There was a nice sense of anticipation building that had a good show biz feel.

"I want Early!" Mr. Finch bawled out in the dark, ruining the mood. He was really sobbing now. Miss Pink pushed him back into the choir line. When she did, her eye caught Miss Betty's, and Betty took it from there. She grabbed Mr. Finch and pushed him behind the entire line of singers. With Mr. Finch out of the way, Miss Pink had the spotlight to herself.

"Are we sinners worthy? The time is now! Blue Jesus! Come forth and shine your heavenly light on this world!" Miss Pink waited. The audience was still standing up in the dark, waiting to see if Early would appear. Nothing happened.

"Blue Jesus, come forth! The time is now!" Nothing. "Blue Jesus appear before your flock!" No Early. I knew he was confused. He expected his pa to be calling him forth. Miss Pink leaned into the manger and spoke softly, "Early, are you in there?"

Early stood up just as Danny Lambert lit the manger with the overhead lights. It was dazzling. The entire audience screamed, and Miss Pink fell off her heels and hit the stage butt first. The choir members on the stage all yelled and backed up; some of them even kneeled. I didn't even try to hide. I jumped out from behind the cross to look at my best friend.

Early was standing in the manger wearing nothing but cut-off shorts. His chest was bare and blazing bright blue in the light. His white hair floated above his head like a cloud. Standing there in the light, my best friend was beautiful. The audience went crazy. Everybody screamed; some started crying. Then it was like everybody got the same idea, and a huge wave of people came running toward the stage.

I'll admit it, I was scared. Christians filled with the spirit are frightening. I saw Matt Williams and Ellerd running toward the stage, too, but there was no way they could stop these believers.

Early stood there in the light and slowly raised his arms. Everybody stopped to watch. He looked from left to right, up to the balcony, back at the choirs, and then back to the audience. He lowered his hands, and everybody sat down. They didn't return to their seats, they just sat on the floor where they were. Then Early smiled. This was magic.

Once again, silence. Too much silence. Oh my God, I was supposed to be talking for Early! I wracked my brain trying to remember the beginning of the Sermon on the Mount.

"Blessed are the poor in spirit, for theirs is the kingdom of heaven!" I yelled. No reaction. I skipped ahead a few Beatitudes. I wanted to hit them with numbers seven and eight before they realized it was me talking. "Blessed are the merciful, for they will be shown mercy!" I was yelling full blast, and I don't know why. Nobody was making any noise but me. "Blessed are the pure in heart, for they will see God!"

"That ain't me talking," Early said, showing that shy smile again. "I can't learn no Bible verses. That's Buddy talking for me."

"Don't tell them that," Miss Pink whispered, then she scurried off stage to cue the colored Baptist Choir. They marched in carrying lit candles and singing "Precious Lord, Take My Hand." Early listened, waiting until they were all onstage, then he raised his arms. They stopped.

"Early! I want Early!" Mr. Finch was sobbing again. I looked over and saw Earl Benson, the pastor of Bluetown Baptist, take Mr. Finch by the arm and lead him away.

"Pa's sad," Early said, and he give a little shrug. "He ain't feeling so good tonight." Early stepped out of the manger, and walked down to the edge of the stage. "Now I got something to say, and I want that y'all should listen tight: I ain't Jesus. If you'uns come here looking for Him, then go home." Early waited. Nobody moved. Still Early said nothing. He waited another minute, then he spoke up, "If y'all are sure you want to be here, then I guess we better get started. I might can help some of y'all. I'm willing to try." Nobody came forward.

"If y'all will form a line, we'll be taking you up to see Blue Jesus, one at a time," Miss Pink announced to the audience. "Imadene, we need us a little music, please." Imadene started playing "Precious Lord, Take My Hand" again. "Early, you're supposed to be sitting in the throne during this part," Miss Pink whispered. Early shook his head, pushed some straw off the manger, and sat on the edge. The Methodist and DCR choirs joined the colored Baptists singing. It was real nice.

There was a stir in the crowd, and I could tell something was happening. It was the Bluetown Baptist Choir marching down the center aisle, heading for the stage. When Early saw them he gave out his biggest smile yet. He motioned to the Bluetown Choir, and everybody applauded. This gave me goose bumps. All the choirs were swaying in time to the music; white, colored, and blue. I don't know why, but I was crying.

I stayed behind the cross watching as people in the audience came up to talk with Early. Nettie Ruth Johnson pushed her way to the front of the line and ran up on the stage. She didn't say a word, just threw her arms around Early's neck. They both laughed, then Nettie Ruth kissed Early and joined the singers on stage. I didn't know the next couple of people that came up to talk to Early, but not much happened. Early talked to each of them, but there wasn't any sign of a miracle.

I peeked at the audience again, and saw Butch Calkins standing in line. His white trash father was behind him, pushing him toward the stage. This was trouble.

When it was his turn, Butch prissed across the stage, looking cocky, and smiling back at the audience. When he got to the manger, he knelt down in front of Early. Early reached out and put his hands on Butch's head. I couldn't stand this. I didn't believe for one minute Butch was repenting his sins. I had to see what was going on, so I walked over to the homecoming throne to watch Butch and Early.

Early bent down and whispered something in Butch's ear. Butch shook his head, and then Early talked some more. All the while this was going on, Butch was fooling with something in his pocket. I saw him strike a match to a string of firecrackers and toss them in the manger. The explosions went off just as Early was standing up. It sounded like a machine gun.

"There's your miracle, Blue Boy!" Butch yelled. "Wake up, you assholes!" he screamed at the audience. "He ain't Jesus! He ain't nothing but a blue retard!"

Butch jumped off the stage and tried to run down a side aisle, but Will tackled him, throwing him to the ground. Matt Williams and Ellerd ran over, pulled Butch to his feet, and hauled him away. The audience was buzzing.

"Fire!" Miss Pink screamed, pointing at the manger.

The firecrackers had lit the manger straw on fire. Several people in the audience started screaming, "Fire," and people started to bolt for the doors.

"Stop! I said stop!" Early yelled. "There ain't no fire!" People stopped running and turned to look. "There ain't no fire," he said again, softer, walking to the edge of the stage. "It burned out."

"Fire needs to eat," Early said, "but there's nothing left. A soul needs faith, and that's why Butch Calkins is gone. He burned hisself out. Does anybody want to talk to me?" Early sat down on the homecoming throne. "I'm ready."

The audience formed another line, and standing at the head was Florence Goss. She looked scared to death, and practically tip-toed across the stage. When she got in front of Early, she tried to kneel, but he pulled her to him and held tight. Miss Florence burst into tears, and Early hugged her even tighter. He stood up, put his hands on Miss Florence's shoulders, pushing until she was sitting on the throne. He leaned over, placed his face next to hers, and they began to whisper.

I knew something special was happening. It was a feeling in the air, like electricity after a storm. It made the hairs on my arms stick up. Everybody in the auditorium felt it. It was just like when the movies go into slow motion. The choir stopped singing, and just hummed along with the music. I moved closer to the throne so I could hear.

"Is it a sin when you love somebody? Is it wrong? Is that why this happened to me? Tell me, Early. Tell me why?" Miss Florence was trying to whisper through her sobs.

"A sin is a hurt against God. You and Miss Dusty ain't hurting nobody," Early said.

"Then why did God give me cancer? Why? It has to be because of me and Dusty," Miss Florence cried. I heard the word *cancer*, and I about jumped out of my skin. Cancer. "God don't like sin. He's been watching us and knowing what we do. Is that why God's killing me?" Miss Florence was getting louder, and Early shushed her. He knelt down and took her hands in his. She leaned over until their foreheads were touching. He reached up and wiped her tears away.

"God don't kill us. God tests us." Early stood up. He seemed to tower over Miss Florence. "Can you be strong for Jesus?" Early asked, letting the entire audience hear him. Everybody leaned forward to hear her answer.

"I think so," Miss Florence said. She didn't look very strong.

"Then say it! Say, I can be strong," Early said.

"I can be strong!" Miss Florence yelled. Everybody in the auditorium held their breath. The choir humming in the background was the only sound. "I can be strong! I can, Early! I really can!"

"I know you can," Early said. He pulled Miss Florence to her feet, stood behind her, placed one hand directly on her forehead and the other over her heart. "Heal this woman, Lord!" Early yelled. He held her tight for a minute, then let go. Miss Florence hit the ground like a sack of rocks. Early wavered a second, then fell back on the throne. Nobody moved.

"I can be strong," Miss Florence whispered. Early reached down, offering his hand. Miss Florence got to her feet, unsteady. Early put his arm around her shoulder. "I can be strong. I know I can," Miss Florence said. She put her arms around Early's waist and kissed his cheek.

"Your cancer is gone. Go home to your family, Miss Florence. You'll be just fine." Early gave Florence a final squeeze, and released her. "Miss Pink, you better help her."

At last the audience got what they came to see; a real miracle. They responded with applause, whistles, cheering, and then everybody got in line. I had to sit down. I felt sick to my stomach. It was cancer, and Early took it away. If only Early had known Mama, things could've been so different.

I'd been sitting on the stage so long my legs fell asleep. When I got up to stomp out the numb, I saw that lady from Alden and her two bleeder kids at the front of the stage. Early saw them, too. He stood up and started shaking his head.

"Yes, you will!" Mrs. Disbrow screamed. "Oh, yes, you will help my babies!" Mrs. Disbrow pushed her kids on stage. "You got to. Help us, please! Blue Jesus, please!"

"I can't," Early said, shaking his head and backing away, "I can't." Mrs. Disbrow wasn't taking no for an answer and pulled her boys across the stage until they stood in front of Early.

"You can, and by God, you will!" she yelled. She pulled her boys from behind her back, and threw them up against Early, knocking him off balance. He slipped, and fell down on one knee. One of the bleeder boys reached out to help him up, and Early screamed when he felt the boy's hands. He pulled the boy to him, hugging him tight.

"Help me, Lord! Please!!" Early cried. He threw back his head and screamed to the sky, "Help me!" Mrs. Disbrow pushed her other son toward Early. He grabbed the boy, and pulled him tight. The three of them stayed tight for several minutes. Early's face was wet with tears. The audience hung on every word, every gesture. Early kissed each boy on the head.

"Did it work? Are they cured?" Mrs. Disbrow asked, her face torn with emotion. "Tell me," she pleaded. Early shook his head. She looked like she didn't understand. "Tell me." Early shook his head again. Then her face changed, from raw to hard. "No?" she asked. Early just looked helpless. "No?" Then she slapped Early full across the face. Early held his ground for an instant, and then collapsed. Nobody moved. Suddenly Early went into a convulsion and started shaking.

"Early!" I yelled, running for him. Miss Pink rushed over, and Miss Emma and Pocket ran up to the stage. "Early, wake up," I said. "Early, open your eyes." I reached out for his hands, but jerked my hands back. His palms were so hot they scalded my fingers.

"Let me," Miss Emma said. She sat on the stage, cradling Early's head in her lap. "Fever," she said, holding her cheek against his forehead. "Child's got fever." She leaned over her son, and kissed his forehead, his eyelids, and cheeks. Early's body was jerking, flopping on the stage. "Early, open your eyes. It's Mama. Early." Miss Emma kept cooing, and after a minute Early's body tensed until I thought he would break in two, then he fell back against his mother's lap. The convulsion was over.

Early's eyes opened, and I could see the fever burning him up. He saw his mother's face. "I can't do no more," he whispered. "I'm sorry."

"There's no shame here," Miss Emma whispered. Leon was on the stage by this time, and he helped get Early to his feet. Early was so weak, he couldn't put one foot in front of the other.

"Get him a drink of water, and let him rest a minute. Then take him over to Doc's," Miss Pink whispered to Miss Emma. "I'll be over and check on him later." She looked up and saw an auditorium full of people watching the drama. She kicked into gear. "Imadene, play!"

Imadene started playing "This Little Light of Mine," and the audience watched as Leon lifted his brother in his arms, and carried him across the stage to the throne.

"Buddy, what are we going to do?" Miss Pink whispered.

"Early's sick. Show's over." I said.

"Not yet it's not," she said. Miss Pink was a woman who had a taste of the spotlight, and she wasn't giving it up. "We've got a show to finish. You've got to help me. Now shuck out of that shirt, and get on that cross."

"You're crazy. Early's sick. I'm going with him." I tried to get to Early, but Miss Pink wouldn't let go of my arm. I yanked it tight against my body so she couldn't get in there for a pinch.

"This is for Early's family. Not you. He's got his mama now. That's the way it has to be," Miss Pink said.

June and July Hosler came up on the stage, joined hands, and started singing "Sweet Little Jesus Boy." That seemed to quiet the audience down, and it really got to me. They looked so sweet in their starched white dresses and hair ribbons.

"Hold still, Buddy," Miss Pink said, and yanked my t-shirt off. "Joe, come tie him down," she yelled over to Mr. Newsom, who was standing at the side of the stage waiting to pull the rope to release his pigeons.

As I stepped on the platform at the base of the cross, Miss Pink turned and faced the audience. She took a deep breath and started preaching.

"Faith is a living, breathing force. We have witnessed miracles today. Blue Jesus did appear. He reached out with his healing hands, and cured the sick. Faith has been tested. Faith is alive!" All the while she was talking, Joe Newsom was strapping me to the cross. "Faith is alive!" Miss Pink screamed.

At that point Danny Lambert cut the lights off, and hit me with the spotlight. The audience yelled. I don't know why. I don't look a thing like Early.

"Say your line, Buddy," Miss Pink yelled.

"Forgive them Father, for they know not what they do!" I bellowed.

Mr. Newsome tripped the counterweight, and that cross shot up to the rafters like a rocket to the moon. It must've been going a hundred miles a minute. We'd forgotten about the counterweights. Early weighs a lot more than me. I screamed every inch of the way up. When the cross hit the rafters, Mr. Newsome pulled the rope on his bag of pigeons, and released them. It sounded like cannon shot when they thudded against the stage. Every one of them was dead. They'd been in that burlap bag and up against the stage lights so long they ran out of air and burned up.

When the cross hit the rafters, I felt my platform come loose. It held for a few seconds, then gave way, leaving me suspended by my arms. I was screaming for help, but nobody heard me over all the singing Christians. The right strap broke first, and then I felt the left slip out of my fingers. I remember falling through space, praying God wouldn't let me die.

I heard a crack when I hit the stage, which must've been my leg breaking, but then everything went black. I do remember thinking, "I've got to have faith. I've got to have faith."

CHAPTER 20

I woke up in Doc Rodger's office with a plaster cast on my leg.
Doc was sleeping in a chair next to my bed, so I coughed to let
him know I was awake. I had a broken nose, one broken leg, a
broken collar bone, and three broken ribs. Doc said it was a miracle I didn't die, because anybody fool enough to let themselves
be strapped to a cross and hoisted up in the rafters deserved whatever happened to him. Then he gave me a shot in the butt for pain
and told me Grandma was on her way. I fell asleep thinking about
Mama sifting flour in our kitchen in Atlanta.

It must've been near dawn when I woke up. I could see a pink-
ish glow coming from the window. I was really confused and
thought I was home. My throat felt raw and dry. I tried to get out
of bed to get a drink, and that's when the pain hit. I remembered
the revival, Early, and falling from the cross. I felt like I was dying.
My nose was stuffed with cotton, and my chest was all taped up,
which made it hard to draw a deep breath. When I tried to move
my free leg, the one without the cast, it wouldn't budge. I knew
I was paralyzed. Miss Florence thought God gave her cancer
because she sinned. When I couldn't feel my legs, I knew God paralyzed me because I didn't believe. That's what started the tears.

"Buddy? Are you all right?" Grandma asked. I felt her reach up and caress my cheek. "I'm right here, honey. Grandma's here." The minute she moved, I felt the weight shift off my leg. "Honey, what do you need?"

Grandma turned on the light in Doc's office. "Oh Buddy, don't cry." Even squinting through the bright light, I could see the worry on her face. Over her shoulder, I could see Will. He looked scared, too. That only made me cry harder.

"I thought God paralyzed me," I sobbed. "I couldn't move."

"I fell asleep on your legs is all that was," Grandma said, chuckling. I was glad she could find some humor in this. "Honey, I'm sorry."

"I don't think it's funny," I sniffed.

"Oh, I don't either. I'm just laughing because I was so scared. Honey, I'm so thankful you're all right. Do you hurt anywhere?" she asked.

"Everywhere," I said. "My nose feels big."

"You busted it, that's why," Will said. "Did Doc tell you that you stopped breathing?"

"We ain't talking about that now," Grandma said. She lifted my head so I could take a drink. Doc has one of those glass straws with a bend in it.

"What about Early? Is he all right?" I asked. The water felt so good on my throat, I slurped pretty hard.

"Early's with his family," Grandma said. "He's going to be fine."

"I stopped breathing?" I asked. "Did I die?"

"Yeah, you did," Will said. "You hit the stage and splattered. Then the cross came down right on top of you. It was a big mess; you and all them dead pigeons. Joe Newsom's a wreck over the dead birds. Says he's going to sue Miss Pink and Mr. Finch."

"Grandma, did I die?" I knew by her face there was something she didn't want to tell me.

"I wasn't there, Buddy. I just know you're here with us now. We're taking you home tomorrow."

"What happened to me, Will?"

"Early saved your life is all. Buddy, you're the biggest miracle at the revival," Will said. "When you hit the stage, we could see you were all broke up. Miss Pink started screaming and pitching a fit, yelling that you weren't breathing. You weren't, neither. I ran up there, and you were as blue as Early. I tried to give you mouth-to-mouth, but you wouldn't draw a breath. Pink leaned over and said she didn't hear your heart. Then she started beating on your chest, screaming that she wasn't going to be responsible for killing you. Doc says that's what busted your ribs. It was scary, Buddy."

"What'd Early do?" I asked, but I already knew. I think I just needed to hear it said out loud.

"He got down on the floor beside you and whispered in your ear. He kept saying, 'Have faith, Buddy. Have faith.' It was spooky. Still you wouldn't breathe, and this is like after ten minutes. Everybody was giving you up for dead. I thought you were dead, too," Will said. Then I think he realized what he was saying. "I felt bad, Buddy. I really did."

"What did Early do?"

"He kissed you. Right on the mouth," Will said. I could hear the wonder in his voice as he said it. "He just kissed you. He put his lips on yours, and you woke up. It was a miracle."

"It was faith," I said.

"If you say so. Maybe it was, just a little," Will said. "I say it was a miracle. Buddy, you're all anybody's talking about. Everybody wants to talk to you. You're the boy Blue Jesus brought back from the dead."

"That's enough of this talk Will," Grandma said, giving me another drink. "It's time Buddy got some rest. Now we'll be back tomorrow afternoon to pick you up. Doc said you wouldn't be ready until after two."

"Did Early really go home?" I asked. I knew there was something wrong. "Well, did he?"

"Not exactly," Will answered. "He's sort of disappeared."

"I think that's enough," Grandma said, trying to shut Will up.

"Where is he," I asked. "Grandma, I got to know."

"Nobody knows," Will said. "After he saved your life, he up and walked out the back door of the community hall. Nobody's seen him since."

"Will, no more. I mean it this time," Grandma said. "Buddy, what do you want before we leave? You need another shot? I could wake Doc up."

"I'm okay, just sleepy," I said. I wanted to sleep so I could quit thinking. My brain needed a rest.

"We'll be back tomorrow. Will's going to pick you up right after school lets out. Now sleep tight," Grandma said, kissing me goodnight. "Will, get me home. I feel like I could sleep for a week."

They turned off the office light, and I shut my eyes when I heard the door shut. I was just about asleep, when I heard the office door open.

"Buddy," Will whispered, "when you were dead, did you see Mama?"

"I don't think so," I said.

"Okay, then. See you tomorrow." And he was gone. This was the first time I'd heard Will talk about Mama since she died. All this time I thought he didn't care. I was going to have to think about my brother some more.

It was a tapping noise that woke me up. I don't know how long it had been going on, but it brought me out of a sound sleep. More tapping. I looked toward the window. There must've been about eight faces pressed against the window, all staring at me. When they saw me open my eyes, they started to really bang at the window.

"Get out of here!" Doc yelled, bursting through the office door, "Y'all get off my porch! Now!" He pulled the window blind down. "I called the law. Y'all are trespassing! Now get out!" he yelled at the window.

This was so bizarre, it had to be a dream. I closed my eyes and tried to think of something good. I caught another image of Mama sifting flour. I have no idea why, it just come to me. I could see the white bits of flour falling like snow, mounding in the bowl. It was a peaceful feeling.

"Open your eyes Buddy," Doc said, nudging my shoulder. "I know you're awake."

"I thought I was dreaming," I said. I ached right down to my soul.

"It's no dream. People been camped out on the street waiting to get a look at you." Doc was feeling my nose, chest, and checking me over. Every touch hurt. "I called Matt Williams. He'll move them out in a couple of minutes."

"Did I die?"

"You talked to Will, huh? I knew that little cuss couldn't keep his mouth shut," Doc said. "Did you stop breathing? I don't know. Maybe. People do that all the time. You ain't all that special." He tugged a bit at the cotton in my nose, which just about killed me. "I'll have to repack this. Buddy boy, I hate to say this, but you'll never be pretty again. This nose of yours is busted up bad."

"Early saved me, didn't he?" I asked.

"That's what they say," Doc said. "Don't you remember?"

"I just remember falling is all. Then I woke up here."

I could see Doc aiming for my nose with some tweezers. When he yanked the cotton out of my nose, I screamed. I felt blood running down on my upper lip, and I started to cry. It hurt, but that wasn't the real reason I was crying.

"You in pain?" Doc asked. I nodded. I was, but it wasn't that bad. I just wanted another shot. I wanted to quit thinking. Doc went to his side table and filled a syringe. It took a minute, but I started to drift, falling through the mattress.

"On second thought, Buddy, I did a pretty good job on this nose. Once this swelling goes down, you may not look all that bad. I got rid of that Harrington bump for you."

I could see Doc talking to me, but I couldn't make sense of what he was saying. His lips were moving, but it was like there was no sound coming out. The magic shot was working. I felt my body quit fighting and give in. My muscles relaxed, but my head kept churning. I wanted to see Early. I wanted to go home. I wanted to rest.

"Buddy, you hungry?" Mrs. Rodger asked. I opened my eyes and saw her leaning over me, holding baby Andy on one hip. He sure has gotten big.

I tried to talk, but my throat and lips were so dry, I couldn't make any sound. She held up the glass with the bendy straw, and I took a huge drink of water. It went down the wrong pipe, and I started coughing, which ripped my chest up pretty bad. Mrs. Rodger put Baby Andy down right on top of me, and lifted my head up so I could catch a breath. When the coughing quit, she gave me another drink. I lay flat again, looking right into Andy's eyes. He was watching, just like he knew me.

"Can you eat something?" Mrs. Rodger asked. "I made macaroni and cheese. I figured soft food would be best." She held out a fork.

"Thank you m'am, but I guess I'm not hungry," I said.

"Well, you been through a lot," she said, smiling. "Look at that baby watch you," she laughed. "I think he remembers you, Buddy."

"He got big," I said,

"Babies do that. He's got a good appetite."

"Can you and Doc keep him?"

"I'd like to see somebody try and get him away from Doc. We're adopting him later this month. Doc filled out the papers, and the judge approved it. Andy's ours, all official."

"He's lucky," I said. "You and Doc will be good to him."

"He's got my heart, Doc's too," Mrs. Rodger said, picking Andy up and holding him tight. "Who couldn't love this baby?" she cooed.

"I don't know. Do you?" I asked. She knew what I meant. I saw her lips get tight, and her face got a little cold.

"Nobody knows. Baby Andy is a mystery. I hope we never find out. Buddy, I don't think I could stand knowing. Whoever did it doesn't deserve this precious child." She held Andy close, kissing his little fingers. She was his mother now. Nothing could change that.

"Are those people still waiting to see me?" I asked.

"The sheriff ran them off hours ago. You've been asleep all day. Doc told me to come in and wake you up. Will's going to be here before long to take you home."

"School started," I said. "I'm glad I missed it."

"Doc says you're going to be out of school for at least three months. He wants you to wait until that cast comes off so he can see how the bone healed. It was a pretty bad break."

Doc came in right then with a pair of crutches. "Buddy, time to get your tail out of bed and try these out," he said.

He helped me sit up and swing my legs over the side of the bed. When I saw I was just wearing my underpants, I got embarrassed. "Mother," Doc said, "give us boys some privacy." It was real sweet he called her mother.

"I guess me and Andy got things to do," Mrs. Rodger said. She hefted the baby on her hip and started out the door. "It was nice having you here, Buddy. Come back and see us when you're better."

I tried the crutches out, and it was clumsy going at first, but I got the hang of it pretty fast. I'm very coordinated. I'm not good in sports, like Will, but I'm still graceful. Mama said I was a nat-ural-born dancer.

"You ready to go, Buddy?" Will yelled, coming through the door all out of breath. "I got football practice, and I can't be late." As he walked in, Doc reached out and smacked him upside the head.

"What was that for?" Will asked, stunned.

"Not keeping your mouth shut," Doc said. "I don't want to hear no more coming-back-from-the-dead talk. It's just going to make folks nervous, and besides, it's not good for Buddy."

"But everybody's saying it," Will said.

"Well, you ain't everybody. You're his brother, and I'm telling you to knock it off. Oh, and one more thing, Will; if I hear of you roughing this boy up, I'm coming out to Aunt Lena's and beat you senseless. Do you understand what I'm saying?"

"Yes, sir," Will said. He was blushing deep red and staring at his feet.

"Look me in the eye when you talk to me, son," Doc said. Will looked up. Shaking hands, they sealed some kind of deal. "You park out back like I told you?" Doc asked. Will nodded, and I could see a look pass between them. "Is Matt waiting on y'all?" Will nodded again.

"What's going on?" I asked.

"You're getting a police escort home is all," Doc said.

"People have been out to the farm looking for you," Will said. "It's because of the revival, and you coming back from the…uh, well, you know." Will cut his eyes at Doc. "Everybody wants to see you."

"Well, I can't see anybody," I said. "And I sure don't want to talk to a bunch of strangers."

"That's why the sheriff is following us home, dummy," Will said. "Now let's go. I got practice."

Mrs. Rodger and Andy were waiting on me at the kitchen door. I'd never been in the back part of Doc's house before. It's nice. He's got a whole lot of books on shelves that are built right into the walls.

Doc went outdoors first and scouted for snoopers. When he said the coast was clear, Will helped me hobble out to the pickup. Matt Williams was waiting on us, leaning up against the patrol car.

"Hey Buddy, you all right?" he asked. I could feel him staring at me, trying to see if I had changed. I nodded. "Then let's hit the road," he said.

It took awhile to get me in the truck. My chest was all taped up, and with my nose packed with cotton, I couldn't breathe right. My cast wouldn't bend, so I had to sit sideways, right up against Will, with my leg sticking sideways towards the door. This was the closest I'd been to Will without flinching in years. Will threw my crutches in the back, and we headed for home.

"Where's Early? Has anyone heard from him?" I asked.

"Nobody knows anything. He wasn't at school, but I didn't expect he would be," Will said. "I went up to the bait farm this morning, but Miss Emma said he never came home."

"He's run away, is what," I said. "He's scared."

"He'll come back," Will said. "I wanted to ask Leon about Early, but Mr. Finch set his dogs on me. I swear, if I had a gun I'd shoot them dogs."

"How's Mr. Finch? Rich off the revival?"

"Been drunk every minute since the revival. That's bait-farm trash. He'll spend that revival money on shine, like as not." Will drove in silence for a bit; then he said, "Don't worry, Buddy, Early's coming back. He has to. He's your best friend."

"I don't know. Before the revival, he told me he was going away. Everything he says comes true. I don't think we're going to see him again."

"Shut up. He'll be back. He's just running scared." Will would miss Early, too. I never could understand their friendship, but at least it made me think my brother had some human feelings deep down inside. The fact that Early liked him was proof enough of that.

Will and I rode quiet for a time. It used to be when I rode in the pickup with Pa, I was always afraid. I know this sounds crazy, but after Mama died, when Pa would take me and Will somewhere, I'd get it in my head that he was going to kill us. Well, at least kill me. I used to think of escape plans. I figured I could push Will to safety, and then try to escape. Every time Pa put on the brakes, I'd get ready to run, but then he'd hit the gas, and I could relax a bit. Grandma's right, I am too high-strung.

Will turned up the dirt two-track toward Gizzy's.

"Why are we going this way?"

"Too many people at the end of our road. Ellerd's keeping watch, but you know how reliable he is. We got to cut across the north meadow. You're like a movie star," Will said, "people want to see you. Isn't this what you always dreamed about?"

"I guess, but I didn't want to be a freak," I answered.

The dirt road across the meadow was full of ruts, and every bounce sent needles of pain through my body. My head was pounding, and I could feel blood trickling out of my nose, running down my lip. I fished for a handkerchief, but all I could see was an oily rag on the floor next to the gear shift. I knew it was crawling with germs, so I wiped my nose with the back of my hand. It came back bloody, not bright red bloody, it was dark, almost black. I've never seen blood like that before. I wonder if this was the blood Early dreamed about?

"There's Grandma," Will said, as he pulled the pickup onto our road. I could see her standing on the back porch, shielding her eyes from the sun, with one hand, working the hem of her apron with the other. "She's been about crazy waiting on you to get home."

"Have you seen Pa?"

"Course I have. I go every day. Nothing's changed, except he's got a friend on the outside sneaking him shine. He was drunk yesterday. Drunk again today. I don't know where he's getting it. Sheriff doesn't know either." Will pulled the pickup right up to the back porch, and Grandma came around and opened my door.

"Buddy!" she said, her face wrinkled up, and I knew she was fighting back tears. "It's good to have you to home."

Grandma helped me out of the pickup, up the porch steps, and into the kitchen. Grandma cooks when she gets nervous, and she'd been working overtime. The kitchen table was loaded down with food.

"I got supper on," she beamed. "I'm gonna feed you healthy, and you'll heal up just fine." Grandma started piling food on my plate.

"I'm not that hungry, Grandma," I said.

"You'll eat," she said, smiling. "Will, get a plate."

"Can't. Football practice," he answered, and was out the door and in the truck before she could answer. Grandma started to yell after him, but just shook her head. "School's on. He's busy."

"I can't go to school," I said. "Doc said so. I have to wait until my cast comes off, and maybe not even then."

"Bet that breaks your heart," Grandma said, giving up a smile. She took a long look at me, and I watched as her smile cracked. She buried her face in her apron and burst out crying. I've never seen my grandma cry like that; not even at Mama's funeral. She cried like her heart was broken. I couldn't say a word. She was crying about me, and that's what hurt.

"Good heavens, I don't know what come over me. I am so sorry, Buddy," she said, wiping her eyes with her apron. I knew that apron was filthy, but this wasn't the time to bring that up. "It's just looking at you now, I realize how much you favor your mother. It got the best of me."

"I'm fine, Grandma. Really, I am," I said. "Doc said I'm not special. He said people stop breathing all the time."

"Maybe some people do, but they ain't my grandson. Doc may know a lot, but he's wrong about one thing. You are special. I love you, Buddy." Grandma bent down and wrapped me in her arms. "I love you so much."

Well, of course I cried. We're not an *I-love-you* kind of family. We don't talk emotional stuff like that. Mama did, a little, but it's been a long time since I heard it. It's nice to be reminded.

Grandma had fixed me a bed in the front room, and as she was tucking me in for the night she whispered in my ear, "Sweet dreams, Buddy. Tomorrow's going to be a great day."

"Mama used to tell me that," I sighed, eyes heavy.

"Did she?" Grandma smoothed my hair back. "I used to tuck her in saying that. I didn't think she remembered."

"Do you miss Mama?"

"Of course I do," Grandma said, kissing my forehead, "but I carry her in my heart. She's always there."

And I fell asleep thinking, "She's always there."

CHAPTER 21

After all I've been through, I don't think I should have to do homework. So what if I'm missing school? I'm a lot smarter than anybody else in my grade. I was tested last year, and I read at a twelfth-grade level, which is really good. I don't see why I can't skip to the twelfth grade, but Mrs. Runyon said there's a whole lot more about school than reading. I guess that's why she sent Danny Lambert out to the house with a week's worth of home-work for me to do.

I saw Danny peeking through the window and motioned him inside.

"Hey," he said, shy-like. "How you doing?"

"How do I look?"

"Busted up," he said. "You hurt?"

"Yeah, sometimes. Sometimes it's not so bad. My leg itches. Doc says that means it's healing."

"I broke my arm once. It itched." Danny put the homework down. "Teacher said you got to do this. Sorry."

"How's school? Anybody new?"

"Same as last year," Danny said. "Football's okay, I guess." He was quiet for a minute, looking around the room, leafing through a *Screen Greats* Mozelle had sent over. Doris Day was on the cover. I caught Danny sneaking looks at me. I knew he was aching to ask about the revival. I didn't feel like talking.

"You better go," I said. "I got to rest. Doc said so."

"Yeah. Sorry." He started for the door, but turned back, the wondering too much to resist. "Buddy, did you really die?"

"Do I look dead?"

"No, I mean at the revival. Did Early bring you back from the dead?"

"That's enough, Danny," Grandma said, coming into the room. Danny jumped about a foot. "Buddy's got to rest."

"Yes, m'am," Danny said, and bolted for the door. We watched him race down the drive, running like his life depended on it.

"Rabbitty little fella, ain't he?" Grandma said, and we both laughed. "Here, I brought you this," she said, handing me Pa's yardstick. "Thought you could use it to scratch under your cast."

Grandma meant well, but there are too many bad memories hanging on that stick. After a couple days of itching, I found that using an old curtain rod works best. It's got a rough end that scratches good.

My biggest problem so far is boredom and missing Early. The night before the revival, he said he wasn't coming back, and I believed him. I've put Will on the case. Since the revival, he's been nice. I don't trust him completely, but I'm thinking on it.

Ellerd is doing a pretty good job guarding our house. Once in a while a stranger sneaks up through the back pasture, but Grandma has Pa's squirrel rifle out, and when she sees somebody she doesn't know, she fires off a shot. When Grandma was in the garden yesterday, a reporter came right up to the house and aimed his camera through the front window. He took a picture of me trying to pee in a coffee can. I could've died, I was so embarrassed. It's hard for me to get to the bathroom with this cast on, and my armpits are rubbed raw from the crutches. I hate peeing in a can, and it's embarrassing enough without anybody watching. Now the whole thing has been captured on film. Grandma got back just in time. She squeezed off two rounds over his head. Man, did he run.

The phone has been ringing off the hook with people trying to talk to me, which is making our neighbors tense because we're on a party line. It's driving Grandma and Will nuts and puts us all on edge. I wish they'd talk to Doc and leave us alone. Last night the phone rang so many times, Grandma just cut the wires. She said the phone company would understand.

June and July came up to the house this afternoon with the homework Mrs. Runyon sent. I guess Danny Lambert won't be back. I think I like June and July more than anybody else in town. With Early gone, maybe they'll be my best friends. They spend all their time looking at my Lennon Sisters scrapbook. They have no idea who the Lennon Sisters are, but they love their dresses. Today I put on my Brenda Lee record, and we listened to it a couple of times. The twins like Brenda.

"Are you sure she ain't colored?" June asked. "She sings colored."

"She's hillbilly. Look at the album cover," I said.

"She's tiny," July said. "Pretty, too. Like a doll baby."

"She got good hair," June said. "I like her."

"Oh Buddy, I almost forgot. We brung you something," July said, after we'd sung through Brenda's "Emotions" about ten times. She pushed the latest edition of *The Dixie Bugler* in my hands, "Don't tell Aunt Lena."

"She said we ain't supposed to talk about the miracle," June said.

"She said it makes you nervous, and you got to rest up. Now we got to get on home," July said. "Buddy, can we come back tomorrow?"

"You can come back anytime," I said. "Turn Brenda off will you? I got to read this."

July cut the phonograph off, and both twins stood there looking at me. I looked up, waiting. June broke the silence.

"I kind of want to touch you, Buddy," she said.

"Me, too," July said. "Can I rub your hand?"

"Why?" I asked.

"You's a miracle is why. You been touched by God," June said.

"Oh, Twins, not y'all, too? Do you really believe that?" I asked.

"We seen it," July said. "Can we? Can we touch you, Buddy?"

Well, what could I say? I stretched out my hand. The girls reached out with tentative fingers, stepping closer. As I felt their fingers on my palm, I waited a bit, then snapped my fist tight.

"Got you!" I yelled, trapping their hands. They cut loose with blood-curdling screams that had Grandma in the front room in two seconds.

"What in God's name is going on in here?" she asked.

"We're just playing," I said, hiding *The Dixie Bugler*.

"Well, quit it," Grandma said. "Twins, I think y'all better run on home and let Buddy rest. Come in the kitchen, I got a chicken rice casserole for y'all to carry up home to your mama." Grandma turned and headed back to the kitchen, the twins trailing after. When they both turned to look back, I give them a wink. They was giggling when Grandma said, "Tell your mama this is her dish, and I'm sorry I'm so long getting it back."

When I knew Grandma was busy in the kitchen, I opened the paper and there was a huge picture of Early. Miss Carla must've taken it right when all the stage lights hit him. He looked good. The headline read "Blue Jesus Raises the Dead!" Under that in smaller type it said "Another Miracle Averts Tragic Accident."

Miss Carla went over every grisly detail, and her story was very dramatic. If I didn't know it was true, I'd find it hard to believe. Thank God she didn't mention anybody Early touched by name. I know Miss Florence and Miss Dusty would get upset at that. This is what she wrote about me: "After Blue Jesus collapsed on stage, emotionally exhausted and physically drained, the revival continued with the participation of Raymond Thomas (Buddy) Dean, whom readers of *The Dixie Bugler* will recognize from the first Blue Jesus Miracle, the Raising of the Dead Baby. Buddy stepped forward to assume the duties of his friend, and commanded the

stage with the presence of a seasoned actor as he stepped on the
cross. His timing was perfection, and he waited until the audience was still before he uttered the enthralling 'Forgive them
Father for they know not what they do' line from the crucifixion."

I really like the part about me being a seasoned actor. Miss
Carla threw that in because she knew I wanted to go to Hollywood. This is my first official review, but I don't think I can show
it to anybody. The thing with miracles is, you sort of have to be
there, or they don't make much sense. Miss Carla told all about me
falling off the cross, and Early bringing me back from the dead.
I'm never going to live this down. I always wanted to be famous,
but not like this. I sure do hope Grandma is right. She said everybody will forget all about this once somebody else in town does
something stupid. But once Tony Dow reads this, there's no way
I'm going to be his best friend.

Miss Carla finished the story up with this: "Blue Jesus was
last seen departing the revival, and at present his whereabouts is
unknown. The sheriff's office asks that any persons having knowledge of Early Finch's whereabouts, please notify them at once.
Burrell Finch, of Finch's Bait Farm, has posted a $500 reward for
the return of his beloved son."

Well, that made me sick. Everybody and their brother would
be on the lookout for Early, trying to get that $500. I just hoped
he'd gone way back up in the hollows behind his house. Early
grew up in the mountains, and I always felt he fit in better out in
nature. Maybe it's his blue skin. He just sort of disappears into the
air. Just when you think you see him, he's gone.

Everybody in the house was sound asleep when we heard the
pounding on the front door. Next thing I know, the lights in the
front room are on, and Matt Williams is standing over me.

"Buddy, y'all got to remember to lock your front door. God
only knows who could come busting in here," he said.

Will come thundering down the stairs in his underpants. He's
not shy like me. I blame sports for this. Grandma came out from
her room, pulling her robe tight.

"What happened to Early?" I asked.

"It ain't Early, it's your Pa," Matt said. "Is he here?"

"You locked him up," Will said.

"He run off," the sheriff said. "He got the keys off Ellerd, beat him up pretty bad, and locked him in the cell. Boys, your pa's escaped."

CHAPTER 22

It's been ten days since Pa's gone missing. *The Dixie Bugler* did a huge story about his escape. The writer who did the story nicknamed Pa "The Crowbar Killer," on account of that's what he used to knock Ellerd out. The fact Pa didn't kill anybody doesn't seem important. Sheriff Williams says until Pa's found, I'm not allowed to go into town. It seems everybody that came looking for a miracle wants to see the boy that came back from the dead whose father escaped from jail. I don't see how I'm ever going to live this down.

Will is taking Pa's escape pretty bad. Of course he blames me. Will's theory is that Pa heard about me coming back from the dead, and just wanted to get out of jail so he could straighten our family out. If that's what Will wants to believe, fine with me, but it's not true, and Will should know why. I'd bet anything Pa was drinking with his jailhouse buddy, and when they were both drunk, escaping seemed like a good idea. Here's some hot news for Will; that's no way to straighten this family out.

I think it's pretty nice of Ellerd to guard our house, considering Pa busted him upside the head and left him for dead. Ellerd said he didn't plan on holding a grudge. Grandma says that's because holding a grudge don't pay as good as the county dole. I'm worried about Grandma. This fuss over me, and now Pa, has got her acting kind of bitter. I can hear her roaming around the house at night, and I know she's not sleeping good. When I call out to her, she says she's checking the locks on the door. I think she's worried Pa is coming back.

The revival was over three weeks ago, and June and July say no one in town has set eyes on Early. Louann came over one day after school. She swears nobody knows where he is. I think Early's just sitting up in one of the hollows, watching the town, waiting for all the fuss to die down before he comes back. Loving his mama the way he does, I know he won't be able to stay away too long. I bet he misses me, too.

This morning Miss Pink came out to the house. She was pitching a fit because Ellerd made her stop at the end of the road while he searched her car. Ellerd thought Miss Pink was sneaking newspaper reporters up to the house. According to Miss Pink, the revival was "a fabulous hit; a real smash!" She's talking real show business these days. That's understandable considering her news. Miss Pink is moving to New York City! She said she's selling her house, packing up three suitcases and her dog, Muffin, and driving north. She's using her revival money to rent an apartment, and said she plans on renewing her teaching license. I didn't even know she used to be a teacher. I wonder what those Yankee kids will think of Miss Pink.

Miss Pink's reason for calling was to say goodbye and thank me for helping with the revival. I can hardly believe this, but Miss Pink says the revival brought in over four thousand dollars. She says that includes money from the tickets, the lawn audience, hot dogs, soda pop, and the cash Mr. Finch got from selling Early's handprints. I didn't know anything about that, but Pink says Mr. Finch got the bright idea to trace around Early's hands and sell the prints for ten dollars. He promised folks that if they slept with the prints, they'd be cured. That's low, even for bait farm folks.

Miss Pink said she was dying for a cigarette, so she helped me out to the front porch so we could talk. She sat in the swing, lit her Pall Mall, and took a long drag. I couldn't bend my leg, so I just leaned up against the porch rail. We watched the cars going down the highway for a time.

"Buddy, I want you to have this money," Miss Pink said, pulling an envelope from her cleavage. When she handed it to me, it was warm and a little damp. That's Georgia humidity for you. "It's one hundred dollars," she said. I couldn't talk. A hundred dollars was more money than I thought possible. This was movie star money. "Well, you earned it. If it wasn't for you, the revival would've been a huge flop, and we'd have had to refund the box office." I couldn't make my mouth work I was so shocked. Miss Pink thought I was confused by her new show business vocabulary. "That means we'd have to give back the money we collected for tickets."

"I know that, Miss Pink," I said. I may not have been to Radio City, but still, I did come from Atlanta, and I was a regular reader of *Screen Secrets*. "How much money is Early getting?" I asked this kind of soft because the last time I brought it up, she got tense.

"Burrell promised me he's opened a savings account for Early." I rolled my eyes at that one. "He promised me, Buddy, what else could I do? He's Early's father. I'm not even family."

"But Miss Pink, you know he's bad to drink. I bet he ain't got two dimes of that money left. Will told me he's been on a bender ever since the revival." My butt was about rubbed raw from the porch rail, so I hobbled over to the swing, and Miss Pink eased me down. She lifted my cast leg and let it rest on her lap. "When Early comes home, he won't have nothing."

"Do you know where he is?" she asked.

"No m'am, I don't. He told me he would be going away. He told me that the night before the revival."

"Maybe it's for the best," Miss Pink sighed, lighting another Pall Mall off the butt of her first one. She sure does smoke a lot.

"Well, I don't think it's for the best. I bet he's lonesome. Do you think he's safe?" This just came tumbling out of my mouth.

"I don't know, Buddy. I pray he is."

We rocked in silence for quite awhile, me and Miss Pink, her smoking, me counting the cars that passed by. When she finished her cigarette, Miss Pink stubbed it out on her shoe and pitched it way out into the yard. She watched it fly through the air, checking to make sure it landed far enough away so it wouldn't annoy Grandma.

"Buddy, listen to me. I don't know that you'll understand this, but I'm going to try. This town doesn't deserve a child like Early. He's really that special. He's got powers we can't understand. Early doesn't belong in this world, and Lord knows, this world can't begin to understand him. Early, himself, doesn't even understand the power the good Lord give him. Don't you think it's cruel to make him try to fit in?" Miss Pink was studying my face as she talked. I nodded right along so she knew I was listening, but I was still thinking about how this town didn't deserve Early.

"As much as we may love him, and yes, I do love that child, Early's better off where he is," Miss Pink said. "The question is, are you strong enough to give him up?"

"He'll come back," I said. "He likes me too much to just disappear. He's just waiting for the excitement to die down is all."

"Maybe," Miss Pink said, "but you know you're going to have to let him go. The more city people that come up here, the further up the mountains the blues are going to go. Pretty soon every blue person will be gone. They're going to be a curiosity people talk about like a memory. Early's too good for that."

Miss Pink was making me cry. What she was saying was true, I just didn't expect it from her. This was the Miss Pink with the beautiful smile.

"I miss him so much," I said, the words catching in my throat as I tried to swallow the tears.

"Of course you do. Buddy, when you were knocked unconscious and stopped breathing, Early bent over you and whispered in your ear. Did you hear what he said? Do you remember?" Miss Pink eased my cast leg off her lap, got up, and held out her hands.

I reached out, and she pulled me to my feet. We stood eye-to-eye, and I realized I'd grown taller this summer. "What did he say?"

"Have faith," I whispered.

"What do you think he meant?"

"I don't know."

"He's your best friend. Think. What did he mean?" Miss Pink was crushing my hands in hers, trying to squeeze an answer out of me. I took a deep breath.

"If I had faith in God, I'd survive." I said it slow, staring straight across into her eyes.

"Have faith," she smiled. "And do you? Do you believe?"

"I don't know," I said. "I want to."

"Early believes. Has he ever lied to you? Ever?"

"No, m'am," I said, pulling my hands away to wipe my tears. "Early never lies."

"Then Buddy, you got no choice. Have faith," Miss Pink said. She leaned in and kissed my cheek. I could feel the big tears building, and I couldn't hold them in any longer.

"But God killed my mama," I sobbed. "Pa said so."

"Oh, Honey, no. God didn't kill your mama, cancer did. It's not the same." Miss Pink pulled me to her, and I hung my arms around her neck and sobbed. "Your pa did you wrong saying that. You've got to believe, Buddy. Especially you. Faith works miracles. You're the proof, Buddy."

I hung on Miss Pink until I felt my tears quit. I didn't even care when she pulled a nasty old hanky out of her purse and wiped my face. I think Miss Pink wears White Shoulders perfume. That's the kind Mama wore. It made me feel good.

"You think you can walk me to my car?" Miss Pink asked, "I'm getting tired holding you up. I swear, you've grown up this summer, Buddy." Miss Pink handed me my crutches, and I hobbled behind her all the way to the back drive. She was trailing White Shoulders and I felt safe.

"Good luck in New York, Miss Pink," I said, once she was sitting behind the wheel.

"Don't need it," she grinned. "I feel confident, Buddy. This move is good for me. It'll be good for you, too, when it's your turn. Until then, try to like it up here a little bit more. It's not all bad."

"It'll be easier with Butch Calkins in reform school," I said.

"For you and everybody else. Now Buddy, before I leave, I want you to look at this." Miss Pink whipped off her straw hat. Hair! She was actually growing little sprigs of hair. "This should make you believe," Miss Pink laughed. "Hair. And it's good hair, too." Miss Pink started her car and pulled a few feet down the drive. Next thing I know, she slammed it in reverse and backed up to where I was standing. "You got to tell the world about Early. He deserves that. Promise?" I nodded. Then Miss Pink floored the accelerator, pointing her car toward New York. I'd never see her again.

It was after supper when June and July came by. Grandma made us some popcorn, and we sat on the back porch, catching the September twilight. It was a good night for popcorn, and as we sat there, I could feel a cold snap coming down off the mountain. Fall was coming.

The twins didn't have any news about Early. July said Pastor Nichols at the colored Baptist had their congregation pray for Early last Sunday, but none of the coloreds know where he is. That surprised me, because usually colored folks know all the gossip in town. I think they pay attention better than white folks.

The twins did report that Carol Disbrow and her bleeder boys have taken off for some place called the Mayo Clinic way up north to get cured. I sure hope it works. Early told me some people are put here to die to teach us about life. He said that's what the bleeder boys had to do. I don't understand that at all.

Will drove up just as the twins and I were singing our way through a three-part harmony of "This Little Light of Mine." He goes out night after night looking for Pa. Every time he comes home, I listen for two sets of feet. I was surprised when Will sat on the back steps and listened to us sing. I knew he was sad about Pa, but Will usually prefers to be alone. When he started to sing with us, I about peed my pants. Will has a strong voice. I'd never heard him sing before.

Grandma brought Will his supper out to the back porch and joined in the singing. We went from "This Little Light" to "Amazing Grace" and we sounded good. Then Grandma started up with "Away in a Manger." That made everybody think about Early and the revival, and after a verse and chorus we sort of died out and just sat on the back porch staring up at the stars. This is the nicest night I can remember since Mama died.

"Lord, y'all, it's pert near nine o'clock. Girls, your mama's going to think we kidnapped y'all. Will, can you carry the twins home?"

"Oh no, m'am, we'll walk," June said, "We ain't afraid of the dark." I saw her look at the pickup and knew she wanted a ride.

"Let Will take y'all. He loves to drive," I said. June and July didn't move. "Go on twins, it's all right."

"Pa wouldn't like it," July said. "It ain't fitting."

"You gals afraid to ride with me?" Will asked. "I'm a careful driver. I promise not to wrap us around a tree." He was teasing the twins. Will could be sweet-natured when he wanted. "Come on. Your pa won't care because it's me. I give him rides lots of times."

"Go on, y'all," Grandma said, giving the twins a push. They tried to sit in back, but Will forced them into the front seat. They wouldn't even look at him they were so nervous. When everybody was settled in the pickup, Will gunned the engine and pulled out of the yard, heading for the back meadow and up the hollow toward Gizzy's. Grandma and I watched the tail lights disappear up the hollow.

"I'm sleeping in my room tonight, Grandma," I said. "I don't sleep so good in the front room."

"Nobody's sleeping these days. You need help getting up them stairs?"

"I'm doing better. I walked Miss Pink to her car and didn't even stumble."

"What was Pink saying to you out there?" Grandma asked. "I seen y'all talking deep. Looks like she's growing some hair."

"She gave me this," I said, showing Grandma the hundred dollars.

"Lord, have mercy. What you going to do with it?"

"Don't rightly know. Save it I guess. Half of it's Early's."

"Pink say that?"

"No, m'am. It's just right. He earned it."

"You're a good boy, Buddy. You're so much like your mama, it almost makes my heart stop," Grandma said. "Now, if you're going upstairs, I want you to get in that bathroom and scrub yourself down. You been too long without a bath. I'm heading out to the barn to check on things."

Grandma gave my hand a squeeze and headed off into the night. There was nothing in the barn that needed checking on. I knew Grandma went to see if Pa was hiding out. I hoped she wouldn't find him. If she did, I sure hoped she wouldn't bring him home. It was so peaceful with him gone, I think it'd be better for me if he never came back.

Getting up the stairs was harder than I figured. I hopped most of the way, hanging on the banister. I really need to work on getting some muscles. When I'm all healed up, I'm going to try to build muscles. Will lifts weights. If I get him on the right day, he might help me. I don't want big muscles like Will, just regular ones.

It felt good to be back in my room. I stood in the middle of the room looking at all my stuff. Grandma says I'm a packrat, but I just like collecting things. I like looking at my bookshelves and seeing all my books and my movie star pictures. As I stood there, I got to thinking about Miss Pink and the smell of White Shoulders. It's funny how a smell can take you right back to a place and time. I was remembering a time when Mama was getting ready for a Girls' Night out in Atlanta. Girls' Night was when all Mama's sisters came to town, and they went out to dinner and a movie, no men allowed. They did this four times a year.

I remember I was lying on Mama's bed watching her get ready. She was painting her mouth. Mama used Hazel Bishop makeup. Her lipstick was named Candy Apple Red, and Mama said it was perfect for her hair and skin tone, like they made it especially for her. Mama had a ritual before she put on her dress. She would straighten her stockings, check her garters, pull her slip down, and then dab on the White Shoulders. She used one dab behind each ear, one at her throat, one on each wrist, and then she put a dot on her fingers and traced the hem of her dress. She said this gave her allure and mystery.

The particular night I remembered Mama was wearing that slip, the one Pa buried, the one I had in my strongbox. More than anything, I wanted to smell her White Shoulders again. I yearned for a trace of Mama's allure and mystery.

I got my strongbox out from the crawlspace, and opened my box of treasures. Mama's slip was right on top. I held it to my nose and inhaled. Nothing. No White Shoulders. I guess that was asking too much. I held the slip up and imagined Mama standing in front of me. I swear I could hear her laughing. Then I noticed one tiny red stain on the lacy bodice. I held it under the light, and there it was, Hazel Bishop Candy Apple Red.

I don't know what it was, maybe seeing the lipstick stain, or smelling Miss Pink's White Shoulders, but I needed Mama more than ever. Sitting there on my bedroom floor in my undershorts, I knew what I had to do to get close to her again. I pulled Mama's slip over my head. I stood up and let it settle around my hips and gave it a shake so it fell to my knees. I remember Mama as being so much taller than me, but her slip felt like it fit. It was snug at the top and hit me right below the knees, just like it did Mama.

I smoothed the slip down over my thighs, pretended to check the garters, and turned, checking the imaginary stocking seams. As I turned I caught a reflection in the mirror. Pa was standing in my bedroom door watching me. He had a gun under his arm, and a jug of shine in his fist. I don't know how long he'd been watching.

I stood up straight and we stared at each other. He was weaving and kept blinking, trying to focus his eyes. I figured he'd been drunk for several days running.

"Rebecca?" Pa whispered, slurring Mama's name and falling up against the doorjamb. "You been watching me from heaven, ain't you? Watching and judging me."

"It's me, Pa," I said, quiet, praying he wouldn't hear and go away.

"What could I do, Becky? I couldn't let her keep the baby," Pa said. He slipped and fell against the door, sliding down to the floor. He put his head on his knees. I could hear the tears in his voice. "Ain't got nobody to talk to," Pa said. He raised the jug and took a hard pull. "Why'd God take you, Becky? He left me with nobody."

"I ain't Mama," I said, "And you got Will. He needs you, Pa." He didn't even hear me.

"Thou shalt not kill," Pa yelled, "but that's what I did. I left that baby in the dump. She said he was dead. I seen it weren't breathing; cold and blue. She said God took that baby because we sinned. That's why I had to get rid of it. But you seen me, Becky, and that's why you come back. You come back to make it right."

My heart jumped, and I felt my knees give way. I fell back on my bed, like someone knocked the wind out of me. My Pa was Baby Andy's daddy.

"An eye for an eye, Becky. An eye for an eye!" Pa threw his head back and howled. "Eye for an eye!"

"Pa, it's me. It's Buddy." I grabbed my crutches and stood up. "You don't know what you're saying."

"I know what I got to do," Pa yelled.

He swung his jug arm wide. It caught my left crutch and sent me sprawling. The fall was like fire going through my body, my broken ribs twisted against my chest, and I felt like I was being stabbed.

"I'm going to hell, Becky," Pa yelled.

"Yes, you are," Will said. Both Pa and I yelped in surprise. I didn't even hear Will come up the stairs. When he got a look at me in Mama's slip his eyes narrowed into slits, but he didn't say anything.

"Will? Son, you scared me," Pa said, trying to get to his feet.

"Ah, Pa, look at yourself," Will said. He reached down and grabbed Pa by his shirt, pulling him to his feet. "Look at yourself," he screamed, pushing Pa's face against the mirror on the wall.

I think this is the moment Will became a man. As for me, I got the same feeling I used to get when we were all in the car, and I thought Pa might try to kill us. I pushed myself back against my bed and pulled myself upright. I started looking for a way to escape.

"I love you, Will," Pa said, starting to cry.

"If you loved me you wouldn't be doing this. My God, Pa, look at what you done. I tried to love you. I watched what you done to Buddy, and I looked the other way. I ain't turning away no more. I'm looking right at you, and I can see what a miserable excuse you are for a man."

"Buddy ain't my son. Can't be no son of mine. Look at him. He's wearing a dress. I ain't claiming Buddy. What kind of boy is he?" Pa asked, throwing his arms wide. The barrel of his rifle hit me square on the left temple, knocking me to the floor. It felt like my head was going to explode.

"Come on, Buddy, get up," Will said, reaching down to help me. "We got to get out of here."

"That's right, get out of here. Everybody leaves me. Don't nobody understand what it's like." Pa was pulling at Will, trying to get him close. "Will, you don't know what it's like."

"Buddy, come on," Will yelled. He reached down and grabbed me around the waist, pulling me to my feet and dragging me toward the stairs.

"Will, I'll try to do better," Pa sobbed. "I know I done you wrong. I'll be good." Will pried Pa's fingers off, and gave me a push to the stairs. When my cast hit the doorjamb, I felt needles all through my body. I yelled out from the pain, and that seemed to set Pa off. "Y'all, get out of here!" He swung the rifle, catching me on the left shoulder. I cried out again.

"Old man, you make me sick!" Will screamed. He turned on Pa. "You don't deserve a family like us, so why don't you do us a favor and blow your goddamn head off? We'd be better off!" Pa grabbed for Will's pant leg, but Will kicked him off. "Just kill yourself and get it over!"

Will got me halfway down the stairs when we heard the gunshot. It was like the explosion happened in my head. I felt like I was dying. That's the last thing I remember about that night.

CHAPTER 23

Pa's funeral was yesterday. I couldn't go because I was at Doc Roger's recovering from a concussion, and what Doc called an extreme case of nervous exhaustion. The service was held at the Comfort Corners Methodist Church. The Methodists were the only ones who'd bury him. All my aunts came home for the funeral and took charge.

Pa didn't get much of a crowd, a lot of flowers, but nobody from town, and only a handful of tourists that said they came to see the boy Blue Jesus healed. I'm still known as the boy that came back from the dead.

I still can't understand why nobody went to the funeral. Pa had a lot of men friends in town. Grandma called long distance to Pa's kin down in Louisiana, and they said they couldn't make the trip. Grandma said there's a world of difference between couldn't and wouldn't, and she hung up on them. My Aunt Dorrie said there weren't even enough white men to be pallbearers, and the Methodists had to get some colored men to help out. If Pa wasn't already dead that'd kill him. Pa didn't take to coloreds all that well. Gizzy and his family went and sat at the back of the church. I bet that made the Methodists nervous. They say Gizzy cried like

277

a baby all through the funeral and had to be helped out of the church. The twins sang "Softly and Tenderly Jesus Is Calling" at the gravesite.

They buried Pa next to Mama in the town cemetery. The twins told me when they lowered the casket into the grave, Will collapsed in tears and refused to leave, even after the grave was covered over. He spent the first night sleeping on Pa's grave, and has been going to the cemetery every day since. That rips my heart apart. Out of this whole mess, I feel sorriest for Will. The guilt is killing him. He blames himself, no matter what people say. He's the kind of boy that needs a father.

I have a hard time sleeping now. Every time I close my eyes, I hear Pa's voice. "I couldn't let her keep the baby," plays over and over in my head. It's not only the words, but the haunted look of his face that keeps me awake. Will and I carry a secret about Pa and Baby Andy, and I need to decide what to do.

Doc Roger talked to me a lot about Pa. He told me about depression and how Pa didn't know what he was doing or saying. He blamed the liquor some, but said it was a mental condition that Pa couldn't control. I don't know what to think. When Doc was explaining about Pa and trying to be nice about it, all of a sudden it come to me I've got a new brother. In that instant, I knew I wouldn't tell Doc the truth about the baby. Unless Pa told on himself, which I doubt, nobody would ever find out who Baby Andy's parents were. I think that's best. I'll convince Will it's best too. I want Baby Andy to grow up as normal as possible.

I woke up with a jerk, pulling away from a dream. I was drowning. I could see a boat floating above my head, but I couldn't reach it. When I opened my mouth to scream, the water gushed in and I felt myself sinking. "Buddy, wake up! It's Grandma." Grandma was holding my arms down. I tried to pull away, reaching for the boat, but she held tight. "Buddy, it's just a dream. Honey, wake up," she said, turning on a light. I opened my eyes and could see the worry on her face. I was confused at first, forgetting I was sleeping in the front room again. "Honey, it's Grandma. Wake up, now. Okay?" I nodded. I could see her gathering her thoughts and knew she was getting the lay of the land before she spoke. "Buddy, we got to talk about your pa."

"Not much to say is there?"

"Buddy, don't."

"Why? He never loved me. It's not like I'm sorry."

"Maybe not now, but later when this catches up with you. He was your pa; he loved you."

"Oh, Grandma, you know better than that."

"I mean it. Buddy, your father loved you. He had problems. He never got over Becky dying. Doc says it was like he was caught in a black hole and couldn't get out. That's what made him drink. The drink made him crazy."

"It wasn't just because he was drunk. It was because of me. He saw me standing there in Mama's slip, and he got disgusted. I could see it in his face. He hated me."

"I'm telling you, your pa wasn't thinking right. That's why he did it," Grandma said.

"I prayed Pa would die. I prayed for that more than once. Every time he beat me, I asked God to kill him. I lay in bed at night begging God to answer my prayers. Then He did. Will thinks it's his fault, but it was me that killed Pa."

"You can't believe that, Buddy," Grandma said. "Your father died because he couldn't get a grip on his life, on what was real. This last summer, he'd been spinning out of control. Then he give up. That's all it is. That's nobody's fault."

"I ain't sorry," I said. I closed my eyes then and turned away.

My mind was churning and got stuck on Pa and the gun. Early's dream about the gun and blood came true. I knew it would, I just didn't think it'd be about Pa and me. I tried to sleep, but my mind was full of ugly thoughts. I had to make myself stop. I needed something peaceful to remember, so I thought hard about the swimming hole. I wanted to dream about something nice. Then I was drifting down Bitterroot River on the inner tube with Early beside me. That's how I slept. That's how I survive today.

When all seven of my aunts, the Harrington girls of Comfort Corners, get together, they're like a force of nature that rolls over everything in its path. They made all the arrangements for Pa's funeral, and when that was done, they went to work on the house. Wanda, Shirley, and Dorrie started cooking. Helen and Ann cleaned the house top to bottom. They had to scrub my room down with bleach to get out the blood stains. All the girls worked on getting my room in shape. They gave it a new coat of paint, yellow, and organized everything. They got all my Nancy Drews out from under the bed, where I'd been hiding them from Pa, and put them on a new bookcase they bought special for me.

When Doc said I was ready, Georgeann and Dawn drove me up to the cemetery to see Pa's grave. I wasn't sure how I'd act. I didn't feel sad. I didn't feel anything. I guess it wasn't real to me yet. When we got close, Georgeann slowed the car down to check for Will. The girls thought he might be visiting Pa. The cemetery has an iron gate and weeping willows at the entrance. All the graves have plastic flowers I used to think were tacky. Now it looked different, pretty somehow. Mama and Pa are at the edge of the hill and can look across the river to the farm. I think they've got the best spot.

No sign of Will. I don't know what I'd have done if he'd been sprawled out on Pa's grave. I haven't seen Will since Pa died. He's been sleeping in the barn and keeps to himself. I think it's important I get Will to like me better. With Mama and Pa gone, we've got to get close. As Aunt Georgeann pulled the car up to the grave, I panicked and made her turn around. I couldn't look. I'd visit the grave later. I'd make Will take me. I had some private things to tell Pa that I could never say when he was alive.

The Harrington girls stayed at the farm for two weeks, and right before they went back home, they called a family meeting. The topic was what to do about me. I wasn't allowed to attend, but since I'm sleeping in the front room, I could hear everything they said. The meeting started with whispers over coffee, but it didn't take long before voices were raised and the discussion got heated.

The general feeling was that I couldn't have any kind of life up here on account of the revival, Pa's suicide, and being such a sissy I got beat up every day. I guess they didn't hear about Butch Calkins going to reform school. The question they wanted to settle was where I was going to live. All the girls wanted me to come and live with them, which made me feel real good. It sounded like Aunt Dorrie was winning. She talks the loudest of all the girls. I was starting to panic. There's no way I'm moving to Alabama. Aunt Wanda was arguing that I should move to Nashville with her because the schools were better. She had them on that one. Aunt Dawn said she knew she was my favorite, and it was only natural that I go live with her. Boy, did that cause a ruckus.

I decided I'd heard enough. If my aunts had thought to ask, I could've told them I didn't plan on going anywhere. Bad as it seems, I had a life up here. It's like Miss Pink said, I had to try to like it. Starting over would just mean trying to fit in and failing all over again. A new town would mean more teasing for being different, for being a sissy. There was no new life waiting for me. It was up to me to make the best of the one I had. Here I had Grandma and Will. They understood me. Here I had history.

Grandma came in from the kitchen. Her lips were pursed pretty tight. "You listening to this?" she asked. I nodded. "Heard enough?" I nodded again. "Then let's get out of here." Grandma helped me pull a flannel shirt on, and we went out on the front porch.

"Buddy, do you want to move away? If you do, I'll understand," Grandma said. "It ain't going to be easy living down that revival mess and now with what your pa done, it'll be even worse."

"Wherever I go, it'll be worse," I said. "I got to stay here and make this work. If I don't, no matter where I go, I'll never fit in."

"Who told you that? Early?"

"I think I figured it out for myself," I said. "Besides, I can't leave you and Will. Who'd tell y'all about Doris Day and Rosemary Clooney?"

"You got my heart, Buddy. You always will," Grandma said, getting a little weepy. Grandma's looking old these days. I think having all her girls home made her miss Mama even more. She never used to cry this much.

The girls were making a terrible racket in the kitchen. The meeting was over, and they decided to bake cookies. The girls yelled for Grandma, and she groaned like she was put out, but I knew better. She loved having her daughters home. She gave me a kiss and went inside. I eased myself down the front steps and went out onto the lawn.

As I stared up at the night sky, I remembered what Early said about some people having to die. He was talking about the bleeder boys, but maybe my Pa was one of those people, too. I still haven't cried about Pa, which is strange. It seems I cry about everything else. I'm sad and all, but it's for the wrong reasons. When Mama died, it was like a terrible weight was crushing my chest and I couldn't breathe. It was like my whole world ended. With Pa gone, everything's opened up, and all of a sudden I can see a future. That's what makes me saddest. When Pa killed himself, he destroyed our last chance to know each other. When he was alive, I always held out hope he'd learn to like me. Now he'll never know what a good person I am. He'll never know if I grow up to be talented or funny or smart or anything about me. Mama always believed in me. She told me so every night when she said "tomorrow's going to be a great day." She believed anything was possible. Me and Pa were different. Our story is about missed chances.

I leaned up against the picnic table and looked up at the stars. I felt that if I stared through the Big Dipper hard enough, I could see right into heaven. Just one mustard seed of faith, and I could see Mama again. She'd tell me what to do. My aunts' laughing carried from the kitchen across the yard. It sounded friendly, which made me believe my fate had been left undecided. The back door slammed, and after a bit of groaning, the pickup engine kicked over. It was Will going out to visit Pa. As the truck headed down our drive, the headlights threw a shadow against the house. In that shadow, I saw my best friend.

"Early?" I whispered. He didn't answer, but I heard the grass rustle, and suddenly his blue face appeared out of the shadows so close I yelled out.

"Hey Buddy," he said. It was like he'd never been gone.

"Where you been?" I asked.

"It don't matter. The question is, how are you?"

"I'm okay. Pa killed himself."

"I know," Early said. He sat next to me on the picnic table, moved close, and put his arm around my shoulders. We sat that way for quite some time. Early was back, and I felt safe. "Did you find the faith, Buddy?"

"I don't know," I said. "Maybe."

"Maybe?" Early said, letting loose with a low laugh. "Maybe? Oh, you got to do better than that."

"Early, did I kill Pa by praying he'd die?"

"What do you think?"

"I'm asking you. You're the one that believes. Did I?"

"Your pa killed himself. He couldn't see the miracles."

"Do you know why?" I asked.

"The baby. You know about that, don't you?" I nodded. "Are you going to tell?" I could feel Early studying my face. I knew what he wanted me to say.

"No," I said. "It doesn't seem right to tell, and it won't fix anything. Doc loves that baby. He'll grow up good."

"So will you," Early said. He jerked his head toward the house. "You got so many people that love you."

"They all want me to go live with them. I'm not going though," I said.

"Good," Early said. "You'll do fine here until it don't work no more. That's when you'll move. You got to grow up first. This is the best place for doing that. You got lots to teach this town, Buddy Boy."

"About what?"

"We won't know until the lesson's learned." I knew he was smiling.

"I hate it when you talk like that. I never understand, and it makes me feel stupid." Early tightened his arm on my shoulders and pulled me close. I was so happy to be near him.

The night air got cooler as a wind picked up and came down off the mountain. It blew a swirling fog down around the house, and Early and I were lost in a cloud. It was a private world, like being caught between hanging sheets. We were alone together, and it was perfect.

"Early, are you God?" I asked. Sitting close on that picnic table with the fog blanketing us, it felt like he might be God. He healed me and saved my life. I had to know.

"No, but He works through me," Early said. "Is that good enough?"

"I guess it has to be," I said. I reached out and took Early's hands in mine. I had to check. His palms were cool and dry.

"Did you find faith, Buddy?" Early asked. His hands clenched mine tight, like he could feel the answer coursing through my blood.

We heard squeals and laughing coming from the back yard, and all my aunts; Wanda, Shirley, Dawn, Ann, Helen, Georgeann, and Dorrie; came running from the back of the house, across the lawn, in their slips.

"We're going skinny dipping, Mama! Don't tell nobody!" Dawn screamed into the night. "Buddy, if you're out here, don't you be peeking at us!" They all disappeared into the fog, laughing, skipping across the meadow and down to the swimming hole. This was my family, and I loved them so much. It made me sad that Mama was missing this Girls' Night.

That's when the real tears began. They snuck up on me sort of quiet, and then I was sobbing against Early's shoulder. I cried for Pa, for Mama, for Will, Baby Andy, and for me. What began one summer day not that long ago came full circle, and I was with Early once again, united against a life that didn't know what to do with us. This summer I learned I'm stronger than I thought. I made a solemn vow to never be scared, and I kept that vow. This summer I accepted I'll always be different. That doesn't scare me anymore. I'm a mama's boy. She was my heart, my strength. That's the miracle I can see. I won't apologize again.

I felt Early's palms grow hot. They were burning my hands, and I tried to pull away, but he held me tight, refusing to let go. Finally I surrendered, and the minute I gave in, that's when my questions were answered.

Early leaned close and whispered in my ear, "Have faith."

I nodded and reached out for Early, but there was no one there. I heard the grass rustle, and thought I saw a blue shape at the edge of the meadow. I could see his hair glowing in the fog, and then he started to fade.

"Early," I called, but the shadow disappeared into the blue night. "Early, I'm saved," I whispered. The grass whispered it back to me, "I'm saved," and I knew it was true. "I'm saved," I said. In the shadows I knew Early heard me. My words had to reach him because I would never see Early again.

This summer Early taught me miracles are always there, it just takes faith to recognize them. When I found the courage to really open my eyes, I discovered myself, a twelve-year-old boy who wants to belong, to believe, to exist. Early taught me miracles, big and small, are the presence of God. I know this is true, because in the miracles, I found hope for a boy like me.

That's the truth as I see it, and I'm known for always telling the truth. Ask anybody.

NOTES

The Blue People of Troublesome Creek really did exist. It started sometime around 1820 with a French orphan named Martin Fugate, who was a carrier of hereditary methemoglobinemia (met-H), a recessive gene trait that inhibits the blood's ability to carry oxygen, resulting in blue skin. Martin Fugate's kin intermarried with the Smiths, who were descendants of Richard Smith and Alicia Combs, also carriers of met-H. Generations later, the Appalachian Mountains of Kentucky, Tennessee, and North Carolina were home to many blue people.

In the mid-sixties a doctor by the name of Madison Cawein heard about the blue people and went deep into the mountains to investigate. He was able to diagnose the problem and discovered a simple cure, methylene blue, which replaced the missing enzyme in the blood. The cure was temporary, but within minutes the skin of the blue people turned pink.

In writing Blue Jesus, I have taken considerable liberties. I was struck by the blue peoples' inclination to isolate themselves from the prying eyes of the curious public. As civilization progressed into the mountains of Kentucky, the blue people withdrew into the mountains and hollows, and ventured down into Tennessee and Georgia.

There are universal instincts in being different. A blue boy with special gifts, and a too-gentle boy looking for acceptance, became best friends. Theirs was a commonality of differences. A lesson for us all.

In memory of
Carla Watkins Trousdale
Loving Mother, Loyal Friend, Librarian
Can there be any higher praise?